"*The True Sources of the Nile* is a vibrant, sensual, moving portrayal of a country in crisis and a heroine in conflict. Sarah Stone has a wonderful gift for conjuring both characters and landscapes onto the page. This is a splendid and engrossing novel."

—Margot Livesey

"Sarah Stone writes in a supple, lyrical style about matters of life and death in this novel, and at its heart the book is about people who will not tell—will not admit—what they know to be true. At once a passionate love story and an accounting of political warfare in Africa, *The True Sources of the Nile* manages to show how closely allied terror and love can sometimes be. Few Americans have witnessed the terrible and beautiful lives of Africans as closely as this narrator has, and as a result this book is hard to put down and impossible to forget."

—Charles Baxter

"Sarah Stone has written a novel of civil and domestic war, of tribal and familial violence–all the more passionate because intermingled: love and death flailing at each other like the pair at the erotically charged center of *The True Source of the Nile*. Whether she writes of San Francisco or Burundi, check-ups or check-points, nightmares or dreams, she does so with authority and in prose honed machete-edge sharp: a vivid, heart-stopping tale."

—Nicholas Delbanco

"This stunning first novel, set in contemporary Africa, begs to be compared to Barbara Kingsolver's *The Poisonwood Bible* . . . yet is distinctive enough to be in a class of its own. Stone . . . brings an authentic voice to this novel of life-and-death issues. Recommended for public libraries."

—*Library Journal*

"Shades of Graham Greene, this first novel is both verdant and ominous . . . although *The True Sources of the Nile* is concerned with the greater issues of passion and unimpeded violence, it is also a meditation on truth . . . full of engaging parallels and paradoxes, the novel is an intricate study of rationality and its mirror image, rationalization . . . an almost palpable sense of contemporary Africa with 'the reddish scent of the dust, the mango and papaya tropical smells, a haunting sense of human tension and of growing things and of languorous obstinate decay.'"

—*Miami Herald*

HUNGRY
GHOST
THEATER

HUNGRY GHOST THEATER

A NOVEL

Sarah Stone

Published by WTAW Press

PO Box 2825

Santa Rosa, CA 95405

www.wtawpress.org

Publications by WTAW Press—a not-for-profit literary press—are made possible by the assistance received from individual donors.

designed by adam b. bohannon

Edited by Peg Alford Pursell

Author photo by Ron Nyren

PUBLISHER'S CATALOGING-IN-PUBLICATION DATA
Names: Stone, Sarah, 1961-, author.
Title: Hungry Ghost Theater : a novel / Sarah Stone.
Description: Santa Rosa, CA: WTAW Press, 2018.
Identifiers: ISBN 978-0-9988014-5-2 | LCCN 2018933255
Subjects: LCSH Family--Fiction. | Brothers and sisters--Fiction. | Sisters--Fiction. | Theater--Fiction. | Mental illness--Fiction. | Substance abuse--Fiction. | Children of mentally ill mothers--Fiction. | Psychological fiction. | BISAC FICTION / Literary
Classification: LCC PS3619.T68 H8 2018 | DDC 813.6--dc23

Manufactured in the United States of America and printed on acid-free paper.

*For Ron
and for my family*

CONTENTS

At the Edge   I
San Francisco, March 1993

PART ONE: THE DARK WOODS

I   Rescue   11
Seoul, May 2004

II   Stage Fright   39
Zanzibar, June 2004

III   News of the World   61
San Francisco, July 2004

PART TWO: OF SHADOWS AND OF RAIN

IV   Ravenous: A Ghost Story   83
Sebastopol, January 2002

V   Dream Boards   103
Santa Cruz, July 2004

VI   Shoreside   117
Santa Cruz, September 2000

PART THREE: THAT HIDDEN ROAD

VII   Six Hells   143
Santa Cruz Mountains and Hell, April 2005

VIII   Train Ride   177
Outside Chicago, June 1974

IX   The Unforgivable Stories   197
Santa Cruz Mountains, June 2005

At the Edge
San Francisco, March 1993

The dark warehouse chills Arielle through her coat and gloves—she and her sisters stare at their aunt as she descends an iron staircase, undressing. Torches cast a smoky, wavering light, half-illuminating the audience, who sit in a circle around the stage. A thin, harsh, persistent music turns the warehouse into a haunted cave. Aunt Julia—Inanna, Queen of Heaven and Earth, according to the photocopied program—has stripped down to her underwear and jeweled armbands. A blue-white spotlight strikes the mirrored floor of the stage, lighting both Inanna and her sister, Ereshkigal, Queen of the Dead and the Underworld, who sits on a throne at the bottom of the staircase. White makeup with sharp black lines and areas of red covers the faces of both queens: they look like warriors, like demons, like the angry dead.

Arielle, Jenny, and Katya have heard about their Aunt Julia and Uncle Robert's performances but have never, until now, been allowed to see one. "They're for adults," their mother said when they first asked. "Putatively."

"Too much sex for us?" asked Katya, and her mother said, "If it were only that." Later, she said, "When you're older you can go, if you still want to, but you'll be sorry." They badgered her this time, though, until she gave in—sooner or later, she always does if they keep at her.

Arielle feels as if she's inside one of her own nightmares, but she can't look away from the stage. Maybe she doesn't even want to. She'll never forget this play—if she can get through it. She's become more and more uneasy as, at each of the seven landings, Uncle Robert's amplified voice gave Aunt Julia—Inanna—another command: "You must surrender your scepter and crown to pass through this gate," or, "You must surrender your golden robe to pass through this gate." Whenever Inanna asked why, he repeated, "This is our way in the netherworld," sounding cold and formal, like a stranger. So at each gate, Inanna dropped something on the stairs and left it behind: her lapis lazuli scepter, her neckpiece, her robe, her dress, her slip.

Now at the bottom of the steps, Inanna takes off the last of her clothing and jewelry and walks onto the stage completely naked. Crouching figures emerge from the sides and move toward her. Movie images flicker on each of the walls behind the audience—one with soldiers in uniforms in the desert and tanks firing, another with planes in the air at night, a third with President—now ex-President—Bush talking, a fourth with a bald man the children only slightly recognize. Someone in charge of the war and too many other things, someone their father hates and goes on about. The bald man talks silently, smiling.

Arielle can see her own breath in the cold air. Aunt Julia might be crying, or is it a trick of the light? The Queen of Heaven and Earth descending into the underworld for her brother-in-law's funeral, and her sister won't let her in. Well, why wouldn't you cry? Arielle's thinking about all this deliberately, trying to stop her fear, to stay separate from it. But the play has made her part of its world, like one of the dreams where she's trapped in a culvert with someone coming after her, on the verge of learning something she doesn't want to know. The old feeling's coming over her, her breathing starting to close up, tears rising in her throat. She takes off a glove and feels around under her folding seat, pressing her forefinger against the metal edge where a rough bolt fastens the legs to the chair.

"Don't wriggle, Arielle," whispers her mother, and she holds still again, but the tears are coming back.

She waits until she can't stand it, then presses her finger against the bolt, hard. In the half-dark, when her mother is watching the stage, she looks down at her finger, the blood very slow, just a drop or two.

The pressure eases, but not enough. Moving very slowly, not to draw attention to herself, she presses until there's enough pain to help. She slides her glove over her bleeding finger and lets out her breath, slowly, the tears receding again.

Ereshkigal, the queen on the throne, wears shimmering deep blue robes, reflected in the mirrored floor, along with the torches and the faces of the audience at the edges. She calls out, "My sister thinks she can come down here without stripping away all she has, even her skin. She thinks, as a Queen of the Light, that she can rule our realm as well, but she will never see in the dark."

After the performance, Julia sits "backstage" in her robe, her heartbeat still quick from the performance. Waiting for Eva and the children, she talks with visitors in the warehouse's old break room, now converted to a place for costume changes but still decorated with relics of the previous era: a defunct time clock, beige lockers, a leftover sign on the wall: "Coffee and tea are free. Please pay into the coffee fund if you wish to use creamer and sweeteners. And clean up your own dishes! Your mother doesn't work here."

Her brother has wandered off somewhere. While she chats with people, her adrenaline rush slowly starts to fade; now she's starving. Eva has explained the biochemistry of performance and post-performance to her. The advantage of having a neuroscientist for an older sister: she can describe all the mechanisms you can't do anything about. But maybe it feels somewhat better to know that the anxiety beforehand fires up the amygdala, which brings in the hypothalamus and triggers the adrenal glands. Somehow epinephrine gets involved, releasing a lot of sugar, and some brain changes take place that hook into the internal opioid receptors. "Which explains," her sister said, "why you and Robert are such miseries to be around when you're not working."

Julia, now sweating through the thick makeup she hasn't had time to remove, smiles and responds to real compliments as well as to ostensibly innocent but barbed remarks. Martina, also a director of an experimental dance-theater company, says, "You so captured the sense of uneven power dynamics. How interesting to bring in Desert Storm."

"Thank you."

"You and Robert always do such intriguing things with appropriation and collaging bits of all kinds of cultures. This one is really quite . . . sometime you must tell me all about what the Kabuki makeup has to do with the Sumerian myth." Bringing in the Kabuki elements was Robert's idea. Julia argued against it, but she isn't going to say so. Martina switches gears. "These idea-driven pieces are so challenging. It's hard to keep them from being either bewildering or obvious. Or both." She laughs. "I focus on the images and the movement. It's so brave, though, the way you two take these big risks. I admire you for even trying."

"Thank you," says Julia, again. Where is Robert? Leaving her alone with the wolves. "I'm so sorry, I have to go find my sister and her kids." She shakes Martina's hand, smiling and thinking, *bitch*, and moves through the crowd. Maybe Eva hated the show so much that she's taken the girls and gone home: she'll call later with an excuse.

Eva said beforehand, "Baby, you know I won't understand anything of what you're doing."

"You can tell me what it felt like to you, though," Julia said. She's hoping to hear that the play is about what you have to give up to make it through, about how it's not too late even when it looks like it's all over. But if she were to tell her sister what she thinks it's about, Eva might agree just to keep the peace, and Julia would never know what she really saw in the performance. Waiting, she feels a little sick, as well as excited, even though Eva's never liked anything they've done. Robert would say, "She doesn't go to the theater, Jules." Julia will be thirty in three years, she shouldn't care what anyone thinks. Still, she wants to hear her sister's verdict.

And the children. Katya, at twelve, might be old enough to make something of it. Eleven-year-old Jenny, though, would just as soon be outside somewhere, playing with animals. And eight-year-old Arielle? Before the performance, Julia wondered if she might giggle uncontrollably once Julia was naked or melt down into one of her helpless tantrums when Ereshkigal had Inanna flayed. What *did* the kids make of the flaying?

Finally, here are Eva and the children, wandering into the old break room, dazed and out of place. They stand for a moment, looking around at all the half-dressed performers with their friends, and make their way through the crowd to Julia.

Eva says, after the initial hugs and kisses, "Ray had to work. He sends his regrets." And, "That was darker than I expected."

"I told you she gets flayed, right?"

"Maybe there was a little more blood than I'd pictured. Didn't you say it was mostly symbolic?"

Julia asks her nieces, "What did you all think?"

Katya, fierce and good-humored, says, "I thought it was cool," while Jenny smiles shyly, not exactly agreeing, but certainly agreeable. Arielle asks, "Why did she do it? To her sister." She has the look of a silver fox, sharp-faced, white-blonde hair and translucent skin, her head tipped to one side. As if she were both intently listening and on the verge of disappearing back into the forest. Little changeling.

Robert joins them, putting his hand on Julia's shoulder. "Why does Ereshkigal have all the gates locked? She thinks Inanna wants her realm. The kinds of people who rule heaven and earth probably think they should own the underworld too. A matched set."

Eva says, "Thanks for that, Robert. I'm sure that answers all the children's questions." She zips up her coat. "Did you write this before the elections? The end of the war?"

Robert laughs, not happily. "The *end* of the *war*. Oh, Eva."

"Fine. I'm going to get these three home to bed. Can you call me tomorrow so we can make Seder plans?" She kisses Julia and Robert and starts off toward the doorway, Katya and Jenny right behind. Robert disappears back into the crowd.

Arielle doesn't follow her mother and sisters, not yet. She can't stop thinking about the play, even with her finger painful and stiffening. Ereshkigal killed her sister by glaring at her, and her servants cut off her skin and hung her on a hook. After Ereshkigal cried for three days, she had her sister brought back to life, but they fought, and Inanna disappeared. The beautiful lights and snowflakes at the very end didn't make it any less sad.

She says, "I never thought hell would be so cold."

Julia wants to put her on her lap, but her niece has a dignity that forbids it. She's not someone you can talk down to. Such a strange child. Julia wants so badly to give her something. "Uncle Robert and I, and the rest of the company, were thinking about this Italian poet from a really long time ago. He wrote a poem in which an Italian poet with the exact same name finds himself, in the middle of his life, in some very dark woods. Which happens to most people, though I suppose I shouldn't say anything about it to you at this point. Anyway, the only way out was through hell, which is all ice at the very bottom."

"Why did he have to go through? Why couldn't he go back the way he came?" Arielle wonders if her finger might still be bleeding. Sometimes she gets carried away.

Julia says, "We should be able to go back, but it doesn't seem to work that way."

Arielle stirs, restlessly. After a moment she says, "Anyway, that's a different story than the play tells. And Ereshkigal could have kept her sister out, if she didn't want her at the funeral."

"Can you keep your sisters out of anywhere they want to be?"

Arielle considers this. "If you owned heaven and earth, it doesn't seem like you'd want a freezing hell. No sunshine. No birds."

Eva comes back into the room, beckoning and calling Arielle's name.

Julia says, "You should go with your mother." And, as Arielle continues to watch her, "Maybe once she had all that, she couldn't stop. Maybe the sunlight wasn't enough for her. Do you know what I mean?" Arielle nods. "So, there's another hell, a very famous Tibetan one, where there are these hungry ghosts. They have tiny heads, tiny necks, and huge great empty bellies, and they gobble away at a trench full of food. Once they've started, they can never stop." Like our family, she thought, but there had to be limits on what you could say to an eight-year-old girl, even this one. Instead, she said, "Maybe Ereshkigal thought Inanna was a hungry ghost."

"Arielle!" Eva's on her way over to them.

Arielle leans forward, suddenly, and hugs Julia so hard her ribs hurt. Julia puts her face into Arielle's hair, which hasn't been washed too recently, and kisses her head. "Sorry about the whole flaying thing." Arielle looks uncertain. "I mean, sorry about all the blood."

"That's okay. I get bad dreams from *Eek! The Cat.* So . . ." She shrugs, thinking about her pushpin at home—the cut from the chair hasn't done it. She needs a little scratch on her leg. Maybe more than a little.

"Arielle! Jules! What is up with you two?"

"Sorry, Eva," says Julia.

"Kumbaya." Arielle hugs Julia again and turns to go with her mother.

"Kumbaya," Julia says, touched, mystified, and hoping that Robert is nowhere in earshot.

She doesn't have a favorite niece, how could she? But her fellow third child, the fox-girl: she's the one who shows up most often in Julia's dreams.

PART ONE: THE DARK WOODS

I

Rescue

Seoul, May 2004

"Itaewon-o district," said the taxi driver, at last. Unnervingly cheerful, he'd pointed out temples and palaces for the previous hour and a half, all across town. The first couple of taxi drivers Eva and Ray had talked to at the airport had spoken only Korean; this one specialized in tourists and military personnel. "Your Yongsan army base is here. Biggest golf course in Seoul. Biggest park in Seoul. All yours."

Through the open window of the taxi blew the smells of exhaust and spicy fish. Neon lights shining their jukebox colors on the street, a nightly carnival. Vendors selling Disney T-shirts, jeweled hair ornaments, silk ties. Brilliant banners covered in *hangul* lettering. Crowds of Korean teenagers and clusters of American boys in jeans and leather jackets, running shorts, or fatigues. As they passed under the lights, their scalps shone under the thin fur of their buzz cuts.

"What if we're too late?" Eva's voice shook, and Ray said, harshly, "You have to be stronger than that." He unbuckled his seatbelt. He felt like a cartoon, the ultimate tourist: paunchy, balding, goateed, irritable. When he looked in the mirror these days, he already felt misunderstood. He could see Eva watching his seatbelt maneuver and deciding she was not going to say one word about his perfectly reasonable attempt to be a tiny fractional bit more comfortable, even if it meant being killed in the wild traffic.

On the plane, he'd been reading about the terrible, newly emerging Abu Ghraib story: he had to incorporate it into the book he was writing on the history of warfare. Maybe, if he could help make sense of this new development, he could stand to know it was happening. Or maybe not. The public nightmare. And then their private nightmare. If only he could *wake up*. He said, "Other people have yachts or golfing or archeological digs. We have Arielle."

Eva said, "It may seem as if it would help to joke about it. But it really doesn't."

"If there's something that does help, please let me in on the secret. Don't wait around for a more convenient time. Now would be an excellent moment."

They passed an immense, elegant palace with a series of roof-tops like wings curling up at the edges above the blossoming trees. "Gyeongbokgung," said the taxi driver. "The first Joseon dynasty palace. First built in 1395; we are a very old country. The palace was destroyed by Japan many times, but when we are invaded, we rebuild. You must visit it."

Eva said. "It's so beautiful." Maybe they could go, if things went well enough. Under her breath, she said, "The innkeeper was beside herself."

"I expect she was worried about being saddled with an incapacitated young woman and her bills. Maybe Arielle's breaking things or attacking people with broken bottles. Unsettling, if you're not used to it. Though if that were the case, the innkeeper would have called the cops, not us. So everything's doubtless hunky dory."

Eva took a deep breath and let it out slowly. The hardworking body—she had to admire its mechanisms, taking in oxygen to reset its autonomic nervous system, expertly shutting off the flood of adrenaline and cortisol. Ray rubbed her shoulder. She bent her head so that her cheek rested against his arm, and put up a hand to the slight roughness of his cheek and jaw, breathing him in. The mint of his deodorant over a musky sweat from the hurry to catch the plane, his dark herbal cough drops, the artificial floral scent of his shampoo— the smells of safety, boredom, old grievances, home.

They'd left the main road and its skyscrapers and could now peer into narrow alleys built before cars, full of people, bicycles, banners and painted signs, photographs of enticing bowls of food.

Ray said, "I always wanted to travel. We could have done almost anything, if we weren't busy raising three rotten kids. Two rotten kids and Jenny." This was meant to be a joke, but they both heard the inadvertent break in his voice.

"Please don't call the girls rotten," she said, dutifully. Her children were—she said this publicly and it was true—the most important thing in her life. Nonetheless, she was not sure she should have had them. Motherhood had always felt like an ongoing chaotic emergency, a frustrating dream in which she never had what anyone needed at the moment they needed it.

Ray said. "Let's think ahead to the part where we maybe get to go sightseeing."

Eva shook her head, thinking, No, but thanks for the heroic effort to teleport us into some madly preferable realm, a tourist heaven, where the good parents go to die.

The taxi whipped into an alleyway and stopped. The driver helped them with their luggage, and they gave him a massive tip, nearly the price of the ride. He nodded with a judicious satisfaction: they'd guessed right on the price of the informal tour. "Good luck," he said. "I am sorry for you, having so many girls. I have five boys. Much better."

They'd behaved as if they were invisible. When they looked at him in shame, he grinned, got back in the taxi, and shot away.

The inn had cracked beige paint, a hand-painted sign. Brown water streamed across the paving stones in front. They went inside, rang a bell at the front counter, and stood side by side. The young woman who finally emerged from somewhere in the back wanted them to pay what their girl owed; Ray said not until they saw her. The woman shrugged and started up the stairs. As they dragged their luggage up five flights, Eva became possessed by the idea that there was a mistake and they must be in the wrong place, but when the innkeeper slid open a door, there was Arielle on a cotton mattress, facing the window, her arms round her tucked knees. At the sound of the door, she uncoiled, turning from one side to another as if under attack. Elegant scroll paintings of mountains hung on the walls, but Arielle had thrown things all over the floor: a tangle of clothes, embroidered cushions, papers, and junk. The back of the inn opened onto a busy street: outside the window, tall gray buildings crowded together; a neon sign right across the way pulsed off and on.

"Arielle," said Eva, starting forward.

"Shoes off," said the innkeeper. She pointed at the polished golden floor and left only after, once again clumsy with shame, they fumblingly pulled off their thick walking shoes.

Eva knelt on the futon behind Arielle, laying a tentative hand on her thin and sour-smelling body. "Arielle, sweetie, we're here."

"Why?" Arielle jumped up and ran for the door. Her father blocked her, and she began circling the edges of the room, fidgeting, not meeting their eyes. When he moved in her direction, she ran from one side of the room to the other, like a marionette cut loose from her control bar, tangling herself in her own strings. Eva reached out to embrace her, and Arielle pulled away. Her lips were chapped, her face and arms covered with new sores and scratch marks layered over the old scars from her cutting years. Her long, matted ashy hair hung around her face. "It's not from smoking ice. I'm just on edge. And don't open the door. The landlady's a spy for the secret police. They don't want us helping the bar girls, that's why."

Eva longed to catch hold of her, to rock her, but when she was in this state they weren't supposed to get within ten feet of her or she could turn violent. She shouldn't have touched Arielle in the first place; she knew that, but it still felt wrong, against all her instincts.

Ray, who knew he had to leave this stage to his wife, closed his eyes but still saw Arielle, her gaunt body and gray skin, the huge dark circles under her eyes.

Eva said, in her lowest, most soothing voice, "Shh, shh, baby." She had to talk deep and slow and keep Arielle talking so she didn't disappear into paranoid fantasies. "Tell us what's going on, sweetheart. Tell us what's happened."

Arielle whispered, "Mom." She huddled against the wall. "I'm going to die."

"Not for decades, baby. I know it feels bad, but this part only lasts three days or so, then a few days of cravings. You can do that. I know you can. We'll be with you the whole time."

"They're *crawling all over me*. Don't you *see* them?" She held out her scarred, bony arms, shaking them at her mother.

"This part doesn't last," said Eva. "We'll find you a doctor."

"No doctors," said Arielle. "They'll lock me up. I'll kill myself."

Eva said to Ray, "We can't get her on a plane like this."

Ray said, "We'll get this under control," and, to Arielle, "You have to eat and take a bath, princess. Your mother will go with you and help you get cleaned up. Give me your cell phone." He held out his hand. Arielle shook her head. "You don't go anywhere without us now. Now *give me your cell phone*." His fiercest, most commanding voice, which none of them disobeyed. Arielle, still not meeting his eyes, handed over the phone. He said, in a low voice to Eva, "You get her bathed. I'll get rid of anything that shouldn't be here."

Searching the room, Ray found the little plastic bag of what looked like crystallized rock candy and the glass pipe, with its smoke-darkened hollow bowl and stem. He bundled them together and taped them with the brown paper and packing tape he'd brought along for this purpose, so no one could find them in whatever faraway trash bin he'd hide them in. Outside, a young male voice called out, "Hot *damn*," and a group of men broke into unmistakably American laughter.

The first place Ray and Eva had gone to collect Arielle was Zanzibar, two years earlier, after they'd reluctantly agreed to her entering a program as an exchange student. She'd been so bored in her high school—at seventeen she was reading her way through Shakespeare, D.H. Lawrence, Djuna Barnes, Sylvia Plath. And the program had strong guidelines. For the first few months of her time there it seemed mostly fine. She'd emailed them nearly every week, her letters increasingly lavish, unnervingly so, one exclamation after another: Making so many new friends! And the place was a revelation! Sunset dhow rides around the mangrove swamps, the sky "like breathing rose petals and honey," dhow rides "where you know you could die but you won't and you look at the black roots in the water and you're really, finally alive. . . ."

In the P.S., she always dropped some new and alarming hint of secret knowledge, like, "Don't worry about Katya—she'll be in touch soon. You know, she needs some space sometimes."

The letters stopped. Her cell no longer worked. Finally, her host mother called: Arielle was out of control and had just missed being arrested. Eva and Ray were on a plane within hours and took her off to a hotel room, imprisoning her in her room till she came down. To explain her pallor, thinness, vomiting, the jittery frenzy that possessed her, Ray had an explanation for the hotelkeeper, "Diabetes. She needs her medication."

And, to Eva, "You cannot tell anyone, at all, about this. It will destroy her future if it gets into her records. No one. Not any of our friends. And definitely not your family—it'll be all over the damn family grapevine in no time. They have zero discretion."

Eva had agreed; she understood his concerns. Of course she talked to Jenny, though she told her not to tell her father she knew about it. "And don't say anything to Katya, who probably couldn't handle it. If you're hearing from her, which I'm not asking about."

Jenny said, peaceably, "Mom, I'm not going to get between you and Katya," and Eva said, "I wouldn't expect you to, but if she were in real trouble, you'd let me know, right?"

Apart from small hints to a couple of her closest friends, the only other person Eva told about Arielle was Julia, since she and her sister told each other everything. At that point they were camping out in their parents' house anyway, cleaning it out, Julia fretting about whether moving them to assisted living had been a mistake. "Couldn't we have brought them home? To live with one of us?"

"We couldn't have," said Eva. "Stop bringing it up, Julia."

"But Mom and institutions. And now that she's finally . . ." Julia trailed off, and Eva said, after a moment, "Were you going to say *okay? Really?*" They began giggling, wildly, and had to go outside to stop, though every time they caught each other's eyes they started all over again.

By that time, they'd spent two full weeks on the clear-out. Their mother, Lily, had covered every inch of the walls, floors, and counters with fabric flowers and hundreds of fans, her carved masks, her own sculptures and collages, mouse-infested decorative cloths, apple-doll arrangements on stove burners, bathtubs buried under several feet's worth of clothes, books, empty but decorative Kleenex boxes, and thousands of clippings. They cleaned, packed, and threw things away.

Eva, at the kitchen sink, scrubbed piles of decorative plates, saying, "If the Collyer brothers had liked really bright colors, their place would have looked just like this."

How much were the family troubles genetic? When Katya, Jenny, and Arielle were teenagers, while she'd been trying to arrange birthday trips to Alcatraz or limit their TV time, they'd fallen into one catastrophe after another. As a family, they seemed to be cursed—first by Jenny's Hodgkin's lymphoma, striking out of the blue in her mid-teens. The other girls started to act out. All through the kids' childhood, she and Ray had tried to figure out what to do. Should they forbid the children all sugar and fried foods? Should they have family meetings with a talking stick? Family therapy? Religion? Their mother had taken the family to services for the High Holy Days, at least, but Ray wasn't Jewish: as a lapsed Baptist estranged from his missionary family, he was wary of all religions. And Eva wasn't much interested. When they celebrated a holiday with observant friends, though, the children loved the Hebrew prayers, the tiny goblets of sweet wine, the candles, the traditional foods. Should they have given the children more of this? Eva's questions drove Ray even wilder: the house had been full of shouting and recriminations.

Secretly, Eva had always felt, on her way to the lab, that she was headed to her real home, where she was an architect of information. She mapped mirror neurons, looking for emotional entrainment, building and maintaining the structures that contained and illuminated knowledge, a place for the next generation of affective neuroscientists to feed on what had already been created, to add their own portion in turn. And, of course, for the last few years she'd been studying the mechanisms of addiction.

She said, "You know, every parent with an addicted child thinks, did we do this, did we not do this? Maybe it was her friends, maybe it was our fighting, or maybe it was society, and she was just going along with the crowd. They were playing around; she wound up hooked. Maybe it was the family neurochemistry, only this generation takes it so much further and harder."

"You're the scientist, sweetie," said Julia, on her knees gathering tiny mouse turds into paper towels and spraying the shelves with bleach, a handkerchief over her mouth and nose. Bags and boxes surrounded her, labeled by Eva: "recycling," "trash," "keep," and "God only knows."

"Okay, the scientist in me says that probably she, like our father and her father, has very intense hedonic hotspots, and that if her own mu opioids and endocannabinoids were functioning properly, she wouldn't need this. Or that she was curious and fucked herself up, with permanent neural sensitization in her brain's mesolimbic systems of incentive salience. And the mom in me says that if I hadn't been so focused on Jenny, on her cancer, if I hadn't—Julia, please, don't say this to *anyone*—maybe loved Jenny most . . ." Eva stood over Julia, her face sad with memory. She seemed to come to herself, wry and in control. "You know, if those mice have Hanta virus, that handkerchief isn't going to do you a damn bit of good."

"Well, if the virus kills us, I hope it kills us quick, before we have to clean out the back room."

Eva thought Ray ought to have known she'd call Julia the very first morning: it was his own fault if he didn't realize that she wouldn't get through something like this without her sister. Though Eva did have to remind Julia not to tell Robert. Because her sister and brother worked together, and often lived together, Julia was apt to say anything to Robert, while Eva and Robert hadn't talked to each other about anything that mattered for years. He never even asked about the kids—he wouldn't want to know all this.

After they brought Arielle home from Zanzibar, Eva and Ray found her a counselor who would keep the file private, as long as Arielle was not a danger to herself or others. They also talked to Arielle for hours about the bad crowd she'd fallen in with. Eva told Ray, told Julia, told their counselor: their youngest girl was too loving and impulsive—she let herself be drawn into things to keep her friends from feeling bad or judged. Arielle, speaking up for herself, said she thought it was more that she'd been trying to focus her mind, to live a bigger, more engaged life. She'd loved the energy of meth, the confidence, the utter wild sense of power, but she knew she couldn't handle it.

She lived at home again, taking an entry-level job as an administrative assistant in a not-too-disorganized nonprofit, cooking her share of dinners, keeping her room clean, seeing a pretty nice boy, and paying a low rent so she could save money to go to college. Her story kept changing, but it seemed her boyfriend had dumped her—she wound up in three months of rehab, for which Ray and Eva cashed in their savings and remortgaged their house.

It seemed to have made a difference though: she turned nineteen without incident. She seemed to be more or less okay, though she didn't take the same pleasure in life as she had. Her yearning for that altered state had ruined ordinary desire. But it could return; she was resilient. This needn't be permanent.

Six months later, she was about to start classes at the local state college, but it turned out that she had requested a refund on her tuition and spent the money on a ticket to Seoul. She'd read a story about the bar girls who lived near the American base and made up her mind on the spot. "I'm ready to give something back, to help the women learn English and escape their awful lives. Most of them haven't had any other choice—someone rapes them and they get thrown out of their families."

She had on a loose long-sleeved blouse and long skirt, covering the old network of razored scars on her arms and thighs. With her newly combed long hair and nonstop energy, her rounded face and body—she'd regained most of the weight she'd lost on the drugs— she appeared to be fifteen, untouched, open-hearted. "But this place I'll be working is so great. It's a bakery as well as a teaching center, so the women can learn a new trade. And there's a daycare too. It's right near the American military base in downtown Seoul, which, of course, is where most of them live."

Her father said, "Absolutely not." And Eva agreed that it was a bad idea. She pleaded with Arielle, getting out the class catalogue for State, showing her what she'd be missing, talking about how she could go to Korea later on, once she had her degree. Ray shouted at her when she pleaded with Arielle, and then shouted at Arielle herself. She was sly, deceiving them, stealing their tuition money. Eva and Arielle cringed, and Eva began to cry. He slammed out of the house, saying, "I'm going for a walk," leaving them behind. When he returned, he began fairly calmly. He told Arielle, "You have no idea of your own strength. You are capable of being anything you could ever want to be. Don't sell yourself short." When she laughed in disbelief, he began to yell again.

"Dad, stop, I can't stand it."

He said, "Well, don't put me in this position. Don't you think I hate it? Tomorrow you're coming with me to court to see the lives of the pro-bono clients."

Arielle went with him the next day, sullenly, and retreated to her room that evening to think it all over.

"Tough love," Ray said to Eva. "You can't pretend it isn't happening. You have to take action." He was warm, generous, expansive with the whole family for the rest of the day.

Over the course of the next couple of weeks, though, Arielle was constantly at them, undeterred by anything they said or did. "I'm going to learn so much more than I ever would in school, and the U.S. owes the bar girls. You know we do, Dad—you know what military bases are like. They destabilize the entire area, create their own mini-economy."

Eva never knew what to say to her when she started talking about politics. Her didactic outrage was so much like Ray's—and so much like her own father's, like her brother's—the whole family on their own soapboxes. Her father had been known to say, when she and Julia and Robert were young, "Everyone in this family would rather be right than president." He'd grin, anticipating the moment. "But who the hell would want to be president?"

She began to weaken: giving way was her role. The family counselor had said, "You have a classic perpetrator-enabler-addict triangle dynamic." They'd only gone to him for a couple of months: he'd held as sacred the whole Narcotics Anonymous world with its ritualized twelve steps, confessions, bad coffee, in-jokes, and, worst of all, spirituality. He wouldn't understand that Arielle might benefit from going to Korea, getting involved in something bigger than herself.

And who could talk her out of it, if her parents couldn't? Eva asked Ray, and—revisiting the question in repeated calls—her baby sister. Though Julia wasn't supposed to know about any of this either. "What does your sister know about child-rearing?" It made Ray crazy when Eva told any of their secrets. "She has all these opinions based on what? Teaching would-be actors to pretend they're someone else?" Julia agreed with Eva that Korea could be a good idea. Arielle had had her troubles but now seemed to be back on her feet, and it would be good for her to have someone to look after.

In the end, Eva said to Arielle she was of age, and it wasn't as if she were free of temptation in the United States. She told her she would help bring her father around.

After another few days of battles, Ray agreed, grudgingly, but he had a few words to say. "Your body is a temple, princess," he told Arielle at the breakfast table, as she picked at her bowl of cereal. "Honor it with daily exercise and good food. Get out and walk in the sunshine every morning. Or the monsoon rains. Or the snow. Go outside and look at the beautiful world and all the people in terrible trouble, all getting through their lives. Do you have boots?"

"I have boots, Dad, I do." She patted his cheek, grinning. "And no secret hollow heels either. Gave all my pipes to Goodwill. Even the nice handblown glass one."

"You think this is a joke?" Before he realized she'd gotten to him again, he'd bellowed, and she flinched away. Had he ever, ever hit her? But how could he yell at her, his broken girl, who kept willfully breaking herself further, as if smashing up a whole palace of treasures. He leaned toward her, taking a deep breath. "You could be anything if you put your mind to it. The world is full of people who have problems they didn't bring on themselves. And people who've recovered from whatever they've done and whatever's happened to them. But you have to put yourself first. Don't get overtired. Don't go out with people who are bad for you. Those bar girls can take care of themselves if they have to. Put on your own oxygen mask first, okay?"

"I always mean to," said Arielle, "but in practice it's more like Grandma and Grandpa's house. I know there's an oxygen mask somewhere, but it's totally buried under a pile of pretty, trivial crap."

He wanted to eat her alive so she would always be inside him and never go into the world, to shake her till her head popped and her stubbornness broke loose. The stubbornness she'd inherited from him: she and Katya were totally his kids, unlike Saint Jenny, who came from some better, kinder universe. "Make a list of what you need to remember," he said. "I'll make it for you."

Their bon voyage presents to her included a Korean-English dictionary, new luggage, B-vitamins, pre-paid phone cards, a spray of Grandma Lily's silk orchids, and a card on which Ray had drawn an oxygen mask. Inside, he'd written. "Stay fed and hydrated. Take walks, preferably in nature. Stay away from addicts. Remember who you are and where you come from. Take days off. Take your vitamins. Have a study plan so that when it's time to come back and go to college, you're ready. We believe in you. Love, Mom and Dad."

"Keep it where you can see it," he said. "Pin it up on the wall and read it every day."

Eva pulled Arielle aside in the airport and gave her an envelope of emergency cash. "Don't tell your father about this, but I want you to know I trust you. Call the minute you think you need anything. I'm so proud of you, baby. I know you'll do great."

The first couple of nights in Seoul, none of them slept much. They stayed with Arielle in her room, Eva lying at the other end of the futon, Ray singing the pair of Elizabethan round songs he'd sung to all the girls as children when they were sick or in pain. They'd thrown out the trash, the ripped and crusted clothing and Ray's card with the oxygen mask, which at some point she'd torn into small pieces and thrown around the room. Cleaned up, Arielle didn't look as bad as they'd feared. Her teeth, thank God, were still okay. There was the scabbing. But that could heal?

When Arielle finally dropped off, Eva asleep near her feet, Ray went down the hall to the room he was supposedly sharing with Eva. The neon lights outside his window flashed. He could smell food cooking: garlic, hot pepper paste. He'd hardly eaten. He stood at the window, looking down at the streets, at the signs in mysterious angular lettering, the people for whom this was home, everyday life, nothing special. It was the middle of the night, but the streets were crowded with groups of men, older, younger, laughing, shouting. And families, too. A mother, father, and three children, right under his window, the boy in a suit like his father, the little girls in stiff pastel ruffles, white collars. Walking down the street, freely, maybe on their way home from some cheerful party. He felt a wave of sadness rolling up through him.

If they were going to be stuck in limbo, unable to imagine any future beyond the next day, he might at least do a little work on his book. He'd brought Keegan's *A History of Warfare*, his yellow legal pads for note-taking, and his *New Yorker*, with the unbearable article by Seymour M. Hersh, "Torture at Abu Ghraib." What had been happening, and who knew, at what level of government, what had been happening? Imperialism, warfare, torture: his very own subjects. He needed to read it again, to incorporate it.

A group of young voices outside, drunk Americans, sang "In Da Club." If he were a few years younger, he'd take off and join them. But then he wouldn't be available if Arielle had an emergency.

He took out his notepad and wrote, "How does the interpretation of events change the 'perspectivity' of a narrative? The U.S. military bases in Japan, Okinawa, and South Korea have become increasingly problematic for these countries. In the minds of the populations, if not the host governments, the line between protection and occupation seems to have blurred. It cannot be denied that the U.S. is, in large part, serving its own strategic interests."

No matter how unbearable the outside world could be, it was still better than thinking about your own family. Because, God, who could stand looking into that particular abyss? The larger abyss—the one out in the world—kept changing from news cycle to news cycle. Right now, it looked a lot like this new Abu Ghraib business.

Undoubtedly Hersh would write his own book. Ray had a different task. If only, while he was in Seoul, he could occasionally sneak away to work on his study of the legal issues around border conflicts: seizure of land; legal and societal consequences for the losers—from the exaction of tribute to the rebuilding of the vanquished; and recompenses, or the lack thereof, for the victims of history. It was time to pull it together, to *finish* it. He'd been reading for years, making notes, writing chapters that didn't quite work together, hoping to come up with a clear overview and argument. He'd had to give up his nonprofit work, but if he could show policy makers the ways that war augmented rather than solved the problems, he could be part of bringing about a world in which war no longer existed. It was a long shot. Nonetheless, it seemed like an effort worth giving one's life to.

The *yo*, a thin cotton mattress, gave absolutely no back support. He paced the floor, watching the world outside his window. The party dying down, finally. But there were still stragglers, pairs or groups of men coming home with their ties loose, faces flushed with drink, arms around each other.

He couldn't remember a time when he had that much freedom or camaraderie. He almost never saw his old friends from the nonprofit days now. After two decades of struggling in badly funded inner city legal clinics, he'd moved into a firm that specialized in contract law, becoming a "corporate sellout" according to the daughter whose therapy, rehab, and legal bills had necessitated the move to his new job. To be fair, he had to admit she'd learned the term from him; it was his own evaluation as much as hers.

He was lucky that he'd been able to make the move at all. For the last few years, he'd been at his new office nearly all the time or, evenings and weekends, visiting the homes of low-income parents of juvenile delinquents, helping them navigate the justice system. He still had to prove himself over and over at work: putting in more billable hours than anyone, uncomfortable when the guys in the office teased him. He'd never be stumbling happily down the street with them either. They were always coming to him with their troubles, their stories, asking for advice. In actuality, they solved their own problems—he merely asked them questions. But they gave him the credit, and he acquired a reputation for kindness, for being able to help anyone. Not something he could stand to think about right now. He crawled under the covers, pressed the hard pillow over his eyes to block out the neon, and tried to empty his mind.

By the third morning, they could at least sit with Arielle on her *yo*, Eva trying to feed her green onion pancake, sliced tangerine, and peeled round Korean pear. "Come on, sweetie, one more bite. You need your strength."

"I'll be sick."

"It feels that way because you're so hungry. Just a little bit and then you'll want more."

Arielle, reluctantly, ate a section of tangerine. "That's enough, that's enough," she cried out, pushing her mother away with both hands.

Ray jumped to his feet. "Let's get outside. Walk it off a little. You can show us the sights, princess."

Outside, the air had a smoky flavor, more than exhaust. "What is that smell?" asked Eva. She and Ray each had hold of one of Arielle's arms, supporting her. Arielle wasn't so much physically weak as raw, the world hitting her directly on her exposed nerves; she jerked as if she were being electrocuted, but she didn't seem to be hallucinating.

She lifted her head, sniffing the air. "Coal smoke. Heating. Under the floors."

Ray said, "I'd hate to see the air quality index," and Arielle said, "Seoul is a world-class city. Right up there with LA and Mexico D.F."

"I like it," said Ray. "Though not as well as Zanzibar."

"Sorry, Dad. Next time, I'll try to lose it in Bali or somewhere. Would that be better?"

Eva said, "Could we not have a next time? I don't want to ask for the moon here."

"Bali for Dad, and the moon for Mom," said Arielle. "If we're asking for the moon, could you send Katya next time? I miss her like crazy, and she's always too broke to come see me."

Was she back, the real Arielle? Ray and Eva glanced at each other, trying not to get caught hoping.

Soon, though, Arielle stopped and peered up at the rooftops. "The government is watching us. They're filming to get it on record. Oh, God, we have to get back." She began shaking; they had to cover her with their sweaters. She moved with a crablike scuttle that earned them all stares. "See?" she said. "You can't tell which of these people are safe."

It was two wretched days later before they were able to go for a real walk. Eva had her eye on the bright silk blouses, a purple mohair sweater with feathers and sequins, but Arielle was pushing forward through the people who flowed around them. She said, "This is the red light district. This is where most of my bar girls work. Worked."

Street vendors shouted out to tourists, offering all kinds of goods, mostly clothing and luggage or food—savory pancakes cooked on grills, pots of fish in red sauce or soups on open stoves. A place of light, air, cheerful commerce. Two Korean riot policemen, bored twenty-year-olds, had their black shields propped against a wall, one squatting, eating noodles, the other smoking and watching the street with an angry half-smile.

How Eva would love to show this to Katya, to Jenny. She felt so far away. And it seemed unfair that they were so locked in their lives at home. What a waste for Arielle to be in the middle of all these wonders while only looking for a way out.

She had to stop judging Arielle, who knew her too well and would see it in her face.

Ray asked, with interest, "So which of these places are cathouses?"

Eva slapped him on the arm.

Arielle said, "Not on this street. This is Itaewon, the main tourist drag. Where our congressmen come to get their suits made on 'fact-finding missions.' Come on, I'll show you the real thing." She started ahead, smiling at a child who stared at them, his fingers in his mouth. "*Annyong!*" she said in greeting, her face skeletal but beaming. He turned and ran.

She led them into a side street; the road twisted and branched. The buildings dropped from several stories to one or two; the colors became browns and ochres, faded and peeling, the signs hand-painted rather than neon or hard plastic. A group of American soldiers, out of uniform, jostled each other, deliberately—one of them rounded off with his fists, ready to throw a punch. "Hall is mad now," said one boy, and another sang out, "Ooo-*ooh*, watch out for Hall." Hall, flushing, dropped his fists and put his hands in his back pockets.

One of the young men stopped in front of Arielle, his hands hooked into pockets, elbows hunched forward. He smelled of sweat, beer, cigarettes. "I know you," he said, drunken, belligerent. He peered forward, having trouble seeing. "Don't I know you from somewheres? Didn't we party with you in . . . in, where was it?" And to his buddies, "Don't I know her?"

Arielle shook her head.

"You know a lot of people *like* her," said the one who'd been teasing Hall. He took the soldier by the arm and said, "Sorry about Williams. He's a little pissed."

"More beer!" shouted one from the back who either hadn't been paying attention or wanted to move things along. The soldiers went on down the street, laughing. Ray had a secret admiration for all warriors, their recklessness, their vivid lives.

Her voice bitter, Arielle said, "A lot of these places are bars. At night you can hear 'Love Shack' and 'Let's Twist Again' out of most of them. This is where the bar girls work. Recreation for our military. Although an American woman has the advantage of costing nothing and speaking the language." Tears came into her eyes; she rubbed them away with her scarred hands.

"You were always such a good student," said Ray, hearing, when it was already too late, his own tone of sad wonder.

So many decisions Eva and Ray had never known how to make. For example, what kind of chemo Jenny should have or what to do when, at nineteen, a year after she'd been pronounced cancer-free but told no private insurance company would cover her for the next two decades, she got pregnant and dropped out of school to go live on a farm with her boyfriend. They'd struggled with deciding whether or not they should bail Katya out of her latest financial disaster, and whether or not Arielle's distractibility, nightmares, and tantrums meant she should be having treatment of some kind. Maybe they were making too much out of a phase.

Or so they thought until blood first leaked through Arielle's sleeves. Eva had made her take off her pink leotard and had seen what she'd done to her perfect body. How old had she been? Ten? Eleven? Somehow it had been going on for years. They hadn't seen it. They couldn't stop it. The therapists couldn't stop it. Eva and Ray had so wanted her to find some other solution, until, finally, she had. It seemed that, at every turn, they'd made the wrong choices.

Ray remembered her in sixth grade building a model of Mission Santa Cruz, constructing the walls from chicken wire, plastering them with homemade adobe. With this came other, painful memories and imaginings of what had not yet happened but might. The failure of Arielle's brain, her kidneys. Prison.

Eva, seeing bad imaginings on Ray's face, couldn't stop her own: a picture of herself standing by a table in some morgue. She couldn't watch any TV show or movie where they had that cheesy, horror-show moment of peeling back the sheet.

More images: the unsullied Arielle who might have been wearing a Ph.D. hood, holding her diploma. Laughing or playing with her own children, handing them grapes and crayons. Whatever she might now become had to grow out of where she was; so many possible doors were closed. They didn't know if they had done this to her or whether it had just happened, a freak of chance or the times they lived in. Were they terrible parents?

Arielle, in turn, read their expressions, the dreadful nostalgia followed by fear and wistfulness, the moment when a pale image of another Arielle joined them—incorporeal but not insubstantial—an alternate-world Arielle, disappointing to no one.

Enraged, guilty, she shook her body all over, rubbing her arms, as if she'd been drenched in sticky oil. "We have to go to the palaces, and, oh, how could I forget? The kimchi museum! Tonight we'll go to

Korea House. We can stuff ourselves at the buffet and watch the traditional dance and drumming show. You'll love it. It's been unchanged for, like, hundreds of years."

Ray said, "Look at what happens when you respect tradition."

Arielle had not managed to distract him. Now she was going to get the lecture.

Her father went on, "They go to school, they study, they carry on through difficulties. This *kibun,* the feeling of the group that must be protected—you know about that?"

"I am the one who's been living here, Dad."

"But you haven't been paying attention, princess. They know how to weave a community together. This respect for tradition helps protect the culture."

Eva took hold of his arm, but he pulled away and went on. "When you take that stuff, it's not only yourself and your body you're hurting. Yes, and it's not only your own family. You damage the fabric of society."

Arielle examined the backs of her hands, the scabbed-over sores. Her mother put an arm around her. "I think a trip to Korea House is a brilliant idea. I'm particularly excited about the drumming. And the food, of course. I've read about that buffet."

That night, after a feast and dance performance, Arielle agreed to be locked in her room for safety, and Eva joined Ray down the hall. Eva undressed in silence until he said, "You're not still sulking, are you?"

"*Damage the fabric of society?* Would that be the corporate-owned politicians and the media-drugged masses you're always on about? What goddamn fabric of society did you have in mind?" She hurled his shirt and underwear at him, then his dress pants.

Tipsy, he let her throw clothes until his belt buckle hit him, at which point he grabbed her. "Those kids can wheedle you into anything. If we stop running to their aid all the time, they'll learn to look after themselves."

"If we stop running to their aid, they could die. Are you willing to let them die on the way to independence?" He bent his head, maybe conceding, but she was on a roll and couldn't stop. "You know, I'm not the one who *dotes* on the girls."

"At least I don't let them manipulate me and then lie about it. You have to be reasonable and firm. A strong parental role model."

She said, breathless, "Strong parental . . . you have to be kidding me. How many nights did they watch you getting drunk? And, if it comes to that, she is far too old to be called 'princess.' It's perverse, Ray. It's unwholesome."

"What a goddamn sick thing to say. Can you even hear yourself?" He had a grip on Eva that she couldn't break. He wrestled her backwards and onto their *yo*—she could feel his growing erection through his clothes.

"Forget *that* idea," she said.

"We're on vacation." He pinned her with his weight. Her body, incurably conditioned, responded when he kissed her ear, her neck.

"Absolutely not." With Arielle suffering down the hall, sleeping the heavy sleep brought on by two of Eva's Ambien, getting up only to pee in a jar?

Ray ran his palm over her cheek, tracing her collarbone, her breasts. He closed his eyes, his breathing rougher. He opened them again. "Stop thinking about her. *Look at me.*"

Eva, watching his reddened face, said, "It was such a bad idea to marry you. I think I've regretted it the whole time." Maybe the biochemistry had left an opening for the harm to their children, but his blame, his rages, had turned the key.

And now maybe she'd finally broken the fragile mechanism of their doomed marriage. Why hadn't she left him when her friends wanted her to, back in her thirties? But she'd had no idea what she was going to do on her own with three kids. Visitation weekends, living in a tiny white box, unable to go to the lab because there was no one to watch the baby. And if she left Ray now, she'd be a single woman in her late forties, living alone in a rented apartment, dating shirtless guys in cowboy hats she met online. Every one of them deeply flawed, in ways she wasn't accustomed to putting up with. And she couldn't even imagine telling these dates about her children, let alone trying to enlist their help. No father loved his girls more than Ray. He had been wonderful all through Jenny's chemo and Katya's financial disasters. And Arielle respected him: he could get her to do things no one else could, like handing over her cell phone or agreeing to be locked in her room.

He said, beguiling, "Come on, honey."

So, the marriage was still on. Was she sad or relieved? Yes, of course. She also resented the manipulation in his voice. "I couldn't relax." But she could hear herself weakening, as always.

"It'll just be the two of us. No thinking about Arielle. I'll say your name. And you say mine." He pressed downwards, a claim on her. "Eva." Kissing her lips—light, quick kisses. "Eva." Her eyelids. "Eva." Her neck. "Eva." The hollow at the base of her collarbone. "Eva. Eva. Eva." When she started to laugh, he knew he'd won.

In the morning, they wandered through Namdaemun street market, examining buckets of live eels, ropes of dried persimmons, sweaters, kitchen equipment, jewelry, and all the possible permutations of ginseng, including soaps, teas, and candy. Eva bought souvenirs. Arielle bought Gyeongju bread for her parents: pastry filled with sweet red bean paste, the top imprinted with a single chrysanthemum. She might be damaging the fabric of society—it was amazing, the stuff her dad said sometimes, did he even hear himself?—but she could still give her poor parents a treat. The worst part of all of this was knowing what she was doing to them. But maybe she could stop.

She had palmed the Ambien and could have gone out the window the night before, gone over to the base and convinced Billy to fix her up, but she had wasted the night wrestling with herself. She had the 10,000 *won* she'd taken from her mother's purse, but she hadn't done anything yet. She might not. She was over the worst of it now, and if she kept going, she could stay clean. Billy might want her to have sex with him if she went over to Yongsan, and she wasn't sure she wanted that. Though she kind of did. "Love my gun more than you," he'd once said, grinning. She was done with him, done with ice, done with that whole part of her life. She could stay in her room at night, go home with her parents, get a job in a kindergarten. Here's your juice, here's your crayons, no, we don't throw sand in each other's eyes, it's story time, everyone, let's get in our circle. She could put the money back, without her mother ever knowing.

Did Eva know? She didn't seem to. How sad was it, that they thought they could keep her inside by locking a door? They were so smart, and so dumb. She squeezed her mother's hand. "You've been very quiet today, Mom."

Eva smiled, thinly. She wasn't sure she had the energy for today, but it wasn't like they had a choice. Arielle seemed all right. And they had already bought their return tickets and a one-way for Arielle; it was just a question of waiting for nothing more to happen. "Have I?" she said. "Maybe I'm a little tired. Taking everything in." She carried her new masks—the Noble Lord, the Foolish Servant, roles they'd watched enacted in a dance performance.

An American male voice shouted, "I'm not going to be ripped off is all." Eva looked around to see a pair of short-haired young Midwesterners arguing with a Korean stallkeeper over sneakers while a friend tried to calm them. The shouter said in an aggrieved voice, "They could be a little grateful." This dislocated farm boy wanted gratitude for his sacrifices. He was, perhaps, not finding the outside world as exciting as he'd hoped it would be.

A terrible wailing siren filled the air from all sides at once, echoing overhead. As if in a sudden rain shower, people scattered and ran for the buildings.

"Oh, no, it's the fifteenth," said Arielle. "Quick." She and Eva and Ray ran to a multi-storied building and pushed inside, the crowd squeezing them against a display of velvet and lace children's dresses, the goods spilling out everywhere, a nightmare of shining excess.

Ray said, "The Civil Defense Drills."

Arielle, apparently unconsciously, stroked the velvet of a child's black and white dress, feeling the silky rosebud at the waist. "Before I came here, I knew about the hostility between the North and South, but I didn't *understand*. Not until I went to the Demilitarized Zone, saw the soldiers, felt the tension."

The crowd shifted, people moving into the building's depths. Ray said, meaningfully, "Korea, of course, is still technically at war, though the resumption of open conflict seems less and less likely. Still, both sides are prepared, which is why they still need our help, though they may not always realize it."

"Dad, is that very inapplicable metaphor aimed at me? Because how gross would that be? Even if South Korea weren't centuries older than the U.S. as, like, a country."

"Oddly enough, not everything is about you. It's not a metaphor: it's a historical set of occurrences."

People pushed past them through the steamy, almost visible air. Arielle said, "My first month here, I was in the subway when the warning blew. I came up to find the place deserted. People had parked their cars, ducked into shops, even squatted by the sides of the road. I walked past a government installation and two soldiers trained their rifles on me, following me and keeping me in their sights. A guy from the Embassy told me later that five years earlier they would have shot me for not going to ground."

Both of her parents turned on her in horror, imagining what could have happened.

"Don't start," she said. "Sorry I told you. I don't need you both at me. We probably all wish they *had* shot me, but obviously they didn't."

Eva was furious, ashamed of her rage, and angrier because of this. "All we ever do is to try to keep you alive. You are our *only priority*. I wonder, sometimes, if you've even noticed."

"I'm really, really grateful, okay? But just stop. Stop now."

Ray said, "Of course we don't wish they'd shot you. But we can't do all the fighting for you. You have to make an effort on your own behalf, princess." Despite himself, he felt a geyser of hopeless rage shooting up through him. He burst out, "Did we spend our retirement money putting you through rehab because we wished they'd shoot you? Do we work day and night to pay all your bills because we wish they'd shoot you? Do we drop everything and fly to wherever you are whenever you need us because we wish they'd shoot you?"

Arielle looked at him in stunned horror, and Eva grabbed him by the arm. "Stop, Ray, stop. I'm sorry I said anything. She's doing her best. You are always *at* them. How can anyone breathe when you're shouting and lecturing and bullying us all?"

Arielle began to cry. Oh, how she wanted that ice rush of power and aliveness, to feel like herself again. She wasn't going to put the money back. Guilty, she cried more.

Eva put her arms around her, saying, "Arielle, don't." How on earth had she so lost control of her tongue? She'd set Ray off too. She *had* to do better. She rocked Arielle, cradling her head where it rested against her shoulder. "Honey, I'm so sorry. I love you so much. I'd do anything for you. Do you know how much you mean to me?"

A fantasy came over Ray: the plane home attacked by terrorists: an explosion in midair, no survivors, metal and body parts flaming in the sky and dropping into the sea. He was ashamed of himself, killing all these reasonably innocent strangers, even in his mind. "This is the end," he said. "This has to be. We can't go through this ever again."

His wife and daughter stared at him, out of identical eyes, a little too close together, Arielle's darkly shadowed. Arielle blew her nose. "It might be the end," she said. "One time it has to be, right?"

They spent their last day exploring the antiques on Insadongil: tiny stores crowded all down the winding street, full of decorated chests, painted masks, traditional pottery, folk paintings. Arielle—who'd found Billy in the night and was now flying—linked her arm through Eva's. The air felt clear and cold, though it still smelled of *ondol* smoke. A bicycle swerved, just missing them. Cars, honking, inched down the packed street.

In the huge central hall of Yeongbin Garden, they rolled *bulgogi* in lettuce, dabbing it all in pepper paste, dipping their chopsticks into all the side dishes, enough food for six or eight people. The rich, dark, chewy beef. A vast spread of different kinds of kimchi: red-flecked, fiery napa cabbage, tangy radish cubes, funky anchovy-laced mustard greens. Bowls of rice and soup, and many glasses of the irresistible, powerful *soju*. Eva and Ray ate and ate. Arielle jumped up to go to the bathroom, came back, pushed her food around with her chopsticks, pulled back long strands of hair, put it up, took it down, and retwisted it.

Now Eva was glad not to have the other girls with them, at least at dinner. Katya would be denouncing the *bulgogi* and telling unfortunate stories about the memories and emotions of cows; Jenny, a quieter vegetarian than her older sister, would say nothing aloud, but she'd look at the beautiful food with so much sadness that it would take a defiant effort to ignore her. How extreme all her children were. They fit, absolutely, in the Zamarin family, unlike her. She wondered how the girls were doing, if Katya were in trouble, whether Jenny would tell them if she'd been to the doctor and found signs of her illness returning.

She checked herself: she was worrying about the other girls to keep from worrying about Arielle. She hadn't been in the bathroom long enough to take anything, had she? And where would she have gotten it? They hadn't left her alone for ten minutes any time the room was unlocked. She tried to inconspicuously get a look at Arielle's pupils. Arielle, though, was moving around too much, piling beef and pepper paste into a lettuce leaf. She pretended to stuff it in her mouth, then dropped it onto her father's plate at the last moment, laughing exuberantly. Surely she was just in a mood.

Ray said, "A lot of older people grew up speaking Japanese as their first language. Couldn't even have Korean names, a culture totally suppressed."

"The Imperial Japanese," said Eva. Money might be missing from her purse, but she couldn't be sure. Probably she'd spent it herself. Horrible, to suspect your own daughter and almost certainly unfairly.

Ray drank another glass of *soju*. "If the Japanese had never been overthrown, what would we know about Korea? Do we accept the narratives of the winners, i.e., the perpetrators? If not, how can we interpret existing evidence?"

Arielle said, "Do we have to?" She began to laugh and couldn't stop. Her parents exchanged uneasy smiles.

Ray said, "It keeps you from getting Alzheimer's, learning new things." But now he was watching Arielle too, wondering.

A short, sobering silence fell over them, in which all three considered whether it was likely that Arielle would live long enough to get Alzheimer's.

Ray cleared his throat, returning to his subject. "Amos Funkenstein said that the aim of the counternarrative is 'the destruction of the adversary's self-image, of his identity, through the deconstruction of his memory.'" He felt himself turning red. Arielle was frowning unhappily. Perhaps she believed he was calling her an adversary, someone whose memory and identity needed deconstructing. His blushing was only likely to confirm this idea. But he couldn't stop himself. If anything, thinking about this was making it all worse.

"Roman Empire," said Eva, coming to his aid. "Ottoman. Standard practice." She didn't always mind his pomposity—she found many of his points interesting, or at least interestingly problematic. For example, why define the strong as "perpetrators"? The Japanese had been an occupying force, but maybe they'd been pushed by history into the position of having to be the strong ones. She thought, If I were a country, I would be a perpetrator. Like Japan. Or the U.S. I would have gunboats. I wouldn't be the enabler. Let Ray do it for a change.

She could feel her mind obdurately turning away from knowledge. Arielle was giddily on edge. Maybe they should never have left her alone in her room, not even with the door locked. Love comes back and back, but not trust, Eva thought.

Arielle had a bout of giggling. Ray remembered her as a teenager, alternately sullen and so charged with eroticism that he'd refused, after she turned thirteen, to let her sit on his lap or hug him for more than a few moments. Her face had softened now; the living blood beat immediately under her skin. Maybe she was okay. Maybe she'd scared herself enough this time. People got over it. They did. They went on and became drug counselors; they scared themselves all over again, every day, watching their clients.

Arielle stopped laughing: she felt insects—she knew they didn't exist—crawling over and through her. She scratched her arms till beads of blood popped up at the edges of her scabs. When she saw her mother watching her, uneasily, she held both hands still. "That's why they can't bear us here, you know? They're still at war—it's all just an armistice. The government wants our troops but the people feel occupied."

"Now who's making historically inappropriate metaphors?" said her father. He felt the joke going painfully flat. "Shall we head out?"

A short walk took them to a familiar-looking palace. Arielle said, the words tumbling out, "Gyeongbokgung . . . it was burned and burned. The Japanese kept invading. And now it's us. Not that we're burning anything. But you see what I mean? You think you're protecting some-one, but you're really enjoying your power. A devil in your ear says, 'We have to do this.' And you find reasons, afterward. Do you *see*?" She stopped, abruptly.

"Isn't that interesting," said Eva, panicking. Over something, over nothing. It wasn't possible. Arielle often sounded wild, talking about war. She couldn't have gotten hold of anything. Maybe this interest in politics would inspire her to go back to school: it would, perhaps, be the happy ending for her to become more like her father. Or like Eva's own father, for that matter. As Philip had aged, he not only lectured less but also seemed to have largely stopped drinking. A hopeful sign for all of them. Meanwhile, Eva could find some in-ear headphones and listen to music all day long as they talked. Arielle was going to be moody; that was part of it.

No, there was the scratching. The mad half-blankness of her eyes. Eva was going to have to ask her. And Arielle would lie to them.

Though they would all be home in a few days, and Arielle back in rehab, with whatever was left of their retirement money, Eva did not see any ending point. Some people's kids recovered. The right rehab, enough repetitions, the right moment. You just had to never give up.

Ray turned sideways, suddenly, startling her. "Will you look at that?"

In two different directions, they could see young women in full, elaborate, snowy-white bridal dresses, like huge sugary cakes. Each bride had a tagalong groom, along with a mob of attendants, family, and the photographer, with or without assistants. One bride whirled forward with a bustle of laughing bridesmaids streaming out behind her, holding her veil and train. A photographer ran alongside, exhorting, and a sulky young man trailed behind the group. The other bride posed in front of a weeping willow near a large pond, out of which arose a pillared summerhouse. Her groom sat on a bench, waiting; her attendants arranged her skirts, veil, and face while she smiled widely, careful of her lipstick, and her photographer called out directions in a peremptory tone.

Arielle said, "They all have Korean wedding dresses and also Western ones. Some of them go all the way south to Cheju Island. For the photographs. It's a huge deal." Her high was slipping away. She began to scratch her arms again, fighting the invasion of burrowing insects. Imaginary, imaginary. Her parents both watched the brides for a moment, wistfully, as if Arielle weren't there, as if she couldn't see them calling up her other, phantom self, the one the drugs had never yet managed to kill.

II

Stage Fright
Zanzibar, June 2004

Julia splurged on a discount round-the-world ticket, a month of travel between leaving San Francisco and landing in New York to start rehearsals. Robert was furious with her, first of all for leaving their own company, but also, apparently, on behalf of the honor of political dance-theater in general. Robert said, "You have some *idea* that going to New York will make you a real actress. You're a real actress here, even if it's not all talk-talk-talk. But fine, go for a year. You're going to hate all that artifice and clawing for position. Let me know when you're ready to come home."

But her new home was out in the world, a bigger life on bigger stages. She promised herself not to call anyone until she was settled in New York, to live in the world without having to describe it to her family or cannibalize it for theater. It was enough to look. In Fukuoka, all the gardens had shrines: Buddhas, exact arrangements of bamboo and water. In Tokyo at night, extravagant palace rooftops reflected the neon lights of the big hotels. Bangkok's mosaics and gold statues, like light shining off the water, said *this is what matters.* Truly on her own for the first time—at thirty-eight! (The three years when she'd lived with Gil in her twenties didn't count, since, obviously, she hadn't been on her own then, or maybe she had been, but it had taken months to realize it.) Immediately she discovered informal guides and phrasebooks, learned how to gesture and pidgin her way through. If you had the accent right, even if you had almost no vocabulary, people could understand a surprising amount. As usual, people stared at her, burst out grinning, wanted their picture taken with her, and confessed to her the secrets at the heart of their life stories.

This had nothing to do with Julia herself but with her long golden hair and oracular, almost surreal beauty. A Venus, a Madonna, an angel whose smile suggested knowledge of a hidden joke, along with the illusion of the acceptance of human frailty. But it was all a genetic trick, her parents' looks combining in an unexpectedly symmetrical and enticing arrangement of features. (An art teacher she'd once had, showing slides, had cried out, "Beauty, my dears, is a matter of millimeters.") Anyway, her looks would be gone in a few years, and she hadn't yet figured out what, exactly, would replace them. Though she could become whatever she was playing, imagine what it was like to be another person, her efforts to develop a personality—what was a personality?—had come to nothing. As near as she could figure out, she didn't entirely exist. On her good days, she experienced herself as a clear glass bowl full of shifting possibilities; on others, she'd begun to have falling dreams, jerking awake in a sweat.

Fortunately, she was learning her lines for *Heartbreak House* and her nightmares faded as she became her character: worldly, tolerant, bossy, generous, amused by everything. Her first role in New York was in a Shaw play, and one that ended in an air raid. But her director had said that he saw it, essentially, as a comedy, if a dark one, and that they'd be focusing on the tricky relationships between the characters. "It will not," he assured her, "be at all preachy or didactic." It wasn't as if she'd been offered a lot of other parts. Besides, Hesione Hushabye was a delicious part. When had she ever played delicious parts?

She took a train north from Fukuoka with Marie and Celeste, two doctors on their way across Asia to join a clinic doing AIDS work, both so young that Julia mistook them for college students. She toured temples in Tokyo with a Danish couple traveling the world: Nicklas, who'd been an administrator with refugee organizations for twenty-seven years and couldn't stand it anymore, and angular, gray-haired, calm Lucia, who'd raised their three children and worked as a legal secretary for a series of bosses as temperamental as her husband.

Nicklas went off to find a cybercafé, while the two women hid out in a tiny restaurant among the collection of restaurants and shops inside the Hakata Station. They ate huge bowls of soft, salty udon noodles with fried burdock root. Lucia confided in Julia that she was thinking of leaving the marriage, except she had no idea who she'd be without Nicklas. If she finally left, would she have some peace or would she spend the rest of her life regretting it? "I know people who've done it and have never gotten over it. They're always telling the story to see how it could have been different. Though of course others are happy to have escaped. So how do you know?"

"Have you tried counseling or trial separation?" Julia asked. Surely there was some available response that wasn't feeble. Wouldn't it be better to be alone than to be miserable all the time? Unless, of course, you were *more* miserable alone.

Lucia said, "We did go to see someone, but Nicklas was wonderful in our sessions. So funny, so thoughtful. I could see the counselor falling in love with him and looking at me coldly: what a bitch, not to be grateful for a man like this. So we finally decided to have not a trial separation but a trial togetherness. We're at our best when we're traveling. Maybe we should just keep doing it until we're too old to have to make a decision."

In turn, Julia confided her mad plan to do real theater at last, how she'd spent far too much on her first trip to New York and the auditions and was now running through the rest of her "life savings," which, what was that really? Almost nothing, and no wonder. How could you save anything from your life? Nobody expected, for example, to store up time. What if, out of every day, you were supposed to put aside three percent of your hours and you'd get to tack them on at the end of your life? By that point, either no amount of time would be enough or you'd wish you'd spent them all in what you'd probably remember as your happy youth.

Julia said, "My brother may or may not ever forgive me. He can hold a grudge basically forever. My relationship with him is more like a marriage than my marriage was. Except, of course not, how could it be?" She felt herself blushing down to her neck, as if she'd made some awful confession, as if there were something perverse and wrong in their relationship. She went back to talking about money, life choices. This move to New York could turn out to be as ruinous as a life of making impossible performances with Robert. She said, "Maybe, finally, I could have done something sensible instead. But I don't have the genetics for that." Here she stopped, again—was she about to spill out the whole bag of family secrets?

Lucia said, "There aren't any shortcuts or safe paths. And since you've given everything up to do this, why indulge these fears?" Julia felt a huge ungovernable love for this stranger. She wanted everyone to be a stranger from now on.

In Bangkok, Julia met Renard, a lovely foul-mouthed journalist from Paris, and spent three days with him. He said, "You should let me make love to you until neither of us can see or walk," but somehow, though she'd felt a mild lust for him, they didn't wind up in bed after all. What he really wanted was to talk about the end of his marriage: his wife's affair, why he'd hit her, his retaliatory affairs, and finally his wife's hacking into his files and email account, her deletion of all his contacts and every article he had in progress. (She had stopped along the way just long enough to forward his most intimate emails to all of his colleagues at work.) "It is not possible that we became those people," he kept saying. Julia should, by now, have been used to how many people wanted to talk to her about their marriages and ex-marriages. This time, she mostly listened. Whenever you opened your mouth to talk about your own life, you made it into a story, and the truth of it, whatever that was, slipped even further away.

Until five a.m. on the last night, when Julia had to go back to her inn, scramble her things together, and catch her next plane, they'd walked through Bangkok's alleys and thoroughfares, temples and palaces, while he told it again and again, from different angles. He added new layers of detail each time, admitting more culpability but also discovering new levels of blame for his now ex-wife.

Her last stop before New York was Zanzibar, inspired by her youngest niece. Arielle had, possibly in equal measure, talents for discovering magic and for self-destruction. The plane landed in Dar es

Salaam, and the cab dropped Julia off at the edge of the city, so hot it wavered under the afternoon sun. Peddlers and beggars clamored for her attention. The Indian Ocean shone a bright, clear turquoise, deepening through a series of greens to a luminous violet. Light-headed and slightly feverish, she boarded a high-speed ferry to Stone Town, soon packed with seasick women. To keep from succumbing, Julia fixed her eyes on the sea until a woman curled into a ball on the bench next to her said, *"Tafadhali"*—please. Julia, using all six of her Swahili words, and an invented sign language, conveyed the idea of rock, paper, scissors to the woman's two youngest children and played until they reached the shore, where the family was claimed by relatives and disappeared.

Stone Town revealed itself as white, white buildings and walls, dhows and coconut palms. Stepping onto the wharf, Julia smelled cinnamon and cloves. Everyone had come here, at some point: Shirazi Persian, Assyrian, Phoenician, Chinese, Sumerian, Egyptian, Omani Arab, Dutch, English, leaving as relics their sad histories and a city of beautiful stone houses or mosques with carved doors, earth houses with thatched rooftops, and children playing in yards full of chickens. A pair of women in black *bui-buis* with hennaed leaves and vines on their hands walked past a donkey nosing into a bucket. A voice from inside said, *What you've been looking for is here.* A double promise: first, that she'd discover what exactly she was looking for; second, that it would appear to her, magically, like a genie in a bottle, an Egyptian amulet in a junk shop. She'd turn some corner and there it would be, waiting for her.

Her hotel room—romantically peeling, with long sheer white curtains around the carved bedstead and a cracked tub that trickled cold water—opened onto an alleyway. She felt dizzy and peculiar, her stomach and head hot. In the night she staggered to the bathroom two or three times to be sick. Around four, after the call to prayer rang through the streets, she broke her promise to herself and tapped out Robert's number on the special cell phone she'd bought for the trip. Fortunately, the room had no reception. The room had already begun to lighten when she fell into the dreamy state that comes with the lifting of misery.

She slept late, did her stretches, and washed in the cold water. She couldn't eat, but she made her way outside, shakily, and tried to call Robert again. Eva would have given her more comfort, but it wasn't comfort she wanted. She didn't have to make up with Eva, in any case: her sister wasn't angry with her for leaving and might not have been even if everything was a disaster. But life was as okay as possible. Their parents seemed to be diminishing slowly in River Valley, rather than dropping off a shelf onto the ocean bottom. And Eva's daughters were doing well *enough*. Arielle was already making progress in her new rehab, a violently expensive but beautiful desert retreat with a strong twelve-step program. She might be waking up at last. Eva and Julia had agreed that having Arielle safe felt as if they'd dropped the old lead coats they'd been wearing for years, instead bouncing along on the moon, noticing what it had been like to be held down by six times the force of gravity.

When Julia failed again to reach Robert, she went back to bed, still dizzy. She was able to get up on the following day, though, and take a dhow ride through the mangrove swamps, trailing her hand in the water that rose almost to the top of their boat. Back in town, she wandered past the museum: the first place her father, brother, or brother-in-law would have gone, full of important information about colonialism and slaveholding. Afterward, she found a small restaurant where she could sit under the vines and slowly eat a stew of chicken and sweet potatoes in a lemon-onion sauce, sharing a table with a pair of American college girls who were very happy to have been nearly arrested in Zaire and even happier to tell the story to Julia. She visited with street vendors and consented to having her hands hennaed, her hair tied up in dozens of heavy beaded braids.

She spent the whole of the next day at the beach—the sea the turquoise-shading-to-green of a tourist brochure, the sand hot and white—where she worked on learning her lines, far from phones or any internet café. The longer she resisted calling, the easier it would be to keep her promise. Some actors wouldn't learn their lines till

they were in relation to the others and knew *how* they'd be playing
the character, but she counted on her primary strengths as an actress:
her nearly photographic memory and the way her lack of any fixed
personality of her own gave her the ability to transform her own ob-
jectives in relation to the impulses of those around her.

She went to Africa House for an early dinner, on the terrace where
all the tourists gathered, and was invited to join a group of strangers
of all ages, brand new traveling friends, telling their war stories, stopping to bargain with the local vendors of tours. Across the table sat
Piers Wright: British, trained voice, very public school. Fortyish, tall
and slender with a nose that took up most of his face, but appealing.
Emphatic eyebrows, hollowed cheeks. His hair creeping back—he'd
be mostly bald in a few years. As if he had a penumbra, he seemed
to take up more than the usual amount of space, but he seemed contained, a warship full of soldiers ready to swarm out and capture the
beach. He caught her studying him and gave an inadvertent smile of
recognition. She smiled back, more widely than she meant to. An actor—almost every man or woman she'd ever been involved with had
been a serious practitioner of make-believe. And he had clearly spotted her as a co-conspirator.

Maggie, a tall woman, perhaps in her early seventies, had brightly
waved chestnut hair and lipstick the color of a red stop sign. Years of
too much sun, drink, and smoke had given her an intriguingly ruined
look. She said to the table, in a firm mid-Atlantic accent, "Darlings.
All of you who are able must go on the Spice Tour. It is the can't-miss
of Zanzibar. And going with new friends is more than acceptable."

"It's pre, per, *prefer,*" said her husband Edward, older than Maggie,
one side of his face pulled down in a permanent sag. He opened his
hands wide to make a shape that would finish the word for him. His
eyes, bright, frustrated, dared them to register pity or dismay, just like
her father, pretending to himself and the world that his Parkinson's
was somehow inconsequential. She had an urge to help, ridiculous
considering she'd left her own parents behind in their terrible, chipper
assisted living; left Eva with her worries about her children; left Robert
to run News-of-the-World Theater. All the while she'd been telling

herself that everyone was fine, to give herself permission to go. She gave everyone at the table a guarded, appreciative smile, admiring them for being unknown, unknowable strangers who had no power over her and could not possibly break her heart.

After a dinner of curry and coconut rice—all of the tourists facing the sunset as the sky turned rose, violet, and orange—she found herself saying to Piers, "I always wanted to do Shakespeare, but it would take a very different kind of training than I had. Where did you . . .?" He didn't look like a romantic lead, though he could have been a Hamlet when younger, an Iago or Mercutio now.

He said, in apparent surprise, "Oh, I'm not an *actor*." The horror in his voice interested her: he was performing an excellent rendition of aristocratic dislike of theater, a faint offense at her mistake. Not only an actor but really first-rate. She revised her estimate upward: Iago or Mercutio with the Royal Shakespeare Company. And yet, here he was in Zanzibar, lying to strangers. Desire for him ran all through her, flipping on the switches in the darkened house.

Late the next morning, Julia, Piers, Maggie, and Edward, in addition to an older Italian man and three young French girls who'd become part of the group the day before, clambered into the old van that would take them on their deluxe spice tour: historical sites followed by a trip into the woods. It was about a hundred and four degrees—the Muslim women in their black coverings moved more slowly, though the tourists walked as briskly as ever, keeping up the pace, making the most of their vacations.

The air shimmered for Julia at the Kidichi Persian baths, as if everything were about to shift and make transparent a hidden reality, but she stood very still, and the stone baths of the ruined harem kept their cold gray. The people around her—tourists with guidebooks, hats, sunglasses; Piers and Maggie and Edward and her whole informal new tribe; the patient and amused guide—remained opaque beings of blood and skin. She closed her hand around the wrist of the still unknown man next to her. His flesh felt safe, comforting. He was now wearing a pith helmet kind of thing that made him look like a ridiculous Hollywood version of an explorer; she was pleased to find herself a little less attracted to him. He, however, flushed and swallowed, when she touched him.

She said. "Not to be incredibly American, but if you're not an actor, what do you do when you're not lying on the beach?"

"That remains to be determined. Some chance or other will present itself."

"Then you're resting."

He said, with a smile, "Unemployed. Resting implies that you will, at some point, be active again."

Leaving behind the stone ruins, they were taken to where they could walk under star fruit trees; their guide peeled slices for them. They marveled at cinnamon bark, and the little tour bus drove them to a stand of trees beside a cluster of small houses far outside town, where they stood together tasting cloves. The world went white. Piers, Maggie, Edward, the rest of the tourists, their guide, curious locals, and every tree and house shone; she saw their atoms dancing. Nothing was separate. A single, shimmering fabric, she and they and all of it. Forms of the living God. Piers put out his hand to her—she saw him as a tall dark angel in white robes, shining with fire. She could feel the ground moving, the others turning to her in surprise.

She seemed to be lying under a shelter, fanned by women, watched by children. The women gave her a pierced coconut to drink with a straw, and when she tried to say, in her guidebook Swahili, that they were children of God—not exactly what she meant, but she didn't know how to say, *You are made of God*—they laughed.

"The heat," she said in English to Piers, who squatted beside her in his ridiculous sun hat, smiling anxiously, with a gesture of helpless goodwill. She considered herself sensibly agnostic, was interested in myths primarily for their illumination of Jungian psychology and their dramatic potential. So she was afraid she might be cracking up. But now, overlaid on her earlier impression of Piers, she had the sense of his other self. Maybe he was her destiny and her trip to Zanzibar no accident.

It was another fifteen or twenty minutes before she was able to stand. They went on with the tour, the others solicitous and full of advice. Maggie told a detailed story about being ill in Nepal; one of the French girls countered with her story of being sick for an entire three-day plane journey from New York to Europe to Africa. The group parted at the National Museum a couple of hours later, everyone expressing too much concern. "Thank you, but I'm fine," she said. "In fact, I think I'm going to go to the Slave Caves at Mangapwani tomorrow, up the coast."

Piers said, "Are you sure you're up to it?" And when she said she was, he said he'd been thinking of going himself and might come along, if it wouldn't be a bother. "Get some rest tonight," he said. "Do you want me to bring you something to eat?"

"That's very kind," she said. "But I can manage."

Piers was smiling at her, wryly.

She smiled back. "Was I indicating?" When he laughed at this, she tapped his arm. "Fine, you're not an actor," she said. "One of these years, you're going to have to confess anyway. Wouldn't it be easier now?"

He gave her a look. In any case, it was too hot and dusty to sort it out in the street, where, if they stood still another moment, they'd be besieged by touts, peddlers, prospective guides, and boat captains. She went home and to bed, not calling Robert, keeping herself awake reading the history of Zanzibar.

In the morning, she felt perfectly fine: at the Caves, she and Piers made their way down the hill from the main road to a dirt path and stone steps and finally squeezed through the claustrophobic entrance to the coral cavern. Sweat sprang out on her temples. As they climbed down the steps, she said, "The Arabs controlled a huge stretch of mainland from here. They sold ivory, slaves, and spices. As if they were all just goods. The slaves came from the mainland, driven hundreds of miles on foot and packed onto boats."

Water dripped from the walls. They stood beside a dark pool in the half-light of the cave, and she imagined the hidden slaves, long after the legal trade had been abolished under British pressure. She was so hot from the walk that her ears rang and red spots floated in front of her eyes.

Piers asked, "How did you wind up in Zanzibar?"

"Sort of a side trip," she said. "You see me, before your eyes, growing up, going out into the world. Better late than never." The next cavern was man-made: cut out of coral, the roof gone. "You can still feel the misery here, can't you?"

He said, grimacing, "The misery I feel is more the misery of freedom."

"Stuff white people like," she said. "The misery of freedom." She lifted her hair off her neck where beads of sweat ran over her shoulders and collarbone.

"Sorry," he said. They turned and climbed back up the stone steps to the dirt road above. "It's a bit thick of us to waltz in, congratulating ourselves for imagining the slaves jammed in here. Your Emerson wrote that at home we think that in traveling we can be 'intoxicated with beauty,' and lose our sadness. But when we get there, beside us is 'the stern self, unrelenting, identical, that we fled from.'"

"Well, he lived in the woods and wanted just a simple life—what did he know?" She felt herself turning a dark red. "Oh, no, that was Thoreau, of course."

"Many people mix them up," he said, his voice very British.

"I *do* know the difference between one Transcendentalist and another, even if I was raised by wolves."

"Were you raised by wolves?"

She laughed and gave him a shy look. "Mostly by my brother. So, yes."

"I don't know when you're acting."

"What else would I be doing?" she asked.

The next day, she broke down and tried Robert until she reached him. He caught her up on the non-progress of the family—no new troubles. She could tell he was waiting to get through all that to ask his real question. "I meant to talk to you about this before you left. Or, no, maybe I didn't. But I'm ready now. Did you see the Seymour Hersh piece on 'Torture at Abu Ghraib' in the *New Yorker?*"

"Robert, for God's sake. I didn't read anything. I was getting ready to go. And now I'm in Zanzibar."

"You're not on the moon, Jules. Last I checked, Zanzibar was still a part of this very small planet. Anyway, I have an idea for a new piece, though I have to work it out for a while before trying it with the company. It doesn't have a part for you anyway, so it's just as well you're not here. It's going to be truly blistering. You'd see if you were here for the performance."

"Robert, of course I'll come. Maybe I'll bring my new friend Piers."

"Uh-oh. What new friend?"

His tone annoyed the hell out of her. Why should she tell him the truth and have him patronize her? She said, "He's a British aristocrat. He sleeps three hours a night and eats only raw food, including steak, because he thinks we destroy our energy by eating cooked things we're not evolved to digest. He inherited something like three million pounds and developed a crazy internet security system and quintupled it. He's invented spyware detectors, ways of using computers and phones to create virtual business structures. He flies to Downing Street to discuss technology futures."

"Jules, for crying out loud."

"Recently he's been buying a chain of super-resorts. It's all about the water. You swim through a mile of interlocking turquoise lagoons to the underground bar. You have your own rustic hut with 800-thread-count sheets on your own mini-island where a boatman brings you your meals. Or you stay in a palace hung with crystal, with a working moat, Indonesian shadow puppets, and dance extravaganzas every night."

"Please feel free to lie to me as much as you like. I think we're paying international roving charges on our cells, but maybe not."

"He *is* British. I think he might be some kind of aristocrat. If we fall in love and become an item, you'll meet him yourself."

"I wish you won't do anything particularly stupid while you're away. Enjoy your vacation. Have a great time, fuck whoever you like, check in with me when your imagination gets out of control."

"I'm not coming back," said Julia. Robert was currently sleeping with Julia's ex-girlfriend, Alyx—another member of the News-of-the-World Company. But that wasn't, apparently, going to stop him from offering Julia free lectures on sex and other helpful topics. Julia and Alyx had been well past their own affair before Robert moved in on Alyx, but still, she and Robert had one of their biggest fights ever when she found out. No one understood bisexuality anyway: people were always implying that Julia and Robert were gay but cowardly or self-deluding, or else straight but trying to make themselves more interesting. So there was some kind of indefinable bi honor at stake in not behaving like oversexed weasels.

It turned out that Julia was not as completely over Alyx as she'd thought. Right outside the rehearsal hall, she'd cried out, "You can have *any man or woman you want*. Why do you do this? No one does this."

Robert said, "We don't have to follow other people's rules, Jules. We're not like them. Come on, be honest. Do you really care, or do you just think you should care?"

She still hoped no one had heard them and couldn't bear to remember it. And maybe it had helped push her out of the tiny and prickly little nest she called home and off to New York. She couldn't go on living with her brother in a corner of an old semi-converted warehouse while he slept with her ex, who she had to see every day at work. She had never been going to forgive him, or speak to him again, and yet, somehow, here they were. Sort of.

He said, now, "I'm not asking you to come home. But you can't be on your own for five minutes, can you? You've already found someone to sleep with and fuss over. Tell me the truth—isn't he damaged in some interesting way only you can repair?"

"I have to go," she said, pretending not to be upset. "I'm going to the Africa House for drinks with all of our new friends. Take care, Robert."

"*Jules*," he said. "Wait."

"I'm waiting."

After a short pause, he said, "I don't know how to do without you. It frightens me. And when I get scared, I get . . . you know. I'm sorry."

Julia hadn't been able to allow herself to imagine what it might be like for him, having her go. "You're the big brother," she said.

"Count on your fingers how long we've been working—and liv-

ing—together. You are the most powerful, the most willful, the strang-
est woman I've ever known. The most beautiful in performance. The
most inspiring to collaborate with on inventing work. And, maybe
unfortunately, my best friend."

"Thank you," she whispered. *Your only friend,* she thought, but there
were depths of unkindness they hadn't yet descended to. She said,
"That sounds like a problem."

"Tell me about it," he said.

After they'd said good-bye and disconnected, she looked at her cell:
the photo she used for wallpaper showed Robert leaning forward—
hands pressed down and shoulders hunched. At the moment Julia
had photographed him, he'd been saying to Alyx, "Find the *why* of
the movement, the story inside." They were rehearsing *Visiting Hours,*
based on interviews with five incarcerated men and women and their
spouses or partners, who'd given permission to have their stories included in the collage. Suspected terrorists, actual murderers, accidental or otherwise, stories of rage and addiction, of the power plays of
guards and system. Five cages of light on stage, striped bars across
the performers' faces, the visitors outside in the half-dark. Despite his
intensity, Robert had a half-smile in which she could read his deep
knowledge of the structures and habits of power, his mix of rage and
wry appreciation, his sinuous, dark life force. Being around Robert
was like standing at the edge of a river as it swelled and burst its banks.
She understood why, at every flood, bystanders were drawn to the
edge of those waters when they should have been running away.

For dinner, Julia went with Piers to the Riviera Restaurant, full of
bright wall hangings and budget tourists. The windows opened onto
the street, letting in the smells of spices, dust, and donkey dung. Outside, tourists strolled through the warm night in shorts and sundresses.
A few well-covered Muslim women had passed by the water's edge
during the day, but almost all of them were gone by now. Candlelight
flickered on the tables, sending shadows up the wall.

They ate a fish pilau with cardamom and onions and a mixed vegetable curry in a golden coconut milk sauce. Julia had three glasses of

the South African wine, much more than she was used to. Piers had drunk the rest of the bottle and part of another. Time to get some answers. It was all very well, in your twenties, to get involved with a charming man or woman lying to you about this and that. She'd always had Robert to go home to, his nasty, comforting jokes about her lovers, his shoulder to lie against while they watched bad movies. That was finished now. No more cruel stories, no more standing on the banks, hypnotized by the rising flood.

She said, "So tell me the truth about your acting."

"I had a year at the Royal Academy in my late teens. It gave me the lingo."

"My mistake," she said. "I thought you were the real thing." She still didn't believe him. No man with a year of study in his teens would have such control over his face, his voice, the modulation of his tones. She still felt his hidden self, still had the feeling of destiny. Though it had seemed like an accident, coming to Zanzibar, maybe there were no accidents.

He smiled and poured out the last of the wine. "I'm a layabout. I have a bit of money from an inheritance. Not much, but I can live a life of pinched idleness if I choose to. Probably I'd be better off if I had no choice and had to stay in jobs I found distasteful, build up my character."

At the table next to them, a pair of lovers drew their fingers along each other's wrists. Julia said, "You don't need money? I can't even imagine that."

"Having money seems to me like being very beautiful. You wouldn't give it up, if you have it, but it's not necessarily the best thing, as you yourself must have noticed. Would I be telling you all my secrets if you were ordinary, even if I weren't a little drunk? You must get your way a frightening amount of the time."

"Judging from family history, my looks will disappear suddenly sometime around the time I hit forty. So I could have only a couple of years left."

"You sound so calm."

"I'm *terrified*. Ignorant as a rock and all right as an actress, but may-

be not better than that. Sort of a dancer, sort of an actress, but not really all the way anything. I could get more training, but the problem is
everything that I'm not as a person. And without my looks, there will
be nothing to mask it. Everyone is always saying how kind I am, how
nice, when really I'm just pretty. But there's no bedrock underneath.
Wouldn't you be frightened if you lost your money?"

"I have a couple of times, in stocks and in real estate. But it comes
back if you work at it."

"When my looks go, that's it. How many fifty-year-old dance-
theater performers do you know? With some training, I could play
Lady Capulet. Or the nurse. Even if I could really act, though, no one
would ever cast me as Lear or Prospero."

After dinner, they wandered down to the open-air market of the
Jamituri Gardens, near the Beit-el-Ajaib palace, the House of Wonders. The air smelled of roasting meat, cumin, sweets, and the sweat
of the crowds around them. A stall keeper, surrounded by his chairs
and chests, was carving a new chair. He seemed to be replicating the
Islamic-African patterns Piers and Julia had been admiring on the
huge doors of Stone Town. When he saw their delight, he began urg-
ing them to buy, but when Julia said that they had no place to put
chairs, he shrugged. "Are you Peace Corps?"

Piers shook his head. He seemed now unable to talk at all. The
man persisted. "Missionaries? Teachers?" When Piers shook his head
again, he said, "Just tourists then." He sounded both satisfied and
woeful.

Piers bought them chunks of sugar cane, and they chewed as they
walked. A pair of lovers brushed past, foreigners, young, uncombed,
feeding each other ice cream, staring at each other's plain faces in
happy awe. Piers put his arm around Julia, and she leaned against
him. His body felt warm, solid—even through their clothes she could
feel the beat of the pulse in his side. With her eyes half-closed, she saw
him as angelic and menacing at once, shining darkly. The next moment, he was himself again.

Back at the hotel, they went to bed at once, holding each other,
shy now that it had come down to it. He rolled onto his back, and she

climbed onto him, staring down at his closed eyes, intent face. The beads in her hair pressed into his chest when she was on top. She gave way to an inordinate, noisy pleasure—a guilty corner of her mind wondering whether it had anything to do with him or came entirely from her own hunger. He moved under her, then above her, in almost complete silence. Her inability to reach him so thwarted and excited her that her orgasms produced colors followed by waves of darkness and light—she had a sense of being blown out of herself into some other state of being. Piers suddenly began to gasp: he came as fiercely as if he'd been with her all along.

A faint light came in from the street, turning the curtains ghostly. They lay side by side, their legs touching. As the place where Julia had been receded, she felt a disproportionate, agonized sense of loss, the pain of forgetting.

They drifted off, dozing and waking, beginning their next love-making with a slow, almost painful kindness. As they discovered the rhythms and movements that matched each other's, the knowledge that she'd be gone soon gave her a sense of time running ahead, unstoppably. The sweetness and imminent loss of this second time, after the disappointment and unexpected violent pleasures of the first, made it more piercing, as if she'd never before fully understood the uses of skin.

Afterward, he said, eyes closed, "That was a different line reading." His voice trailed off as he slid down into sleep.

She sat up, pushing aside the lace canopy for a better view—the glass lamp was very dim. This was it, the moment when fate had become her friend. She imagined him visiting, once she was settled in New York. The leaves of trees shading brownstones casting shadows over them as they walked together. Maybe he'd see her perform and begin to consider a return to the theater. Waiting backstage for each other if they'd seen the performance too many times to sit out front. Most people weren't actors, didn't think of being actors—except in some vague fantasy of stardom and universal acclaim—and would live their whole lives without stepping out under the lights and becoming someone else.

The world seemed too much to face alone. With Robert, she'd had nearly two decades of performances, spectacular or humiliating moments, sudden discoveries. On her own, she'd watched the sun rise over a hidden Buddha in the mountains of Japan and gazed out at the crowds outside the window of her cheap hotel in Bangkok while a man killed chickens in the corridor. She hated it that no one shared those memories. With Piers, she'd seen the caves where the slaves were kept a hundred years ago. They'd eaten cinnamon bark together, and she'd seen his other self.

He lay on his side now, breathing softly, his face slightly puzzled, as if he were working out some problem in his dreams. The amplified recording of a bell sounded for the 4:00 a.m. call to prayer from the mosque down the street. He sighed and turned, eyelids twitching, the corner of his mouth lifted. Julia stretched out beside him, closing her eyes.

When she was small, Robert had said, "Wait here," investigating before he allowed her to cross streams or streets, climb trees or the side of the house. The *work* he'd put in to get the company going, to haul them out of their ordinary, unimaginative, doomed life and into the one he'd imagined for them. She closed her eyes and seemed to see him gesturing to her to wait as they approached a bridge, but ahead of them she saw another brother, older than either of them, turning back to wave. He had bushy eyebrows and an unreadable smile, was already halfway across. She was surprised to realize she'd always had two brothers and had only known about one.

She woke and saw Piers watching her. "Tell me the truth, really, about your acting," she said.

Piers said, "God, you're persistent." And, when she waited, he said, "I will tell you, on two conditions." She nodded. "No advice. No trying to rescue me." She nodded again, a little less certainly. "I was an actor for nearly twenty years. My stage fright was no worse than most people's. And then, one night, none of it made any sense. Not in an intellectual way, not the usual questions about why we put ourselves through the misery of auditions, rejection, and the mockery of old schoolmates embarked upon decent, regular lives with children and jobs and pension funds. I'd been through all that, from time to time, of course, but none of it was in my mind. There had been some bad notices—not for the first time, naturally. Somehow, though, in the middle of a performance of *Merchant,* I became Piers and could be no one else, not then, not ever again. It was *over.*"

Once started, he couldn't seem to help telling the entire story. As Bassanio, he didn't have much to do in the first part of the opening scene, and somehow, listening to Antonio's "I hold the world but as the world, Gratiano—a stage, where every man must play a part, and mine a sad one," he'd become aware of the audience, an enormous, potentially vicious animal. He stood on stage, cold and sweating, staring at his colleagues. Allan and Jonathan and Paul moved easily through the set of a Venetian street at night. But it was all pretend. "I am Sir Oracle," said Allan, and, "Thou shalt not know the sound of thine own tongue," said Paul. The speeches went by very fast: Paul and Jonathan would be exiting in a moment. Piers felt his lines floating somewhere outside his mind.

In fact, when he thought about it, it had started in the wings, people whispering, "Piers, are you quite well?" Nodding, a kind of laugh, trying to pass it off. Sweating, clammy, his throat closing, knowing that this wasn't the normal thing, the normal nerves.

Allan said his own line, "Is that anything now?" and Piers stared at him, swollen tongue filling his mouth. Concern on Allan's face, a whisper from the prompt box, "Gratiano speaks an infinite deal of nothing, more than any man in all Venice."

His memory of the moment was foggy, yellowish: the stage lights blurring, Allan picking up the line, "Perhaps you'd say Gratiano speaks an infinite deal of nothing, more than any man in all Venice." And, when the silence continued, "His reasons are as two grains of wheat hid in two bushels of chaff: you shall seek them all day ere you find them, and when you have them they are not worth the search." He took hold of Piers' arm, kindly, and patted him. Not part of the blocking.

Piers stood there like one of Medusa's suitors, trying to think how and where it had been lost. The weekend notices. *Samuel Rosen's thinly unremarkable Shylock . . . A curious failure of attention in the second act . . . Adriana Lang seems more than usually petulant, as well she might, choosing among such an undistinguished crop of suitors . . . Piers Wright, dreadfully miscast as Bassanio, seems to feel the role of the passionate suitor as a waste of his slight but genuine comic gifts, which work well enough if tightly confined and directed. Alas, the acid delivery and vamped-up comic timing that have worked for him before, playing Dadaist Tristan Tzara in* Travesties, *for example, make him a strange choice for a romantic lead.* He could remember *that.* Clammy. Sick. What was his next line? His tongue, the size of an arm, choked him.

Allan—looking right into his face—began to freeze in turn. Time had stopped: he felt that only he and Allan knew what was happening. Anyone in the audience who knew their *Merchant* well knew that he'd slipped. The cast and crew knew it. But they might all still think it was a normal drying up, that Piers would catch on in a line or so. Soon, they would know that this was something else. Next the waiting, breathing, multiheaded beast out there would know it. His toxic unbelief was already spreading like oil in a stream, breaking the spell, slicking it over with the ordinary, the everyday world, where one defining failure or mistake can change everything that comes after. The hardest thing he had ever done was getting off that stage, a nightmare obstacle course, before collapsing into a ball in the wings.

When Piers finished telling Julia his story, he put his head into his folded hands. She could imagine him on stage, where he had stood, night after night, though it hadn't until that moment been *Piers* under the heat of the lights, his vision reduced to a fog. All those judging eyes, a sea of them, waiting. She cupped her own hands over his, trying to imagine what it was like to be so thoroughly yourself that you could no longer be anyone else.

She bowed her head, hiding her envy. Also her disappointment. He wouldn't want to sleep with her again after this. They didn't, after they confided in you—so soon, so deeply—except for the truly desperate ones who would then propose marriage. He was not her fate, and she wasn't his. Once again, she was lost in the world, on her own, set free.

In a moment, Piers, no longer a stranger, would look up, ready for the sympathy that he deserved. She paged through her memories, hunting for one that would call up the right emotions. Not the level of sympathy appropriate to the loss of a house, a grave illness, or the death of a family member. A gentler expression, not overdone. Years of improv at rehearsals made the process almost instantaneous: she returned to the uncomplicated empathy she'd felt for Renard in Bangkok—all his secret emails exposed to his colleagues by his enraged wife—and she could feel her face take on the look of tender understanding she now felt. Ready, she lifted her head. Piers might or might not perceive the work involved, but experience told her that he would, in either case, accept her offering.

III

News of the World
San Francisco, July 2004

We were the News-of-the-World Theater Collective, moving from city to city together; we were all married to each other and to the idea of what you could pull from the streams of the news that ran over and around and through our lives. We wanted no one to ever again let that information splash over them without thinking, so much unnoticed linguistic and conceptual sewage. Selene and I were with the company for six years, starting in '98: in the Tenderloin, in various cities during the year when we were touring by bus, and back home in San Francisco, where it all broke apart for us.

"It turns out that we weren't as essential as we thought," I say to Selene, not for the first time. I'm brooding and tidying up our corner of the living room of the sixth-floor Omaha flat where we're crashing with Tina, a dance-school acquaintance, who stayed with us in San Francisco when she was on tour. "It was Robert and Julia's company all along. Or maybe just Robert's. The rest of us were superfluous."

"Please stop using that word, Jessie," says Selene. She's dressing for an audition to play Ado Annie in a dinner-theater revival of *Oklahoma* and would like me to move on. But Tina, a bit too curious, has been asking why we left. We've said that we had director trouble, which is true enough. We can't possibly tell her, or anyone else, what actually happened. It's not clear to me what comes next, though we did have to go. But I miss the company.

We began working with the news by accident. The beginnings of the collective were rough, improvised. Selene and I'd just gotten to-

gether when we met Robert Zamarin as part of an impromptu guer-
rilla memorial protest in downtown San Francisco, the week after
Matthew Shepard's murder. After the protest, Robert said he and
his sister Julia were putting together a small dance-theater collective:
would we be interested in joining them?

The collective's first performance that meant anything to anyone,
before we even had a name, took place in the living room of the
tiny Turk Street apartment the co-directors shared. Robert was our
primary director, impresario, and writer. Very tall, short dark curls,
his hands and face pale against his dark turtleneck. His face had
a Cubist look, as if it had been smashed with a hammer and put
back together a little too quickly. A small gang of neo-Nazis cruising
Santa Cruz's Beach Flats had jumped him when he was fourteen,
a smart-mouthed, half-Jewish kid who hadn't yet reached his full
height. They'd seen the blue numbers he'd taken to inking on his
forearm. Real numbers, from people who'd died in the camps. No
one had been able to get him to stop: the outrage of others, their
efforts to explain what was wrong with what he was doing, were
central to whatever he was after. And his broken nose and damaged
cheekbones hadn't discouraged him.

We set up chairs at the perimeter of the room, so we were surrounded by our tiny audience. Selene and I mimed lovemaking and
fighting, pinning each other's arms and baring our teeth. We dripped
red paint over each other and let it run down onto the newspapers
we rolled on. I slid across her, my breasts against her belly, my legs
imprisoning her. She shook me off onto my back and let her dark hair
fall across her face, aware all the time of her beauty as a theatrical
element that had to be managed to prevent it from being distracting.
Boyce—a Midwestern farm boy, a dancer who'd turned to the theater
in his thirties—moved toward us, his hands held in menacing positions: starfish, fists, a pantomimed knife thrust.

Meanwhile, at the back of the room Robert read Milton in an
ominous voice. "First, Moloch, horrid king, besmeared with blood /
Of human sacrifice and parents' tears . . ." Julia climbed a rope toward a hook we'd hung from the ceiling. Our audience shifted and

sighed, their faces expressing a yearning for it to be over. A yearning we shared.

And then Robert, in a moment of inspired desperation, made use of one of the Theater of the Oppressed methods he'd been fascinated by since long before we began working together. He combined a Newspaper Theater practice with our dance. Dropping *Paradise Lost* and picking up a section of a smeared newspaper from the floor, he read from it, rhythmically. I wish I could remember the passage. Something violent and ordinary you'd never notice if you read it on the train, in the bathroom, over breakfast, on a break. If you felt a little sick afterward, you'd put it down to too much coffee or a too-sweet breakfast muffin. But when Robert read it, it got through.

In response, Julia, Boyce, Selene, and I began to improvise, pulling each other into new shapes, geometric and tense. We could feel the audience, a live entity, breathing with us for the first time. From that time on, Robert, backstage center, would read lists of the dead from a current war or border conflict, or vivid stories of local crimes and disasters. Julia, upstage, responded with facts and statistics about the oncoming water and food shortages, tsunamis, desertification. (Not all bad news, of course. We had delicious celebrity gossip, miraculous rescues by loving dogs or self-sacrificing strangers, and sometimes messages from the dead, as reported by tabloids in a slow news week.) Boyce and Selene and I, with our bodies, made news of dance—or vice versa—trying to find new ways of embodying, without miming, the texts. Our strategies to get people to *hear* the news worked for years, and we thought we could do it forever.

Selene's and my final rehearsal with the company—we didn't know it was going to be our last—was for a piece we knew nothing about ahead of time. Julia was gone, apparently on her way to do mainstream theater in New York. Nobody could understand her ability to suddenly turn her back on everything that had ever mattered to her, her cheery good-byes and refusal to say when or if she'd be back, Robert's silent rage. The company never had much to say about which of Robert's ideas we were going to be carrying out, but ordinarily he wasn't mysterious. He was more likely to call us at six a.m. if he had a new idea. This time, though, all he said was, "Rehearsals start Tuesday."

On the Monday night before rehearsal, Selene and I were in bed playing gin rummy. We played a lot: board games, cards, noisy sexual dramas complete with costumes and role-playing. Because we lived in a huge, rotting Victorian in the Haight and had five roommates—an actor, two dancers, and a painter—we had a lock on our bedroom door for privacy and thick hangings on every wall.

In my favorite game, we became theatrical impresarios and put on Shakespeare's plays for "acclaim points": *King Lear* was worth more acclaim points than *Cymbeline,* for example. I'd picked up an appetite for the Shakespearean world as a kid in Marin, on family trips to the Renaissance Faire, with its marketplaces, pageants, and stages in the woods. I was frightened and appalled by the masked figures of the sins, especially Gluttony, with his great belly, long pink tongue, and lascivious grin. But Queen Elizabeth had made a procession to that pageant stage every year, with all her courtiers. Her audience, dozens of twentieth-century Californians (most of us dressed as sixteenth-century peasants, shopkeepers, or low-grade gentry, though a few obdurately showed up in shorts and Hawaiian shirts), sat on hay bales and shouted, fervently, "God save the Queen!"

"Maybe Robert is planning to do something fun," Selene said. "For once. He'd better break it to us slowly or there'll be revolution." We were both naked, propped against the pillows, our cards in our laps, legs resting against each other.

I said, "Maybe he'll read the spring fashion news and you can strut your stuff for us. It'll be all about the power of beauty and how you make them suffer with longing."

"I'm getting a little old for that stuff," she said. "You idealize me, Jessie."

"I'm past that stage."

"You *do,*" she said, pulling her leg away from mine. "You keep saying to me I'm the most beautiful woman in the world, and it's nice, but it's also pressure. I was pretty in my twenties. Now I'm interested in other things."

"You'll always be beautiful," I said. "Even when you're a white-haired old thing, strangers will still stop in the street to stare at you." Her fall of black hair, the way her cheek curved down to her lips, her rounded, slightly overripe body—all of this would have made her a star in any seraglio. As for me, I looked like a scrawny, smart-ass kid, and people often mistook me for a boy. I was a painter before I was a dancer, before I began acting: most often, I play the part of the aston-ished victim, the one the audience is supposed to identify with.

She dropped all the cards on the floor, and lay on her side, back to me. I looked down at her from above, seeing how the bedside lamp—a handmade affair of old seashells we found at a thrift shop—illuminat-ed her eyelashes against her cheeks. I was a little miffed, but decided to let it go. It made me puff up with pride that this stunning creature belonged to me, that I was the one who gave her pleasure, looked after her. But it wasn't such a bad deal for her either. She requires a lot of looking after, my Selene, like a large and sometimes bad-tempered Persian cat, needing constant attention, unable to tolerate unpleasant food or too much sunlight or wind, easily lost in strange cities. I put my arm around her, and she snuggled up to me, the length of her body against mine.

When we arrived in the Mission the next day, the usual guys stood on the corner in front of the Dollar Store next to the building that held our rehearsal space. Unshaven, staggering, given to fights. They tended to wear old army fatigues or jeans, caps pulled over their eyes. One of them said, "Honey, can I have a light?" An old guy, the smell of fear, anger, and alcohol drifting off him.

She turned toward him, her face opening up. She doesn't smoke and certainly didn't have a light, but she was going to find some way to help him, talk with him, and maybe listen to his problems for the next hour. I put my arm around her shoulder and began steering her in the direction of the gate over the gallery door. "Not tonight," I said.

He looked at me in surprise, as if he hadn't realized I was there until I spoke. He said, "I wasn't talking to *you*, Jack." I smiled at him, and shepherded her inside.

We reached our performance space by walking through a nonprofit gallery and climbing the rickety stairs to a room behind the gallery's office. Our space could hold up to thirty chairs, which we set up ourselves on show nights. The gallery downstairs displayed work by new young artists—pieces that sometimes set our minds on fire and sometimes embarrassed us—vials of bull's blood and photos of blurred fields or pointillist cityscapes.

Though our performance room was a blank box, the gallery had a huge wall of windows, the light slightly dimmed by an iron gate, looking out onto the dirt and primary colors of Mission Street. I always felt a little suffocated, leaving it all behind to go up into the windowless white room.

When we saw the huge photos Robert had pinned on the walls of the performance space, Selene wheeled around, staring. She'd refused to look at the pictures when they first appeared online. Now she gagged, then swallowed. I put my arm around her.

We'd all seen the images, but not like this. Robert had spent something, getting color photos blown up so that the humans in them were larger than life size, the camouflage of the fatigues showing brown and green, the blood bright against skin and floor. Naked bodies, smeared with mud or shit, some clutching each other, lying in piles. One man crouching in fear of a black dog, a hall of shiny metal doors behind him, his hands up almost across his face. Bags over the heads. Raw wounds, bandaged or not. Soldiers with guns and smiles, a girl with a leash. Another girl in fatigues crouching beside an anonymous body, half covered here and there by bloody cloth. The scissors she held next to the fresh wounds. A man in fatigues beside her, both of them wearing dark watch caps. Her face, her tilted head, her smile, the gloved hand giving a thumbs-up. There she was again, over the body of an unshaven, bandaged man, his dead eyes closed, ice packed up to his neck. Her smile—what was that smile? She was the one I couldn't look at. It was like suddenly coming up against a funhouse mirror.

Robert leaned against a wall, dramatically enacting both the seriousness of his determination to carry out this new idea and his attentive interest in our responses. The room felt inhabited, a cold excitement like an electric field: walking up to the pictures was like pushing through occupied airspace, as if there were a humming in the walls, other people outside the spectrum of our vision, talking at sound frequencies above or below our range of hearing.

Alyx, Vân Anh, and Boyce sat on the floor, glum, their faces shuttered. Boyce began to do stretches, his face in his knees. He was such a farm boy, even in his big city leathers and chains, that he hardly ever said a word. Vân Anh, the youngest member of our company, was swift-moving, self-sufficient, often wickedly funny. She'd grown up in the Laurel District in Oakland and had studied dance at Mills. Today she wore leggings, an A's T-shirt with the sleeves torn off and the neckline ripped, a leotard, and boots.

Alyx, who'd only been with the collective for a couple of years, pulled strips of rubber off her sneakers. A skinny girl in her late twenties, she usually sang or did beatbox and toning, her readings incantatory. In her strange, wandering voice, any newspaper or advertising fragment sounded like a call to another world. She'd been sleeping with Robert for months, which of course we all knew about though it was apparently supposed to be a secret, just as we'd known a couple of years earlier when she and Julia had been "secretly" involved. They were alley cats, the Zamarins, though Julia at least usually stayed away from members of the company. Robert, though, was a different story.

It seemed that one of us should intervene, if it weren't already too late. Neither Alyx nor Boyce would say anything, and we had a very small group for this early rehearsal, though perhaps Jake, Jolene, or Lisbeth would be joining us later. Or Robert might be keeping the show small. Julia would at least have told us what we were up to. We hadn't understood, before she left, quite how much she made it all happen. Her sometimes scatty willfulness had made her seem more decorative than she was, less of a load-bearing pillar.

LaVerne might step in. In her fifties, originally from New York, she'd been a dancer and an actress for more than four decades: everything from Mary Zimmerman and August Wilson off-Broadway to the sorts of impressionistic pieces where performers climb up and down ropes to the accompaniment of electronic music and obtrusive lighting. She appeared with multiple local companies and we were lucky to have her at all. After Julia left, she'd said to Robert, in front of us all, "We're a collective; maybe we should make decisions together about what we're going to do next."

Robert, in his newly savage way, had said, "Dears, as far as I'm concerned, every one of you could run the Royal Shakespeare Company. But as it's worked out, I happen to be the director of *this* company. So could you try trusting me?" He'd gone to Juilliard, unlike the rest of us, and was a wizard with funders—we relied on him far too much for our basic support—but in the old days he hadn't thrown his weight around like that.

I said, "It's too fresh. Why don't we take a break from current news? Why not do the Crimean War? How about My Lai? I'm not sure what we're going to add to these photos. We could stand naked in front of them and do nothing. Anyway, I don't know who would come to the performances, or why. Maybe creeps getting off on the pictures." I tried to keep my voice firm; my body shook when I stood up to Robert. It might be that, coincidentally, my hours would be cut, or Robert would be unable to support me in getting a particular teaching job, or not a single one of my ideas would make it into the new performance. With Julia gone, no one could keep him in check.

He said, "Children. We perform the news. Yes?"

Alyx said, "It's our job, right? To bear witness to the things our audiences don't want to see or think about? But they come to us because, at some level, they count on us to show them what they already know. What a relief it is to stop denying it all. And once they face it, they can take action." Her tacit job in the company was to say to Robert what no one else could get away with: sometimes he'd even listen to her. Right now, she was handing out the party line.

"Probably, mostly, we get people who enjoy feeling indignant and then heading home to the suburbs," I said, frowning.

Selene, either because she was genuinely upset or wanted to distract Robert, gave a huge sigh and reached out to him. He put his arms around her, and she rested her head on his shoulder.

Years earlier, back when I was a painter, I'd had sex with men sometimes. I still occasionally feel a flicker of attraction, but it's very diminished, and none of the people I used to sleep with seem quite real now, even the ones I wanted badly at the time. I've always been faithful to Selene. I've never been sure whether she was faithful to me. She'd said, a couple of months earlier, after a particularly exhilarating rehearsal, "If you and I were to have a baby, maybe Robert could be the father." I was afraid to ask if she'd ever slept with him or if she was thinking about it: he certainly acted in public as if she belonged to him. And he wouldn't let his relationship with Alyx slow him down.

I did sometimes say to Selene that we could leave and go elsewhere. New York, Chicago, someplace where we weren't always negotiating how to maneuver around Robert.

"What other company would take us both on? And could you go back to just dancing after this?" she said. Because of Robert's genius at getting grants, none of us had to work more than part-time at day jobs during show times. We temped or taught a class, sometimes a theater intensive over the course of a summer, but none of us had to wait tables or work full time. And to what extent were all of our best ideas a result of Robert's suggestions and prodding?

Robert gently wiped Selene's face with a handkerchief. "My baby."

Before I could stop myself, I said, hearing my own voice as sullen and spiteful, "*My* baby, technically speaking."

He looked over at me and said, "Jessie." A comical reproach, so full of complicit amusement that I found myself returning his smile. So there weren't going to be any consequences; instead I would be masterfully forgiven. He turned to the group. "I have readings for you all. Selene, you can start with the trial transcripts." He handed out a stack of articles, and we sat down with them.

We read more or less in silence for a while. Vân Anh said, "Are you going to read these during the performance?"

"I want to watch you work first," he said, his tone inviting us into a marvelous and serious game. "Then I'll know if we read from these or find something else."

For the next hour and a half, we traded articles, lying on the blue exercise mats, moving to uncomfortable folding chairs, standing for a while, leaning against the walls, careful not to touch the photos. The air stirred around us, an invisible crowd. We had food, but no one was eating.

We read about the special access program, an entire secret military life, no checks or accountability, with both a daylight and a shadow structure: "the white guys," making speeches and denying all knowledge, and "the black guys," who had hidden power and unlimited approval to capture, interrogate, and kill "high value targets."

The detainees were moved from prison to prison so that even the system itself often lost track of where they were. Almost every source pointed out that information extracted by torture was likely to be useless invention. Most of these pieces said very little about the stuff that had been all over the TVs and daily news—the ongoing sexual party, the lurid details of who was sleeping together, who had gotten who pregnant. The guards had been told to "soften up the detainees," but who were the others in these pictures, in the testimony? What might those insane, cheerful, proud smiles be expressing?

I caught myself trying to imagine how to dance this and was afraid I'd humiliate myself by throwing up in the rehearsal hall. At least this would be a genuine, human response. Or else the result of a *desire* to have a human response.

I said, "There is nothing we can do to add to, explain, or ameliorate any of this. It would be disgusting. We're not going to change anything by doing a dance; we'd be like a lot of head lice. Even if it were news no one had noticed. Which, hello, not so much."

Robert stood grandly before the photographs. "This is what's happening, here and now. There will be a few scapegoats. Then the whole country gets to forget it ever happened, to take it for granted." During his explanations and exhortations, the magic usually kicked in—the sense he, as no one else, could create of including each of us in a charmed inner circle. "The mechanisms that foster torture will continue untouched. We need to find a way to make people *pay attention.*"

"Ten or eleven people at a time," I said, putting down my article. "Unless we get a full house. And who's going to want to watch this? I don't think we should do it."

Vân Anh said, "Do LaVerne and I have to be the ones, again, to bring up the role of racism in this war in the first place? Could anyone else do it for a change?"

"It's intersectional. Of course." Robert gave a small bow, one that said he'd thought of every possible objection or angle before any of the rest of us.

"Oh, please," LaVerne said.

"I knew when I came in today," he said, "that I'd be attacked. Often those with the least confidence in taking on artistic challenges are the most vocal in resisting them."

I said, "I didn't say I'm not up to it. I said it would be pointless."

Selene poked me in the side, and Alyx said, quickly, "It depends on what we're after, doesn't it? Who do we want to see this piece? People who know about it and haven't been able to take it in, or people for whom we could illuminate it in some way?"

"The strays and the converted," Boyce said.

Selene said, "I wish we could do stories about heroism and self-sacrifice. Maybe if we gave people a positive example, we'd inspire them to change their lives and the world. We could show people dying for each other and their beliefs. We could do Joan of Arc." She had a very Joan-of-Arc expression as she said this. It was easy to picture her suffering and determination as the flames rose up around her.

"You have an original mind," Robert said. "That's your charm. You are a lovely creature with no clue about anything, and somehow that becomes your great strength."

She turned to look at him, her face taking on an expression of betrayed fury. She opened her mouth, but Boyce leaned forward. "Hey, did you realize that Jessie looks like her?" He pointed at the central photograph, the girl crouching over a man's body. Bandages covered his face. She beamed as if she were being photographed on Christmas morning, showing off her favorite present.

Robert smiled, his eyebrow up again, as if this were part of his plan. Maybe he was just quick to catch a cue. Selene sat back, breathing deeply. She looked down at the pale, polished wood of the floor and drew patterns in the dust with one finger.

Robert pointed to Boyce. "Lie on the ground with your arms behind your back." He turned to me. "Kneel beside him. Menace him
in some way."

"Absolutely not." I picked up my jacket and headed for the door.
"Come on, Selene."

"Jessie," said Selene. Any evidence of anger had disappeared. We'd
find out later if her fury had gone underground, if she developed a
migraine. She'd been having a series of them after a demonstration
where we'd been stuck in the hot sun. I'd told her, before we went out,
that she'd be better off staying home, but she's never known her own
limits.

Boyce said, "Let's try it out. Maybe we really can touch people in
some way, maybe this will make them take some action, like Selene
said."

"What action would that be?" I said. Selene had a pleading expression. I put down my jacket. Boyce lay down, pulling his sweater over
his head as if it were a hood, and held his wrists together. I knelt over
him and pushed him in the shoulder, hard enough to roll him to the
side. I pulled back, feeling a little sick. Our hungry, invisible audience
waited.

"That's good," said Robert. "The rest of you can be guards." He
looked at Selene, who dropped to the other side, lying next to Boyce,
her arms behind her back.

Robert looked at LaVerne, who picked up the articles and flipped
through them. In a newscaster's voice, she said, "The President 'is sorry that people seeing these pictures didn't understand the true nature
and heart of America.'" She frowned and tried again. "The Secretary
of Defense has described the detainees as 'unlawful combatants.' As
such, he says, they 'do not have any rights under the Geneva Convention.' It sounds like I'm being ironic." She tried an ordinary voice:
"Seymour Hersh says, '. . . of course, Saddam tortured and killed his
people. And now we're doing it.'"

Boyce curled into a ball and began to inch away, leaving me kneeling over Selene, who pressed her wrists together and arched her back.
I leaned across her, placing a spread-out hand over Boyce's face,

against the wool of his sweater. Selene and I caught each other's eyes and dropped our poses.

Alyx, still sitting on the floor, said, "It's not believable." She shook her head, helplessly.

Boyce said, "All we're doing is re-enacting it. Why don't you stand there and read the accounts of Milgram and those experimental subjects who went on turning up the shocks? Jessie could work the controls."

Robert said, "Jessie, you're a guard. Tie up Selene."

I unbuckled my belt, slid it out of my jeans, and wrapped it around her wrists, pulling it through the buckle. She jerked in surprise, though I was trying to be gentle. We'd played some bed-games with velvet handcuffs and blindfolds; now it was as if a nightmarish version of our private life were happening in public.

Trying to act as if this meant nothing to me, I said, "The prisoners should be wearing fewer clothes."

"Why don't you take off *your* clothes?" said Boyce, muffled by his sweater.

"I don't believe you as a guard," said Robert. "You're a Girl Scout, learning to do rope tricks. Stop trying to make us like you. Think of the worst thing you've ever done."

Looking around the room, I could see that everyone had been sent back to—what kind of memories? I realized I didn't know most of their secrets, though we'd been working together for ages. Boyce had broken his father's nose once, but that was retaliation, when he was finally big enough to protect himself and his sister. Selene hadn't spoken to her parents in five years—she came from a part of the Midwest where some people still think there's something wrong with us. I tried to think of my own worst thing, but everything seemed so low-grade. I'd left one scary, pathetic girlfriend by refusing to return her calls or emails. I'd given away a friend's secrets in sixth grade—her bed-wetting and eating spoonfuls of sand—and pretended not to know who had made her subject to endless tormenting. When my friends were shoplifting in junior high, I hid out in another part of the store, in case they were caught. Robert was right: every gesture I made, on or off stage, showed my cowardice and yearning for approval. I couldn't be dazzling, but I could be *nice*.

Above me, in the central panel, the girl grinned. She'd stepped across a divide, and the photo proved it. She was a citizen of a new country now.

A channel opened up in me, like water pouring in, the starving watchers both inside and outside. I yanked on the belt, tightening it around Selene's hands. Her back arched again, a painful-looking spasm, and she rolled over, the belt beneath her, her shirt twisting up to reveal her skin. After a moment, I raised my thumb, smiling up at Robert.

There was a long silence, the rest of them staring at me. Selene shook herself free and backed away. Alyx put her arm around her. Robert didn't seem to know what to do next. "Not the thumb," he said, finally.

"The thumb is really . . . she should do it," said Alyx. She spoke with some urgency, and I could see the others nodding, even Selene. No one was looking at Robert. They were watching me alertly, waiting to see what I'd invent next.

"I think we have to have the thumb," I said.

Robert stood up very straight, making himself taller. "Don't start enjoying this," he said. "That would be taking it a little far."

"I'm not enjoying anything." My head floated above my body. If the thumb had been his idea instead of mine, he'd be insisting on it right now.

"You're not such a good girl after all, are you? You see you can cause pain and like it." He changed his tone, squatting beside me and placing his hand on my arm in what appeared to be a kindly gesture. He murmured, comforting me, "I know how hard it can be to mix your work and personal life and what it must be like to be in your position. I want you to know that you do have an essential role in the company. We have to have a Selene, but think how impossible it would be to put on a show without people like you as well."

A wild red rage blew up and through the top of that open channel—pouring out of my head, out of my mouth. It felt wonderful.

"Take your fucking hands off me," I said, my voice shaking, hissing into his face, feeling myself become monstrous, my face a distorted mask. "I feel *violated* when you touch me. You don't know a goddamn thing about me or my relationship or anything else at all. Don't call us at six in the morning anymore. Don't touch either of us. Don't pretend you care about me in any way, shape, or form, or that you want me in this company for any reason besides that I'm here to look after Selene. At least I'm not a person who *lives* to be admired and then behaves like a totally pathetic, bullying *brigand.*"

All the air went out of me—it had seemed I was saying something, but I realized it was all stupid. Brigand, who said brigand anymore? I didn't know if I even believed what I'd said or if I'd tricked myself into letting Robert set the terms of my defiance. He was so much smarter than I.

Everyone stared at me as if I were radioactive. Selene began to cry. Robert's face had gone very still. "You'll need to come and talk to me in the morning." It was clear from the unmitigated coldness in his voice that he was planning to fire me. "First thing." He said to everyone else, in an almost normal voice, "We'll call it quits for the night. Go home, do some freewrites, see what you think. We'll start again in a couple of days and I'll have some choreography for you, based on what I've seen here."

He usually said, "Good work!" no matter how bad we were, and for that moment, however often we heard it, we felt a wonderful sense of absolution. I'd left so many rehearsals and performances remembering that, after all, I loved to be in his company, and there was no one more magical. He began unpinning and rolling the photographs, Boyce starting from the opposite wall, working their way toward that central panel.

On the way home, Selene said, "Are you crazy." It wasn't a question. I shrugged, and she said, "I can fix this, if you let me." We were on a night bus: drunks and crackheads, kids in their fishnets and piercings on their way to the clubs, teenagers inhabiting their story about their gang life. Selena always sat by the window. I took the aisle seat, between her and the world.

I said, "I do believe I've remembered the worst thing I ever did. All of them. It's things I *didn't* do. People who were hoping I'd look after them. My mother, after her diagnosis. She was living with two cats in a little condo at the end of a long and nauseating bus ride to the hospital; she hinted she'd be better off staying with someone, and I pretended not to understand her."

I'd never told anyone about this, not even Selene, and I looked down as I spoke. My voice was low so no one else would hear, and I half-hoped she wouldn't either. "I was in *Medea*, a small part, but a big production, my first real chance after college. It seemed that if I let this opportunity go by, I might not have another one. Sometimes a neighbor took Mom for her chemo, and I told myself the woman was the sort of person who doesn't have enough going on in her life and needs to be helpful, that I was doing quite a bit by going to visit my mother for a couple of hours once a week, calling her every few days on the phone. That we all have different sorts of gifts—I was an artist, not a caregiver. I didn't know what to do for her. I thought my mother might live a long time, and I couldn't imagine having her with me. In the end, it was only six months. But even those weekly visits made me crazy with nerves."

Selene touched my leg, and I took a quick look at her face. Selene, who wouldn't even have left a sick stranger alone, couldn't comprehend what I was saying. She might well have wondered what it would mean for her in the future.

I said, "Now I send a little money to various organizations and write some letters or emails. I go to demonstrations if they seem safe. But what have I ever risked to try to stop what we're doing? I sit in my house and let the cattle cars go by. I'm a cold person, Selene. There's something damaged inside me." Maybe I was hoping she'd contradict me, tell me how my loving her proved I wasn't cold, and I'd say she was the only one. But she just took my hand. I went on, "Don't even think about getting in between me and Robert. I'm through with wheedling and giving in and letting you be charming for me."

Selene, looking doubtful, squeezed my hand. She didn't think I could overcome him, but she was wrong. I knew where his soft underbelly lay, and, for the first time, I was willing to put in the knife to get my way. His power lay in his ability to charm and confuse us, never to go after more than one of us at once, to put us in the position where we didn't feel safe defying him. Inside, though, he was as frightened and ashamed as anyone, afraid he'd lose his command over us, afraid we'd stop worshipping him. If I kept showing up and doing my parts, he would have to let it blow over rather than risk a full-out insurrection. He'd be able to see I wasn't afraid of him anymore. If he interfered with me, I might say anything to them about him. His control over the company would be gone.

That night, Selene went to bed before me. I sat down on the couch at nine and found I was so tired I couldn't get up to wash my face. Our housemates came and went, on their way to bed. The air felt thick, as if we'd brought the hungry watchers home with us. My mind, half-dreaming, turned over images from the photos. The bag over the head. The smeared bodies. The dogs. The ice. The thumb. The grin.

Finally, I decided to skip face-washing and turned off the living room light. When I went into the bedroom, a woman lay in my bed, the covers pulled up to her chin. On her side facing me, an odalisque, a stranger. She opened her eyes.

"Hey," I said. "Are you *naked* under the covers?" I'd meant it as a joke, but found some part of me shocked at the idea. As soon as I said it, I felt as if it were possible that I might not know her. Did I, really? Who was this woman in my bed? Had we ever really known each other? She looked familiar and unfamiliar at the same time. It was a little sexy, but more frightening. Was I supposed to climb under the covers and sleep beside her? And I didn't know who I was either. I didn't recognize myself.

"Of course I am." She smiled at me in what seemed like obscene invitation.

"I don't think I can get in there if you're naked."

"What are you talking about?" The smile went away. My sense of dislocation was worse. She said, "Jessie?"

"I don't think I know you. I can't get in bed with a stranger." I was and wasn't play-acting. It felt real. I can't remember now what I thought I was doing.

She gave me a look that said she was tired of this. She threw back the covers. A well-fed, pampered, muscled adult body—wrinkled nipples, strange patch of pubic hair, soft belly. I let out a scream.

She sat up and grabbed the covers, shielding herself. "What's the matter with you? What are you doing?"

I couldn't say anything. I shook my head. Selene, who never has to ask what I'm thinking, began to cry. And that was a little bit of a pleasure, though I wasn't admitting it to myself. She was seeing herself through my eyes, frail and weak—stripped, for once, of her beauty. I didn't say anything, just stood there.

I put my hands over my mouth and ran into the bathroom, dying to get clean. I was afraid some member of the household would intervene or come in to find out what was happening, but no one did. I washed my face and neck several times.

When I went back to our room, she'd curled up, facing away, the covers over her ears. Nothing was inside me, around us. Selene and I were absolutely alone. By now all my feelings for her had returned, and I couldn't entirely remember that other state. I was Jessie Brown, who'd been the football mascot in high school and who longed for a day at the beach with no knowledge of anything happening anywhere in the world.

When I climbed into bed, though, and tried to put my arms around Selene, she jerked away from me. "My feelings are hurt."

"We were sort of playing, right?" Maybe that's what we were doing. Just another game.

"You looked at me and screamed." Her voice was blank, no emoting at all.

I moved closer, nuzzling her hair. "My leopard, my Selene, sweetheart." After a while, she started to relax, though she still held herself away from me.

"We're not going back there," I said. She didn't answer for a while, and I said, "Selene, we're done with those people. With that company."

If I'd thought about it, I would have assumed we'd have an argument that would last for days. I was willing to fight as long and hard as necessary. There was no way I wouldn't win—when it came down to it, she couldn't live without me either. Instead, there was another period of silence. I couldn't see her face, and couldn't tell whether she was angry, sad, frightened, reflective.

Finally, she said, "Yes, okay. But I want to have a different kind of life. I want to be able to move around, to go wherever the good parts are. I don't want us to always have to perform together."

I nodded, nuzzling her ear, making a trade that now seems as if it's going to cost us plenty.

At first it seemed we could join one of the other SF companies, or get in touch with old pals in New York or Chicago, but our network has thinned out over the last few years. Most people have kept moving, and they still know each other in ways that we don't anymore. We've agreed that we have to widen our net, to audition in more cities. By October, we found ourselves here in Omaha. Who knows where we'll be by the holidays?

I'd forgotten what daily life in the theater is like for most performers: waiting tables during the day, taking time off for auditions, getting commercial work sometimes, very occasionally the work we want, but more often than we like, no work at all. It's all too easy to drop out of one category and into another. When you've been playing regional dinner theater—whether it's Ado Annie in *Oklahoma* or a junior hyena in *The Lion King*—it becomes harder and harder to get other kinds of roles, and in the process, the very nature and intent of your performances begin to change.

And Selene's and my games, in and out of bed, seem to have ground to a halt. A couple of times, in cheap hotels or at Tina's when she's away, I've tried getting out the masks and boas I brought with me, or the dice that tell us which parts of each other's bodies to kiss, but Selene said, not long after we left San Francisco, "I think we've outgrown all that, don't you?" We fight less, but we're more sharp-tongued about small irritations and no longer tell each other everything. I'm pretty sure that, during our unsuccessful weeks in New York, she was sleeping with other people. Being with her will always be better than being alone, though, and maybe every couple gets to this point sooner or later. My hope is that we'll get over it again. Maybe in a year or two, if we're lucky. Or it may take something bigger: there's a kindness I see sometimes in longtime couples where one or both of them has been close to death.

I try not to think about the night in San Francisco when we made the decision to leave. And I try not to remember the next morning, making love for the first time with the new feeling of separation between us. By any real measure, it was a small, irrelevant event. No prisoners held on leashes with the threat of death over them, moved from prison to prison so their families couldn't find them, hooded and standing on boxes, thinking the wires attached to them were live and they'd be electrocuted. No one beaten, no one having lit cigarettes pressed into their ears.

Even if someone were to say that I could have done all of these things, under the right circumstances—if I'd been told to "soften them up" by a higher command, if I thought they were my enemies— they'd be wrong. If I'd been in Milgram's lab, I would have refused to deliver the shocks, or at least the highest level of the shocks. But I didn't know who I was during the torture improv or when I didn't recognize Selene. And I wasn't willing to take one more step down that road. I still don't know what I might be capable of if I lived indefinitely in the country of the strong.

PART TWO: OF SHADOWS AND OF RAIN

IV

Ravenous: A Ghost Story

Sebastopol, January 2002

County mental health services has set up Unit 8 in a converted farm-house west of Sebastopol. The doors stick, yellowed curtains hang in the windows, and bright reproductions of Czech folk paintings—framed in unbreakable plastic—decorate the walls. In one, a huge barefoot boy stands on a curly field of flowers, holding a miniature village on a platter. In another, giant roosters in long dresses throw snowballs at each other in front of hills covered with snow-capped huts. Katya thinks the choice of reproductions shows a secret sympathy for the potential beauty of madness, undercutting the regimens of logic, therapy, and pills.

She's sworn to keep confidentiality, which she does, but she sees the descriptions in the charts she updates. *Patient hallucinating. Patient v. delusional, poss. switch to Ziprasidone?* She answers the phone. "Mental *Health*, can I help you?"

"Is this a joke?" she'd asked Dr. Steiner on her first day, and he'd said, frowning, "No, no, that's how the phone must be answered, write down the date and time, please."

It's pouring outside, a miserable, apparently eternal, cold and heavy rain, and she's on the phone with Dr. Steiner—he's worked an all-nighter at Riverview inpatient and won't be at the clinic until the following Tuesday. "Reschedule all my clients, will you? Thanks . . ." He hesitates, then settles on "dear." Fast and guilty, he says, "I have to run."

"Yes, Dr. Steiner," she says. "I'll call them all right away."

She doesn't hold it against him that he doesn't know who she is—so far as she can figure out, he never learns the names of the temps. She's been at the clinic for almost two months, but he's only in once a week—he spends most of his time on Riverview's locked wards. Damned if she knows how he can listen to all those stories all day, everybody weeping or suicidal or thinking the government is trying to kill them. Still, she feels at home around the clients, with their wild reconstructions of reality and sudden losses of control—they remind her of her own family, though it's all more out in the open here. Except for her Grandma Lily maybe, who'd been hospitalized a couple of times when she was younger. The family doesn't talk about that, and she seems more or less okay now. Katya's decided that the difference between crazy and noncrazy is whether you can keep it to yourself. Also, of course, the brain chemistry.

Dr. Steiner has no openings for weeks, which means an extra month or so before they get their meds checked, and plenty of the clients don't have phones, even the ones with homes. An Angel of Efficiency would handle this, as she'd handle everything—appearing and disappearing in a cloud of undiscovered particles, her cape covered with circuitry.

When Katya, at twelve, had realized she was probably some kind of superhero, she'd tried jumping off the back balcony (broken collarbone), reading minds (grounded for two weeks for the guesses she'd made aloud), and turning invisible (a ducking in the algae-filled school culvert, but at least it wasn't sewage. Probably.) Now she has a short shock of pink and blue hair, snakes tattooed up her arms and across her belly, a prime wardrobe of thrift shop miniskirts and pea coats, but no discernible superpower. Once again, she's begun actively looking to find it—she has less than a month before her twenty-fourth birthday—though obviously she hasn't mentioned this to anyone.

Rose Corten arrives at 9:20 and is so agitated that she waves her arms in the air, shouting, "But I don't have any meds!" She's a thin girl, about Katya's age, known for doing street drugs, complicating her daily cocktail of lithium and anti-psychotics. "Doesn't he know that?"

Katya would like to put her arms around her until Rose's heartbeat slows, but it's against the rules. "You can go to Psychiatric Emergency Services."

"Have you ever fucking *been* to PES? They make you wait for hours! It's an hour and a half each way on the bus from here, and do you know what they give you? One fucking day of meds! One day!" Rose stomps over to the door, gripping the frame with both hands, giving it a bang with her head.

Katya calls out to Estella, one of the MA therapists. Estella's superpower is to make anything she suggests seem reasonable: by the time she's done, Rose is on her way to PES with a book on energy healing to read on the bus.

At lunch, Katya sits in the back room with Estella and Sukey, another therapist, a loudly exuberant woman with waves of black hair and rhinestone-studded glasses who specializes in child molesters and violent offenders and sings to keep herself going. The rain hits the roof in a constant thrumming rhythm, interspersed with spattering when the old drainpipes get overloaded and dump an extra shower of water onto the metal roof of the storage shed alongside the clinic.

Sukey's eating a supermarket chicken that smells of lemon-pepper and garlic, and when she offers them some, Katya has, for the first time in a long time, an attack of chicken-desire. She says "No, thanks," thinking of Adriana, one of her younger sister Jenny's chickens. Adriana has a big white puff of feathers on her head and a surprised way of responding to the sound of her own name. Jenny, twenty-two and four years cancer-free (though uninsurable for the next two decades), lives about half an hour further out in the countryside: married, with a two-year-old and a baby, a mother goat and three kids, a llama, a dog, three cats, and about a dozen chickens. A farmer, studying to be a witch and herbalist, Jenny hasn't eaten meat since she'd gotten sick. Her plan is to turn the hens to pets when they get too old to lay. Katya stopped eating meat along with her, for company at first, later because of Jenny's animals.

On Katya's last visit to the farm, Rex, a big brown and gold rooster with spectacular tail feathers, ran up and down outside the coop, screaming with rage and regret; he'd made the choice to go out for the day and visibly repented when he saw the inside chickens being fed. Katya could be anthropomorphizing. He definitely wasn't smart enough to realize that Jenny would feed him in about five minutes.

She shakes extra hot sauce onto her bean and cheese burrito. Estella has a tuna salad with a dressing that comes in a spray bottle. She applies it in one quick sweep. "Two calories," she says. "If you don't spray too long. Eventually you save enough for a chocolate bar."

Katya says, "Hell, make it two bars. Especially if you're not putting blue cheese dressing on the salad. You save even more that way."

Sukey says to her, "You do math like I do math. I'd hate to see your bank account." She pulls apart a thigh and drumstick, torquing the bones and giving them a quick snap. A little trail of vein hangs out of the knot of fat and gristle, and *still* Katya wants that chicken.

"Wait till you're our age." Estella pinches her belly. "At least five inches, right? And that's the bad kind of fat. Once I hit 185, I stopped weighing myself. But I get up and look in the mirror every morning to see if I've become fatter overnight. There are these long blue veins that break at my scars."

Sukey laughs. "It's all sliding downhill. Sooner or later I think all the skin and fat will fall right off and I'll be a medical see-the-organs doll." She shimmies, demonstrating. "Are we scaring you, honey? How old are you, anyway? Twelve?"

"Twenty-three."

"Woo-hoo," Estella says, and Sukey chimes in. "Twenty-*three*. I can't even remember being that young. You haven't started to live yet—it's all ahead of you."

How Katya would love a drink. Bad, in the middle of the day. January! She and her family had, as usual, spent almost the whole month on their freewheeling celebrations of Hanukkah and Christmas. Lots of candles, holiday lights, a big tree at her parents' house, too many presents, too much food. How gray January is. She'd even thought, briefly, of going on a diet.

She says to Sukey and Estella, "I was married, once. Didn't last very long though. I think it was the influence of the Elvis chapel that tempted us into it." It was during Jenny's cancer, a long, out-of-control weekend away from it all in Vegas. It had all been too much—the hospitals, washing out Jenny's pans with their nearly transparent half-cups of bile, Jenny's puffy face and old-woman walk, the sense of the impending chasm ahead. Sometimes, without ever having planned it, she'd bolt. She and Suzanne had wound up "married" that way, too, not legally of course—but in a surreptitious ceremony performed by a priestess they met at a solstice ceremony on the beach. Katya loves getting married. She'd do it every year if she could. But the timing had been terrible. She only half recalls her parents' exasperation and Arielle's sentimental delight, but she remembers Jenny's face when they came home and announced what they'd done: the hard flash of the pain of being left out, immediately covered by a pretty great imitation of enthusiastic surprise.

Sukey asks, "What's an urban child like you doing up here in the sticks?"

"I wanted to be close to my sister's farm. Anyway, it's okay up here, apart from only seeing my friends every three weeks and all the men driving pickups and seriously wearing cowboy hats and boots like they mean it. My last temp job before this one was on the 28th floor of an insurance building in downtown San Francisco, in the financial district. None of the windows opened. I spent my days stuffing mailers—the guy in charge showed me what order they were supposed to be in. *Three times.* One of the long-timers whispered to me, 'Be glad you're not stuck here,' and I said she wasn't either. Though sometimes people are."

Sukey and Estella drop their eyes, their whole faces tending downwards. Maybe they'd like to be working someplace where people were actually getting better. A bigger clinic, a private clinic, who knows whether they felt stuck at Unit 8? It's possible that Katya's superpower is a gift for saying the wrong thing. Or getting herself into huge messes: everything from having spent all her money without realizing it to suddenly throwing a whole rack of fur coats in every direction to grabbing hold of a woman who was smacking her kid on the ear. And she's gotten herself fired too many times for telling bosses exactly what she thought about the lousy way they treated their employees.

She doesn't know when to stop, that's the trouble, though nothing's happened for nearly two years now, so maybe she's over it. At some point, it should all be far enough in the past for her to leave temp work and find a real job. The temp people don't seem to care, as long as you're breathing and can type, and the jobs probably assume the temp places have vetted everyone. She wouldn't hire herself, that's for sure.

After work, resisting the urge to go to her sister's farm and slog through the mud, helping with chores, doing anything to avoid spending the evening by herself, she heads home. She's living in an efficiency on the second floor of a block of apartments that look across Highway 12 to Sebastopol's graveyard—headstones bulking under cypress trees in the moonlight, bunches of artificial flowers.

The apartments sit in a block around a cement pool protected by a chain link fence. Inside the fence, decorative planter boxes had once softened the effect. But people threw them in the water sometimes, possibly as a drunken joke, so the management took them out. Now the place looks like a prison yard, if a prison yard had an oblong turquoise pool in the center. Occasionally a rat falls in and drowns, the body floating in the water overnight or until someone can fish it out.

A few years ago, a guy drilled holes in the walls and ceiling of one of the apartments, spying on his female neighbors, but he's gone now, and anyway he lived on the opposite side of the complex. Still Katya imagines those eyes—though it's not rational, she sometimes checks her walls to make sure they're intact.

There's a note from Morning Katya in the middle of the floor. "Pay the BILLS! Don't go to PRESS BOX! Do the LAUNDRY!" Evening Katya thinks, "Water is for horses; Dickel is for drinking." She crumples up the note from her stingy, controlling morning self and tosses it toward the garbage pails against the wall. It misses "Recycling" and ends up in "Landfill." Too bad. It's party time.

She decides not to call Jenny, but finds herself punching the numbers. Just a short call. "Hi, sweetheart." She can hear wailing in the background. "How are you?"

"Hanging in." Jenny laughs in that way that means she isn't quite. Paul, in the background, now appears to be galloping and whinnying. The baby is still wailing. Jenny, off the phone, makes soothing noises.

Katya says, quickly, "I'm worried about Arielle. She needed more than a month in that inpatient place. I don't think a meeting or two a week is going to do her. I get these weird phone calls from her. Do people know she's maybe not doing so great? You know the parents and I never get anywhere when we try to talk. Could you talk to Mom?"

Jenny hesitates. "Of course, but I'm about to make dinner for Paul and feed Caro. And I'm behind with getting all the animals in for the night. Can we talk about Arielle another time?" And then, off the phone, "Shh, sweetie, I'm getting there, let me get this undone."

"That's fine, I can call back later. Would an hour be good?"

A short pause. "You know how important you are to me." Jenny has a soft voice, even when she's being firm. "But I can't talk every night, Kat, I just can't. Brandon's home and everyone needs feeding and there's getting the kids to bed. And I have to get up super early tomorrow because it's a market day, so there's boxing up the eggs and the goat cheeses and the lettuces. I know it must seem like not having a job would leave a lot of time, but some days I'm lucky to have half an hour. And I'm spending it all on the phone. Why don't you come out instead? Not this weekend because Brandon's parents are coming, but next Saturday. We can hang out and chore together. Would that be okay?"

Jenny is sending her away, reasonably—she has so much life, and Katya is so greedy for her time and attention. The abyss opens up, a panic of abandonment. It's like falling into a dark tunnel. Katya says, "Of course, of course, that would be great. I'm sorry, Jenny. Can I . . . how often would be okay to call?"

"Maybe twice a week? Would that work?"

"Twice a week is great. Thanks. Go feed everyone, okay? Kiss Caro and Paul from me, and say hi to Brandon." She doesn't want to miss one minute of Jenny's life. She wants to hear her voice every day, to live on the farm, to memorize her, to swallow her up like an animal getting ready for the coming winter. And it's no use calling Arielle—she's on the road somewhere, her cell phone lost. Arielle will call when she calls.

Katya heads out to the Press Box for a couple of hours, and, on the way back to her place, stops at the all-night supermarket where she buys a roasted chicken, eating half of it right there in the car, tearing into the sweet greasy flesh, straight out of its foil pan. The tendons in the legs, the dark bits of liver along the backbone, the greasy paprika-speckled skin, the slightly dry, stringy breast, the cracking of the little bones. Somehow she would have died without eating it: it was the chicken or her, and so what anyway? The whole world does it. Is she better than the whole world?

She spends most of the next day at work thinking of the chicken, torn between squeamishness and a new surge of desire. At home, she eats the rest, then, erasing the evidence, washes and washes the pan, the sink, the table, the counters.

The chicken smell seems to be in the carpet, the table and chairs, though she's taken out the garbage, left the windows open—she gets out rubber gloves and cleaners and scrubs it all down again. As she crawls into bed, she almost sees something moving, out of the corner of her eye, a shadowy, chicken-shaped flicker. When she turns toward it, it's nothing, a trick of the eyes, and she turns off the bedside lamp.

In the morning, she leaves another note for Evening Katya in the middle of the floor: LAUNDRY! BILLS! FIND REAL JOB! NO PRESS BOX!!!

Her tattoos covered by a turtleneck and her hair brushed into tidy blue and pink swirls, she answers the phone, updates charts, greets the clients. She can't believe she ate a chicken.

People do it all the time—no big deal.

Not the same people who've been sent to jail for lying down in front of bulldozers or throwing paint on fur.

Just because you're the same person doesn't mean you're the same self. A tiger lives inside, and it needed some meat.

Oh, please—this was yet another voice (annoyed, smoking on the iron balcony, black raccoon eyes and an old black trench coat)—there is no tiger inside you. The worst kind of lie is a lie you tell yourself.

That is so not true. That is such a piece of rhetorical bullshit.

You're a piece of rhetorical bullshit.

Katya wonders if everyone has these fights in their head or if she's losing it. Brian Pierce comes into the waiting room, his coat dripping from the rain. Maybe in his forties, black hair and beard, eyes reddened at the edges but with wheels of brown in bright blue, his face weathered, probably from spending too much time on the streets, though it could be outdoor work. A pretty regular guy, except that he's wearing a hand-hammered copper helmet, like a stranded Viking. She doesn't remember what's wrong with him exactly. "How're you doing there?" he asks. He says, with an air of sharing a confidence, "Tricyclics are a problem," and she wouldn't argue that, but he goes on to say, "I know the future, usually. But the tricyclics stop the brain waves."

"What happens when you take them?"

He has kind, wise, only moderately mad eyes. Is this man crazy? "A thick feeling, like being underwater. The signals can't get through, the density is wrong."

"Electrical signals?"

"When I wear copper, it blocks unwanted entrants. Aluminum foil would work, if it didn't rip. You need a certain openness to read futures, but the beings are always looking for a way in."

She asks, "Like ghosts? Aliens?"

He looks at her like she's patronizing him. *"Please.* Not ghosts or aliens. Energetic beings. Who knows where they come from? But they leave washes of memory on top of your own. Blurry. To read the future, you need to get to where you can see the shape of everyone's life in the round. Otherwise it's only blips."

"So everything has already happened? We don't have any choices?" Katya has one eye out for the therapists. She's participating in his delusional state when she should be bringing him back to reality.

"Time is a *continuum.*" She wishes that anyone she ever dated would look into her eyes with such beautiful seriousness. "The present is over

before we realize it's been here—each moment holds the whole past
and every future possibility. What I read is just likelihoods, but not on
tricyclics."

On the wall behind him, the giant boy holds his platter of village:
identical houses each with a pair of windows like eyes, surrounded
by round trees. Bones stick up around the platter's edge, all sealed in
a turquoise bubble. The tidy rows of puffball clouds all around him
seem to belong to the same world as Brian's continuum of possibilities, even the clouds that have fallen to earth, where they lie in cozy
piles among the fleecy trees and soft hills.

"Okay, Brian," says Sukey, appearing at her door, catching his eye,
and heading back into her office. On his way, Brian puts a finger out
to touch Katya's arm. A shock runs through her, not static electricity,
not lust, some current of recognition. He leans down and whispers,
"What are you doing tonight?"

"Going out drinking," she says. "Realistically."

"You want company?"

"Sure." She writes down the address for the Press Box. It's not
like it's an actual date. She's regretted almost any man she was ever
involved with, and, come to think of it, she's regretted the women
too. She has the worst goddamn taste, like a broken compass that
always points somewhere slightly left of due South. She's not getting
involved—they're having a drink. And though she has to keep confidentiality, she doesn't remember anything in her instructions about
not socializing with clients. The therapists, obviously, would have to
avoid that. All afternoon she considers reading his chart but manages
to resist.

That evening, she takes her usual seat toward the end of the bar,
breathing in the smoky air, drinking two bourbons, and waiting to see
if Brian shows up. She buys everyone a round, and they toast her. The
men—one regular, Jacob, a gray-haired, wary man, and two strangers—argue about whether Northern California should secede from
the South and take its water with it. When they run down, Katya asks
Ramona and the men, "Do chickens have souls?"

Jacob says, "Do I have a soul? Do you have a soul, Ramona?"

Ramona smiles and wipes down the bar under the moose antlers with their fur of dust, the signed photograph of bodybuilder Bev Francis, the mirror. The red, green, and yellow lights of the jukebox gives the room a faintly sad air, like an institutional Christmas.

One of the strangers clears his throat. "On the TV once, I saw an evangelical show where a woman said she and her sister had this chicken, the only pet they could afford. Called it Lucinda. Dressed it up in little aprons, hats, dresses. But one day it ran out in the road, and the cars ran right over it. So there was Lucinda, all smashed up, one eye kind of hanging out."

Katya pushes her glass across the bar and then pulls it back before Ramona can refill it. She's hoping Brian doesn't show up, but she wants to take it easy, in case.

"They carried the body into the kitchen, crying and crying. They laid that chicken out on a board, anointed it with oil, and kneeled down to pray. And when they opened their eyes, what do you think they saw? That chicken had been healed. Their faith raised it right up again and healed it." He thumps his glass down on the bar and bursts out laughing. So does his friend. They drum their hands on the bar and clap them against each other's in the air. Having put one over on everyone. Or having told a "true" but totally ludicrous story. Or having repeated an out-and-out lie.

No one thinks the chicken was healed. But she can imagine it so clearly. Why shouldn't you believe that chickens could have miracles? If you believed in miracles, that is, and if you didn't, what a sad, sad statement about your life, and no wonder you were in the bar every night.

Ramona says, "When my oldest daughter was four, some idiot told her that cows have friends and enemies, that they hold grudges, that they love their babies and fight and wail and look for them when they're taken away, that they even worry about the future. I said, 'Please tell me who figured out that cows worry about the future and how. They, like, make five-year plans? I'd love to see a cow's five-year plan.' But my daughter said, 'From now on, I'm not eating any more animals. Only cheese sandwiches and hot dogs.' So I let her live on sandwiches and hot dogs. It only lasted a month anyway."

"You didn't tell her hot dogs are meat?" asks the stranger who told the story about the miracle.

"We think we're protecting them, but it doesn't work out that way." Ramona's superpower is her burr of a voice that, though she sounds nothing like Jenny, has the same effect. Her voice surrounds them, as warm and soft as if she'd wrapped them in a car blanket and they were all going home, late, sleeping in the back seat with rain against the windows and the blur of headlights going past.

Maybe Katya's superpower is the ability to name other people's superpowers. Not a top-drawer superpower, like flying or invisibility or shooting flame, but better than the power to make sure the dishes are done every night or the uncanny ability to realize when a bill has gone missing in a pile in the house and to make sure it gets paid on time.

They all sit in silence, drinking and listening to salsa on the jukebox. Brian comes in, still wearing his helmet, now with an ancient sheepskin coat that makes him look more like a Viking than ever. Katya wonders what she was thinking. In relation to anyone else at the clinic, he'd seemed pretty sane. He sits beside her and nods to Ramona, who says, "Can I help you?" Not too friendly.

Katya says, "This is my friend. Brian."

"Okay. I'll serve you if there's no trouble."

"No trouble. A glass of some kind of stout would be nice," says Brian, mildly.

"One for me too." Katya reaches for her wallet, but Brian, majestically, waves his own and takes out a five. He winks at Katya, with those brown-in-blue eyes, and she falls immediately in love with him. He's her father's age! He's a nutcase! She shouldn't have had those two bourbons. But when Ramona delivers their ale, Katya takes a deep drink of hers and says, "We were talking about the souls of chickens. Brian, do you think chickens have souls?"

He says, "Chickens, yes. Ducks, absolutely. Fish, I don't know. Octopi definitely. I read in *Scientific American* about this lab. The fish were disappearing. They put a researcher in overnight. Nothing. They set up a closed-circuit camera. That night the octopus unscrewed the lid of its tank, climbed out, jumped across the lab, opened the fish tank, ate a couple, closed it up again, and jumped back into its own. Of course, you'd have to think that the ability to conceal your crimes means you have a soul. Maybe the octopus was just really smart about staying out of trouble."

The other men are grinning: Brian's making their night. One guy, when Brian's head is turned, makes a little loop around his ear with his finger.

Katya jumps up. "Brian, what about a walk?"

"Sounds good," he says, and she goes out thinking that, whatever else, it may be easier for her not to go to the Press Box in the future. But she sometimes thinks she feels about the Press Box the way a real Jew would feel about *shul.* The place where you're most yourself, the place where you go to be with your tribe. She never had a *bat mitzvah*, though, and on her very occasional visits to some synagogue, she stumbles over the Hebrew transliterations of the prayers, feeling like an imposter, an idiot. All those names for God, and that's just the beginning. A real Jew would pray all day long, celebrate all the holidays, know something about the six thousand or whatever pages of the Talmud. She is so not up to it.

She wants to take Brian home, but what if he stabs her with her big vegetable knife or strangles her in bed? She should have read his chart. They go, instead, to the graveyard, walking between the stones. The fog has settled in, a wispy dampness that soaks them invisibly. The thin moon still shines brightly enough for her to make out headstones. Annie Chalmers 1860-1892. *Mother* and *Father*—two great flat stones side by side. And John Peterson 1958-1996, that grave covered with offerings: half-melted Valentine's Day candies, Easter eggs, a felt-pen-decorated baby doll, clumps of flowers, messages on a balloon: "We miss you, John," and "I want my Johnny back."

Brian strolls along, hands in pockets, the collar of his sheepskin coat turned up. "I used to have a pet chicken I called Beth. On a farm—*bad* idea. My mother said not to get attached, but I wouldn't listen. To teach me a lesson, instead of selling Beth when it came time, she took me out in the yard, told me to chop her head off. I cried, said

I wouldn't. She said no more meals in that house until I did. By the next day, I was so hungry I would have killed one of my brothers. So I picked up the ax and did it. Beth ran here and there, her neck spouting blood. A few seconds, but I dreamed about it for years."

"Oh, God, how terrible for you," says Katya. This level of childhood trauma is way above her pay grade. She wishes, for a moment, for Sukey, for Estella, to tell her what to do.

"I didn't eat her. By that night, my mother had to let me eat something else. I never have eaten chicken after that."

"You're a vegetarian?"

"No, I eat beef, pork, like that. Just not chicken."

"I'm done with all of it." Really done. No more Lucindas or Beths. Also no more omelets. Or anything produced by those wailing cows. So at some point, she'd already had her last dish of cow's milk ice cream, her last triple crème cheese. If she'd known it was the last, she might have enjoyed it more. Or maybe less, who knows? She asks Brian, hesitating, "Do you think all that with Beth affected you?"

"You mean, did it drive me nuts? No, that's my biochemistry. But it made me sad. The world has no pity on children." He taps his helmet and puts his arms around her. "I hear their broadcasts every day. Really, I need an exorcist, not a shrink, but the county doesn't cover it."

They stand still. He kisses her, slow and exploratory, his lips soft, one hand holding her head lightly, the other stroking her cheek. She opens her eyes and sees his face, blank with concentration, his eyes half closed. He's kissing her with his whole self. No performing, no irony, nothing held in reserve. He asks, "Do you live near here?"

"Right across the street." She's gone way too long without this.

Inside the efficiency, she slides the note from Morning Katya under the bureau by the door while Brian pulls at her shirt and says, "Take all this off."

They strip quickly. He has strong shoulders and arms, a furry pot belly. She puts her hands on him, touching his belly's softness.

He draws back at her tattoos. "You're covered in snakes."

"Protective snakes. The kind people want for aphrodisiacs."

He looks doubtful, but his erection doesn't waver. His visible amazement in remembering the astonishing business of flesh on flesh makes sex with him like being present at the beginning of the world, though it doesn't last long.

Afterward, he lies beside her, holding her and threading a strand of her hair through his fingers. She's drifting off when he begins to shudder. "No, no, no," he cries, bounding out of bed and running to a corner of the room, crouching there, head rocked forward between his knees, arms stuck straight out ahead of him, his hands flapping.

She jumps up herself, squatting beside him. He shouts in an incomprehensible language, thrusting the invisible away with his hands.

"Brian, it's all right. It's Katya. Can you hear me?"

He goes on shouting. The downstairs neighbor pounds on her floor. What has she done to him? She runs her hands over the cold, goose-fleshed skin in front of her, the body that had made her so happy minutes earlier.

"Pray, pray, pray, pray," he says in a desperate monotone, rocking back and forth. Is he praying, or does he mean she should pray?

Loudly, she says, "God or Goddess or whoever, please protect and defend this man."

More agonized, he shouts, "Pray, pray, *pray*."

She prays, aloud: "Protect all the children. And the animals. And all beings everywhere. Especially Brian and me." The prayer started out well but has become a little selfish toward the end.

It seems to work, though. Brian jumps up and climbs on the futon. He crawls under the covers, curls up in a ball, and sleeps until morning, while she lies beside him, awake for most of the night. When she does drift off, her own headless chicken pursues her from room to room. She dreams its life: crammed into a cage with dozens of others, beak cut off, feet grown to the wire mesh, squawking stupidly, seeing whatever chickens see out of their chicken eyes.

She starts up in bed, fully awake. She should hide the knives, just in case, but she's afraid to move. Are they going to sit and eat breakfast together? She starts running over menu options—cereal would be fastest, but seems a little cold-hearted; pancakes imply commitment. But she must have fallen asleep because when she wakes, he's gone.

He's left a small pyramid of colored stones and pieces of gravel on the kitchen counter, along with a torn scrap of paper with his phone number.

At work, she pulls out a pile of charts to update, hiding Brian's inside the others. For about two hours, she fights the urge to read it, but around eleven, her decent side loses. Brian has been hospitalized eleven times for psychotic episodes and suicidality. Medication notes and descriptions of their side effects fill the pages, along with his history. His father shot himself at the dinner table, in front of the family, when Brian was seven. In his teens, Brian had trouble with delinquency and showed the first signs of schizophrenic affect. He's started a few college courses here and there, and even finished a couple, studying first history, then psychology, and finally philosophy. When not in the hospital, he lives in the house his mother left him and sometimes rents out rooms, though tenants, disturbed by his occasional shouting in the nights, usually don't stay. He gets a monthly social security check and the occasional odd job. Notes by different doctors describe Brian as prey to religious delusions and hallucinations; he believes he knows the future and the past and considers his father's suicide to have been caused by demons who sometimes come back to torment Brian and urge him to kill himself as well.

Katya puts the chart away and, when Karen emerges, says, "I'm going out for a ten-minute break."

She walks down to the end of the street and looks out across the dark gold hills, cut through by Highway 12, telephone poles, and golden hills enlivened by clumps of grazing milk cows. A much dustier version of the world than the Czech paintings, most of which were painted on the back of panes of glass, originally, the artist learning over the years what the picture would look like when turned right side round.

For a few minutes, she imagines calling Brian—trying out different things she might say, none of which, in the end, seem preferable to silence. She can't stay here after this, but if she leaves this job, there'll be nothing else up here, and she'll piss off her temp agency. She could

wait tables at one of the two health food cafés or even one of the ta-
querias, though probably not unless she works on her Spanish.

Or she could go back to the city and drive up sometimes on weekends to see Jenny and her family. She remembers the Mission at night:
going to see experimental performances in converted garages, and,
if they were her aunt and uncle's shows, or shows by their students,
feeling like a vicarious part of their world. Best of all was sitting over
garlic fries and ale at the Phoenix, people on all sides, as her friends
made plans for their possible futures. A couple of years ago, they'd
laid it all out on paper: Zadan planned to sell transformed and muti-
lated Barbies on the web, Corinna to open her own street cart, Mary
to start a graphic zine for teen runaways. Then, as now, Katya didn't
exactly have a set of specific and measurable goals. Probably she's like
a cow in this way—she can worry about her future but has no capacity
to plan for it.

Just before the end of the day, she types up her two weeks' notice
and leaves it on the break room table. Unless he makes a special trip
in, she'll be gone before Brian's next appointment. Before she leaves
for the night, she says to Sukey and Estella, "You need a less terrible
person for this job."

Sukey laughs, and Estella gives her a hug, first offering open arms
and an inquiring look to see if she has permission. "None of the temps
stay. It's not really personal. You might want to go back to school or
something anyway."

Katya doesn't even argue with this. The whole older generation
thinks that whatever's wrong with her can be fixed by more school. As
soon as she gets home that evening, she picks up the phone and says,
as soon as Jenny answers, "I'm sorry to call? Is it okay? Do you have a
minute? I ate a chicken."

"Katya. Wow." A short silence. "Do you want to tell me about it?"

She whispers, "Jenny, I think I see a little headless ghost, running
through the apartment on its drumsticks. It might be haunting me."
*Katya was very delusional this morning and her cognitive processes seemed to be
impaired.*

It takes form as she describes it. "I do, I do see it." The chicken, headless, its glazed, roasted skin shining, lurches into the heater, falls down, and is up and running, blindly. "I don't want to live with the ghost of a chicken."

"Well, show it the door."

With the phone tucked into her shoulder, she opens her front door. "O.K. It's out—it went over the railing. Oh, God, it's in the pool."

The chicken thrashes in the water, pale and phosphorescent in the halogen lighting over the apartment building's uncleaned, unheated pool.

"Can you get it out?"

"*I* can't do anything." But the chicken flops onto the side of the pool at the five-foot mark, then runs out past the mailboxes and across the highway. "Good, it's in the graveyard. That's fine. Thank you, Jenny. I really needed your help."

"Be cool, Katya. Take care. And maybe watch out for the bourbon?"

"Unless it sees me first. Give my love to Brandon and kiss the kids for me."

"Turn on the radio or something. Read some philosophy." Jenny has two superpowers: staying alive and being the person everyone turns to in their crises. Ninety-eight percent of the time she says the exact right thing. But not always.

Katya says, "I'm too young for philosophy. It's better if you start when you're old—it's the opposite of ballet."

She hangs up, says to herself, "Well, I called Jenny, but I will *not* go to the Press Box." Through the open blinds, headlights shine, flashing up the wall. Across the highway, somewhere in the blank and impenetrable graveyard, the ghost of the chicken is crashing headlessly into gravestones. Katya shuts the blinds, grabs her peacoat, and is out the door.

When she gets home from the Press Box, around one, she doesn't go into her apartment but crosses the highway to the cemetery and walks up the drive to where the hearses park. Under the waning moon, ghosts flit and sparkle, some kind of visiting going on, grave to grave, but Katya can't make it out. The whole thing seems comforting, like a display of white holiday lights in the trees downtown. Although this is the first time she's seen these ghosts, all of this feels inevitable—her chicken has given her a ticket to the other world. She makes her way between the graves, not disturbing the dead, who ignore her, making their rounds, table-hopping.

When she doesn't fight it, she doesn't mind the chill. She sits against the side of a stone, not on the grave itself, and closes her eyes. From somewhere behind her comes a muted scratching, claws on rock. When she looks around, she sees a gray cat leap away and streak across the highway. It's been watching the headless, luminous chicken as it silently rubs a drumstick on a headstone. The chicken moves toward her, and, when she stiffens, jumps away again—she's startled it.

"Why should I feel bad?"

The chicken edges forward, body cocked to one side. A few pinfeathers, slightly shriveled in the store's grilling-oven, cling to its bluish-rose breast.

Katya says, "You want me to say I regret eating you? Sure, of course. Get on the bottom of the list. I used to let Jenny chew bits of asphalt from the street, when Mom wasn't watching. Kids swallow all kinds of things without getting cancer, right?"

Wings jutting up and back, the chicken crouches before her. When she reaches out a hand to touch it, it flattens itself against the ground. The rest of the dead shimmer by; she can't make them out as clearly as she can her own chicken.

She says, "Believe me, I've done worse things this very week."

The chicken gets up on its drumsticks, edging backwards.

"You're a goddamn judgmental stunted dinosaur. I think your superpower is guilt."

The chicken turns and hobbles behind a stone. Katya calls out, "I am not going to apologize to a chicken, alive *or* dead."

The chicken, as if she had in fact apologized, reappears triumphantly. As she says, "You shouldn't waste it on me—maybe you could go visit a few CEOs or politicians and work on climate change or something," it gathers itself together, clenching its skinny wings, and jumps into her lap, curling up between her knees. She puts down her hands to stroke it but can't feel anything. A cloud passes over the moon, and she thinks she can hear the whisperings of the dead, though she has no idea what they might be saying to each other.

"All right," she says to the chicken. She gets to her feet. "I'm going home. You can come or not, it's up to you."

She sets off between the graves, and, at the edge of the cemetery, looks back. Behind her, the chicken, less pale, rosier than before, hobbles at top speed, taking little jumps and lurches forward, at each step leaving behind a claw-shaped imprint of phosphorescent light.

V

Dream Boards
Santa Cruz, July 2004

CAST OF CHARACTERS

PHILIP: a former professor of psychology, now 86, with advanced
Parkinson's. The oldest child, and only boy, with three younger
sisters and high family expectations, he began drinking heavily in
high school. In college, he studied psychology to figure out what
was wrong with people. His work was always focused on research
and teaching; he never saw a patient and was always highly skep-
tical of therapy. He originally explored the psychological causes
of warfare. Later, he studied compulsion and the various mechanisms of delusion and denial, and finally innovations and alternate treatments for schizophrenia and other reality disorders. In
River Valley, he will use a walker, but not a wheelchair, and has
recently returned from another stint in the hospital. He's also on
blood thinners for his heart condition and wears a number of
gauze bandages where his skin was torn in his most recent fall.
LILY's husband.

LILY: an 80-year-old artist, she has as much trouble walking as PHILIP.
She has been living in the U.S. since she was eleven, when she was
sent away from Warsaw. Initially, she stayed with a cousin, who
found her unnerving enough that she soon delivered her to her first
institution, the Los Angeles Orphans' Asylum (classes in the Boyle
Heights facility, though, post-earthquake, they lived and slept in
the basement of St. Vincent's). She is on several medications now,
though her primary condition (generally, but not always, diagnosed

as schizophrenia) is considered to be substantially in remission, with no significant relapses since her sixties. PHILIP's wife.

JENNY: PHILIP and LILY's middle granddaughter, 22, cancer survivor, farmer, apprentice herbalist and witch, mother. Before her Hodgkin's lymphoma, which at first the doctors thought was a return of her earlier bouts with mono, she'd been a cheerful, practical child and then an unusually agreeable teenager. She'd shown an early talent for looking after people and animals and for putting together entertaining school lunches for herself and her sisters. She often did other family members' dishes when they were busy. On weekends, she sometimes woke up early to make muffins or batches of brownies. Everyone turned to her to resolve disputes. She was more likely to be an audience member for the little plays Katya and Arielle put on than a participant. She never said so, but she didn't see the point of the family's endless theorizing, pretending, and making things that couldn't be eaten or used. After her lymphoma, she was, if anything, even more herself and completely unwilling to spend another minute solving useless equations or sitting in a classroom while her life ran out. Now she has long, curly brown hair and an easy laugh. She's the person in the family least likely to deliver a lecture, on any subject, or to make an unkind remark.

ACTIVITIES DIRECTOR

TIME: The present
PLACE: River Valley, an assisted living facility in Santa Cruz, California
STAGING: The home has high ceilings and trees outside the window. This scene takes place in the activities room, with its art tables and holiday colors, possibly including decorations from the most recent or upcoming holiday. Other residents could be suggested by puppets or projections.

[*Lights up on* LILY *and* PHILIP, *making the current art project: cutting out and collaging images for dream boards. Their boards are projected behind them on the walls. The words and images should be legible.*

PHILIP's *dream board—collaged from* World Watch, Earth Island Journal, Earth First! *and so on—shows images of harvesting, the Maldives and Seychelles, rushing full rivers, and other pictures from a flourishing world with its islands still above water. However, it also contains facts about chronic hunger and predictions about the disappearance of rivers: i.e.* World Watch's *"The Nile, the Ganges, the Amu Dar'ya and Syr Dar'ya, the Huang He (or Yellow River), and the Colorado are each so dammed, diverted, or overtapped that for parts of the year, little or none of their freshwater reaches the sea."*

LILY's *dream board is a collage in pale pinks, grays, and shades of blue: a flamingo that appears blind, dipping its head behind its coiled neck; part of a bulbous palm tree; their middle child, Eva, at about ten, wearing mirror sunglasses and looking like an angry star who doesn't want to be seen; a spray of pale pink blossoms shot in infrared with a tiny cutout of the head of Elijah Wood as Frodo floating in the trees; a fragment from a Japanese painting of a bird on snowy branches against gold leaf; the head of a laughing but anxious boy, a stranger clipped from a magazine; some bits of podlike blossoms and gray bulbous shapes; a bit of faded pink blouse behind a bed lintel; their youngest daughter, Julia, as a dreamy five-year-old with some kind of pipe or hook in her mouth, looking into space as if she'd seen a ghost; and, on the diagonal from the blossoms in the bottom corner, a swarm of what appear at first to be pink fish, but turn out to be a huge flock of flamingos in blue water—hundreds of them clustered like an infestation, a tornado of birds.*

From offstage comes a young woman's voice: the ACTIVITIES DIRECTOR, *explaining.*]

ACTIVITIES DIRECTOR:

The dream boards are a chance for you to consider what you most want in your life and to put your desires out into the world as an intention. Find images that represent your ideal life and future and make them into a collage. Be lavish here. The more specific you are, the more powerful this exercise becomes. How can you call your vision into reality? What would it look like for your dreams to come true?

LILY:

Ouch! [*rubbing her hip*] Oh, I cannot wait for the next surgery. Damn. My Vicodin is up in our room.

PHILIP:

Do you want me to get it for you?

LILY:

I can get it myself, thank you. Where is that child? She was supposed to be here two hours ago. [*doesn't move*] Don't you want anything cheerful on your board? I wish we had gone to Paris. We could still go. We could stay at the Hotel Carillon and have *quails ballottine* and walk on the Champs Elysées.

PHILIP:

Maybe not this year.

LILY:

You are such an old crabcake. [*to the audience*] I absolutely love this man. I would die for this man. [*to herself*] How is it possible for a person to be in this much pain and still be walking around? Why can Jenny not get anywhere on time? Maybe she was in an accident. Maybe she and Paul and Caro were rushing over here, and for once they remembered to get my brie and brioches, but as they pulled into the parking lot, a big delivery truck was backing up and Paul was poking the baby and she burst out crying and Jenny turned around just as the truck…well, I don't like to think of it. It breaks my heart. But I'm an old lady. I'm the last person in the world you should tell you're coming at 1:00 when you have no such intention. I wouldn't have rushed my lunch if I'd known.

[PHILIP's *tremor is giving him difficulty in cutting out the pictures. Now his face falls into blankness, his eyes unfocusing and jaw hanging open. He shakes himself and returns to full coherence.*]

PHILIP:

You finished your lunch at 2:30. Jenny meant to be on time. She'll be here soon enough. It's a long drive for her. And I don't think she's bringing Paul and Caro this week. So probably if she was run over by a truck they're safe and sound with their Dad. Meanwhile, I'm happy to go get your pills, if you want.

LILY:

It's important for me to train this body of mine. I so want to be able to look after you. Eva says I'd be in less pain if I didn't stay up watching TV till all hours. She wants me to go to bed with the lark and get up with the chickens. Bless her. She has such energy. Aren't you proud of her? [*pause*] Not that I'm not proud of Robert and Julia, of course. Goodness, all that creativity. Not so practical as Eva. I think she's getting secretive. There's something she's hiding about the grandkids. And Arielle does seem fragile. Doesn't she? Don't you worry about her? Do you think, assuming Jenny isn't lying dead in the road somewhere, that she'll tell us what's happening? She won't tell us. If she even comes. [*pause*] Is that true, about the rivers drying up?

PHILIP:

The National Center for Atmospheric Research analyzed 925 rivers. More than a third of them, including the Niger, Ganges, and Yellow River, are drying.

LILY:

I want you to put one thing on that dream board that has nothing to do with climate change, world hunger, or war and torture.

PHILIP:

There's nothing on here about war and torture yet. I'm trying to figure out how to represent peace and human rights. Without putting in any pictures of people holding hands.

LILY:

This project is not designed to grind our noses in the dirt. It's a dream board, not a reality board. It's not good for you to be so angry all the time.

PHILIP:

Why, exactly, are they having us do it at all? A particular form of cruelty visited on the old by the peppy young.

[JENNY *enters and kisses each of them.*]

LILY:

What a nice surprise, dear. It's been such a long time since we've seen you.

PHILIP:

She was here the first Tuesday of last month. And the month before. And the month before that.

LILY:

I was so afraid you'd been killed. Would you like to make a dream board? You put down pictures of everything you want in life, and it magically comes true. Wouldn't that be nice? I'm so glad nothing's happened to you.

JENNY:

I'm sorry I'm late, Grandma. It's so hot, and I had to water everything by hand, and the restaurant deliveries ran late, and one of my clients is getting divorced and I couldn't prescribe for her till she'd told me the whole story, and Paul bit someone at preschool, and I had to go pick him up and take him over to daycare and talk them into letting him stay for the afternoon. But I did get your brie and pastries. They're in the fridge. What would I like on a dream board? Maybe a new irrigation system for the back lettuce beds. A better-quality baby bouncer for Caro. Pretty trivial stuff. Maybe I'd cover the board with magic clocks so I could extend every day for seven or eight hours. And use them to sleep. I like your boards better. Though you need human rights on there, Grandad.

PHILIP:

That's just what I was saying.

LILY:

Ouch! [*rubbing her hip*] Oh, no, oh no, oh no.

PHILIP:

Should I get your pills, or are you going to do it?

JENNY:

I'm happy to get your pills, Grandma. Tell me where they are.

LILY:

You'd never be able to find them. [*to* PHILIP] It grieves me that this body of mine will not do what you all want it to do. It really causes me great pain that I cannot be the woman you would like me to be. The wife you truly deserve to have.

PHILIP:

If you'd like me to get your pills, just say so. [*A standoff.* LILY *stares at him.*] Okay then. [*He stands, grips his walker, and moves forward in a kind of run, nearly falling as he heads toward the door.*]

LILY:

Take my walker. It's better.

PHILIP:

I don't want your damn walker.

LILY:

It's better! You have such a damn hard head. Come back here and give your blushing bride a kiss. Come here. Come on. Come and give me a kiss.

[*He turns, slowly, having trouble getting his feet to work, and makes his way back, gripping his walker. She half rises, leaning over her walker, takes his cheeks between her hands, squeezes them, and kisses him on the mouth. He gives a small laugh and kisses her in return.* JENNY *watches.* PHILIP *exits.*]

LILY:
I so love that man. Do you know how much I love that man? My biggest fear is of dying first and leaving him alone. What would he do without me? I shudder to think of it.

JENNY:
It'll be a long, long time before you die, Grandma. I don't think you have to worry about him outliving you. Did you talk to him about the wheelchair? Because River Valley said if he keeps falling and having to go to the hospital all the time, you two won't be able to stay here.

LILY:
Why do you think he's going to die? How do you know I'm going to outlive him? Are you predicting the future now? Reading crystal balls?

JENNY [*takes* LILY's *hand*]:
I didn't mean to upset you.

LILY [*sullenly*]:
I'm not upset. We talk about where we'll be buried. We talk about who will go first. Why do you think I will outlive your grandfather?

JENNY:
Maybe you won't, Grandma. Maybe you'll die at exactly the same moment. I'm sorry I said anything. I promised Mom we'd talk about the wheelchair today.

LILY:

I want you to tell me what you see.

JENNY:

He's half in the shadows, most of the time.

LILY:

Oh, that's just dementia. An ugly word, really, for something that happens to all of us sooner or later. Couldn't they come up with a better one?

JENNY:

How about befogged?

LILY:

Befogged. I like that.

[PHILIP *enters, slowly, the pills balanced on his walker. He leans down, grips the bottle, and hands it to* LILY. *She takes two.*]

LILY:

Your granddaughter thinks you're going to die.

PHILIP:

I'm struggling not to say, "We're all going to die." Whoops. Just did.

JENNY:

There are traditions that believe in preparing for the next life. Rules to live by in this one, stories about the next: gods and goddesses, demons, great tests to endure. Because, truly, we are all going to die. We are.

PHILIP:

We endure plenty of tests right here.

LILY:

Well, this talk is a little morbid for me. When I die, I am going right up to God, and He will fold me in His arms and say, "I'm sorry for all that pain I caused you, my child. I was testing your spirit. And my, didn't you fail that test?" "I'm sorry, God," I will say. "I did everything I could. I just wasn't up to it, that's all. I could not be brave enough. I'm sorry I wasn't what you wanted me to be." I just hope He will take away that pain and reunite me with all the people I ever knew. And we will dance in Heaven.

JENNY:

That's a beautiful picture, Grandma.

PHILIP:

We'd better get her up to the room before she falls asleep.

LILY [*rouses herself*]:

I am going to finish my dream board, thank you very much.

PHILIP [*to* JENNY]:

Don't think we have too much idea what we're preparing for.

JENNY:

Grandad, can we talk about the wheelchair?

PHILIP:

No wheelchairs. [*looks at* LILY, *now nodding off*] Your grandmother won't have it. We bought one, but she said I kept crashing into the furniture. And I did maybe run into people once or twice. It's out in the hall now where it can't hurt anyone. Don't look like that. [*softly, looking at* LILY] Your grandmother's a wonderful woman. Everyone tells her their stories. She has a whole group of women here who worship her. They'd do anything for her. It's amazing to see.

JENNY:
I know, Grandad.

PHILIP:
I never believed the soul survived the body. But I'm willing, now, to think that part of our consciousness might continue to exist in some form. It would be nice to think it wasn't all a waste.

JENNY:
A waste? Hundreds of students, years on the school board, all that research. All the letter writing and marching and phone calls and years of you making peanut butter ginger noodles when you were shelter host. As far as I can tell, you never wasted a minute. And if your wheelchair isn't working for you, we could get you another.

PHILIP:
No more wheelchairs. [*shrugs*] I'm proud of my children. We raised three great kids. And Eva raised three great kids. Everything else seems to have faded away.

JENNY:
So what would you want now if you could have anything at all?

PHILIP:
I'd like my children and grandchildren to be happy and live good lives.

JENNY:
For yourself, Grandad?

LILY [*opens her eyes*]:
He'd like to take his lovely wife to Paris, that's what.

[*They look at her, but she's drifted off again.*]

PHILIP:

When we moved here, I thought since I wasn't doing the meals and house cleaning anymore, I'd have time to read again.

JENNY:

Why don't you put a picture of a book, or a whole pile of books, on your dream board?

PHILIP:

Not too realistic.

JENNY:

It doesn't seem like too much to ask, when you're eighty-six years old. One book. One thing on that dream board that's for you.

PHILIP:

Would that make you happy?

JENNY:

You're only going to do it if it's for me? Okay. Yes. It would make me happy.

[PHILIP *pages through the magazines, holds one up, and begins cutting it out. He can't get the scissors to work, looks to* JENNY *for help. She takes it, cuts it out briskly, and hands it to him.*]

JENNY:

Thomas Berry. *The Great Work: Our Way into the Future.* That's it? That's what you want?

PHILIP:

Would that be acceptable to you?

JENNY:

Whatever you want, Grandad.

LILY [*waking*]:

What does your Grandad want? He wants a nap with his bride right this minute. He wants to help her get her old bones out of this chair and to take her on a fast elevator ride upstairs for a nice sexy nap.

PHILIP [*puts down the picture of the book*]:

So much for that. It was terrific to see you, Jenny.

JENNY:

I'll see you next month, Grandad. I'll call before then, of course. Meanwhile, I think I'd better help you get up to your room.

PHILIP:

We can manage it ourselves. It's going to take us a little while. You go on home to your family and your farm. Thank you for your faithfulness, Jenny. I know it's a big drive for you. Go on now, before you get caught in rush hour. We'll be fine. We're used to this.

[JENNY *kisses them and exits.* PHILIP *stands, holding onto the edge of the table, and grips his walker.* LILY *tries to stand, fails.*]

LILY:

Now don't rush me. You always rush me.

PHILIP:

We have plenty of time.

[LILY *tries to stand, fails, tries again, finally manages to get up. She takes hold of her walker, turns to* PHILIP *in triumph. He lifts one hand, slowly, puts it on her shoulder, and leans on his own walker again. They turn toward the door. Lights out.*]

VI

Shoreside
Santa Cruz, September 2000

Shoreside is all greige: greige linoleum, greige walls, greige blankets on the hard thin beds. Arielle's still sick and shaky, unfocused. Last night was the worst. She wrecked everything. She should be dead, but instead she's surrounded by people so crazy they have to be locked up in here. Gina, a woman she sort of remembers from last night, is giving her a tour. Gina's oldish, maybe fifty or sixty, but she has cat's-eye glasses, leopard-patterned leggings, and a blouse covered with tropical flowers. Her graying hair sticks up on one side. She seems like she doesn't give a fuck. Still, she's explaining everything to Arielle, and she only seems a little weird, not full-out bedbug.

She says, "Breakfast in a few minutes. That's your first chance to start earning points. We get a point for staying in bed at night, a point for sitting through community meeting or talking in group, a point each time we take a tray of their food and consume at least eighty percent." She laughs, for no apparent reason, and Arielle semi-laughs with her. To do well in Shoreside sounds like hard work, with as many bullshit hoops to jump through as high school.

A big guy shoulders past, and Arielle squeezes up against the wall. Are any of these people murderers?

Gina says, "Don't worry about Gary. You should stay out of his way when he's going off. But he doesn't mean anything by it."

This feels distinctly uncomforting. Maybe he means well, maybe he doesn't, but the real question is what kinds of damage he might do. For all she knows, she's already damaged herself. The hospital psychiatrist wouldn't let her go home, even when her mother said they could look after her, even when Arielle pleaded to go back to her own room. The psychiatrist told her parents, "You're not objective enough to evaluate the situation." Now Arielle's trapped here for at least three days. Who knows what could happen in that time? Maybe she really will go crazy.

Gina leads her down the hall, saying, kindly, "Sometimes we can smell salt air during yard exercise. And when we get enough points, there could be a walk to the beach." She takes Arielle into her room and opens her nightstand: everyone's nightstands, beds, and footlockers are identical, as if they've all joined some weird army. In her drawer, Gina's made a small altar with a sand dollar and piece of kelp.

"With enough points, you can earn weekend furlough or even get out altogether, to the halfway house near the lagoon. Then you can get up in the morning and walk to the sea."

"How many points is that?" Maybe it's okay to have fewer choices. Maybe Arielle doesn't want weekend furlough. Maybe she doesn't want to go home. Even though some of these people scare her, she can't hurt anyone in here, including herself. No one will let her near a razor or pills. No one will look at her with anxious pity.

Gina takes Arielle to the nurse's station and asks how many points it will take to get to the halfway house. They're busy and try to brush her off, but she won't go away. "Wouldn't it be motivational? For us to know?" she asks an aide whose nametag says Rebecca. Fingernails of a Manchu empress, tracings of red-blue veins across her nose and cheeks.

"You'll have to discuss your situation with your doctor, dear. The important thing is, you keep your end of the contract. You know what you need to do to get points. Just stay on track. We'll let you know when you hit your targets."

As Gina and Arielle walk away, Arielle asks, "Didn't they ever tell you how many points you need to get to the halfway house?" It comes out more rudely than she'd intended. She smiles to make up for it.

"Well, maybe it's my mind, or maybe it's the medications. I know what matters, but the details get away from me. And the staff likes to change the rules from time to time. It helps us all remember they're in charge. But they're doing their best, within their own limits."

Though it's ungreat not to be able to just walk out—the doors all locked, their windows threaded with wire, and a double-locking area between doors, like an airlock in a spaceship—still, it feels as if this could be a kind of temporary home, a working system. Because despite people like Gary, it might be safer here. She cannot stand the idea that, sooner rather than later, she's going to have to face her parents and explain what she was thinking last night. And her friends are going to be through with her now that everyone knows how she betrayed Jasmine. She's so fucking toxic. She wanted to quit living before she poisoned everyone around her, and last night will only have made it so much worse.

In the common room, there's a bearded guy rocking back and forth in a chair. Gina says to him as well as to Arielle, "It's like school. The real purpose isn't to learn history or science. You learn getting up every morning. You learn sitting in the chair. With that skill set, you're ready to go to work."

The guy says, "Do you know what can *happen* if you distract me? You'll end *all of this.*" He makes an explosion with his hands, blowing out his breath. The poster behind him reads, "Peace Begins At Home," a brown and a white hand clasping each other over an obviously feeble-minded dove.

Gina guides this lost child down the hall, back to her own room. She needs to check on Marjorie, to make sure she's up. The aides will be rougher with her if they have to wake her themselves. Arielle looks puzzled, as if she's trying to shake off a dream and wondering if she's now in another dream. She seems less unhappy, though, so Gina doesn't tell her how, before the meds kick in, she's learned to close her eyes and hold the sand dollar and kelp to her nose, turning her back to the wind with the sand blowing against her legs, sand crabs burrowing at the tideline. It's better to downplay the shadier aspects of this place for someone seeing it all for the first time. She herself is fifty-three and since her teens has slipped back and forth. In and out the window.

Each time, they lock you up again. The state hospitals, the locked facilities, the meds. Sometimes you can stand your life in exile from the world and then sometimes not one more day. Your lungs close up. You'll die in a cage.

In the middle of the night before, loud crying woke her; she'd tongued her bedtime sleeping pill instead of swallowing. Some nights, she prefers not to be put under, even if it means hearing the muffled calling of other sleepers flailing in their beds. Maybe those others tongued their meds too. If they catch you, it's the shot in the ass instead. And, of course, you lose points. But the drugged sleep is too thick. The pills make you groggy for hours in the mornings.

She got out of bed and went to investigate the commotion. The nurses' station rose up out of a cold, blank space that branched into corners. A fluorescent light flickered badly, the floor smelling of piss and strong chemicals. In the first of the patient chairs, the aides and a guard stood over a girl of fourteen or fifteen. Arielle, though of course Gina didn't know her yet. She was shaking and weeping. She should have been in Willow Grove with the other kids, but that place often had a shortage of beds. Probably she was pretty in a better moment. Now she was a sick mess, her long silvery hair matted, her eyes shadowed, her skin gray.

The security guard who came with her in the ambulance stood over her at the nurses' station like a kindly but disapproving uncle. "You want to look after yourself. Your life is a gift from God, you have to make what you can of it."

In the second chair sat Jonathan, who was sent down to State a few months earlier—a crowded barracks of a place where, in Gina's experience, the food is even worse and most of the doctors are trainees. He wouldn't have been allowed back at Shoreside if he hadn't been doing better, but it sure wasn't apparent last night, as he sat restlessly in his chair, uttering long strings of curses, his eyes unfocused.

Stan, one of the middling aides, bustled around. "Jonathan, let Sherry and me do your vitals and you can go to bed. Right down the hall from your last room. Aren't you *tired?*" His voice when he said "bed" was full of longing.

Arielle had her hands over her face, crying. She was *loud*.

"Now, come on," Sherry said. Not one of the good aides. She'd recently chopped off her hair, a ragged inch long all over. On Sherry's shifts, the number of fights rises dramatically. Patients wait around the corner, singing, "I dream of Sherry with the light brown hair," and flee when she approaches. They tell her they're in love with her, that they can't stop thinking of her. Behaviors that can be written up but that don't cost points. Jack said to Gary one day, "I'm going out on a limb here, but if it's at all possible for you guys, let up on Sherry. She found out her husband's been spending hundreds of dollars a month on 900 calls and massage parlors." When Gary told this to some of the others, Ed said, "We'll let up on her when she lets up on us. Someone give her the memo."

Sherry talked to Arielle as if she were talking to a two-year-old, "Can you calm down? I can't put you to bed yet. So we're going to have to restrain you sitting up if you can't calm down. I can't give you anything, your body's had enough tonight. Vodka, ibuprofen, Ambien. And decongestants. Really? Decongestants?" She looked up from the report, grinning. "No shit." When she saw Gina, she asked, "What are you doing out of bed? What's going on here?"

"That's what I've been trying to figure out. That's exactly the question. 'Crazy Nights' for forty, please, Alex. What is, 'What am I doing out of bed and what's going on here?'"

Arielle, despite the terrible shape she was in, laughed. Right then, a voice inside Gina—it felt like one of the trustworthy ones—suggested she look after this little nuthouse virgin. The child could maybe be taught not to make a career of it. Gina said, "I heard a ruckus. My meds aren't working and I'm awake." She turned to the girl, "If they mistreat you, you can call the patient advocate. This is a *regulated* snake pit, but you have to know your rights."

"You can tell her all about her rights in the morning, Gina. You're going to lose some points if you don't get back to bed right now. The doctor can adjust your meds on Tuesday." Sherry made a note, probably writing her up. Patient was delusional. Patient laughed inappropriately.

Gina winked at Arielle. The girl undoubtedly saw her as a middle-aged woman in a Victorian nightgown with a pattern of small rose-colored sprigs and torn lace. A round, pinkish face, puffy but not too battered. If she looked crazy, people wouldn't tell her their stories. Nobody runs from her, if you don't count her own children. "I'll look you up at breakfast, toots. Order the full brunch menu. The Belgian waffles are primo."

"Get *back to bed*, Gina. You just lost two points, and you're about to lose more."

"Jonathan," said Stan. "Would you hold still for your pulse? What the fuck is with you people tonight—is there a full moon out there? You don't want to be sent back to State, do you?"

Arielle, feeling both shy and like death on a stick, makes her way alone into the breakfast line—Gina said she had to go wake up a friend. At the pass-through window, they hand Arielle a breakfast tray with a plastic number 46 and a boiled egg, carton of milk, bowl of Special K, orange juice, and coffee. The dining room is right across the hall. At the door stands an aide, whose nametag says "Dace." She has the face of a very sad horse, her hair raked up into a ponytail that only adds to the effect. As everyone enters, she eyes each tray, maybe to make sure they haven't dumped or pocketed anything while she was checking off someone else. When it's Arielle's turn, Dace makes a mark next to 46 on the sheet on her clipboard. "You're new, aren't you? Make sure your number's visible on your way out."

Inside the huge dining hall, the iron-mesh windows reveal a small, trodden-down yard with one tree in the center and some bushes by the fence. The patients look like a bunch of zombies—blank-faced or smiling creepily to themselves or talking at random, grimacing. Arielle thinks, "They're just *people*," but she can't help flinching. Wondering, do I look like that? Will I, if I keep taking their drugs? And, if any of them are murderers, who would it be?

A few teenagers sit together at a table by the back wall, but Arielle, unshowered, feels way too gross to sit with them. What if they don't want her there? What if one of them knows Jasmine or Danny? They aren't like her, anyway. A couple of them wear sleeveless tops, flaunting their old and new scars right out in public. She pretends she hasn't seen them and sets down her tray at a long table in the middle of the room. No one talks to her. Why would they?

"Wow." Gina, in the doorway, makes an entrance. "Where's my huevos rancheros? Didn't I order the Eggs Benedict? What kind of Epicurean banquet do you have for us?"

Dace writes on her clipboard. "I'm not in the mood this morning."

"Are you on daytimes now?"

Dace scowls. "I'm apparently on any damn time they like."

"Sorry."

"Yeah, well, thanks for the thought."

There must be eighty people in the dining hall, coming and going with trays, sometimes way too close. Some of them walk like zombies, too. It's probably just luck if no one spills coffee all over you. Suddenly a guy comes up behind Arielle and leans over her: she jumps half out of her skin. His long, craggy face and cold, vacant eyes make him look like a vampire. His open shirt flaps over checked pants, his tongue darts out, licking the corners of his mouth. "You want that coffee, miss? Because if you don't, I want that coffee."

Gina smacks down her tray, across from Arielle. "Let her eat, Thomas." He ambles away to the next table, where they seem to be used to him. A woman hands him her coffee, matter-of-factly. Gina says, "Can I sit here? Unless you're tired of my company."

"Sure." She's hyperaware of how she looks, the way she reeks.

Gina flourishes her napkin, a duchess about to embark on her morning feast. "Well, let's get a good look at you. Aren't you a little beauty?"

Arielle can't help smiling. It's the kind of off-the-wall thing her Grandma Lily says all the time. She's spent years in places like this one. Now it's Arielle's turn. If she goes on living, none of this will be a secret from the world. Everyone will know she's the kind of person who has sex with her friend's boyfriend and then tries to take the coward's way out. Probably because she's actually crazy. Like Grandma Lily. Her grandmother acts almost normal a lot of the time, but she's definitely whack. Arielle shoves away her breakfast tray.

"They're not going to poison us." Gina breaks the top of her runny egg and examines it. "They're more worried about keeping us quiet, so we can't get underfoot in their wars." And, when Arielle doesn't know what to say, "You have noticed there are seventy or so wars going on out there? You want the list?"

Gina seems like a member of Arielle's own family: losers and idealists. What is it Aunt Julia always says? "We come from crazy." It's so awful that Arielle starts laughing.

"You think it's funny, do you? Ready to live yet?" Gina eats three quick bites of her egg with an expression of determination.

Arielle pokes at her cereal and eats a bite. Does she have to eat a slimy egg too?

"According to their lights, they may even be protecting us," Gina says. "But they can't do anything about the dreams."

Arielle can't put this remark together with whatever Gina was saying before, but she's willing to try. "The dreams. I know about those."

The Gina who was showing Arielle around seems to be replaced by someone unfocused who keeps looking off into space. "If you listen, the dead will tell you what's really happening. But if they possess you, it's bad. If they start to get inside you, start singing right away."

Arielle tears her toast into pieces. She could dip it into the egg, mess it up, and make it look like she's eaten a full breakfast.

"Especially musical numbers. It interrupts their frequency."

The P.A. system announces, "Last call for breakfast. Numbers 75 through 99 should *already be* in the dining room. Last call for breakfast."

A woman appears next to them with her tray, smiling. Four hundred watts. The sight of her seems to bring Gina back to herself. "Arielle, this is my best friend, Marjorie, who is saner than you are. Marjorie, this is Arielle, our new little nutball who's legitimately terrified of this place and everyone in it."

Marjorie says, "It's not so bad in here. You get used to it. Not like State."

"We don't want her to get used to it."

"But why can't I have my own clothes?" Arielle shrugs in her too-large flowered dress and old sweater: a snake imprisoned in dry skin, needing to scrape it against rock.

"Too hard for them to do laundry if they keep track." Marjorie's about forty, with shoulder-length black hair. When she smiles, she looks as if she's holding a secret under her tongue, waiting for it to melt.

Wasn't there a song that the little badger Frances sang, in *Bread and Jam for Frances*, about the slipperiness of boiled eggs? A story Arielle's mother read her over and over. And then Katya memorized it and pretended to read it too. They will all be better off without Arielle around. But why couldn't she have done this cleanly, so they could be sad for a while and then start getting over it? She begins to weep. "I want to die. I deserve to die."

"The way I look at it is, you will," says Gina. She strokes the matted strands of Arielle's hair. "Don't let them see you cry. I'll tell you the rules later. But it's important. Dry your eyes, eat your breakfast, don't make any disturbance. Here come the aides."

Arielle sits up straighter but can't stop crying. A white-haired guy stands and hurls his tray, just missing them. The dining room hoots in joy and alarm. Someone else throws a tray. An alarm sounds and aides come running. Breakfast is over and the aides take away the ringleaders. To give them more drugs? To put them in solitary confinement? To punish them in some unimaginable way? Arielle has no idea, but, introduced to breakfast theater at Shoreside, she's stopped crying. She heads out with Gina and Marjorie, waiting in line to show their trays at the door. "Be Here Now," says a poster covered with sixties-looking flowers, and it seems like a possibility.

Gina and Arielle follow Marjorie to the art room, where the Tuesday poetry session is beginning. The room's crowded with people Gina's surprised to know, the living and the dead. She asks herself, *What does it say about me that these people are my friends?* Her inability to keep the worlds apart landed her here. No one wants to hear the messages of the dead. She has to learn to lie about their bone-chilling visits if she wants to build up her points.

The poetry lady flies around the room, exclaiming cheerfully whenever anyone manages to write words on paper. She wears clothes she's painted herself and hats with cherries, birds, flags with lines from old poems. "A poem must not mean, but be," says a flag on today's hat, a nest of robin's eggs on top and a plastic lizard crawling up the side. On the back of the hat there's another flag: "The Holy Ghost broods over this wide world with warm breast and with Ah! bright wings." Gina enjoys the poetry lady, though she often forgets to give them points for their work and attendance. Still, she lets Marjorie paint uninterrupted, peacocks with human eyes in their tails or creatures crushing the moon.

Arielle, looking unhappy but absorbed, seems to be writing a play with illustrations. Gina, taking a peek, can read much of the huge round handwriting. A jaguar named Alicia haunts a waterhole. While waiting for prey to show up, she steals her tiger friend Jasmine's boyfriend, Danny, also a jaguar. The jaguar Alicia repents, but no one will forgive her, and the play ends with her crouching over a bottle of pills, saying, "When I am gone, please remember only the good I did." Arielle scratches this out, furiously, and writes something else Gina can't make out. At least she's not sitting and crying.

She still needs her spine stiffened, so Gina takes her to the employment workshop late in the afternoon. The workshop's run by Jack—one of the best aides, one of the getting-ready-to-be-a-doctors, not one of the no-one-else-will-have-mes. He has a fuzzy beard and is very good about giving points. He passes around blank forms. "Since you all aced the interview practice, it's time for employment applications. I'll help you write in your job histories." Many of his clientele are wandering around, staring, mumbling. They rest their heads on their arms and sleep—in the room, but not of it.

Gina could fill out the form with the places she's been fired from, but the meds blur her sight and writing is hard for her. At one point, she read all the time and took notes. Every conspiracy or lie about the wars has been named in a book. People read about war with some part of their brain she doesn't understand. Their reptile selves should be howling in alarm. Maybe she'd be like the rest of them, if she couldn't see and hear the dead, their pleas for help.

Jack places the form on the table in front of Arielle. "Why don't you give this a try? It's an exercise, but it could come in handy. What would you like to study, when you go to college? What do you picture yourself doing later on?"

Arielle leaves the form on the table. "I like to dance. I like to do gymnastics. We're reading *Macbeth* in school. We have this substitute teacher who says she falls asleep over it every night, which goes to show what a sick waste of time high school is. How can you fall asleep over *Macbeth?* I could study to be a performer like my Aunt Julia. But then I'd be broke all the time and get behind on the rent and be evicted and get crappy reviews and think I've wasted my life. Or, I could do real work like my mom and go sit in a climate-controlled lab with no windows, doing research. Or get a regular, meaningless job with databases and client meetings. I could write down everything I eat and save some bonus points for popcorn at the movies on the weekend."

"Adulthood looks worse from the outside," says Jack. "I remember that. Most days it's not so bad while it's going on. Why don't you think of the most unrealistic dream job possible and fill out an application for that? You can't get what you want if you don't know what it is." He raises his voice. "*Ed.* Please fill out your own form and let Lynn fill out hers." He moves across the room, calmly.

Gina whispers to Arielle, "You need to learn to have your existential crises in private. You're only here on suicide watch. It doesn't matter what's happening in your head. All you have to do is sit up, smile, and go to meetings. Then you can get out."

"I can't." Arielle shakes her head, stubborn as a cat.

Gina pushes the form toward her. "You can. You just think you can't."

"Well then, if you know the secret to everything, why are you still in here?" Arielle asks. Gina doesn't have an immediate answer.

Saturday: first visiting hours. Arielle is still under observation, having failed her 72-hour test. She happened to mention that she didn't know for sure that she wouldn't do it again if they let her out. This is true. She's heard people jumping off a bridge sometimes change their minds midway and want to live, but she can't imagine coping for the rest of her life. What are her friends saying? How long would she have to be away before people stopped hating her?

Her parents come to the common room, bringing—oh, God—her grandparents. This is so sad she might die right on the spot. She looks at the stained linoleum, carefully folding the loose fabric of the rabbit-patterned fleece pants they've given her. She's in a room full of people like her, who don't know how to be with their families anymore, if they ever did.

Her mother hugs her, but doesn't know what to say. "How are you, baby? Are they feeding you okay?" Her tone of voice, reproachful, contained, frightened, says everything her words don't. Arielle's father says almost nothing. Better than she hoped for: he can really go on a tear when he starts lecturing. Her mother has brought homemade shortbread, which she keeps passing around. Arielle takes one and holds onto it, her throat too tight to eat.

Grandma Lily takes a double handful, saying, "Oh, I shouldn't eat these. Now don't let me have more. On the other hand . . ." She laughs. "Don't you dare try to stop me." She inspects the greige linoleum floor: its stains and scratches display a long, sad history. "They could do a whole hell of a lot more with this room. It's not that much better than State, if you ask me. I did my time in these places, but I'm done now. Finished, *fini*, over. No more boiled chicken and rice, no more people shaking you awake at dawn, no more creepy men trying to sneak into your room." Arielle's mother seems to want to break in, but Grandma Lily, without appearing to notice, switches course. "The best place was Blossom Ranch—why are these places all named as if you're out for a jolly vacation in nature? It had real curtains and furniture. Lace. We ripped it up quite often, of course, so it had to be cheap stuff. But they'd replace it after. An elegant experience."

Arielle's mother sighs. The common room, it's true, is beyond depressing, with its crappy schoolroom chairs and ancient television encased in hard plastic. A strange unbreakable mirror half-covers the wall by the door—are they supposed to learn how they look to the outside world?

"I don't understand," Arielle's father says, directly. "How can you be so unhappy? You have everything to live for."

"*Ray,*" says Arielle's mother. "Arielle, are you getting enough to eat?" She reaches out, almost touches Arielle, draws back. "Please look after yourself." Arielle can see the anger she's trying to disguise: all the work she's done, raising Arielle up, wiping her nose and butt, taking her to dance class, and Arielle wants to throw it away. Her mother hates to have people waste her time, and who could be wasting her time more desperately than her wretched youngest daughter?

Lily says, "Oh, all you people have no idea. Our girl is experimenting with emotional dramas. You don't mean it, do you, honey? It's like the Greeks, the *heresias,* young people taking on emotions and philosophies to decide how to live. A much better question than *whether* to live. They're all looking for the meaning of life. But it's not something that already exists. You have to make meaning by hand in your own little workshop."

Arielle's grandfather clears his throat. "First Arielle's getting her biochemistry sorted out. Rewiring the misfiring circuits. Then we can work on meaning."

"Meaning comes first," says Lily, at the exact moment that Arielle's father is saying, "Meaning is overrated."

Arielle tries to eavesdrop on some of the other family conversations in the room. The people from outside talk about sports, grades, jobs; the people who live here parade their own views of reality. Or they say nothing at all, like her. She doesn't think she has a view of reality. But maybe she does, and it's invisible. Or maybe she's swimming in her family's view, like a fish trying to get out of its bowl. The thought of herself as a fish, banging against the glass, hiding inside the little ceramic castle, makes her smile.

"There you go," says her father. "It's really not that bad, is it?"

Gina notes that after visiting hours, Arielle won't eat her dinner. She saw the family's offerings. Homemade shortbread cookies and—produced right at the end of the visit—a woolen hat and a biography of an Olympic gymnast. She watched the little tableau from the hall, the

normal family grieving over their perfect child. The mother repeat-
edly passed around the box of cookies, trying and failing to keep her
hands away from her daughter, touching her hand and squeezing her
shoulder. Arielle, her shoulders hunched and hands clenched in her
lap, stared at the floor, trying not to flinch. The father looked from
the other patients to Arielle, inspecting her anxiously. And the grandmother! Well, she was a piece of work.

Arielle sits at the table, poking at her meatloaf and suspicious gravy,
rearranging the mashed potatoes to cover the food she's not eating.
"My mother's starting to hate me. How poisoned do you have to be
for your own mother to hate you? She pretends not to, she fusses over
me, she has all kinds of plans for my success. She doesn't know it's
already over for me. I'm not going to live that life."

"At least you talk to her. And hate is a little strong. Maybe she's
ambivalent." Gina takes her napkin, folds it, and begins to tear out
a circle. "I have two children. My daughter wrote a letter saying
that it's better for her if we have no further contact. Her therapist
encouraged her. My son and his wife screen their calls so I can't get
through."

"That's awful. What did you do?"

"Oh, blunt. Well. Why not? I don't know, Arielle. I was always in a
lot of trouble myself—and children don't forgive the mother. They're
good kids. I wish they would tell me what I did so I could make it better. But sometimes there isn't any better." She holds up a torn circle of
napkin, the edges ragged. "At least you talk to your mother. So this is a
medal. When you wear it, you and I will know what it's for."

Arielle puts the medal in her buttonhole, but her face shows a dark
panic. "You all look after me, but you shouldn't. You won't when you
know what I'm like. I'm not a person, I'm a disease."

Marjorie strokes her shoulder. She and Gina exchange glances, and
Marjorie says, "We're all done for already. There's no one left to in-
fect. Maybe the animals."

Gina says, "You don't want to die. You want your impossible family
to die so you can be free to be your own little poisonous self. That's
okay. It's natural." She's trying to hurry it up a little. She hates to miss

the beginning of *Jeopardy*. She doesn't know who to root for unless she knows their stories.

Gina has finished more than ninety percent of her food, which is the same as one hundred percent for points purposes. "Tell Dr. Schiller that you had a realization in the middle of the night. Tell him you were lying there feeling abandoned, and you wanted to commit suicide, and suddenly you had a memory of being in your crib. No, better make it your bed. You were crying for your mother, and no one came. Don't say any more. He's going to want to have a part in your realization. You're looking to discover, with his help, that your suicidal urges are meant as a weapon against the mother who wasn't there."

Marjorie says, "Damn, you're good."

"Aren't I though? What a career I could have in the shrinking business."

Arielle stares at them. "It's not that they don't give and give—but it all rots when it hits me. It's not their fault." The tears spurt out.

Gina gives her shoulder a squeeze. "Say all that to Dr. Schiller. The tears would be good too. Probably if they injected the brain of a chimpanzee with whatever you've got going on, it would attempt suicide too, and come up with a good story to explain it."

Marjorie smiles, kind, not too involved. "It's like malaria, or colds. You won't be sick all the time, but you'll be susceptible. The hard part is remembering that it's temporary."

"That's it. When you sit around dreaming about it, you waste your brain. You have a nice little brain, Arielle. Think of something else to do with it."

"I can't." She bows her head, still crying. Gina jabs her in the thigh with a fork, hard enough to bruise.

Shocked, Arielle stares at Gina, who smiles and nods. "There you go. Step one, like I told you at breakfast, learn to keep it together at meals. And in group, too. Never let them see you like this. Get out the first minute you can, and then stay out, no matter what. If I'd known this at your age, I'd be president of General Motors by now. I'd have a big house by the ocean and wake up every morning to the sound of waves and seagulls."

"You don't think we need therapy?"

"Dr. Schiller would slowly ask you leading questions until you discovered all your feelings for yourself. It'd take him around two years. Maybe ten. He's a pro. But so am I in my way. I've just developed my own techniques." Gina stands up, brushing off blue checked polyester pants. "Could we get down to the common room? We're going to miss *Jeopardy*."

But two aides flank Gina—Sherry and a new guy. Sherry's weird self-cropped hair stands up in peaks. She's wearing denim overalls, as if she were about to muck out the stalls. She grabs Gina's fork. "Minus ten points for violence," she says to the new guy. "See if she needs to be put in restraints."

Gina, at once, puts her hands in front of her body, drops her eyes, and stands limply before them.

Arielle says, "She was helping me."

"Bobby here is going to take you to the nurse's station to get checked out. You need to make some friends your own age, honey. The back table would be a good place for you."

"I don't want to sit with the cutters. I like it here."

Marjorie says, "Nothing happened, Sherry. We were having psychodrama practice."

"And that's minus two points for you for inappropriate response to violence. If you're done eating, you need to be moving down to community meeting."

Sherry says to Gina, "Come with me. I'm going to write you up, and then you're going to be talking to your doctor about whether or not you need to be back in State. If it were up to me, you'd already be on the bus." Gina goes along in silence.

On Thursday afternoon, Gina and Marjorie find themselves, with fifteen or so other patients, slowly circling the tree in the yard under an overcast sky. Two aides sit on the bench close by, making sure that everyone keeps moving. From outside the fence come the traffic sounds, brake noises, horns. Sea air filters intermittently through the gasoline and exhaust. Someone has threaded an old pink ribbon through a fence hole. Marjorie touches the ribbon every time they pass.

Gina says into Marjorie's ear, "Don't let them see you looking, but there's a gap in the wooden fence behind the chain link. If you climb the fence, you could stand on the broken board, and go over. If we can't get the points, that's an option. In the halfway house, you could paint all day long. That's how Steven made it out."

"And then what happened to him?" asks Marjorie. "We're not equipped. They don't let you into the halfway house without the paperwork. You've spent time on the streets. You remember what it's like. Better if we could earn the points."

"My points are shit. But I'm trying to build them up again." Suddenly, Gina feels the cold. Billy, who hung himself in his bathroom that winter, is beside her. Then invading her, freezing down through skin and muscle to the center of the bone. Having given up on his own life, he now wants hers. Regret—his? hers?—replaces bone marrow, takes over cells. Tears roll down her face. She can't move.

Marjorie puts a warm arm around her. "What is it? Don't stand here, we'll get in trouble."

"He wants me to come with him," Gina whispers.

"Tell him you're busy. Come on, let's sing something." Marjorie begins, under her breath, to sing a song the dead particularly hate, "Hello, Young Lovers." Gina, slowly, sings with her, and Billy, enraged, disappears.

An aide shouts at them, and they move. They pass the tree, where Marjorie touches the pink ribbon, a crumpled satin the color of a baby blanket. Dace blows her whistle and everyone moves toward the door, waiting for her to unlock it, to let them back inside.

The art room is locked, so they go to the common room. Arielle is already there with some other patients, watching a TV show with five girls in a house trying to get something or to hurt each other memorably—interviewed by the camera, telling each other's secrets.

"We were making plans to escape," Gina tells her. Not too quietly. No one listens to you when you're not whispering.

Marjorie sits at the scratched table, its fake wood peeling off in strips, furiously drawing on notebook paper. Black birds descend on a pulpy sculptural shape. She's said she wants to get the world inside down on paper before her mind goes altogether; after years of meds, she feels pieces of herself floating away like icebergs. Gina watches as Marjorie brings the birds into existence, some pecking the pulpy shape, others flying away with pieces of whatever it is in their mouths.

"A searing comment on today's society," says Gina, studying the drawing. "Or perhaps any society."

"'My Heart is Being Eaten by a Bevy of Ravens,'" Marjorie answers. She laughs. When she's smiling, she could sell California oranges to Florida.

"The ravens are good." Gina says, "If we follow every one of their rules, we could get enough points for the halfway house. Real birds nest in the eucalyptus around the lagoon." Marjorie, still drawing, shows by the tension in her shoulders that she's listening. Arielle, though she seems to be looking at the TV show, is now listening as well, glancing at Gina.

Gina says, "Once, my kids and I were taking a train across the country." She doesn't like to speak of her own children, now semi-functional scrabbling professionals who pretend she doesn't exist. She's tried to help them wake up. Broke Tim's TV, though that was to protect his kids from the propaganda, and she wasn't exactly in control when she did it. Anyway, it's a bad mistake to talk about children to Marjorie, but now she's started.

Arielle leaves the TV group to sit with them. Gina goes on, "Andrew was about three. He was fine with the train *to* New York, and pretty good about all the sightseeing. Almost over his tantrums. But he couldn't believe we then had to go all the way home again. Somewhere around Missouri, he said, 'All done train, I get off now.' I had to hold onto him to keep him from jumping through the door."

Marjorie puts down the pencil, her face going empty. "My babies," she whispers.

The aides would say, "You never had any babies, Marjorie." The doctor would say, "What do babies represent to you, Marjorie?" Gina takes hold of her friend's hand and waits.

Arielle, nervously, takes the other hand, looking at Gina to find out what to do next.

Marjorie, weeping, repeats again and again, "They killed my babies." No one in the room pays any attention.

Gina thinks anyone meeting them on the street, in one of Marjorie's bad moments, would believe her friend to be the sicker of the two. Not only because she weeps over the babies she thinks she's lost. Even at her best, she's busy imagining her jungles, moons, peacocks, underwater caves full of fronds. She's the one, though, who keeps them on track when she's all there. It's been a while since Gina's amygdala monster kicked in, using her face and body for screaming and smashing things, but she can't count on it not happening again. Marjorie's the one who can sometimes get to the real Gina, underneath. When Gina tired of the whole thing and killed herself, almost a decade ago at State—a long slice up the arm from a loose shard on a window assembly—Marjorie found her, called for help, and made her get out of bed and face the days until she was willing to go forward on her own again.

Arielle says, "Should we call someone?" She's twisting around, looking over her shoulder, as if somewhere in here she can get help.

"That's the last thing we should do." Gina puts an arm around Marjorie's shoulders. "I'm sorry, sweetheart." Right now Marjorie's a ball of misfiring neurons masquerading as memories. Five, ten minutes, and she'll forget, and she'll be Marjorie again. When it's Gina's turn to go off, it will be Marjorie's turn to hold her. "Let's take a little stroll around the palace corridors before they give us our meds."

Arielle helps get Marjorie to her feet. "Does she need a nap? Or a walk outside?"

"No napping in the daytime. And it's not outside hours."

Arielle looks at the windows, and, for the first time since she's arrived, Gina sees her face full of longing. The late September sun, the shadows of the trees against the dirty glass, the flickering reflections of the cars going past.

On Arielle's last Saturday in Shoreside, Katya and Jenny sit with her in the common room. She's going to be released Monday, ten days after her admission, not so much thanks to her own efforts as the dictates of their insurance, though following Gina's instructions with Dr. Schiller probably didn't hurt. Arielle can see that her sisters have decided not to reproach her or ask questions—maybe they're under instructions from her doctor. They sit on either side of her, each holding a hand. The hands keep asking, through the unrelenting strength of their grip, "How could you do this to us?" She feels like a war criminal.

To top it off, they've brought more shortbread. Baked by their mother, who never bakes anything. The cookies, in a plastic container, sit on Arielle's lap.

"I'm thinking of something," Jenny announces.

Katya asks, "Is it animal, vegetable, mineral, or none of the above?"

The sisters, and sometimes the rest of the family, used to play "Infinite Questions" while sitting on Jenny's bed in the days after a chemo cycle, as she became well enough to want to do something. When you had the time, why stop at twenty questions? With enough questions, you could come up with the answer to anything. They'd establish whether the item was real or imaginary, something they had seen or only knew about, in this world or another. Some items were easy, and you could get there in a couple of dozen questions: the mother duck in *Make Way for Ducklings*, Grandma Lily's wedding ring, Napoleon's thumb bone. The custard they were all having for dinner (during Jenny's cancer, the whole family wound up eating like invalids). Some questions could go on for days. Grandma Lily had kept them guessing for a week before Arielle guessed the concept of the Tibetan Buddhist deva realm. Not the realm itself but the original idea of it: the thoughts in the minds of those who'd first started to imagine all those gods. There'd been a trip to the library in there, trying to figure it out.

Gina enters the common room, and marches up to the sisters. The aides watch, warily. She takes Katya by the chin, turning her head this way and that, as if performing a medical examination. She does the same with Jenny. She nods and says to Arielle, "Nothing is inevitable. Maybe the wars. But not for you. Sometimes people escape."

"Probably not though," says Arielle.

Katya shifts in her chair, bouncing forward, as if Gina had hit the switch and booted her up. "I don't think wars are inevitable. Just because we've always had them. We always had slavery too, right?"

"We still have slavery," says Gina. "Don't you children read the papers?"

"We still have *exploitation.*"

"Your chocolate. Your shoes. Look it up."

Katya won't let go. She never does. "It's not on the same scale, though, is it? We don't have whole societies based on people owning other people."

Arielle frees the hand holding Katya's and opens the plastic tub, offering them around. "Mom made pecan shortbread." Brown along the edges, dry, crumbly, not enough nuts and too much sugar, the butter a little rancid, practically no flour. How can you mess up shortbread? An intense pang attacks her. She misses her mother. Couldn't she maybe, in the end, be forgiven? It's possible that she might not be totally toxic. Maybe just toxic in waves. Because here's Katya, and you can't call the way she's acting untoxic. And Gina can be a little toxic. But, as Grandma Lily would say, aren't they all fiery and remarkable beings of the human realm?

"Slavery was a whole institution," says Katya. "It seemed permanent. But nobody thinks it's part of life anymore. It's not *inevitable.*"

"Katya." Jenny's smiling affectionately, in the tone she uses when the kids she's babysitting pour syrup all over the floor or tear up rolls of toilet paper. She never yells at anyone. But she's the only person in the family who can get anyone to dial it down.

Katya's about to continue anyway, but Jenny catches her eye and shakes her head. Katya grins. "Okay, I'll look up chocolate and shoes." She takes a cookie, bites into it, and says, "Jen, maybe you could give Mom some cooking lessons."

A few feet away, Gary begins licking the big, unbreakable slab of polished metal that serves for a mirror. His face pressed against the surface, he turns his head slowly from one side to the other, nose smashed flat, watching from each eye the movement of his tongue across the glass. He arcs forward, vomiting against the metal plate, still watching himself. Dace leaps up, grabs his arm and, as he begins to struggle, blows her whistle. The door bangs open and aides pour into the room; he's so big, it takes three of them to get hold of him. Even in restraints, he towers over everyone. As they wrangle him through the door, he twists around to look down at the sisters and winks. "Sweethearts, you wouldn't believe how hard it is, being me." But he's still struggling; he can't seem to help it.

Jenny and Katya, as if they'd rehearsed it, stand in front of Arielle, who says, "Gary's not going to hurt us. He doesn't mean anything by it." Her sisters look at her, then out the door at Gary, but it's over. The aides are hustling him away down the hall.

In the car going home on Monday, the family plays car charades, a made-up game they treasure chiefly for its unnecessary difficulties. Arielle, not quite up to it, looks out the window. How wickedly beautiful it is. Some of the trees don't seem to have gotten the message that they're in California and are going red and gold, dropping leaves. A blue heron stands in the lagoon, the water shining around him. Even the piles of garbage by the road seem remarkable. It is all made out of itself. It all means something. Unless that's the drugs.

She touches the folded note from Gina in her pocket that she found in her nightstand drawer as she was gathering her things. Gina's handwriting is terrible: the words go up and down the page, around the edges. "A spiral staircase . . . don't go down it . . . don't imagine how to die . . . that's making it real . . . go up the steps . . . take one step up not down then one more . . . other people are there, plus you have to eat . . . if the dead come remember to sing and they don't like jokes . . . go to the ocean if we run away . . . just kidding! don't read this doctors! . . . we will find shells and maybe we will see you . . ." Gina's drawn something that looks like one of Marjorie's ravens.

So when Arielle thinks about going back to school, worrying about what she'll say to Jasmine, whether she can avoid Danny altogether, what they will all think of her, that's going down the spiral staircase. Thinking of Gina and Marjorie, maybe that's a step up.

Her sisters jostle each other. "*Memento!*" says her father. Should he be watching them in the rearview mirror while he's driving?

"Way too easy," says Katya, and their mother, either cross or pretending to be cross, says, "Let's see you do better then."

Arielle would like Gina and Marjorie to escape. She would like to go to the sea with them. In this thing called real life, her family argues, laughing. She looks out the dusty car window and sees the cypresses, the waterline, and the college students back in town for the beginning of the new quarter.

In her mind, she can see Gina, sneaking into Marjorie's room late at night, getting ready to wake her. Machinery would be humming in the hall. An ice machine. Or the Thymatron IV ECT system, charging up. Gina would have her kelp and her sand dollar with her. Where would they go? Would they wind up at State? What would happen if they were caught?

That's a step down the staircase. It's no good to think this way. Someone would take them in. Maybe they could come live with Arielle's family or with Grandma Lily and Grandpa Philip. The family keeps saying the grandparents may not be able to stay in their house much longer, but maybe they could if they had their own aide to make everyone meals. And Grandma Lily could teach Gina and Marjorie to live outside again.

Arielle thinks of the two of them, waiting for their moment when the halls are quiet, Gina stretching out beside Marjorie, her arm across Marjorie's stomach, her face against her back. In a little while, everyone will be in bed. Then they can go. The noise of the machinery will cover them. The alarm won't sound until they go through the door. The living are drugged, and the dead can't stop them. Maybe, once they're out, and everyone can see that they're not so much crazier than anyone else, they can convince the halfway house to let them stay. Maybe they can live there together, and then, every day, Gina can walk to the sea.

PART THREE: THAT HIDDEN ROAD

VII

Six Hells

Santa Cruz Mountains and Hell, April 2005

CAST OF CHARACTERS

EVA: An affective neuroscientist, mother, 42 years old, analytical and fairly successful, though also disorganized and late everywhere. She has an air of permanent anxiety, particularly about her children.

JULIA: EVA's younger sister, a 39-year-old actress, attempting to find a place for herself in the New York theater world, currently visiting her sister in Santa Cruz.

LEOPARD, LION, and SHE-WOLF

KILLER

GHOST

RAMA, LORD OF DEATH

HADES

ERESHKIGAL, SUMERIAN QUEEN OF THE UNDERWORLD

HUNGRY GHOSTS

HARPIES, GORGONS, including MEDUSA, and ARMED CENTAURS

INHABITANTS OF THE CHAMBER OF ENDLESS TORTURES

TIME: April 2005

PLACE: The Santa Cruz Mountains, off Highway 17, and several underworlds

STAGING: All scene changes can be accomplished by lighting, shadows, projections, news footage, and sounds (as in the murmur of the boiling river of blood or the cawing of crows).

SCENE I: THE SANTA CRUZ MOUNTAINS, OFF HIGHWAY 17—THE DARK WOOD/THE HUMAN REALM

[*Lights go up. A spring evening.* JULIA *and* EVA *wander at the edge of a road in the dark wood, the trees menacing. The occasional house floodlight or car lights from the road give the sense of the presence of ordinary life.*]

EVA:

I don't like leaving Arielle right now, but I had to get you out where we can talk in private. We have to decide right now, or better still, last week, what to do about Mom and Dad. River Valley's not working out for them.

JULIA:

They're too old to adapt to a new place. And this is way too big a subject to get into right before Seder. Let's talk after tomorrow. We'll have all morning: everyone will take off and leave us with the dishes.

EVA:

We could have another emergency anytime. Dad's fall last week was such a nightmare. The hallucinations. The hospital. I keep waking up remembering that *angry* surgeon saying, "Your father just told the staff he's rescinding his DNR. But he's too fragile. If we have to give him CPR, it will crush his ribs. In my opinion, he's not competent to make this decision. You can reinstate the DNR, but you have to do it immediately. He could go at any time, and if the DNR's not in place, you'll have to live with the consequences." Three a.m., and I couldn't think. How could I say, "Yes, go ahead and kill him"? None of you could help me. I appreciate how supportive you were. But I was the one who had to call the surgeon back and have him yell at me. Then the next day, Dad was okay. Okay-ish. He said, "There seems to be an awful lot of falling down around here, and then there's a fuss, and it seems I'm at the center of it."

JULIA:

I know, Eva, but you can't keep going over and over this. There've been all these falls, but he's still *himself.* When he gets dehydrated, he starts hallucinating. All anyone has to do is make sure he's drinking enough. I'm sorry you had to go through it. But moving Dad won't make him less stubborn.

EVA:

I put a water bottle holder on his walker. But the aides don't remind him to drink. How can they be so busy that they can't do the littlest things? River Valley's saying they have to transfer him to the skilled care wing. That's preposterous: they just want to charge us eight thousand a month. I'm going to move him and Mom in with us. We'll get a part-time aide, and I'll take charge of his care.

[LEOPARD, LION, *and* SHE-WOLF *appear at the edges of the stage and begin a dance that's sometimes beautiful, sometimes ugly, but always frightening. Although the two sisters don't see them, whenever the women move toward open space, the animals subtly herd them away from the road and more deeply into the woods.*]

JULIA:

You've got to be kidding me. If Dad needs skilled nursing, we have to find a way to pay for it. Eva, I cannot deal with talking about the folks right now. I thought you wanted to get me out of the house to talk about Arielle. I'm worried about her. She's so spacey, and she keeps going off for naps.

EVA:

That's another thing. We're in a bit of a rough patch. She hurt her ankle dancing and wound up with a doctor who didn't know her history, obviously. He gave her an oxycodone/acetaminophen mix. But now she's with a new doctor, and we're getting her off the medication.

JULIA:

Oxycodone? Really?

EVA:

It's fine. I'm keeping a close eye on her. Don't tell the rest of the family. Ray overreacts to everything. And Katya's just like her father. They don't need to worry, and you don't need to worry. What you and I have to do right now is to talk about Mom and Dad. If River Valley moves him to skilled care, they'd be separated. They'd hate that, Jules. They would be so much better off spending the rest of their lives, however long that is, with me and Ray.

JULIA:

You can't take them on. Has Ray said yes to this?

EVA:

He will. We're in this up to our neck anyway. I'm the one everyone calls in the middle of the night. If I had Mom and Dad with me, I could get up and look after them myself, and go back to sleep after, instead of lying awake fretting about them. And Arielle too. We can't afford to put her back in rehab, and in the daytime I don't think it's the right solution. But in the middle of the night? All of this feels like a fist around my heart.

JULIA:

So with you and Ray at work, would Arielle wind up taking care of Mom and Dad? I mean, what the hell? You literally can't do this with one part-time aide. Mom and Dad have access to a dozen aides at River Valley. You'll be too exhausted and overwhelmed to take care of them, let alone Arielle. She needs you to put her first, Eva. And neither Robert nor I can look after the folks. Robert's useless, and I can't be here more than every couple of months. Even then only for a few days, maybe a week. I'd love to think I'm the person who will give up everything and devote myself to the family, but we'd all go mad. I'll get a second job, I don't care what it takes.

[LEOPARD, LION, *and* SHE-WOLF *move in concert, a solid wall facing the sisters, who, without seeing them, hesitate, then turn and walk the other direction, onto a path leading into the woods.*]

EVA:

It could be good for Arielle to have someone besides herself to worry about. And they'd be fine with a caregiver for the days and us looking after them at night. Don't argue, Jules. I'm going to try this. If it doesn't work, we can go to board and care.

JULIA:

I won't try to stop you. But I think it's a terrible idea.

[LEOPARD, LION, *and* SHE-WOLF *surround the sisters from behind, edging them closer to the trees, down a side path.*]

I don't love walking up here—it's kind of creepy. I'd rather be walking around in town or on the beach. I also don't love it that Robert and I are going to be teaching in these mountains next summer. The Scheherazade Institute. I think it's down in a hollow somewhere around here. Aren't there a lot of serial killers in these mountains?

EVA:

That was the seventies. And only a couple, really. You're such a city girl. You run all over New York—is there any neighborhood you won't go to, if there's some weird little theater piece happening? But you're afraid of a few trees. Another fifteen minutes? It's good for us to be out here. Researchers find lower levels of frustration and negative emotions when people walk in nature. Doesn't it drive you crazy to live in New York?

JULIA:

I love being right in the center of it all. Theater, music, art, people. It's even better than I'd hoped. As for my situation, everything takes the time it takes, right? I'm waiting tables and going on auditions. Don't look at me that way. It's not like I'm roofing in Phoenix in August. It's an amazing city, and I'm part of it. In a weird way, I'm happy. I might try for some voiceover gigs to get money for the folks. You can't really want to take them. What about your work?

[LEOPARD, LION, *and* SHE-WOLF *steer them more deeply into the woods.*]

EVA:

It's true that when there's no one in the house, I can live on twenty-four hour time. There's nothing fogging my brain, nothing stopping me from getting up at three a.m. to work on ideas. I can stay at the lab until midnight. Ray is okay, as long as we're not fighting. It's almost like being alone. But if any of my beautiful, screwed-up kids are at home? Then I'm spending most of my time and energy on family anyway. I may as well take in the parents. I'm drowning in tasks, even with them in River Valley. And I've wasted so much time already. But it doesn't matter about the lab, not really. There are other people to do the work.

JULIA:

How have you been wasting time? You've done so much research. All those published articles.

EVA:

I mean real work. Finally we're figuring out how to map the mirror neurons. The anterior cingulate fires when people watch others in pain—I think we've found empathy, Jules. Imagine what it would mean to discover how we dissolve the boundaries between ourselves and the world, if we found the neurological basis for ethics, for non-violence. Then we could come up with real interventions. [*pause*] You don't like this, do you? You want people to go to a play and see the light, you want to make art that stops people from being crazy. I'm not sure that's how it works. Look at Mom. Her life's been all about art.

JULIA:

Don't tell her I told you this? She says, "It's all about the language we use. Dementia is such an *ugly* word. Why use such an ugly word for something that happens to everyone, sooner or later?"

EVA:

She said that?

JULIA:

And not just once. Last time, I said, "Mom, can we talk about this?" She said [*imitates a threatening, nearly hysterical voice*], "That's enough of this subject for now." And then she started humming.

[*She hums, imitating the sound of someone drowning out an idea.* EVA *walks through the trees.* LEOPARD, LION, *and* SHE-WOLF *crowd* JULIA, *pushing her to follow. Without seeing the animals, she resists them and steers her sister back toward the road.*]

JULIA:

Maybe I should stop indulging myself in New York. Maybe I'm just saying to myself that we'd drive each other mad if I came back, but we wouldn't drive each other any madder than any other parents and children. They've done so much for me. Maybe it's time for me to grow up. Why should you be on duty because you're the oldest girl?

EVA:

Why should you be on duty because you're the favorite?

JULIA:

The perks of that position wore off years ago. Which means I have a ruined character for nothing.

[*Eva takes hold of* JULIA's *arm, guiding her directly into the woods.* JULIA *gives way.* LEOPARD, LION, *and* SHE-WOLF *dance.*]

EVA:

See that glade up ahead? Can we spend a few minutes admiring the trees? Pretend we're twenty and discovering the magic of nature. With the concession to middle age that we don't have to take off our clothes.

JULIA:

Okay, madam expert on the neuronal correlates of consciousness, what can you tell me about Mom? Do you think it's just aging?

[*During the following speech,* KILLER *appears in the trees and begins shadowing them, keeping out of sight.*]

EVA:

If it's Alzheimer's, it starts in the temporal lobe. The hippocampus, mostly, so the first sign is forgetfulness. Then the disease spreads into the neocortex. You forget what you did last week, you forget what you're supposed to do tomorrow, you forget names, faces. When the neocortex gets involved, a whole range of cognitive functions start to go. There's a test for it, but Mom said she doesn't want to know, and River Valley says she's still capable of withholding consent. Meanwhile, she's taking seaweed pills she read about in one of her health newsletters.

JULIA:

I heard something. Someone's here with us.

[*Looks around, anxiously, but* KILLER *is hidden behind a tree.*]

EVA:

It's the woods. They're full of squirrels and birds. We're much safer than if we were wandering around Hell's Kitchen.

JULIA:

Believe me, the main danger in Hell's Kitchen these days is the price of the real estate. Or if you stumble into Marseille or someplace and wind up eating dinner. Dollar for dollar, you'd probably be better off getting mugged, though the memories wouldn't be as pleasant.

[KILLER *is closing in on them, taking out his gun.*]

EVA:

I told her if it's Alzheimer's, we might be able to slow its progress with medication, and she bit my head off. Neuroscience can describe the mechanisms, but it doesn't tell us how to make her take the test.

JULIA:

Jenny said she's been giving Mom rosemary. It has some kind of Carne acid or whatever, and it's supposed to slow it down. And she's giving her energy treatments every day by phone.

EVA:

Seems like you know more about my children than I do. [*pause*] Dad used to say nature designed us to die before sixty. I never thought he'd be someone who'd rescind his DNR. Truthfully, though, we're not ready for him to die either. And Mom would go on forever if she could.

JULIA:

At what point would she stop being Mom? She still knows who we are. She still knows who she is. How much would she have to lose before she stopped being herself?

EVA:

Who else would she be?

[*They cross the stage and exit,* KILLER *behind them.* LEOPARD, LION, *and* SHE-WOLF *continue their dance among the trees. Blackout.*]

SCENE 2: FIRST HELL [ANGER/THE REALM OF THE ANIMALS, THE LIVID MARSH]

[*Lights up.* EVA *and* JULIA *are alone, on the ground, in a cold, bare place of blue flames that sometimes seem to be icicles or marsh light. Crows caw sporadically in the background. Two pools, Lethe and Memory, lie a short distance apart.* EVA *and* JULIA *are distinctly alive though dazed. In the hells, the dead wear masks and the demons have fantastical makeup.*]

EVA:

Were we robbed? Are we dead? My throat is so dry.

JULIA:

I keep sinking into the ground.

EVA:

We could be dreaming—the level of apparent paralysis, coupled with activation of the arousal systems, suggests a response to the stimuli around us.

JULIA:

What on earth are you talking about?

EVA:

I'm scared.

JULIA:

So am I.

EVA:

It's so cold. And yet I'm parched. Look at those pools. Is it true you shouldn't eat or drink in a dream? No, that's only superstition. Like black cats being bad luck.

[RAMA, LORD OF DEATH, *appears at the back of the stage. He has three eyes and a crown of skulls. The calling of the crows comes more frequently.*]

JULIA:

It's the land of faerie where you can't eat or drink. Those pools could be dangerous. Or they could save us.

EVA:

Something in my mind is trying to get to awareness from long-term memory, but it's triggering the amygdala instead. If I could breathe. If I could think.

RAMA [*descends and inspects them, slowly*]:

What are you two doing here? How interesting. You shouldn't be here yet. Jumping the gun a little. To coin a phrase.

JULIA:

We want to go home. Please.

RAMA:

Everyone thinks they want that. At first. How nice to have you here. Things have been awfully dull. Such an endless parade of the dead. A population explosion. I shouldn't wonder if you two feel a little confused. You're not truly dead yet, but probably you will be soon. I'd place my bet on "very soon." This place is full of demons.

JULIA:

Why are we here? I feel sick.

RAMA:

I'm not surprised.

JULIA:

It's so loud. Can we please go somewhere more peaceful?

RAMA:

Not right away, I'm afraid. Whether or not it's better than this for you in the end will depend on which ring you're assigned to. You might get fiery sands, rains of fire, ice . . . there are a lot of possibilities here. But we have a few games first. Please take out your pencils: there will be a short quiz. Choose a pool, drink, and see what happens.

[*He disappears.*]

EVA:

I don't trust him.

JULIA:

I don't know what other choices we have. The Pool of Memory. Lethe. I think it would have to be the Pool of Memory.

EVA:

What is that scum on top? It looks contaminated.

JULIA:

If it's a test, we should drink from the one that looks worst.

EVA:

The Pool of Memory. I don't like the sound of it. Let's try the other one. It's so clear. And feel how cool it is. It's lovely. [*She cups her hands and drinks from Lethe.*] You look familiar. I know you, I think.

JULIA:

God help us. Drink from this other one, quick, before you get any worse.

EVA:

I'm not thirsty anymore. I feel happy now. Sweetheart, I'm sorry, but remind me of your name? Isn't that strange, that I don't remember our names, or anything about us, and yet I remember you. We were playing a game. Tag, I think.

[EVA *tags* JULIA *and runs away laughing.* JULIA *chases her, can't catch her, kneels, cups her hands, drinks from the Pool of Memory.*]

JULIA:

How much I'd forgotten. Mom and Dad. Robert. The girls. Arielle. Oh, crap. Eva, come back! We have to get home right away.

EVA:

I don't want to know, whatever it is. Why be so serious?

[*She runs around the stage, tags* JULIA *again. The noise of the crows builds to a crescendo, then stops abruptly. Blackout.*]

SCENE 3: NEUTRAL ZONE

[*In front of a curtain.* HADES *and* ERESHKIGAL, QUEEN OF THE SUMERIAN UNDERWORLD, *stand alone in a spotlight.*]

ERESHKIGAL:
They're useful to me alive—I want to send them home.

HADES:
I plan to keep them. It will be better, for them and us, when they're dead. Rama already had them drink from the pools too soon. Who knows what kind of trouble that will cause?

ERESHKIGAL:
I'll deal with them right away. They needn't disturb you at all.

HADES:
I'm against letting people go back. It never works. Like that singer who came looking for his wife. And then the Italian poet. Fortunately, hardly anyone reads him anymore, and they don't believe him when they do. But when he went back, he spread all kinds of disastrous half-truths. Mortals may forget their lives, their families, themselves, but they hang onto all the misinformation they've ever been fed. It balls up the processing.

ERESHKIGAL:
Just straighten them out.

HADES:
They don't trust me, after all the propaganda. They think they're being punished by their circumstances; they think they're here forever.

ERESHKIGAL:

They say there's a path out of this place for us, too.

HADES:

That's a myth. Not for us. And the humans can only go on, not back. These two are no use anymore. The dead who drink from Lethe know nothing. The dead who drink from the Pool of Memory are only interested in their own stories. We may as well set the demons on them and then get them processed.

ERESHKIGAL:

You can take their memories before they go back to the overworld. The greatest and darkest of the gods can't be afraid of a pair of mortals. What power do they have, compared to you?

HADES:

I would be willing to have us each talk with them. Meanwhile, I'll send them to the Chinese Chambers or maybe the Tibetan realms. Let these two get used to the place a little before I talk with them.

ERESHKIGAL:

You're going to get them first? Then you make the first impression.

HADES:

You can go first if you like.

ERESHKIGAL:

Thank you.

HADES:

And I'll have the last word.

[*Blackout.*]

SCENE 4: SECOND HELL: DENIAL/LUST AND GLUTTONY, THE
REALM OF THE HUNGRY GHOSTS, THE ILLUSION OF PARADISE,
GOLDEN FERTILITY AND WEALTH SUCCEEDED BY VIOLENT
STORMS

[*Lights go up.* HUNGRY GHOSTS *dance around troughs of food. All the* HUNGRY
GHOSTS *have large bellies and proportionately tiny heads, perhaps with long, skinny
necks. In their dance, they reach for, claw at, and attempt to swallow the food. Sometimes they fight over it. Some of the ghosts are engaged, from time to time, in grotesque
copulations. Sometimes they roll or lie in heaps on the ground, blown by what seem to
be storms. Despite the troughs and the storms, the lighting and set or projections should
create an illusion of great opulence and an excess of enticing food and erotic imagery.*]

EVA [*lunges toward a trough*]:
I'm starving.

JULIA [*grabbing her*]:
What is going on? What are you doing?

EVA:
Look at this feast. Aren't you hungry?

JULIA:
Don't eat anything in a place like this. It's a totally basic rule. Oh, why
didn't you read more fairy tales?

EVA:
A place like what, exactly? [*approaches a series of* GHOSTS: *all dodge her.*]
Excuse me. Excuse me. Excuse me.

[*After three or four tries,* GHOST *turns to her, still cramming food.*]

GHOST:
I'm sorry, I can't stop. The more you eat, the hungrier you get, but I
didn't figure that out in time. Don't start.

EVA:

Can you tell us where we are? How did you get here? Where did you come from?

GHOST:

It's easier to say what I don't recall than what I do. I don't remember my name. I don't remember what I did out there, or what it looked or smelled or sounded like in the world, or even if I had a family. I must have had parents, but I don't remember them. Maybe I had brothers and sisters. Maybe I had children.

[GHOST *dives for a trough and begins fighting over food, but then he stands, lets the hand holding the food drop to his side and seems to come more into focus.*]

This isn't the worst neighborhood, by far. We had a guy once, a suicide, who'd spent centuries as a bloody thornbush torn by harpies. I ask you, is that fair? He was miserable in life, and so they made him a thornbush. Who's running this place? What's wrong with them? Some people seem to get out. One day they're here, then they're gone. Things have started to come back to me, over time, unless I'm inventing them. I always had my eye on the next rung: came in early, stayed late, let myself be seen. Sent out email memos at two a.m. to let everyone know I was still working. They gave me awards. Not the big ones, though it seemed as if it could all happen for me if I kept at it long enough. But awards for what? What did I do?

[*He looks longingly at the food, brings it to his mouth, drops the hand again, brings it back to his mouth.*]

JULIA:
We don't have time for this. We have to get out of here.

EVA:
Oh, God, I'm starving. I can't help it. We have to live down here—we

have to start learning the ways of this place. And we need some nour-
ishment.

[*Moves toward a trough, but* JULIA *stops her.*]

JULIA:
I'm ravenous too. It doesn't matter. We have to go home to your kids.
Don't eat. Chew my arm if you have to. [*She and* EVA *bite at each other's
arms and shoulders.*] That helps a little. Do that, if you think you're going
to eat the food.

EVA:
Did you hear him? He said this isn't the worst neighborhood down
here. We could be in even more trouble if we leave. [*pause*] Did you
say I have kids?

JULIA:
We have to look for a door, an exit, something. If we can get back to
the pools, you can drink too, and then you'll remember everything.

[JULIA *moves around the edge of the stage, looking for a door, then returns to* EVA,
who now has a mouthful of food.]

JULIA:
Stop that. Don't eat any more of it. Spit it out. Cover your eyes—or
look away. Remember something from our lives. Your children.

EVA [*swallows the food*]:
Perhaps I married a prince. We had a chocolate ganache cake, with
rum in the layers. Almond whipped cream. I wore a ball dress, and we
danced in a glade with all the birds singing.

JULIA:
That's not what I remember about the glade. You're hallucinating,
Eva. See if you can picture Arielle. When she was a child, she loved

building things in the sandbox and drawing. She loved to draw eyes—to put in the pupils exactly where they should go, to recreate reflections. She needs you to get home. Katya and Jenny need you. Our parents need you. How can I remember everyone when you don't? You're the one who's with them all the time.

EVA:
I can see you believe what you're saying, but it doesn't mean anything to me. I'm sorry.

JULIA:
All of those memories must still be inside you somewhere. You couldn't be yourself if they were gone. For crying out loud, Eva. You're the good one. We have to find those pools again.

[*A painfully bright light shines at them from one side of the stage, and a dusky one from the other.*]

Doorways—look. Hold my hand so we don't get separated. Wait, it's too bright over there. This way, quick.

[*They run toward the dusky light, offstage. Blackout.*]

SCENE 5: THIRD HELL—THE ICE-PALACE CAVE OF ERESHKIGAL, SUMERIAN QUEEN OF THE UNDERWORLD

[*Lights go up on Hel. On the banks of Gjöll, the Wailing River, sits the ice-palace cave of* ERESHKIGAL, *A palace full of Hel-trees.* ERESHKIGAL *sits on a throne at the back of the stage.* JULIA *and* EVA *stumble out of the wings.* ERESHKIGAL *appears to be a statue.* EVA *and* JULIA *disregard her.*]

JULIA:
No pools. So much ice. I'm so cold.

EVA:

And there's no food.

JULIA:

We have to work out the rules. Why are we here? Are we being punished? How do we get out?

EVA:

If we're dead, we don't owe the living. All those people you described have to look after each other now. No further claims can be made on us.

JULIA:

You think they can make it without us? And maybe we're not dead. Remember the demon?

EVA:

If this is a delusion, we're either going to wake or die, at some point. And if not, we get to find out, at last, what it's like out there. Endless exploring with no one to stop us, no bodies to slow us down. We'll discover the connections between systems. And we'll know what it all means.

JULIA:

That's a fantasy, like the idea of a guy in red with a pitchfork. Anywhere we go would probably be more like that place with the starving demons or ghosts.

EVA:

We got out of there. If we figure out what we did, we may just keep ascending.

JULIA:

Or we may wind up tearing each other to pieces or buried head down in ice, once we're really dead. I remember that, in one version of the afterlife, if you were sullen in the sunlight, you lie under slime forever.

EVA:

All of that is just poetry written before anyone knew anything. How can you help being sullen in the sunlight if you have a serotonin deficiency and they haven't figured out what meds you need? All those poems and myths were the equivalent of saying, "Snap out of it." They gave it to us all nicely done up with meter and images that burned it into our unconscious. Well, there. Look how much I do remember. Everything important, I think. And I'm not torturing myself with the rest of it. We have to find those pools again, and this time you can drink from the one that lets you adapt to this place.

[ERESHKIGAL *stands.*]

ERESHKIGAL:

You two are a gift. Here you are, seeing what the living never see, and with, perhaps, the chance to return to the sunlit world.

JULIA:

We can go home?

ERESHKIGAL:

You might have that choice. When you were attacked, you stumbled out of your world and into this one. You must act before you are killed down here and become subject to the rules for the dead. If you return, you will be found injured but alive. If you go on, you will become inhabitants of this realm, and your bodies will be found in the woods.

EVA:

Where would we go on to?

ERESHKIGAL:

You wouldn't like it. You would disappear and no longer know yourselves. I think I can arrange for you to return to your realm. On one condition.

JULIA:
What do you need?

ERESHKIGAL:
I wouldn't say need. But there is a small favor you could do for me in return.

EVA:
I could think better if we had something to eat.

ERESHKIGAL:
Down here, we eat the food left for the dead. Not so much of that anymore. When there's nothing else, we eat clay and ash. You need to know who I am if you're going to be of use. I'm known as Ereshkigal, Queen of the Underworld, though I've tried different names over the years. Nephthys in Egypt, Kali Uma in India. The Norse knew me as Nef-Hel. I've been down here a long time. My sister came here once. She banged at the gate like an empress claiming her last realm. Naturally I lost my temper—anyone would.

JULIA:
I know this story.

ERESHKIGAL:
Not my story. No one up there knows what really happened, or why I did it. When she came down here, stripped to the skin and bent low, she still hadn't lost her pride. She gave me a look out of the corner of her eye that said, "You can take everything, but I'm still Queen of Heaven and Earth, and you're still Queen of Clay and Ash." Something exploded in me—I flew into such a rage that everything that happened afterward seems like a dream.

[ERESHKIGAL *begins pacing.*]

When I came back to myself, I was in agony. Above, nothing flowered, no crop ripened, no children were born. Her servants came, at last, and begged for her life. There was nothing I would more willingly have given, but it was too late. I wanted to keep her by me. I offered them everything I had, but they turned their backs. They poured the water of life on her and took her up into the sunlight. Why did they ask me to restore her, when they could do it themselves?

[ERESHKIGAL *is now circling the sisters, who draw closer to each other, holding hands.*]

The rules demanded a replacement, so her consort comes down to spend six months a year here, his sister the other six months, but they don't speak to me. Every time one of them goes back to the world above, I send another letter with them. All return unopened. I have no faith that these letters are being given to her. After all this time, if she read what I had to say, her heart would relent. I need messengers I can trust.

[ERESHKIGAL *takes each of their right hands between her own, in turn, and folds it over an invisible letter. Once they each have it, she nods.*]

JULIA:
If she knows you sent us, how will she receive us? No offense.

ERESHKIGAL:
Remaining here would be so much riskier.

JULIA [*aside, to* EVA]:
She's offering us a way to get home by helping them make up.

EVA:
I don't think we should get mixed up in this. No one here is telling us the truth.

JULIA:
Shh. [*to* ERESHKIGAL] Yes, we will. We will do anything you ask of us.

ERESHKIGAL:

You'll be messengers, but it's not simple. Part of your task, in getting out, will be to remember what matters, not to be won over by flattery or discouraged by gloomy predictions. There is a door opening for you now. Don't forget.

[*A dark red light shines from one side of the stage. The sisters run to the door. Blackout.*]

SCENE 6: FOURTH HELL—DEPRESSION/ACEDIA, THE REALM OF THE JEALOUS GODS, DIS

[*Lights up. Dis: heaps of broken rock inhabited by* HARPIES, GORGONS, *including* MEDUSA, *and* ARMED CENTAURS. *A river of boiling blood, full of the spirits of the violent, murmurs upstage.* EVA *and* JULIA *mop and fan themselves during the scene.* HADES *strolls onto the stage, avoiding the river.*]

HADES:

I'm Hades. Of course I know who you two are.

EVA:

Is that river on fire or—oh, how vile—is it blood?

HADES:

My apologies for the surroundings. I was going to meet you in my own palace, but it's under repair. Workmen everywhere doing something noxious with hammers and a terrible-smelling spray. In any case, you have to learn to live with conditions. Take my case. If I may. The two things Cronus, my father, was best known for were marrying his sister and eating his children. There was a prophecy, you see, that one of us would dethrone him.

[HARPIES, GORGONS, *and* CENTAURS *climb about the rocks behind him.*]

People always want to know what it's like to be eaten by your father.

Even when they don't ask, you can see it's the first thing on their minds. By the time I arrived, the girls were all there: Hestia, Demeter, Hera. Demeter, of course, was only one of the big sisters then. I couldn't have imagined she'd have a daughter like Persephone.

EVA:

Persephone is your niece?

JULIA:

Shh.

HADES:

You'll get used to our ways. We don't have as many choices as you do, living down here. Anyway, after me came Poseidon. Then Zeus—but he wasn't inside Dad with the rest of us—he was born in secret in the night, raised on milk and honey by Mother Earth and her nymphs. Of course, we didn't know about the blessed little bugger until he saved all the rest of us. He has never, to this day, been able to refrain from mentioning it in conversation. "That was around the time when I was escaping Dad by turning myself into a serpent and my nurses into bears." "That was around the time when I gave Dad the poisoned mead and he coughed you all up." Not that I'm not grateful. Eternally. I thought I might get to take over, eventually. I was the biggest, the strongest, and the smartest of all the children. In my mind, I practiced the brilliant vision, the magnanimity, the sheer reach that I'd need when it was my turn to be Lord of the Universe. Not virtues much in demand down here.

EVA:

Could you tell us what virtues are useful here? Are there ways to be in less—less agonizing regions of this place? To get out?

HADES:

I'll get to you two. I'm not quite finished.

JULIA:

Yours is a wonderful story. But we really need to get home.

HADES:

If you interrupt again, there will be no possibility of you ever getting home. I was getting to my idea that I might run the oceans. The family says to me, "Oh, but you have all the jewels and minerals for yourself." The hell with that. In the sea, the sunlight comes through, you have every kind of creature and frond. Tide pools. They gave those to Poseidon, though I'm older than he is. And smarter too. Why am I the most hated of the gods? Did I want this job? Get me out of here, give me a week's trial as Lord of the Universe, and you will see in me the breadth of vision and generosity of spirit I practiced for so long when I was living underneath Dad's ribs.

[HARPIES, GORGONS, *and* CENTAURS *begin to fight.*]

You see what I have to put up with. People should try spending nine months a year down here in Erebus in an empty palace listening to the ghosts of the dead twittering like bats, the screaming of those being tortured in the fields of Tartarus, and the endless joyous singing and laughter of the revels of golden Elysium. People don't understand how rough it is.

JULIA:

It sounds like a long, hard time. And there's no way to change it?

HADES:

That would be my point: we each have our fates. Yours went sideways for a bit, but it's about to get back on track.

JULIA:

Can you send us to the place with the pools so my sister can recover her memory? And then we can go home?

HADES:

In theory, you get a choice, but it's complicated to have two of you at once. And you made your choice already. You played a little Russian roulette out there in the woods. Now you're in the Great Beyond—a very earthcentric term. Naturally, you have cold feet, but we're going to arrange for your deaths—a detail—and you may then have the option of heading up toward eternal light. It's a bit of a haul, but it's your only option.

EVA:

Listen to him—we could get out of here, we could go up and on.

JULIA:

But we've been told we can go home.

HADES:

Are you suggesting I don't know the rules?

JULIA:

If we're not dead, if there's any choice at all, can you let extenuating circumstances be a factor?

HADES:

Most of the dead have extenuating circumstances. Yours are maybe around the fortieth percentile.

JULIA:

Please. I'm begging you to make an exception and send us home.

HADES:

That's not your home anymore. Your sister is ready to face that fact.

JULIA:

She's confused; it'll be okay when she remembers what we've left behind. Please.

HADES:

If you insist, you can do this the hard way.

[*Blackout.*]

SCENE 7: FIFTH HELL—AVARICE/ANGER, THE REALM OF HELL,
THE CHAMBERS OF TORTURES

[*The lights go up on* JULIA *and* EVA. *Projections on three walls show scenes of torture, possibly including paintings, photographs, and silent video images. The feeling in the scene is more of grief than of horror. Phrases appear on the screens or on stage as back projections or in a news crawl: Wind and Thunder, Grinding, Flames, Ice, Dismemberment by Chariot, Tongue-ripping, Pounding, Torso-severing, Skinning, Maggots, Mountain of Knives.*

Dancers move around the stage in pairs and triads: the tortured are boiled in oil, cut apart by knives, burnt, disemboweled, sawn into pieces, their eyes gouged out, and their hearts dug out of their bodies. Again, a feeling of grief and yearning for escape on the part of the TORTURERS *and the* TORTURED. *The crows are cawing, sporadically.*]

JULIA:

Where are we now? This is worse than anything so far.

EVA:

I can't bear it.

JULIA:

We have to hang on to who we are so we don't lose ourselves. We have to concentrate. It seems like we can get out of these places if we think the right kinds of thoughts. If your husband and your sister were drowning, who would you save?

EVA:

You can always get another husband. Hey, I know that joke!

[*A doorway of light opens at the side of the stage. The* TORTURERS *are now start-ing to take an interest in the two sisters.*]

JULIA:
Your kids need you. Katya, Jenny, and Arielle. They're all such live wires. A little fucked up, but you know, they're young. It's amazing how people can grow out of things. They need your help, Eva.

[*The* TORTURERS *come closer.*]

EVA:
It's over. They're here.

JULIA:
We'll run through them. Hold my hand.

EVA:
It's no use. I'm sorry.

JULIA:
Close your eyes. Take my hand. I'll pull you.

[EVA *shakes her head, frozen. The* TORTURERS *are almost on them.* JULIA *takes* EVA's *hand and pulls, but* EVA *can't move.*]

Eva! Do one of Jenny's energy things. Imagine a taproot. It's going all the way down from your body to the center of the earth, through this underworld into the earth's crust, to the shelf above the earth's molten core. Fasten your taproot to it. Hold on hard. Make a light circle around you. Don't let them in.

EVA:
I can't. Don't you understand?

JULIA:
Just hold on to me then.

[*A flame-like spotlight springs up around* JULIA. EVA *doesn't move.* JULIA *embraces her. The circle of flames follows her, but it's only big enough for one, so they're each half in and half out of the circle.*]

EVA:
It's not covering us.

JULIA:
Hold on to me. Concentrate on making the circle bigger.

EVA:
I can't. I'm not going to get you killed.

[EVA *struggles free of* JULIA *and flings herself out of the circle of flames, in the direction of the* TORTURERS, *leaving* JULIA *alone, now completely enclosed in the circle. The* TORTURERS *descend on* EVA *and attack her with their instruments.* EVA *falls, while* JULIA *tries and fails to break through the circle of flames. Blackout.*]

SCENE 8: SIXTH HELL—ACCEPTANCE/PRIDE, THE REALM OF
THE GODS, HADES:

[*Lights up.* EVA *and* JULIA *are alone, once again in the cold, bare place of blue flames and icicles beside the two pools—Lethe and Memory.* EVA *is now bathed in a blue spotlight.*]

JULIA [*tries to touch* EVA's *face but can't enter the blue light*]:
Oh, now. What made you do that? I can't feel you. You're not—what are we to do?

EVA:

If I'd had time to think, I might not have. But maybe it's not the worst thing.

JULIA:

If they could send us back from a half-state, why not from this? Because I don't know what to do for your kids without you. Or for Mom and Dad. You'd want to go back, if you were yourself. The kids are worth everything they cost you.

EVA:

All I want is to find a way to go on up, to that place Hades was describing. It will be like living inside a lake of pure thought. Maybe you go back and see if you think all those kids are worth everything they'll cost you. We could compare notes at some point.

JULIA:

Eva, you're not yourself. You were, are, a wonderful mother. And the kids are wonderful too. There's something askew in their brains. But maybe that also makes them poetic and impassioned, with remarkable ideas and impulses. Like Katya, okay, she's prickly but fab, a tattooed hedgehog of principles who can hardly manage daily life. She makes up her own ethics and believes in direct retribution. Arielle, I don't know. There's a demon on her shoulder. But she's fighting it. And Jenny's a very funny, very practical angel. Animals follow her around. Wild dogs eat from her outstretched hands.

EVA:

I might not mind knowing those people.

JULIA:

Drink and see if you can get your memories. Then we can build our case to the gods.

EVA:

I'm not going to think about it. I'm going to do it before I change my mind.

[*Kneels at the scummy Pool of Memory, cups her hands, brings them quickly to her mouth, and drinks.*]

I remember, I remember everything. I remember studying *drosophilia*. A fruit fly has about a hundred thousand neurons. A human baby has about a hundred billion. It makes sense to think you can understand a creature with a hundred thousand neurons. But it's crazy to think you can understand a creature with a hundred billion, or any systems they invent. I remember a pigeon, on a park bench, puffing up his chest and cooing in his throat. I remember Katya, Jenny, Arielle. Oh, God, I want to go back.

JULIA:

We won't take no for an answer. What else can they do to us?

[ERESHKIGAL *enters and puts her hands on* JULIA's *head. She holds out a mask to* EVA, *one of those the dead wear in the underworld.* EVA *takes it but lets it hang by her side.*]

ERESHKIGAL [*to* JULIA]:

My sister will help you, I think. The only requirement is that you deliver my message. [*to* JULIA *and* EVA] Hades sends his best wishes. Unfortunately, he appears to be sulking. [*pause*] You two have been together a long time. Not as long as those who live into old age, tiring of each other and the world. You're luckier than you know to part friends. Now you have what you might think of as five minutes to say your farewells.

JULIA:

Help us to go back together.

ERESHKIGAL:

That possibility is over. Your sister is on this side now.

JULIA:

What if I go and do the heavy lifting? She can come along as a spirit who appears to us sometimes. At least to the kids?

ERESHKIGAL:

The only spirits up there are the strays who got lost on their way here. [*to* EVA] The climb will be painful. [*to* JULIA] You'll wake up in your old body, with some additional impediments. But they too may be useful to you.

JULIA [*panicking, to* EVA]:

How am I going to face your kids? What will I say to Ray? And how will I deal with Mom and Dad? Robert? I've never lived a minute of my life without you.

ERESHKIGAL:

Don't worry, you only have fifty or so years left up there. Though you will have more work to do when you return here and before you start the climb. Maybe a couple of centuries. Not long.

EVA:

You're saying the future is determined?

ERESHKIGAL:

Do you really want to spend your last few minutes together discussing philosophy? [*to* EVA] You will remember her longer than she remembers you. And you will remember this time with us. [*to* JULIA] You will not remember this. Though you might have dreams.

JULIA:

You could at least tell me now what things are like. And Eva will remember, so tell her. You're saying it's already happened, or happening somewhere else, or pre-planned? There's no free will?

ERESHKIGAL:

Why are you all so obsessed with "free will"? When you pose it that way, you're looking in the wrong direction. But you do not exactly have what you would think of as choices.

JULIA:

Then what's the point?

[ERESHKIGAL *laughs, ruefully.* LEOPARD, LION, *and* SHE-WOLF *enter and begin to dance.*]

EVA:

You're getting shadowy—please listen. I'm sorry you have to go back alone. But it's not complicated, just hard. You can do it. You were always great at those improv games of yours.

JULIA:

Right, like any of us are ever going to be happy again. Not to guilt trip you. [*pause*] Remember me as long as you can? Or maybe it's better if you start forgetting all of us as soon as possible. Apparently, I'll be here in fifty or so years, if all goes well. And then following you in a couple of centuries. A blip.

EVA:

I don't know who we'll be by then. How much will we have to lose before we stop being ourselves?

JULIA:

Who else would we be?

[EVA *puts on her mask and she and* JULIA *back away from each other, toward opposite sides of the stage. A dusky light shines from the direction* JULIA *moves in; a painfully bright light from* EVA's *direction. They exit, still facing each other. Lights out.*]

VIII

Train Ride
Just outside Chicago, June 1974

Eva, hot and sticky in the train's intermittent air conditioning, thinks the objects outside could be part of a dream: they all seem to mean something. Why is there a flowered couch sticking out of a dump? What was wrong with it? Maybe someone was redecorating, or maybe they ran away without paying their rent and their landlord threw it out.

The train goes on rocking, hour after hypnotic hour, the trance broken by jolting stops and whistles. Long empty stretches of land, the occasional farm with its ragged fences and brightly painted tractors or combines. Eva doesn't point out what she sees to her brother and sister—who would care? Julia, predictably, had a huge tantrum when she woke up this morning and discovered she couldn't hop off the train whenever she wanted. Now she's sleeping and snoring quietly, her warm face in Eva's lap, her blonde hair sticking to her cheeks in wisps. Her eyelids flicker.

Robert, in the seat opposite them, props his feet on their bags, absorbed in his paperback of classical mythology. He turns a page and gives a half-smile, as if having his suspicions confirmed. He's a teenager pretending to be a grown-up, too world-weary to be amazed. Dad put him in charge of this trip, because what choice did he have? But Robert's gotten scary in the last couple of years: tall and pale, with dark hair and eyes and a cold way of telling you what to do and not accepting no for an answer. Bullheaded. People think he's much older than fifteen. Julia worships him, but Eva is done with all that.

Eva passionately wants to go home, not the new, ruined home, but home when their mother was still there, when the family was still what it used to be. She misses her parents, she misses her room, she misses her street, and she misses taking all of that for granted. What she wants is to go back to the time before she knew what it was like to lose the feeling of home.

She will be starting sixth grade in the fall, and she hopes to learn a lot this summer. She's been reading the *Encyclopedia of Our Earth* Dad gave her for her last birthday but is taking a break so she won't finish it too fast. She wants it to last the whole train ride. The book helps keep her from thinking about the days and weeks before Dad put them on the train. Molten rock from the earth's mantle constantly wells up between the crustal plates. Piles of rocks known as lateral moraines collect at the sides of glaciers. The food chain in the sea starts with plant plankton, eaten by animal plankton, eaten by small fish, eaten by bigger fish, eaten by seabirds and sea mammals.

They pass a great rockslide, the train dislodging more stones as it passes. Hills, scrubby fields, dark reddish-brown rivers, neatly planted rows of corn or cabbages, interrupted by stations, bustle, announcements, crowds of people. More tracks, more crossing signs. Collapsed bridges, deep ditches. This is the first time she and her brother and sister will visit their uncle's farm without their parents. She's not going to think about that. She looks forward to seeing his pigs and cows and the stupid but beautiful chickens with their black and white or chestnut feathers, their head plumages or red combs, their weird rivalries and sudden festivals of flapping around in the dirt, bathing in the dust.

Outside the train, the world flashes by. Sonja sees telephone poles, an old flowered couch sticking up from the top of a landfill pile, and furniture warehouses full of the accoutrements of domesticity—whatever non-actors use to set up the stage sets of their houses, before they forget they're playing a long-term role and start thinking of this performance as their life. "The artist and the madman seek the same end: to order chaos, to search for meanings," said Augusto Boal. "That was what God was doing on the very first day of the Creation." Not that she, or any of the troupe (so far as she knows) believes in God, and neither does Boal. But they practice the same unreasonable levels of devotion as mystics and monks.

And maybe the same level of madness. Sonja has not only returned to Simon Magus, *again,* despite all her promises to herself and her mother, but last night, she actually married him. She's a moron. Or a genius. Drowsy from lack of sleep, she feels herself pleasantly embedded in the jokes, rivalries, and games of the troupe, many of whom are still drunk after the wedding. Everyone thought the marriage a great escapade and toasted her and Simon through much of the night.

The train trip, a honeymoon, an adventure, a chance to practice Theater of the Oppressed Forum Theater in the world, was Simon's idea. It was Sonja's idea to marry on the train. She's still wearing her thrift-shop dress with its faint smell of another bride's rose-musk perfume. A yellowing Victorian gown, or a knock-off, with a high lace collar, embroidered bodice, and long lace-trimmed sleeves. The lace is torn at the neck, the edges of the sleeves, and along the bottom of the skirt. She also wears a crown of silver foil branches woven out of an old Christmas decoration. Richa, a minister of the Mother Earth church, wed her to Simon, legally, in the middle of the car. Sonja danced down the aisle, and Simon danced toward her. They made up vows on the spot. They promised to be honest, to be faithful to the truth of the moment, and to dedicate their marriage to justice and the pursuit of uncovering reality, whatever the cost.

This morning, despite their mixture of continued drunkenness and hangovers, the troupe has been running through games, warming up. Simon, even if still a bit drunk, is dazzling, his long hair pulled back in a ponytail, his muscled body showing through his tight black T-shirt and jeans. His strong nose and his way of cocking his head to the side make him look like an eagle searching for a place to land. But his voice is soft, and he has a tender manner and smile.

The two of them consummated their wedding in a train toilet, a brilliant, memorable event that took place both in the physical world, more or less in the damp metal sink, and also in the transcendent world of fallen angels, with a radiant shower of trailing sparks and the kind of pleasure that leads her to daydream about last night all through the morning exercises.

Clearly, he loves everyone today. That's Sonja's doing. Something to be proud of. He leads the troupe through the Antiquated Telephone exchange, Puppet Sequences, and an Atmosphere of Snow. Next up is Immigrants. Everyone begins as statues. Clara stretches out on the filthy train floor, wretchedly holding out her arms for help. Marina, not to be outdone, drops to the floor beside her. Bruce and Lisabeth extend their arms, their expressions painfully sympathetic. Most other people have left the car. A small audience remains, pretending to read while observing them in interest or with unpleasant expressions of judgment.

Her mother's said, about Simon, "He certainly thinks well of himself," and "This Simon—you say he's a joker? He's very suited to the stage. Though he takes up more space than we have in this living room." Sonja loves his grandeur. With Simon, she'll never have an ordinary life. What will her mother say when she finds out they're married? Sonja will call her from Chicago and say, "Be happy for me." No, that's an opening as big as a barn. She'll say, "This is the right thing for us." But she doesn't know whether it is or not. And her mother will pick up on that right away.

Finally, in Union Station, Chicago's huge terminal, the Zamarin kids can move freely. Eva holds Julia's hand, to reassure her and to keep her from running away. Robert allows his sisters pizza and donuts for breakfast, just because he can, to remind them he's in charge. They tear into their food like wild kittens, who are basically very small tigers, since tigers and cats are both part of the Felidae family, though tigers are in the Pantherinae subfamily and house cats in the Felinae.

Across the way, at a row of pay phones, stands a woman in a wedding dress, looking like a ghost of a nineteenth-century bride. She's not so old, maybe in her twenties, with wispy curls twined up around her face, a silver crown that sparkles under the lights. All her features seem crowded together, which gives her a surprised expression, as if she's climbed out of an old painting and found herself in this echoing terminal. If she were a real bride, she'd be at a party, surrounded by people, dancing and drinking champagne. Maybe she's a crazy person. The thought shuts Eva's mind down: crazy is one of the terms she will no longer allow herself to use, even in her own thinking.

After they climb back on the train, Robert lets her hold the tickets. A fake concession, which she accepts because it would be undignified to refuse. Being responsible for the tickets turns out to be a weight, though. She checks on them again and again while making sure Julia holds on to her or Robert as they make their way from car to car.

Time has a way of stretching out on the train. Their only excursions are occasional trips to the toilet cubicle with its dubious, sticky floor, or the snack bar with its array of treasures that cost too much to buy, though Robert does allow them each to choose a candy bar. Grandly, with the air of doing them a great favor.

At home, walking by a playground, Eva sometimes looked at younger children and imagined what her own kids might be like someday, how she'd look after them. It will be nothing at all like this family, that's for sure. In the week and a half since Mom was committed, Eva, Robert, and Julia haven't been allowed to visit. She had a knife, and Eva got it away, and it could have been worse. Eva didn't mean to hurt Mom. She dreams about her mother's face at the moment she grabbed for the knife, her look of betrayal.

Dad said none of it is her fault. "Eva, you mustn't worry about all this. You did your best." He sighed. "Sometimes I think Robert and Julia are most of all your mother's children, just as you are most of all mine. You and I, we like to think about things scientifically. Your mom is magical when she's doing well. Probably this business with the knife started as a kind of performance and just got out of hand. More out of hand than usual. You understand what I mean, don't you?"

Eva nodded. She didn't, but she loved that he thought she was like him.

"The doctors will help her, and she'll be all better again. Sometimes it's just a question of recalibrating our brains, biologically." He gave a sad smile.

What Eva did might have wrecked the Zamarin family. It doesn't help to think about it. Meanwhile, she, Robert, and Julia are on their way to their uncle's. To get them out of the way, though no one's said this, exactly.

Sonja, on the phone with her mother, finds she can't say she's married Simon. Union Station towers over her, classic and magisterial, a reproach to impulse and indecision. People are staring at her bedraggled dress and crown. She'd have told the truth right away except that her mother said, as soon as they greeted each other, "I wish I could have had adventures myself, but by the time I was twenty-four, I was already tied up with your brothers and you. It was all diapers, baby food, spit up, someone crying. I thought, I'm not twenty-five yet, and my life is over."

The sad, affectionate, spiteful yearning in her voice haunts Sonja. She pictures her mother sitting at the old red Bakelite kitchen table, surrounded by her collection of salt and pepper shakers: the penguins, the cop and robber, the cacti, the kissing gnomes. Sonja is past saying things like, "I didn't ask to be born," or "You could have adventures now," or "But what about when you say that we're the great treasures of your life?"

She'll find another pay phone at the next stop. Meanwhile, she offers up one of the stories her mother claims to like, knowing her mother will inevitably say something jagged and painful afterward. Sonja still wants to tell her everything. "We went back to one of my favorite exercises, playing animals. The Joker gives us each a piece of paper telling us what we are. The first time I did this, I had no idea there'd be a male and female of each species, that Simon had the other jaguar. That was before Andre left. Simon wasn't the Joker then. As animals, we eat, we drink, we fight, we show whether we're greedy, secretive, aggressive, or timid. We sleep, we wake, we search for mates, as poetically, surreally, or realistically as we want. But the Joker reminds us we have to be faithful to our animal's way of behaving, we can't stop to observe the others. Once we've found each other, we replay our lovers' meeting in the center of the circle, and the others guess who we are by crowing or roaring. It was funny, Mom, we had one couple we couldn't guess at all. What kind of animal were they? Turns out they were human. Anyway, that was when Simon and I first took an interest in each other, as jaguars."

"I'm glad you're having fun, doodlebug. Keep in mind that you don't have a big window left for finding someone who's good father material. Having children is the greatest joy in life. I wouldn't want you to miss out on it."

"Our train's about to leave, Mom. Have to run to catch it. Love you!"

"Love you," says her mother, who believes in both love and God, though she rarely attends church and never remarried after Sonja's father died.

The trip's taking longer than Eva ever imagined, and there's a guy making very weird faces at the end of the car. Neither Robert nor Julia notice that he's talking to himself. Is he a problem or not a problem? She finishes the *Encyclopedia of Our Earth* and accepts Robert's offer to trade it for his book of mythology. This book doesn't take her mind off the family at all, but it has its uses. When Julia wakes up, demanding a story, Eva tells her about the Minotaur with his bull's head and monstrous man's body, trapped in his maze, starving for boys and girls to eat. "His father was a magical white bull, a gift from Poseidon," she says. "This king was supposed to sacrifice him, but his wife . . ." Now how was she going to tell this story? It wasn't a book of mythology for kids, that was for sure. "How about this one? It's about Nessus. He's a centaur. Do you know what that is? He's sort of the opposite of the Minotaur: he has the upper half of a man's body, and the lower half of a horse's body."

"Why does he?" says Julia, piercingly. She leans against Eva, their bodies sticking to each other, to the train seat. Her face is focused, taut, as if she can turn herself into a single point of concentration and so understand these mysteries.

Eva pages through this story, checking how it will read aloud. Nessus is supposed to carry Herakles's second wife, Deianira, across a river and instead tries to run away with her. Herakles shoots him with a poisoned arrow, but dying Nessus gives Deianira his tunic, dripping with poisoned blood, telling her it will work as a love potion. The book stops the story to explain that in another version of this tale, she mops up his blood with a cloth and weaves it into a cloak. Which, either way, gross. Then Deianira thinks Herakles doesn't love her anymore, so she gives him the cloak. The book doesn't report on his response. What would he say? "Oh, yes, dear, thank you for this bloody cloak— how thoughtful of you"? The cloak burns him until he builds a huge bonfire and climbs into it, which persuades the gods to step in and rescue him.

Julia tugs at her. Eva says, "Just a sec, Jules. This might not be a good story for you."

"Why isn't it a good story?"

Robert's laughing, not even pretending to read the far more interesting and useful encyclopedia. Eva asks him, "Of all the wives you could run off with, why pick Herakles's? And why would Herakles trust a centaur when he'd fought another centaur in the first place to win Deinara?" (Eva pictures her as having a fairly horsey face.) "Why didn't the cloth burn Deinara when she was weaving it? And if the gods were going to rescue Herakles, why wait all through his miserable feeling of burning until he actually lit himself on fire?"

Robert shrugs. "Maybe it was fun for them, seeing him burn. Maybe they just didn't give a damn. You can be so terminally literal, Eva. It's a great story. Go on, read it aloud. Julia will love this story."

"It's ludicrous." Eva offers the book to Robert, but he's not ready to return her encyclopedia. She wants to read it again as part of her project of learning everything.

"I will love this story," says Julia, with determination. She'll do anything Robert says. If Eva let him, he'd start acting this out with her, which would be a disaster. To try to keep him from giving Julia nightmares, Eva sometimes plays their dress-up games, their adventures in other worlds and re-enactments of myths and fairytales, trying to steer their imaginings in less frightening directions. But what she most loves is to lie in a patch of sun and look at the shapes of things. How leaves move in the woods. The patterns of the sun through branches. The way the ocean changes color right under the surface. How light moves across the ripples of a creek, and oil slicks coil in rainbows on the surface of a puddle.

The guy at the end of the car talking to himself is louder, angrier. "You have to keep your promises," he says. "What good is anything if you don't keep your promises?"

"Let's move closer to the dome car," Eva says. "Let's grab our stuff and go." She gestures at the guy with her head. Robert sighs, indicating that she's overreacting, but he shoulders the bags without complaining, while Eva takes Julia's hand.

As they walk through the cars, a wicked-looking man, like a crooked jockey, begins following them. "What a little beauty you are, sweetheart," he says to Julia. "You're going to be something, aren't you? Your mama must be a hottie."

He scans the train, but their mother is far away, of course. And Eva thinks that, at fifty, maybe she's not as much of a hottie as she once was. Eva's tried to imagine her mother's life in Warsaw, the Los Angeles orphanage, the place where they've now committed her. Impossible. When she and Eva's father met, he was teaching psychology in San Francisco, and she was in a hospital remission study, a success story, a star. "How beautiful your mother was," he's said, though not for a long time.

Eva's not going to think about any of this, she just isn't. She says, "Our mama looks like me and my brother. And my sister's *five years old*, asshole."

The man reddens and walks past them, straight out through the front door of the car, and a group of people bursts into applause. "Oh, brave," says a man with a very long brown ponytail and electric blue eyes. He and the twelve or so people with him appear to have scraped up their clothes from a fifty-cents-a-pound bin: old skirts, loose pants, polka-dot ties, bowler hats, everything too big or too small, colors and patterns so mismatched they seem to vibrate. Wild manes of hair half pinned up or flowing down their backs. Eva's amazed to see the woman in the wedding dress here. She can't help smiling, as if she's an old friend. Up close, it's clear that the dress is ripped. The foil crown is completely ridiculous. But Eva feels happy to know the woman has friends—she can't be a crazy person, right?

The man says to the others, "This child could teach demechanization—what was the dominant will in that interaction?"

"Protection of the sister," answers the woman in the wedding dress. She's smiling back at Eva, and although signs from the universe are not statistically valid, it feels like good luck to see her again.

"Sit down with us," says the man with the ponytail, waving to the others to make room for them.

Robert asks, "Who are you?" and the man says, smiling even more broadly, "In Theater of the Oppressed, we have no leader, just the Joker"—he gives a little bow—"who can direct, participate, comment, and change roles as needed. We play games and rewrite history. The great Brazilian director and activist Augusto Boal was kidnapped, tortured, exiled to Argentina, but he's invented this new theater, and it will change the world."

Sonja watches Simon posturing for these children. "They don't want to know all that. Give them something to eat." She gestures at the troupe: now that she's married to Simon, she has a certain authority she hasn't had before. Everyone rummages around and produces crunchy foods in foil and plastic bags. She doesn't remember what she has in her own bag, but when she opens it, she finds oranges, chocolate, and plantain chips.

As the children sit down, she learns that the tall dark-haired boy is Robert, gawky but fierce. He studies the troupe members as avidly as if he might be called to play any one of them on stage. He's a young raptor himself. Seeing him with Simon makes her feel uneasy about both of them, in some way she can't quite name.

The middle girl, Eva, is out of place, nervous, as if she might be afraid someone will ask why they're traveling by themselves. Maybe these kids are homeless. Maybe they're orphans. They look shell-shocked, like people who haven't yet started to believe in their losses.

The little girl, Julia, is a peach, and a piece of work. When she sees that Sonja has chocolate, she smiles deliciously, half-closing her eyes, her long eyelashes against her cheeks. Sonja gives them all handfuls of plantain chips. She's practicing having children: she could raise a whole house full of them. And Simon better get ready to prove her mother wrong. Sonja gives him a non-newlywed look.

He says to the children, as kindly as if he understands himself to be auditioning for fatherhood, "I would like to do an experiment with you—an educational experiment, but not at all boring. Would you like that?"

Robert says, "I still don't know your name."

"I am the Joker, but you can call me Simon Magus." Young Robert apparently feels that eating chocolate has relegated him to being just one of the children. He swallows quickly and stands, broadening his thin shoulders, ready for action.

Simon isn't quite ready to begin. "But no teaching is valuable if it's free. So there needs to be some kind of exchange."

Eva starts to gather up her bags. Sonja, curious to see what will happen, and wanting to help out these lost children, unwraps more chocolate and holds it out to her, along with an orange.

Robert leans forward and takes both the candy and the orange, then breaks off pieces of chocolate for his sisters.

Eva says, "We don't have a lot of money."

Simon laughs. He's unbearably sexy, without being exactly handsome. And he's hers. It might be that she'll spend the rest of her life with him. That could happen. He says, "You could give us something else. An object you care about."

"Okay, then," says Eva, her mouth full. She reaches into a bag and pulls out a book, a mythology compendium. "We don't need this anymore."

Julia lets out a wail. "Not the Minotaur!" Robert pulls it away and gives it to Julia, then hauls out another book from his shoulder bag. An encyclopedia, the cover decorated with different views of the world and its strata, a tree on a floating island of grass, an erupting volcano, frolicking dolphins and other sea creatures. Eva starts to lunge for the book but contains herself.

"Excellent! We could use a few more facts," Simon says. "You give us your encyclopedia and we'll teach you to change the world. Fair enough?"

As Robert's handing it over, Eva asks, "What exactly are we going to do?" She's suspicious, that one, rightly so. She shrugs as if to say she doesn't care about the encyclopedia, but from the way her eyes follow the book, it's clear how much she loves it. Unlike her brother and sister, she's painfully transparent.

"Leave their book alone, Simon," she says. But Simon's ignoring her. He didn't like it that she gave the company a command and they obeyed.

He tucks the encyclopedia into his duffel bag. His voice is still quite sweet, insofar as Simon is ever sweet. "You change what happens on stage and you can uncover the causes. You can stop being a machine, stop reacting according to your habits. We play games with power and status so we learn to recognize them and how they work."

The troupe are already stretching, starting to warm up. They lean over to touch their toes, reach their arms over the backs of the train seats, do lunges. The children finish eating and stand over their bags as if unsure whether they're staying. Robert is alert, Eva wary, Julia holding the book of mythology to her chest as if it were a beloved stuffed animal.

Simon sweeps his hand through the air, a grand theatrical gesture. "In Forum Theater, we re-enact an event; someone intervenes; we try a different solution; we see what worked or didn't; we try another. Yes? Shall we do this? Why don't you start by thinking of a time when you, or someone you know, faced an instance of oppression, where you or they felt helpless?"

Eva says, "We don't want to play this game."

Simon's voice grows even kinder. "You'll see. You'll feel much more powerful after."

Robert suddenly offers, "My mother's father and mother were separated in Warsaw, at a train station in 1942. He never saw her again, or

knew where she was, until he was digging a pit for bodies at Treblinka
II and saw hers among them."

Eva, too late, claps her hands over Julia's ears, and Julia clings to her,
bewildered, her anxious face asking *why?* Why dig a pit for bodies,
what is Treblinka II, how can this happen? What a disaster—they
should have left as soon as they saw these people. Their parents don't
even know that Robert has told Eva the story. They told him when he
was thirteen, so probably they plan to tell her as well in another year
or so. But Robert told her as soon as he heard it himself. A family
secret this Simon Magus is going to take for himself, she can see that
already.

Robert says, "If he'd refused to throw her in the pit with all the others, the guard would have shot him."

She'd like to think he'll regret having chosen this story, though
probably not. When he first told her, she said it was a terrible story,
and he said, "It's the only kind, really. Everything else is a lie. Even
the fairy tales, the real ones, not those wretched Disney versions. Birds
peck out the stepsisters' eyes, and they dance in red-hot shoes at the
wedding until they fall down dead. But this is realer than that."

Is it, though? Who told the story to their parents? Their grandfather after the war? She doesn't even know if he lived through it.
Someone who knew him then? Eva has imagined her grandparents as
like her mother but sepia-tinted: bunched up in a cattle car with too
many people and nothing to eat or drink, separated at the train station, her grandfather not knowing where his wife was. She's allowed
herself to imagine the cattle car, the separation on the platform, the
smell of the dirt and the feel of the shovel. She hasn't yet been able to
step over the brink, to enter into the moment when her grandfather
recognized his lost wife.

But Simon Magus, the Joker, is already there. He stands in the
swaying train, fishing out a carved wooden walking stick from under
the seat. "Here is our shovel. I will be the guard. Who wants to try to
take the role of the husband? What might he do differently?"

No one in the car is reading anymore: they're all paying attention to Simon Magus, surrounded by his troupe. Some seem interested, others irritated or upset. But no one says anything. Julia's face is reddening, ominously. Eva can't carry her out of here on her own. The woman in the wedding dress, Sonja, is packing up the rest of the treats in her bag. From her look of fury, Eva thinks maybe she'll help. They'll leave Robert and Simon Magus alone and the three of them will go to the dome car and wait this out.

One of the men from the troupe says, "I'll do it." He takes the stick-shovel and stands in the aisle.

Simon Magus is going on again, apparently for the benefit of the Zamarins, but perhaps more to his own troupe. He talks like a teacher lecturing students who don't quite understand what he's been saying, "In Forum Theater, there are no spectators—only spect-actors: anyone can be a protagonist at any time. If you see another solution, you can shout 'Stop' and enter the scene, taking the part of the protagonist. It's not a debate, but a theatrical enactment. Do you know the difference?"

When Robert nods, stiffly, his face proud enough that Eva thinks he must not have followed this either, Simon Magus continues, "The performance can be realistic or symbolic, making use of images to find the underlying situation. Perhaps an extrapolated ritual, a metaphoric ritual. But for now, let us, out of respect for the historical seriousness of the subject, begin this realistically."

Sonja taps her foot, her arms crossed. Robert nods again. If Simon Magus is explaining to his people how to explain, he could be doing a way better job of it. But Robert does this too—always reminding his sisters how much he knows, how much they don't yet know.

Simon Magus takes up his position as guard, making his hand into a gun and pointing it at the spect-actor holding the shovel. This man, now turned into their grandfather, looks down into the ditch full of bodies that was the floor of the train and sees his wife. He throws down the shovel and crosses his arms. Simon Magus shoots him, and he falls, heavily.

Julia burrows into Eva's side.

"Oh, now," says a middle-aged woman on the train, but when the troupe ignores her, she looks at her shoes. There are no other children in this car. Just one baby at the far end, its mother busy feeding and fussing over it.

Simon Magus asks, "How did that solution work? Do you have doubts about the way the oppressed protagonist behaved?"

Sonja steps forward, facing down Simon. "We've had no warm-up. Shouldn't we start with some Image Theater? These children know nothing about suggesting subject matter."

Robert scowls. He hates it when people call him a child. He shouts, "Stop!" He steps in and picks up the stick-shovel, then strikes out at the hand that's a gun, showing how his grandfather could have protected himself but stopping just short of hitting Simon Magus.

"Magic!" shout two or three people from the troupe at once, and Simon Magus explains, "Sometimes people come up with a solution that's not possible, so we call magic on them. Symbolic or realistic, we have to find something that can work in the real world. Let's go again." He takes the stick from Robert and holds it up.

Sonja puts her hands on her hips. "Are we following a path of liberation or fatalism here? Is this aggression or oppression?" She sounds like she's memorized the line but is using it at the wrong time.

Another woman, older, with longish gray-white hair, has had enough. "Augusto Boal wrote about the Jewish doctor who said that nothing could be done after the transportation. But what about choosing a different moment? Could people have resisted wearing the Star of David, the move to the ghettos?"

"We resisted. Some of us resisted." That's another troupe member, tall, bearded, like Abraham Lincoln in jeans. Not anything like old enough to have been there, so Eva can't think what he means. He stands behind Sonja. "But how often have the Jews saved themselves by lying low? What does resistance look like, with our history? My grandfather, in Birkenau, gave all his food to his wife and daughters and starved. But then they wound up in the gas chambers. With these kids' family history, there's nothing that can be done."

Simon Magus, in his gentle, compelling voice, says, "There's always something one could have done. Again." He stares at the bearded troupe member, who stares back for a minute or two, then sits down.

Another man takes up the stick and looks down at the floor of the train, his face registering the invisible body of his wife.

Julia cries, "No!" and, "Liars! You're making it up!" She sobs, spattering, out of control, thrashing in her seat like a great snake, while Eva tries to hold onto her. Sonja starts in their direction, but stops as if she has no idea what to do next.

"We have to get her out of here," Eva says to Robert. He looks at Julia, then at the troupe members.

"Now," she says.

Robert, sighing, leans down and picks up Julia, one hand under her hips, the other holding her head against his chest, a firm grip. She weighs a ton, as Eva knows, but Robert does a lot of push-ups. "Don't be such a baby, Jules. We'll take you to the all-glass car where we can see the trees. You are way too old for tantrums and too young for temperament. So cut it out. I mean it." Julia wails in his arms. He shifts her to one side and picks up a pair of their bags and hangs them on his other shoulder.

Eva drags the small suitcase and their lunch bag, following him. Simon Magus raises his voice over Julia's cries. "If you can work the situation through to the end, you will be released from it."

Robert stops, blocking Eva's way to the door, looks back over his shoulder toward the troupe, his face full of longing. She sees how much he wants to go back and have another try at it. Julia cries more loudly. Her tears started from real upset, but she's exaggerating her sobs now. The tantrum has become a chance to get attention, as if she were part of the play. Oh, God, what a family. Eva would love to run away and never come back, but she can't leave Julia alone with Robert. How would he take care of her? Eva pinches him. "*Go*," she says. "The dome car." She wants to say to him, You are going to be in so much trouble. But who would he be in trouble with?

Sonja can't stay to watch Simon trying to win back the children, who are heading to the front of the train. She catches up her bag and walks as fast as she can in the other direction. He isn't father material even for vicarious children. In the bathroom in the next car, she takes off her wedding dress and crown. They won't fit in the trash, and the window doesn't open. She rolls them into a ball, tying up the dress with its own sleeves, and stuffs the ball in a corner. She washes her face and as much of her body as she can in the sink but rejects the feeble air dryer, wiping herself off with a clean T-shirt. She has one more change of clothes before she has to find a place to do laundry. She considers wearing a dirty shirt instead, but she feels foul enough already. On her Dark Side of the Moon T-shirt, a shaft of white light strikes a prism, refracted into a rainbow. What if this were the first and last day of the shortest marriage in history? At least she'd never have to tell her mother about it.

Someone knocks on the door. She calls out, "Be right there," then combs her hair, applies eyeliner, zips her bag, and goes out. Simon. He's never before come after her when they've had a fight. "Hey," he says.

None of the rest of the troupe are in sight. It's just her and her new husband. She says, "So what the hell was that?"

"Being faithful to the truth of the moment."

"'There's always something one could have done'?" She wants him to explain what he meant, what his intentions were, to make it all so clear that she will go beyond forgiving him to admiring him and blaming herself for her own shortsightedness. Forum Theater: a protagonist with a wish and the will to exercise it, an antagonist with a desire or need to thwart that wish, a crisis with danger and opportunity, and a defeat. And in the defeat lies the opportunity to step in to find a solution. But she doubts he has a satisfactory answer. And as soon as he tries to justify himself, or explain, or show how she, or the troupe, or the children are in any way to blame, she might just take her bag and disembark. And this time she's not coming back. "Well?"

Simon just stands there. Not a jaguar, not the Joker. A twenty-seven-year-old guy in a too-tight T-shirt, his face unhappy and bewildered. He looks down at his hands, turning them over and then back again, as if they might have the answer on one side or the other.

Robert moves through the next car, shifting the weight of their bags and stroking Julia's back. "Quiet now. What a complete pain you are. We're going to go see the trees. Can you please get a grip?"

"I can get a grip," Julia murmurs into his neck, crying a little more softly.

"That was amazing, though," he says, still angry but also lit up. "What was it they called that? Theater of the Oppressed." He shakes his head, lips moving as if he's re-enacting the scene.

Eva doesn't like his frightening, total focus. He needs to be thinking about Julia, but he's gone somewhere else. Robert's caught an infection from these people: something in that game has hold of him. She pictures the troupe continuing with the story they've stolen, the ghost of her grandfather stuck there, handed over to strangers by his own grandchildren.

The train sways, and Eva grabs the back of a seat to keep her balance. Robert, ahead of her, carrying Julia and the bags, bends his knees and absorbs the movement without stopping. Eva misses her encyclopedia and all its crucial information about the world. She'd like to unspool time, run it backward and then forward again, like the film strips her teachers show in class, the sprockets rattling. If she could go back to the moment before they began playing the game. Sonja has chocolate and oranges in her hands, a pleading look, she wants so much to help them. Eva steps in before Robert can take the food. *No thanks*, she says, *we appreciate it, but we don't need anything*. But Robert accepts the chocolate anyway, and they're all eating it. He's telling their grandfather's story.

Stop!

Mom is at the kitchen sink, slowly washing a few dishes, breakfast half cleared away. She's been silent and strange the past few days. When she talks, she sometimes makes sense and sometimes says scary things about sin and darkness. It's better if she's not alone too much, but she shouts at them if she thinks they're watching her. Eva wants to keep her company without making her nervous, so she's reading the *Santa Cruz Sentinel*. So many families are having troubles. But problem children may be about to get aid in the Pajaro Valley Unified School District. The coordinator "appealed to residents to tell him of any youngster, who may be from one day old through school age," whether they don't speak or can't be understood, move awkwardly or can't walk, don't seem to hear or don't listen. Those who run into things, those who have difficulty reading. Anger, fits of crying, constant fighting or "other behavior which is not easily explained." Help may be available. "They should be identified as early as possible, he says, so special training can be initiated early, if it is required."

The water in the sink keeps running. Something in the room feels odd. When she looks up from the article, there's Mom holding a long, sharp knife, regarding her as if she's the enemy. Eva drops the paper on the kitchen table, its morning plates full of crumbs and yellow streaks of egg, an ordinary mess. This time, though, instead of running toward her mother, she stands where she is and says, "You don't mean that, Mom, wake up, please." No response. Mom isn't there. Someone else has taken her place.

Stop!

This time, Eva turns to run from the kitchen. There will be no fight. Mom won't get hurt. The family won't be wrecked. She'll call her father and help will be available. But Mom, or the someone who's taken her place, runs the other direction with the knife—going for Julia.

Stop!

Eva grabs the newspaper and holds it in front of her, lunging at Mom. She wraps the knife in paper so it's harmless. Mom comes back to herself, and, seeing how upset Eva is, takes her into her arms.

Magic!

They enter the Great Dome car, and the trees outside are beautiful and distant. Inhuman. Robert bounces Julia up and down, making up a story in which the trees talk and dance when no one is listening. But the trees are just themselves, busy with photosynthesis, taking exactly six molecules of water from their own roots and six molecules of oxygen from the air and making one complete molecule of glucose, feeding themselves. It's perfect in a way Robert and Julia can never understand.

IX

The Unforgivable Stories

Santa Cruz Mountains, June 2005

VISITORS

I lay against the passenger seat of our old VW bus, holding onto my new canes: iridescent aluminum with red-purple swirls and rubber tips. Robert stared straight ahead, concentrating on the gravelly, twisting mountain road. The bus jolted over a pothole, and I cried out. I said, "Sorry," and he answered me, tersely, "I know you can't help it. But I'm driving as carefully as I can, Jules." He rolled his shoulders and cranky neck, tossing his head like an old horse about to charge. He looked a decade older than he had in early spring, his face thin and cross.

Though it was mid-afternoon, giant redwoods blocked the June sunlight from every side. It was hot even in the shade. Branches lay across unmarked roads, and dogs barked in unseen houses. We'd be arriving a few days ahead of the students, along with the other companies chosen by the Scheherazade Institute for a summer of teaching and making new work. It had seemed as if life without Eva, with a hole torn in the world, would be equally hard anywhere. But returning to these woods, these mountains, was a mistake. I hated them, as if they had killed my sister.

The woods had an ancient, dark, indomitable quality. The farther we went, the more my dread grew. I wished I could remember my last conversation with Eva. Some talk about our parents, I think. And another, crucial, discussion. About the children? Like the tail end of a dream, the memory hung around the edges of my mind: I'd be about to get hold of it, and then it would slip away again.

After the attack, I'd woken up, bit by bit, in the odd dislocation of finding myself in a hospital, with everyone crying and acting strangely. They'd told me we'd been shot and had both been out for nearly a week. For the first couple of days I was semi-awake, and then awake and in fierce pain. In all that time, when I asked where Eva was, everyone pretended she was still unconscious in another room. Two months later, though I was no longer on my hands and knees howling, I still hadn't forgiven any of them for letting me think, even for a minute, that she was still alive, that there was hope.

Redwood branches brushed up against the windows when we rounded a particularly tight turn. "I don't know how to live in an Eva-less world," I said and began to cry, convulsively.

Robert glanced over at me. "Jules, I can't help you with this. If you want to wallow, you have to do that with the rest of the family."

"It's like a hurricane, or a great earthquake, has torn everything down. Now we have to learn to live in the wilds, with no roof or walls."

"We'll go back to work, and we'll get through it."

The wave of grief began to subside. I blew my nose and wiped my face, considering Robert, who seemed both familiar and strange: tall, spooky, broken-nosed, a kind of Cubist portrait. He had our father's dark hair and pale skin as well as his gloomy passion for world-saving; our mother's beauty and dramatic flair. The firstborn child, articulate and reckless, a never-ending geyser of ideas. We'd spent our whole adult lives working together. But if I could have only one sibling, I would rather have had my sister.

As we'd driven down from the city, kids in cars had honked and waved: our VW bus had "News-of-the-World Theater Company" in blue and scarlet letters across the shellacked newspaper veneer. The entire back of the bus was crammed with everyone's luggage and an assortment of old props and costumes. The lead car in a mini cara-van, including the old sedan, full of other company members packed in together like a clown car at an out-of-luck circus. Ordinarily when we were all on our way somewhere, the bus would be full of gossiping, complaining, singing company members, but though everyone had been agonizingly polite, clearly no one wanted to ride with Robert and me right now.

Another hard corner, another slap from the redwood branches against the windows. I said, "I shouldn't be here. I don't even know if I can perform anymore."

"There are whole companies where people do spectacular pieces from wheelchairs."

I'd meant I was afraid I couldn't stop crying. I said, "No wheelchairs."

"You don't have to have a wheelchair if you don't want one. We'll figure it out." The old Robert had awakened in the morning with a puppy's amazement at the world and all its bright variety of things to smell and taste and investigate. Now he looked his age, coming up on fifty. He'd lost at least as much weight over the last two months as I'd gained. On the rare occasions he sat down for a meal, he regarded his plate of food as if some witch had put it there to plump him up so she could pop him into her barbecue pit later on. He'd swallow, painfully, say he didn't have time, jump up, and leave. And there was no Eva to talk to about it. I was never going to have a conversation with her again.

We turned onto a smaller, more pitted road, bumping our way down the mountain. As we passed near a hand-built shack with a "PRIVATE! NO TRESPASSING!" sign, a pack of dogs threw themselves against the fence, howling. Under the canopy of interlocked redwoods, a half-dusk overtook us. We'd heard rumors about survivalists and serial killers, men who left behind letters composed in dramatic and intriguing codes. Our own killer was out here somewhere. I might find him again and somehow take revenge. Or he would finish me off this time.

Robert sighed. "This maybe isn't the best time, but I have to talk with you about Alyx."

"We don't ever have to go over that again. I already forgave you, Robert. I'm prepared to support you both. The thing she and I had: it wasn't important." I was going to add that I appreciated that he'd at least waited until she and I were through—this time—but fortunately stopped myself. Why dredge up the past?

He said, "No, I mean, I need to break it off with her. I can't handle any relationship right now, but I don't want to throw things off for the company by making drama."

"And you want my advice on getting rid of her without upsetting her."

"It sounds so cold when you put it that way. But I'm going nuts here, Jules. And I think she might be wanting to settle down with me. Maybe you could talk to her."

"Seriously?"

A thin, tank-top-wearing, crop-headed little toughie, Alyx had a way of propping her elbows on her knees and her chin on her hands and staring as if she were an anthropologist from another planet, sober and above judgment. And in the next moment, she'd give a reckless grin, a dare, an invitation. "Get into trouble with me," that grin said. "I am going to take you places you never knew existed." I couldn't picture her settling down with anyone, let alone my impossible brother. During the first couple of years we'd worked together, she and I hadn't exactly been friends. To our own surprise, we became lovers for three intense and discombobulating months despite my own rule against getting involved with any company members, then we broke up in a raging argument where it wasn't entirely clear who was breaking up with who or why it was necessary. It was all emotion: accusations of dependence or manipulation, ugly assessments of each of our worst characteristics in the name of ultimate honesty. Afterward, we didn't speak for a while, outside the rehearsal hall.

We'd tried to keep our affair secret from the company, though I wasn't sure whether we'd succeeded. Robert knew. And a year or so later, not long before I left for New York, the two of them got together. I was mad, I admit it. Maybe it was part of the reason I'd left. But sex had always been part of his method of getting to know people's possibilities and limits. For me, the need to constantly be with someone had been about how ashy the world felt whenever I was alone. I was working on that.

I asked him, "What exactly do you picture me saying?"

He smiled: wistful, ironic, a lopsided grin. "It's kind of a woman thing. Maybe you could point out the disadvantages of being with me. Who knows better than you?"

"Maybe. We'll see."

"Give it a try." A wicked smile, drawing me in. His intensity made him seem as if he gave off a humming vibration, a swarm of bees or an imminent explosion: in any conversation, he was focused completely on the person in front of him, all attention, but also storing up their thoughts, mannerisms, stories for future use. I felt a melting sensation in my chest, stronger than anything I'd ever felt for a lover. Though what I felt for Robert was not at all erotic. More as if I were being killed.

I wondered again if I could return to professional life, after two months crying, eating pasta and sweets, and holding one or another of my nieces. The one good thing about being back in the Santa Cruz mountains was that it was only a half hour drive to River Valley, and we'd be able to work visits in and around our teaching and rehearsal schedules. It was painful to see our parents. Dad was grieving terribly, and Mom kept thinking that Eva had gone on a trip somewhere. Family members were split on reminding her or letting her live in a world where Eva was off having a great time, but I was never going to lie to her "for her own good," the way the family had lied to me.

Eva's family was undergoing dramatic changes. Ray, fragile, explosive, had quit his corporate law gig and was planning to set up shop on his own. Jenny, as usual, didn't say much about what was going on with her. The calmest and steadiest of Eva's children, she kept her crises as invisible as possible. But she had dropped a word or two to let us know that she and Brandon were having marital trouble. Katya had been arrested and given probation for spray-painting swastikas onto a hog-processing facility and resisting arrest. She'd lost her apartment, her job, and—thank God for small favors—the awful boyfriend she'd been dating. She had a new barista job and a room in a house full of activists in San Francisco's Mission District. Arielle, not working, staying with Katya, still seemed to be doing better than anyone else.

She'd been beyond wretched but in the last month or two had found a kind of equilibrium. We told ourselves Arielle had taken her mother's death as a kind of wake-up call, that she'd found a way toward something like peace. (What did we think—that she was meditating? With, maybe, a side order of Tibetan chanting?)

And Robert and I hadn't done well apart. While I was in New York, he and the company had written and performed a piece about Abu Ghraib to tiny, hostile audiences and scarring reviews.

NEWS OF THE MUD

Robert Zamarin's earnestly energetic little News-of-the-World Theater troupe—unfortunately minus the enlivening presence of its leading lady and other longtime players this season— seems to have descended into ever more self-referential, didactic circles. The claustrophobic set, its walls choked with newspaper clippings and enlarged photographs of uniformed soldiers and half-naked victims, matches the unremittingly dark and aggressive mood of the production. A number of new company members, who haven't yet found their footing, either literally or figuratively, seem to be unpleasantly surprised to find themselves in this high-toned but fairly muddy slum. Turning their back on both the pleasures of narrative and the challenges of nonlinear or experimental forms, the actors declaim their news stories, history, and statistics as if accusing the audience. Even the lighting and occasional flashes of music are unremittingly somber. Without the visual surprises, tonal changes, moments of playful humor, and vivid choreography of previous News-of-the-World pieces, a performance meant to enlarge our understanding of the world instead boxes itself into a painful solipsism full of loud emoting.

Though Robert and I didn't discuss the review, I remember being very upset, thinking he'd be enraged by the word "solipsism" and the one-sided description of the production. I felt impatient with the troupe, as I had when I'd seen the show, and annoyed, as usual, by my demotion from artistic partner and co-director to "leading lady." (Local newspapers, if and when they review us, have always described me as "Robert Zamarin's sister," or "Robert Zamarin's beautiful sister.")

My own reviews were not much better, and I was aware of Robert on the other side of the country possibly triumphing in them, undoubtedly seeing them as evidence that I should never have left News-of-the-World and could not make it outside our bubble.

NO HEARTBREAK IN THIS HOUSE

The casting is the weak spot of the Titan's well-meaning production of *Heartbreak House*. David Benson, perhaps too much the old-guard icon, is surprisingly one-dimensional and unconvincing as Captain Shotover: he seems here a would-be Brit, whose plummy manner fails to conceal a certain hollowness. Though he should provide the heft, the bass note, of the performance, he seems to have lost interest in the hard work of acting and appears to be showing up more out of force of habit than of conviction. Newcomer Julia Zamarin, though developing the aging loveliness to make a believable Hesione Hushabye, lacks the wiliness and force of character to carry off the part with any real flair. Sylvia Tanacross as Lady Utterwood is splendidly fey, but her efforts seem wasted, most of all because of Howard George's direction, which seems to waver from scene to scene, sometimes falling into a sententious, anti-war solemnity, at other times rising several octaves to become a shrilly arch domestic drama. Shaw's real bite, however, is gone, his wit muffled, and we are left with an endless, dreary tea party.

I agreed with this assessment of my castmates, though I would have been less harsh. The logical conclusion was that the reviewers were also right about me. Except how could a thirty-eight-year-old show *aging loveliness?* A fifty-year-old, maybe. But thirty-eight? Why did my family get old so fast? And did I not have force of character? I'd wept over the review: I had been afraid that it was Robert who made me wily and gave me force of character; I had been determined to stick it out, in love with the exacting broken-mirror world of Off-Off Broadway. Oh, how all this had mattered to me then, before Eva was gone. But I still didn't know whether and how my brother and I could work together again.

Our company hadn't always been awful: we'd toured the country with *Afghanistan / Iraq: Invasion Dances* and had been mentioned in sometimes surprisingly large-circulation newspapers. There was a clip from *Prison Stories* on YouTube, which had received more than eight thousand hits—nothing for YouTube, huge for us. Once upon a time, we'd had a handful of European performances in tiny experimental houses, at another, a short Japanese tour in alternative spaces, with thirty to fifty people in most audiences, many of them quite enthusiastic. At least fifteen or twenty. But we seemed to have lost whatever we'd had. We had to get it back, and we had to get it back now, with the second chance the Institute could give us, no matter what kind of shape we were in. I, for one, didn't have a whole lot of other choices, or, if I did, I wasn't up to going after them now.

We'd called our prospective new piece *Hunger* in the grant proposal and pre-performance publicity and promised a startling juxtaposition of texts and images, "news and anti-news." Whatever that meant. So far, our entire preparation for the piece consisted of scheduling performance dates, piling up research material to bring to the Institute, and sending our venues a poster with some ominous stick figures against an abstract background that faintly suggested a starving crowd. We were essentially starting from scratch and would have to work long, focused days to make our deadlines. I had never felt less like working in my life.

One more turn, and we found ourselves looking down the rutted road to a dirt parking lot full of old cars. Beside the lot sat the central lodge of the Scheherazade Institute, an immense, gabled rotted barn of a building, encircled by a redwood deck outfitted with picnic tables. The building, with its huge Comedy and Tragedy masks fixed above the door, looked as if it had been cobbled together in the middle of the night and might crumble back into the earth in daylight. Our new quarters lay at the bottom of a green valley, a wall of the giant redwoods rising up the hills in every direction, surrounding us.

Less than an hour away in one direction, vacationing crowds ran in and out of the tame waters of the Monterey Bay and screamed happily on the Ferris wheels and roller coasters of the Santa Cruz Beach Boardwalk. Less than an hour away in the other direction, in enormous gray-white buildings, people assembled semiconductors and debugged software. In the deep woods, the 24/7 virtual world seemed imaginary, a faraway dream. Even under very different circumstances, these woods were no place for city people. Everyone in the company knew when to look away from certain gestures in which money passed from hand to hand, where to find the cheapest tacos or *Pad Khee Mao*, how to live illegally in warehouses, and which sites had the best housesitting gigs. In these mountains, none of that was going to be of any use.

I struggled out of my side of the bus—Robert knew enough not to try to help me, and everyone else averted their eyes. On my canes, with my new, slow, leg-dragging walk, I had joined the ranks of the semi-invisible, along with the homeless and the very old: people's eyes skittered over me, as if it would be a faux pas to register me, maybe controlling their natural urge to gawk, maybe afraid of the possibilities I represented. When they did acknowledge me, their gestures became large and performative, and I found myself performing in return.

Alyx, Boyce, LaVerne, and Jolene piled out of their car, stretching. Vân Anh and Lisbeth were finishing up other commitments and would be arriving over the course of the next day or so. I didn't understand exactly how we would function without Jessie and Selene, who'd been part of the company since before it was News-of-the-World Theater, but they were gone and that was that. LaVerne stood beside the car, wearing a long embroidered dress, her braids wound into a crown, surveying the scene with appreciation. Jolene had a new set of tattoos—a rise and fall of birds across her arms. She could never have a straight job again, maybe, but that was true of most of us. And those birds could be beautiful in performance.

Alyx touched her toes and bent to each side, acting casual. She and I were having trouble meeting each other's eyes. When the group had convened in San Francisco before starting our drive, she'd said, "I am so, so sorry about your sister." The others chimed in, and there were tears and hugs. Now Alyx said, "Here goes nothing. Can you believe this place?"

I said. "Look at those trees. Look at that creek. The wildflowers. Is that lupine?" I had no idea what lupine looked like, but it sounded like something you'd find in the mountains. My heart rate had risen, being near her. From the outside, you wouldn't have any idea why she could make a person so crazy. In our performances, she often played a watching role. She'd do her little stick-like dances, a small bag of dry bones, a marionette, and the audience would begin noticing how she rattled and spun, not quite part of the action, not quite separate. Sometimes she'd perch somewhere on the stage, her face and body expressing critical hyperawareness of the other performers. If the audience didn't know how to feel, how to take something, they might find themselves looking to her for clues. She could undercut anything happening onstage, which made it possible for us to get away with wildly sentimental or didactic moments. Alyx, a ghost of detached observation, stood in for the audience so that they might even think, "Wait a minute." Or "These people have a point."

And yet in bed, she was another being altogether, an otter sliding through water, without judgment or thought, devoted entirely to pleasure. She made me feel as if it might be possible to be alive again. Nonetheless, I was not going to get in between her and Robert, not in any way known to man or woman. Let them work it out for themselves.

Alyx leaned against the dusty car. "We can admire the scenery as the place falls down on our heads while we sleep."

I waved a cane, largely. "Not a problem. I believe we're sleeping in the woods."

"At least Julia's back," said LaVerne. "Last year was way too Jacobean. Now we'll have some dancing and jokes again."

Other people looked chastened, though LaVerne didn't. Were they worrying about me not dancing? It had never been my forte. "Now you'll have some *sturm und drang* again," I said. Everyone laughed. I smiled and bowed: we were like a *commedia dell'arte* scene, just getting out of our cars. I couldn't imagine what rehearsal might be like.

Everyone took in the Lodge, the dirt parking lot, and the meadow. Six men in Elizabethan rags, their shirts dirty and torn, staggered in circles, their dialogue coming so fast that they stepped on each other's lines. These would be the other instructors—students could study/ perform with us or with the Cambridge Shakespeare Company. Not, by any means, the most well-known or respected of the local Shakespeare companies. Fairly uneven, though they sometimes had unexpectedly memorable productions. They were, I suppose, like us. I didn't know the other troupe, the Kundalini Dancers, whose mission statement mentioned Awakening the Inner Goddess.

On the ground near the men in rags, a girl appeared to be sleeping, a ghostly, lovely creature, her hair and skin so pale they were almost white. A young man sat on a stump beside her. "That's my noble master! What shall I do? Say what? What shall I do?"

At the far side of the meadow, a dozen naked people of all ages and sizes lined up, silent and tense, then began hiding behind each other, one after another. Some of the company, the younger women, seemed to have great gymnastic abilities. The older ones, like any aging dancers, had to find compensations, make up in expressiveness for what they lacked in flexibility or stamina. First they hid one at a time, then in twos and threes, enacting the terror of shame. One man stood facing an invisible audience, as if waiting for a firing squad. Three women, refusing to hide, formed into a pyramid, while two others, their bare bodies sweating in the summer sun, edged around the line, crouching, singing a low, grim, wordless song.

My skin prickled. Members of our company, not particularly prudish, blushed.

Boyce said, "Are those teachers or students?"

"I think they're renting space," said Robert. "There's a category called 'Visitors.'"

LaVerne said, "Please let them not be our students."

"They seem like they know what they're up to, whatever it is," Alyx said. "Look at this place. What a hole. What are the students paying for this summer?"

"A lot," I said. "But not for the décor. It's up to us to make it worth their while." She and I looked at each other, then away. I was working out a sisterly smile, but it came too late, and she was watching the naked people again.

Boyce said, "Serious, *serious* doubts about this gig," and Jolene poked him. The general manager of the Institute appeared at the doorway of the Lodge: Lenore, a big woman in her late fifties with a great deal of deep red hair piled on her head and secured with chopsticks. We made our way down to her, and she clasped our hands in hers and began to give us a tour of the building and its immediate surroundings. The Institute had begun in the 1920's as Camp Hope, she said, a charity organization designed to improve the characters and prospects of rough Irish kids from San Francisco and Los Angeles.

When something went badly wrong with the administration, a boy's organization had taken it over. Some of the boys, and even a few counselors, left early and unexpectedly, some of them trying to frighten their fellows into going as well. After one boy disappeared— his body found two days later in the creek bed, where he'd apparently fallen in the dark and broken his neck—the camp closed for more than a decade. It reopened as the Mind-Body Institute, began to offer movement and bodywork classes, and then Lenore, with the help of generous theater lovers, had invented it as the Scheherazade Institute, a combination theater school and retreat center.

Much of the information on the tour was news to us, since we'd never seen, though we'd always heard about, the Scheherazade Institute—famously uncomfortable, famously useful as a way to land better teaching jobs than any we'd ever had, with very decent pay. We'd be teaching two four-week intensive sessions that the Institute had titled "Experiments in Action: Dance-Theater Improv" and "Dance-Theater Production." The Institute promised, in its advertising, that students who signed up for both four-week intensives could help with and appear in the company's next show. We'd met the students briefly, months earlier, during the audition process, but we'd have no idea what we could do until we saw them in rehearsal.

Lenore led us around the Lodge and out toward the cabins. She also gave us the times for meals and the sign-up procedures for rehearsal spaces. The one phone in the office was available for brief calls, by special arrangement, and only from 9 a.m. to 8 p.m. We'd need phone cards for long distance. Shuddering slightly, she said that if we were ill, we needed to keep to our rooms, and if we were sick for more than a day or so, we'd need to get a room in town. She said, "All hours and regulations are posted in the dining hall. There aren't any exceptions, I'm afraid. You know how artists get, if you allow any leeway at all." Her laugh, a deep contralto, suggested a vast but vaguely unpleasant tolerance.

We made our way across the wooden bridge over the creek, up the dirt path into the redwoods, clambering over roots and rocks, pulling ourselves up steep patches by hanging onto tree trunks. I couldn't keep up; I was trying not to pant audibly as we climbed. I'd been in physical therapy practically every day for the first month I was awake and had sheets of follow-up exercises, but it was going to be a long haul, mastering and being mastered by pain. I'd had the usual dancer's aches, but this was something else. My level of pain felt uniquely terrible to me until my first post-hospital trip to a drugstore, when I stood in the aisle surrounded by dozens of painkillers, thinking, well, hello, honey, welcome to the real world and where have you been all these years?

I had to tuck one cane under my arm and use the other to pull myself forward. Step, drag, step, drag. A nice even dance step, though it could use a touch more variation. People were finding it hard to match the slowness of my gait, like being tied to an old record, played at the wrong speed, the voices drawn out agonizingly. Stopping to wait for me, everyone pretended to be admiring the view.

Lenore said, "You'll be three to a cabin—you can make your own arrangements. We haven't finished the insulation yet; we're hoping to do it later this summer. Or perhaps next summer, though that won't do you much good." She laughed again, looking around, investigating us for signs of temperament.

"Are you a theater person?" I asked.

"I'm a singer," said Lenore. She stopped in the middle of the path, placed her palms on her diaphragm and inhaled deeply, her great rib cage expanding as she sang, "When I am la-iad, am la-a-a-aid in earth, may my wro-o-ongs create, no trou-ou-ble, no trou-ou-ble in thy breast." Her voice could have filled San Francisco's War Memorial Opera House; a half dozen crows, startled, flew up through the trees.

"Dido's lament." She started up the hill again, briskly, and we arrived at a fork in the path—up the hill to the left sat a set of little A-frame cabins. Unfinished, no more than shells with cutout openings for doors and windows, a small deck. There might be room for three cots for our sleeping bags, with perhaps a foot of room in between them. Off to our right, at the edge of a side trail that led up the creek and deeper into the woods, sat another A-frame, a bit hard to see from the main path.

Lenore said, "The students will be in the dorm by the Lodge, but we've found it better for the companies to have their own places." She laughed. "What with the construction, it's worse than usual this summer, I'm afraid. Each cabin has a composting toilet out back. Some people set up bucket showers, but there are also two showers with hot water upstairs at the Lodge. No sign-ups for those. People take their chances on that." Her minatory look suggested this was our first test.

Robert said, "I'm sorry, but this is impossible. My sister is injured. She needs a bed, easy access to a bathroom. I called about this."

I couldn't believe he was saying this in front of everyone, or that he'd secretly tried to make arrangements for me. We all had sleeping bags. I'd assumed I was going to have to make this work.

Lenore said, "Alas, I'm afraid it's all we have. I'm so terribly sorry. But I don't want you to worry if you don't feel able to do it, dears. We have a couple of companies who couldn't be accommodated this summer but are very eager to be here. Of course, there's something about being at the Scheherazade Institute, and, if I might say so, about having *been* at the Scheherazade Institute. But it's completely your choice. You don't have to let me know right away. Take the afternoon to think it over." She smiled.

Bluffing, I thought. What would she tell the students if we took off? But she clearly knew we wouldn't. Probably this happened every summer. She didn't have any idea what was wrong with me; for all she knew, I'd pulled a muscle dancing.

"We don't need the afternoon to decide," I said. "I'll be fine. If the company is fine?" People nodded, dubious, and I went on, "We're delighted to be here. Very honored. Robert?" I poked him in the side, my face saying, We don't have any other choices right now. He shook his head, but what was he going to do?

Aloud, he said, "LaVerne, you and Lisbeth can have one of the cabins up the hill, and Boyce can be in the other. Jolene, you'll share with Vân Anh when she arrives. Alyx, Julia, and I will take the cabin to our right. It's closest to the Lodge."

"You're the boss," said Alyx, and began to walk back to the car to get her things. This power play was some part of his master plan. Did he really want to break up with her? Did he want her to get back together with me? Did he have some more complex idea going on?

My immediate impulse was to spend as much time away from the cabin as possible. Not the Lodge, full of students, no place to be when one of the uncontrollable attacks of tears seized me. And *not* these woods. There was no place to go. There was no one but Robert to go to. Panic surged up in my stomach, my chest, closing everything down. I took his arm, pressing my forehead against his shoulder, feeling the heat of his skin, smelling his faintly spicy sweat, his tea tree shampoo. I restrained an urge to bite him. I didn't know myself anymore.

Our own cabin, semi-obscured by redwoods, was another triangular A-frame, the doorway and two windows empty spaces. Someone had begun to drywall the cabin and then apparently been called away to another project—a couple of chalky panels covered one wall, a single piece of insulation was tacked up on another, beginning to shred, the silver paper peeling back to reveal yellow batting. The cabin jutted out to the very edge of the creek.

Trying to catch my breath, I sat on the fern-covered, mossy bank, dipping my fingers into the trickle of summer water running over and around river rocks. An old tire, some rags, and half of a chair lay in the path of the creek, which swirled around their algae-covered shapes, making a small, unscenic waterfall.

Robert rolled out his sleeping bag on the cot right in front of the door, the worst, least restful spot. He believed that certain responsibilities came with being director: not only pushing everyone past their limits as artists and breaking them down until they became capable of work they'd never previously imagined, but also ensuring the physical safety of the troupe. Whatever his faults, he never used his position for small advantages.

Alyx and I would sleep on either side of him, with about a foot between the cots. Robert went back to the bus for another load, and we began to roll out our own sleeping bags. I said, "Well, this is awkward."

She still wasn't quite meeting my eyes. She looked down at her cot with a small, fond smile. I wasn't sure whether the smile was for Robert or me. "Somehow it seems as if there should be a new word for this. Awkward doesn't begin to cover it."

"So do you know why he's come up with this arrangement?"

"I never know what he's up to. I thought maybe you'd have some clue."

Maybe this was part of his plan to break up with her. I was going to say, if I kill him, you could dispose of the body. But it might not sound as if I were joking. And should I be joking? Sometimes, with the nieces we found ourselves suddenly laughing before looking at each other guiltily, as if Eva would mind, as if we'd betrayed her.

I hoped that rehearsing, finally being back at work, would make me tired enough to stop the nightmares. After the attack, during the weeks I'd been in a coma, I know I dreamed, violently, but it all evaporated as soon as I woke up and began the slow business of relearning to live in a world where I had let Eva be killed. I had *felt* what was coming in those woods—not that we were going to be shot, but that something bad was on its way. I could have insisted and gotten us both out alive. I wished I could remember the attack. Or the dreams. (Something I was supposed to do—what was it?) When I tried to reach the memories, my mind became a dark, swirling space. But I couldn't leave it alone. The dreams, and whatever obligation they held for my waking life, still called to me from outside the edges of my mind.

On our way down to the Lodge, we heard the crows calling harshly in the trees, drowning out the sounds of the creek. The redwoods had a thick, inhabited quality, lumps and knobs cropping up unexpectedly. Summer poison oak crowded the sides of the path. The golden air filtering down through the redwoods flattened, lost some of its color. High, light cries filled the air. Not bird cries. They sounded like words, echoing back and forth across the valley and through the trees, but I couldn't make out what, if anything, the voices were saying.

For our first dinner at the Institute, we entered the enormous kitchen and drew table names written on scraps of paper. A woman from the naked company presented each person with a metal dish printed with Barnum & Bailey posters and containing the names of the tables. The company was here officially after all, though their materials hadn't made it into our packets. The office had given us an addendum, which included more rules and Naked-Nude-Human's mission statement, all about nature and culture, the naked and nude, the confrontation of innocence and shame.

Overhead, the raw wooden ceiling beams rose in a pitch that reached its apex in the Great Hall next door. The kitchen itself had an eight-burner stove, a walk-in refrigerator. A few interns, hair in scarves and hands in rubber gloves, pulled pans of chocolate chip cookies out of the oven.

Some people drew a table in the steamy kitchen, others of us wound up out on the deck. I had a winning lottery pick: I'd be sitting at Arden, a table overlooking the meadow on one side and the pool and hot tub on the other. The creek bounded that side of the property, the forest rising up on all sides behind.

Many of the kitchen tables were empty—the students wouldn't arrive for a couple of days, and the Institute staff sat by themselves, away from the rest of us. Most of the deck tables had filled up with a mix of instructors and paying visitors. Robert was nowhere to be seen. He wasn't going to start skipping meals altogether, was he?

I filled my plate with spaghetti in a thin marinara sauce and salad from the vats on the counter and then had to decide whether to carry it myself, with one hand, seeing if I could get by with only one cane. I tucked the other cane under my arm and began lurching across the floor, looking for Arden, but didn't make it three feet before a stranger said, "May I?" and took my plate away, smiling.

"Thank you," I said, and tried to hurry out to the deck, the kind stranger following behind.

Arden had some *Tempest* people—including Caliban and Prospero—and a few of the naked people. I sat down, shaking hands all around, and the naked woman who'd been talking smiled at me in welcome. I'd guessed, from her manner with the others, that she was the company director. In her late sixties or early seventies, she had a broad, reddish, sunburnt body, brown around the arms and shoulders, pinkish in the rolls of flesh on her back and belly, freckled across her breasts. She had a big plate of food, not fighting her middle-aged hungers. Did they perform anywhere? Wouldn't I have heard about them? It hurt to imagine their physical dangers and slights, but I admired this director, radiant in her skin, even with the bones wearing away and cartilage dissolving into her blood.

Eva had said once, "Oh, Julia, why are you so smitten by every huge narcissist you meet? I swear, you collect these people," and I'd answered, "I like to be around people who revel in being themselves." And when she sighed, I asked, "If you don't like narcissists, how do you stand being a part of this family?" She laughed, not happily, and pulled a strand of my hair.

Tears prickled around the edge of my eyes and I pinched myself, hard. Caliban was asking the director, "Isn't it painful, to be so exposed?"

The naked girl across the table from him—a redhead in her twenties, her face freckled, her body spattered with velvety moles—said, "It's like turning to face the monster in your nightmare, when you realize that you can't get away from it by running." She blushed, red spreading up to her hairline and down her neck and onto the tops of her breasts. The whole table watched, and in pretending not to know that she was being watched, she blushed harder.

Alyx came out of the kitchen, headed toward Arden with her tray and a look of tense resignation. I made room for her at the table, smiling and swinging my hair over my shoulder. She smiled back, a complicated smile that seemed to encompass our whole history, including her opinion of my vanity, as well as the difficulty of our new relationship, maybe even her pretense that we were, and always had been, buddies. Sisterly. With her dark hair and pale skin, her watchful look, she had sometimes reminded me of Eva. But when I'd said this to Robert, way back when he first started up with her, he'd said, "Please don't make this any more unfortunate than it already is."

And what did she see in us? She'd admitted she liked my divergent mind, my inability to sort things out, morally, intellectually, in terms of my emotions. "You look so calm and wise from the outside," she'd said, mischievous. And Robert? I don't know, but she watched us both, all the time. Well, we love an audience, don't we? We're most ourselves in front of one.

The crowded table, the bland spaghetti and damp salad, and the endless discussion had really gotten to me. Surely I was over-reading the situation. "Hey, roomie," I said, regretting the remark as soon as I'd said it.

She gave me a look of acknowledgment: she wasn't any happier about our inadvertent ménage à trois than I was. At least she'd met my eyes this time. We were making progress. She set down her tray next to me, took her chair, and began to shovel in her dinner—for such a tiny creature, she ate like an orphan in the workhouse.

Her life had made it impossible for her not to root under rocks in the darkest possible way, a secretive creature, judging silently, even while smiling or offering up excessively courteous remarks. She almost never talked about her history, but I think that, like us, she came from crazy. Once she'd said something about her father smashing the glass pane in their door after her mother had locked him out, and then her parents throwing their wedding rings into the woods, hunting uselessly for them afterward. They used to refer to each other, she said, as "My future ex." Another time, in the middle of the night, she said that she sometimes wondered about the effects of a life of professional make-believe, and I could see her, when she was occasionally temperamental in rehearsal, scanning herself for signs of her genetic inheritance: maybe someday she would no longer know where the edges of reality lay, what she was making up, and what truly existed.

Prospero, still Prospero even in jeans and a white shirt, tore off bits of French bread and rolled them into balls. He had an apparently habitual expression of deeply humorous awareness, as if he knew what the world was like and yet had forgiven it and everyone in it. I couldn't even imagine the level of understanding it would take to encompass the unforgivable world. I knew it was possible: I just didn't know how a person would get there. He said, "The essence of acting is nakedness under the mask. You all seem to be reversing this. Fascinating."

"Hair, scars, and lumps," said the director. "We're holding up a mirror to the audience. No airbrushing here."

I was wishing they'd sit on newspapers or towels, rather than directly on the benches. These oozing, primordial beings. Maybe the opposite of distortion is truth, or maybe it's another kind of distortion. They seemed embedded in their ideas, their politics, like scarabs in resin.

"That's what we do," said Alyx. "Performing the news. A different kind of mirror."

A young Shakespearean, bearded and graceful, said, "Why be an actor if not because you can't bear being who you are?" From the outside, at least, he appeared boyishly unburdened.

The director answered, "And yet you don't escape the limits of your body, your voice, your physical being. You're Ferdinand, aren't you?" The boy smiled. "No one would cast you as Caliban or Prospero or even as Miranda, except perhaps as an experimental gesture." She turned to Prospero. "And you will never be Ferdinand again."

Most of the table averted their eyes. Prospero, performing rueful acceptance, bowed, saying, "It always comes down to the audience loving us. And maybe to our testing that love."

I said, "We're not so interested in being loved. Or liked for that matter. For us, it's about *making something* that never existed and, in the process giving people what—if they only knew it—they sometimes need worse than food or medicine."

Despite there being no students yet, the din flooding out onto the deck was incredible, as if we were inside the Lodge itself, with people laughing and shouting. The Kundalini Company seemed quite large and close-knit: almost all women—mostly white, mostly young—with long hair and batik dresses or harem pants. They moved back and forth between the tables, laughing and acting out anecdotes using undulating hip circles and fluid snakelike arms.

I was thinking for the thousandth time that what we did (for a living? As an obsession?) was partially out of a bewildered curiosity about the lives of others, partially about the pleasures of pretending, and partially about a ravening hunger for love and attention. All these theories were ways of dressing up our need, like taking a wolverine and decking it out in a little hat and matching sweater.

Prospero folded his arms, nodding at me. "Without what we do, without our *stories,* people would spend their whole lives going to work, eating chips in front of the television, bopping around on YouTube, and suffering all the cheery tortures of an unnamed hell."

Fighting the sense of being caught in a waking nightmare—the word "hell" producing an inexplicable panic, an immediate sense of the loss of my sister—I bent my head over my food. Eva had so despised what we did, though she tried to be fair. She'd said once, years earlier, before so many things had gone wrong, "I hope you don't take this wrong. But I wonder sometimes. My kids make things up, they play games, dress up in costumes and pretend. But then when they're about twelve, the real world starts to click in. It's as if they begin to wake up. Or sometimes people stay in a half-sleepy pretend world well into college. But you and Robert . . .do you ever wonder what happened?" Her intent inquiry: the scientist determined to get to the bottom of things.

"You mean why didn't we grow up like normal people?" But no one in our family could exactly be said to be normal. Though probably it depended on your definition.

Eva had patted my arm, to show she was trying to help. Her eyes showed so much intelligence, but there was a wall partway in, like looking at the reverse side of a one-way mirror. You could never see into her hidden places.

When I finally pulled myself together, the conversation had moved on—an argument over happiness and meaning, whether theater brought meaning to a life, whether parenting might, what about work that mattered? A doctor's work had meaning, but what about an artist's? All of that kind of thing.

Alyx had a sympathetic expression I couldn't bear. I said, "Have you seen Robert?"

"Wasn't he here earlier?"

"I didn't see him."

"He *has* to eat," she said, and I nodded. We were more together on this than we had been on almost anything since she and I were lovers. I didn't know why she was with Robert. He was probably the most important person in my life—certainly now—but I couldn't imagine deliberately choosing him out of millions of men in the world. I wanted to ask her what she thought she was doing. But of course I was left with my own silent speculations and amateur psychologizing.

I said, "Let's go see if he's somewhere in the Lodge. There's still time for him to get some food."

We cleared our trays into the bins, scraping leftovers into the compost, handing our dishes to the people on the dishes shift, and heading into the great hall, an enormous, beamed vault that smelled of smoke from the fireplace, a hint of old sweat from years of rehearsals and performances, garlic and oregano from dinner. The room had been designed for banquets or meetings but now it had a stage at one end. Dancers ran from side to side, leaped, crumpled, lay still, rose again, in front of an audience of folding chairs, empty, except for their director/choreographer, who was taking notes, and a dancer, in sweats, leg warmers, and a neck brace, drinking juice and practicing cautious stretches.

Alyx and I made our way into the corridor—old dark wood hung with show posters—and peeked into a prop closet full of half-broken coffee pots, plastic swords, helmets, hats and cloaks, and half-burnt candles, all of it smelling of must and stage makeup. The locked door next to the closet had a hand-lettered sign saying, "Private."

Alyx said, "If I were paying what the students are paying, I'd mind the hell out of this place."

"Maybe they'll find it romantic. Artistic."

"Julia, did anyone ever tell you that an excess of optimism can be really annoying?" We were walking upstairs—a short phrase that hardly expresses what it was to make, in front of Alyx, a complicated clamber with my canes under my arm, holding onto the rail, getting the legs up one at a time. Alyx said, her tone changing, "Are you doing okay?"

"As okay as anyone would expect." I didn't want sympathy, exactly, though I'd be lying to myself if I said I didn't want people to be aware of my situation, to refrain from chattering away about wonderful outings with their sisters or to ask me to do things that would make my physical situation worse. Though I myself kept ignoring the warnings my newly stubborn body laid out for me in the form of new and greater pains.

She said, "He could be up at the cabin," and I answered, "There's nothing to do there. And we're upstairs now, so we may as well look around."

Two small rehearsal rooms had been abandoned in a hurry, chairs pushed all over, empty cups left behind. Both the second-floor bedrooms had open luggage, clothes thrown over the bed or chairs, the chaos of visitors whose toiletries also filled the counters of both bathrooms. The far end of the hall opened into a parlor, crammed with old furniture, with huge dormer windows on three sides. The remaining wall held a pair of Chinese scrolls, ancient mountains, a rainstorm, over an old piano. The air was full of thick spices, a dark, unforgiving smell.

Under the windows that faced the road sat an altar draped with purple cloth, scattered with used tickets and arranged with old linotypes of actors and actresses I didn't recognize, a rusty oversized key painted with what could have been bloodstains, a set of sugar skulls, and a clear plastic box jammed to its brim with ill-assorted objects. Through the plastic, I could see a primitive Venus carved of brown soap, artificial flowers, Japanese soda cans, and Styrofoam packing pellets. Handmade cloth puppets lay across the top of the box. Incense and votive candles burned away on the altar.

The altar felt inhabited by a tangible sense of wrongness, of avidity, the borders between worlds deliberately elided, the hinges on the doors between broken open. Alyx said, "I hate this room—it's totally creepy. I can't be in here." Without waiting for an answer, she walked out.

I couldn't seem to move. Over the altar, the air shimmered, a dark gold light, and I saw, or imagined, a shining, cold, beaked presence appearing in the air, several feet high, its topaz eyes staring at me, blindly, as if seeing past me to another reality or as if I didn't exist.

A primitive terror possessed me, the feeling that I could be swallowed by whatever it was that watched and never come back to the world. The thing fixed its eyes on me but there was no communication between us. I wanted to cry out but, as in a dream—aren't I dreaming then? I asked myself—couldn't make a sound.

I don't know how long this lasted. A few minutes. Forever.

Then it was gone and Alyx was calling from the hall, "What's wrong with you, Julia?" A question far too big for me to begin to answer.

She came back, tugged at my arm, and we bolted, a slow business in my case, even with her help.

Out in the meadow, my legs and hips aching, we stopped and looked back.

"Did you see it?" I asked.

She shook her head, staring. "What did you see?"

"Nothing. Something I imagined. That room upset me."

"It got to me too," she said, "Don't tell anyone about this. Nobody would understand."

"I didn't think you cared what anyone thought. And what is there to tell? We're just children, scaring ourselves."

She said, very low, "I don't like it here. The whole place feels like an invitation to mischief."

"Like we need an invitation."

"Wouldn't you think we'd all be nicer to each other? I mean, given that our whole lives are about revealing the structures of cruelty and deception?"

"I don't think it necessarily follows," I said.

She put a friendly arm around my shoulders, and we walked

through the dark meadow toward the porch with its lanterns, round Japanese shapes that moved in the breeze. Pools of light slid back and forth, their edges very black. We could see, as we approached the Lodge, the whole company leaning against the edge of the railing—tossing small sticks in the direction of the creek, some kind of contest, evidently.

IMPROV

On the night before our students arrived, I woke several times in the black, completely lightless dark, hearing the rustling of animals in the woods. How had I known not to walk in the woods with Eva? Why hadn't I been stronger with her, stopped where I was, refused to go any further, pulled her back out with me? I kept turning over, as quietly as possible, trying to find a position that hurt less. My brother and Alyx were breathing deeply, each in their own too-familiar ways.

There's something oppressive about sleeping bodies when you're wide awake, your brain full of 4 a.m. chemicals. You're afraid of disturbing them, maybe jealous, feeling entirely excluded from the world of rest. Though I wanted to get up and out of there, I was afraid of my own clumsiness, the possibility of kicking someone in the head as I tried to make my way out of the cabin. Maybe the shining beaked thing was somewhere out there. A double fear: either I might be going as mad as my mother or the presence was real. If those were my choices, I wanted the thing to be real. I wanted to call Eva for advice: but I would never talk to her again.

That thought was always like being dropped into a deep pit, falling through space. A sense of her Eva-ness came over me all at once—her particular mixture of sharp humor, focused intelligence, and loving impatience. The feeling that she was always about to escape, that no matter how you tried to catch hold of her and keep her, she would find a way to disappear. I began crying again, silently, into my pillow. I had to stop, or I would wake Robert and Alyx: I focused on breathing exercises until I finally became drowsy.

Toward morning, I was carrying a letter but had forgotten what it was and who it was for, though not that it was urgent. I found my way into a dark corridor, the walls entirely covered with wooden cubbyholes, none of which had names on them. A feeling of anxiety possessed me, all out of proportion to the situation.

I awoke to the sounds of Robert and Alyx having sex, outside but not far enough from the cabin. They were trying to be quiet and had perhaps not noticed or had forgotten the cutouts in the walls that served for windows. If I slunk out, they'd know I'd heard them. It was both arousing and revolting to hear their breathing, their suppressed moans. I remembered the way Alyx would lash from side to side as she came, the thrill of having to hold her down. When we were finally done, she'd turn over, and I'd wrap myself around her, both of us sliding into a blissful, trusting rest.

I rolled over, pressed a pillow over my ears, and tried to go back to sleep or at least to pretend until it was time to wash in the cold water bucket we kept behind a sheet above the creek. When they came back in, I was on my stomach with my eyes closed, breathing as regularly as I could, but I suspected they knew I was pretending.

Eventually we all made a show of waking up, made our way stiffly through the morning fog, joined up with the rest of the company, sat with whomever we had drawn at the tables, and worked our way through piles of scrambled eggs, hot cereal, toast. Those who ate, anyway—most of the women in the company, and now Robert, subsisted largely on nutritional bars, fruit, half-salads, or vegetable soup. I had half a bowl of cereal. Too much pasta in the last few months, combined with my not having figured out a way to dance, had started to make my clothes tight. Not that I was really wearing anything with a waist band—I was living in knits, mostly rehearsal clothes, sweat pants and pullovers. Robert, once again, ate almost nothing, and I didn't feel like eating even my small serving of oatmeal. The prospect of meeting our new students made the morning too exciting, and too nerve-racking.

Ariel sat on the porch railing, swinging his feet, singing. "Come unto these yellow sands, and then take hands. Curtsied when you have, and kiss'd the wild waves whist." Soon enough, he'd be getting to those bones lying full fathom five and "nothing of him that doth fade but doth suffer a sea change."

Here's what was on my mind that morning: we had a lot of logistics to balance. We'd have twenty-four students for the first month, fewer than a dozen staying on for the production workshop and the show. I had pre-teaching nerves. Who was showing up—how would they get along with each other? How would the group settle in? Who would be the ones with the great needs for attention, who might be hanging back or have performance issues they hadn't faced?

Lenore apparently couldn't keep assistants. Tracy, the girl currently holding the position, was always off wandering the woods or hanging out doing nothing much. "Oh, yes!" she'd said in the first few days, whenever anyone made a request, and then, when reminded, "Right, right. I'll get on it immediately!" And then nothing would happen. But at least she was agreeable. So we were on our own, administratively, which we were used to and mostly preferred, though it would have been nice, given how long it took to get into town, to have a reliable source of supplies.

By 9:00, we were checking in the students and getting to know them—Jason, Tanikah, Jon, Roxanne, Sherrie, Mel, Johanna, Marcus, Phoebe. Right now, they were, of course, strangers, undifferentiated from each other, disguised by their scarves and piercings, their costumes. They inhabited their bodies with a tentative impulsiveness—one girl was doing downward-facing dog on the porch—more fluid, less defined, maybe less professional than the prospective Shakespeareans, arriving at the same time, who seemed to have had quite a bit of training: they showed it in their carriage, their voices, the precision of their gestures. But as we met the students, I realized that though I'd mostly been right in my guesses, some of those I'd thought were ours went off to the Shakespeareans, and we had one or two of the incipient pros. Maybe they were looking to loosen up or expand their theatrical arsenal.

Tanikah, a theater arts major from Berkeley in her early twenties, small and compact, with a New York accent, said, "I hadn't expected so many *white* people," and LaVerne said, "Early days yet. I'll let you know if and when it's time to run." They exchanged smiles that said this was probably going to be okay, or at least okay enough. ("Good enough for government work," as one of the teachers we'd worked with used to say after rehearsals for a student performance.)

Jon, a handsome boy in his late twenties, long blond dreads and a sunny face, earned his living delivering medical marijuana and had been to two or three colleges, none of which had quite worked out. He'd told me all of this on the phone, engagingly, while he was deciding whether or not to register. During his check-in, he said, "Is somebody doing yoga lessons yet? Because I could totally do free drop-in early morning yoga in that meadow."

"You can never have too much yoga," said Tracy, who was, alarmingly, helping out with the sign-ins. I was going to make sure I procured copies of those sheets before she could squirrel them away somewhere we'd never see them again.

Sherrie, a triumphantly girlish woman in her fifties, who'd been born Stan and only been Sherrie for the last five years, wanted to make sure that we knew to use the pronouns "sie" and "hir" which sie preferred. I had already begun thinking in female pronouns, was going to have to adjust. Sie was very trim, with long hair, expensively dressed, hir children grown, finally able to pursue hir lifelong dream of acting.

Every student who came in shifted the nature of the group as a whole and added to the kinds of work we could do. Ideally, we would have a company of thirty people. What couldn't we do with all those bodies and souls?

They all went off to the dorm, those who were here—a few would be arriving late. At 10:00, we began our work together. We went around the room, each person coming up with a gesture and sound to go with their name and the rest of us echoing that. I fell for them immediately, in the semi-parental way teachers fall for their students. No, not parental: you feel free to let them make their own mistakes and decisions. So maybe it's like the fierce appreciation you'd have for a grove of redwoods or a stream.

We had the smaller rehearsal room, a converted storeroom with a single window, dark redwood walls, a concrete floor with an old shag carpet, and costumes and masks piled in a big trunk and hung from hooks. Feathered masks lay in a heap on the floor. A plastic pig snout hung underneath a bowler hat by the window. Outside the window, some of the naked women rehearsed in the meadow by the pool.

Robert introduced the structure of the summer. "We're glad to have you with us. You're bringing in all kinds of experience, backgrounds, and interesting knowledge. We're going to start right from the beginning, to get a common vocabulary. We'll open with energy and focus work, trust games, learning to listen, learning to react in the moment. You can't be somewhere else when you're on stage, not even in the moment that's supposed to happen fifteen seconds from now.

"Later we'll move into bridge work, bringing in some elements of Theater of the Oppressed, including Forum Theater, Rainbow of Desire, and then we'll make short pieces, solo and group. For those of you who will be staying on for the performance—and it's not too late to sign up for the second half of the summer as well—talk to Julia about that if you'd like to, and keep an eye out during this early work for elements we can use as we begin the second half of the summer and the preparation of our hunger performance."

He wasn't kidding—we needed everyone's input. We'd been collecting statistics and information, looking for surprising anecdotes and approaches, but we were hoping for new material from the students. All summer, we'd keep coming back to the question of hunger, or hungers, which we'd explore along with questions of power and theatricality. And, of course, technique. Because you don't need less technique when you're doing political work, you need at least as much. Though of a different kind.

As he talked, I was thinking about all this, and what I'd be saying if I were running the orientation, but I also found myself highly aware of Alyx. We sat in a circle on the floor—most people sat on the floor—a couple of us were in chairs. She had her feet in a diamond shape and was holding them while pressing her back forward, inconspicuously stretching while she listened. Her face had the peaceful lines of a creature who'd been thoroughly sated in the night, but I tried to tune her out.

Robert always took over the introductions, the explanations of new projects. In earlier years I'd sometimes tried to make sure the company or students were hearing from me as well as from him. But my efforts made things awkward, often turning into a low-key public power struggle. These days, I mostly stayed in the background, giving way to his bold, electric charm and ability to sum things up with great concision and force.

After all, I was an essential member of our theatrical and teaching partnership, the one who reined in or softened the most ludicrous ideas, the one who looked after the students emotionally. It would be nice if Robert could be kinder. He could be kind to me, of course, or Alyx, and sometimes he was great with our nieces or with the company members, if I were there to catch the rough moments. But he was often difficult with students, wanting to scold them into improving. Also, less forgivably, he found their moments of clumsiness to be an offense against the art form he loved.

In the beginning, though, he could bring the whole group together, convey the sense of the urgency and delight of what we needed to do. He said, "I'm about to teach you the most important thing you'll learn all summer . . . the failure bow. How do you feel when you've failed? Show me with your bodies, say what you'd say."

"I failed," said someone. Boyce said, enthusiastically, "I screwed up!" The students were slow at first, then entered into it, bending down, staring at the ground, melting with shame. "I fucked up!" "I failed!"

"All right then," said Robert. "Now stand like winners. You've just had a triumph."

People put their hands on their hips and squared their shoulders, or raised their arms in victory salutes, and Robert cried out, "Say it again! Louder!" He pumped his fist. "I failed!"

We all strode around the room, making our victory salutes, chests out, crying out, "I screwed up! I failed!" Robert said, "Do this whenever you make a mistake! You took a risk! You learned something! You failed! Woo-hoo!" The students giggled at first, tentative, embarrassed for us as well as for themselves, but soon they'd be making mistakes on purpose for the pleasure of celebrating them. Jon especially loved this. He cried out, "I fucked up!" several times in a row, looking into each of our eyes in turn to see that we were celebrating with him. It was impossible not to return his smile.

As for me, as I made the way around the room on my canes, struggling to lift my arms to say the words, for the first time in my life my body seized with performance panic. The full deal: trouble breathing, such terrible nausea that I had to briefly leave the room to be sick in the hall bathroom, cold sweats. I said to myself, maybe it's the flu, maybe it's food poisoning. I'd always been secretly proud of myself for never really having stage fright, had pitied Piers and every other sufferer. I believed I had no self to be self-conscious about. Now, though, I had a sense of people *looking* at me, that I wasn't up to this, and everyone knew it.

When I limped back into the room, slowly, Robert said, under his breath, "Don't do anything that hurts. Sit down if you have to."

I whispered back, "You don't have to pamper me, Robert. I can look after myself."

But the fear continued until, half an hour or so later, Lenore stood in the doorway, beckoning to me, her face forbidding. My first thought was that she somehow knew Alyx and I had been in the altar room— but had anyone said it was off-limits?

When I reached her, she held out a couple of pieces of paper. "Someone called for you in the night. And again first thing in the morning and again just now. Katie, I think. She said she had to talk to you directly. Then, this morning, that she'll be driving here with— Ariel? She said they'll need a bed right away."

"What else?" My bones had gone hollow, and I leaned on my canes.

"This is unacceptable," said Lenore. "No overnight visitors. No out-of-hours phone calls."

"They're company members," I said. "They're late arriving and don't know the rules yet. My apologies. I'll tell them as soon as they get here." Maybe it was nothing, why leap to conclusions? Katya had been fired again, the two wanted a vacation, they didn't realize the situation here and thought they could come to the mountains and hang out in the hot tub.

Then why had Katya called in the middle of the night? Maybe Arielle was doing drugs, and Katya wanted to get her away from her crowd. But she'd been clean so long. The sense of some painful memory or undone task tugged at me again.

Lenore had a grand nod—Elizabeth I of England could not have had more magisterial dignity. The chopsticks in her hair dipped and rose with the movement of her head. "The cabins are all full. You'll have to fit them in."

"Is there any way they can stay in the Lodge? We can pay the visitor fee." We couldn't, but what was more debt, given our load? An enormous floating creature, a kind of translucent paramecium that traveled with us everywhere, hovering over our heads and humming to us, "I can never be paid off" and "You will never retire."

"The rooms are full." And then, relenting a bit, "No one is using the parlor now."

"The room with the altar?"

"That's the only space if you can't get them into a cabin."

They couldn't be up there. Unless, maybe—could the altar be rearranged or disassembled? Reluctantly, a step at a time, I went upstairs, bracing myself for the wrongness, the beaked presence. I hummed under my breath, feeling like a madwoman on my way to the attic. "Come unto these yellow sands, and then take hands." Something I'd heard recently, but I couldn't place it. I stood outside the room for a long time, thinking of the girls, then pushed the door open.

It was a room, that was all. An old altar with some draperies, sugar skulls, burnt out incense and candles. The scroll paintings on the wall, the old piano, all of it entirely sad, faded, unremarkable. I worried again about what was happening with Katya and Arielle but said to myself, it has to be okay. It's probably an impromptu vacation. Don't make a drama out of everything.

I went back down to rehearsal, where Robert was leading warm-up games: sound ball, word-at-a-time stories, fortunately/unfortunately—it was all about getting everyone into the center of the room, having them realize they could jump into the circle before they had an idea, that something would come to them. There was no point in interrupting—one of us needed to keep our focus. Time inched forward, minute by minute. Company members showed students how to mirror each other, exactly, then with distortions, and finally in exaggerated amazement at the beauty of our reflections. We sculpted each other, then took turns leading and following, dancing each other around the room, the followers with their eyes closed, moving blindly.

Robert said to one shy girl, Mel, "Jump in, dear—you're not going to get any better by hiding in a corner. Don't worry about being clumsy. Lots of people are. You have to *use* that." She ran out in tears, and I made my slow way out after her, and wound up hearing the whole story of her family. Robert reminds so many of them of their fathers, which shouldn't surprise me anymore. I was trying to pay full attention to Mel, but most of my brain was dedicated to the girls. But no one was in jail or the ER. Maybe Katya had called around ten, and Lenore had exaggerated.

Mel, her whole story witnessed, said, "Fuck Robert!" and I agreed. "He's right about my being clumsy, though," she said, looking up at me out of the corner of her eyes, hoping I might disagree.

"You're still looking for ways to use your particular gifts. You have some unusual ways of moving. You're resisting the obvious, which is already great. So you have to make what you're doing even greater so people can see how surprising and memorable those moves can be. Pay attention to when and how you undercut fluidity, and think about what the quality of 'clumsiness' might mean, which of your favorite performers make use of unexpected and startling movements." I was saying to her almost what Robert had, in different words and a different tone, but she threw her arms around me, and with all that settled, we went back into the rehearsal hall.

I realized I had to tell Robert what was happening and whispered to him at midmorning break that the girls were on their way. He had an expression of surprised annoyance, but there was no time to talk it over.

Late in the morning, we were in the middle of a session of "Complete the Image." The students, paired up, each frozen into positions

in relation to each other, created silent mini-scenes: a mugging, someone caring for a sick child, two people staring down at a mysterious
object on the ground, working with each other's body language. One
would unfreeze, choose a new position, and start another scene.

Katya appeared in the doorway, a denizen of another, more terrible world—her eyes red behind her new cat's-eye glasses, her face
smeary, her clothes filthy. I wanted to run to her, but there was no
inconspicuous way for me to move quickly across a room. She was
staring at us, a little glazed, unsure.

The students didn't seem to see her, but Robert, who'd been traveling the room observing and sometimes stepping in, became one of
the statues, gazing at our oldest niece a long moment. He clapped
his hands and said, "A wonderful morning, people. Let's break for
lunch. You've done a splendid job, you're much better at staying in
the moment and reacting to your partners, not anticipating or planning ahead. This afternoon, we'll move on to some demechanization
and power dynamics exercises. Really first-class work today." The students, and even some of the company members, shone at his praise.

As people filed out to the kitchen, they either scrutinized Katya or
looked away. Robert and I pulled her in the other direction, into the
empty corridor that led to the stairs, the pale overhead lighting useless
against the rough wood of the walls so that we seemed trapped in a
dark forest grove. She smelled—of vomit, fear, sweat, and the metal-
lic, chemical tang of hospital disinfectant.

She told her story in a whisper: fast, fevered, the individual words
almost indistinguishable. "She's in the car, I can't leave her for too
long—they say she's stable, but I'm afraid of what might happen if
she passes out. She's been staying with me—she says she can't sleep
since Mom died. But, you know, I have, or *had,* all these housemates,
so we've been living in the same room, and *still* I didn't even know
some moron doctor prescribed her oxy this winter after she hurt her
ankle dancing. She told me this morning that after Mom died she
started taking double doses. It made her feel things were okay. That
life was okay, and she was okay, and it was possible to feel good. Then
yesterday my genius little sister figured out she could smash a few pills

up and get a super high all at once. She's not making a lot of sense. I'm hoping she's not . . ." Katya cried quietly.

It came back to me all at once, a painful flood of memory. The oxy prescription. That's what Eva had been telling me on our walk: she'd wanted it kept secret from Ray and Katya. If I'd only worked harder at remembering, I could have helped Arielle. This need never have happened. I was crying too now, but Robert was furious.

Katya began again. "She did it in the bathroom. And I heard her knocking things over when she passed out. If I hadn't been home. Or gone in." She looked straight at me. "She wasn't *breathing*. She was going blue. I couldn't wake her. I dialed 911 but I didn't have time to talk. I said she wasn't breathing and gave the address. If I hadn't had that CPR class in jail. There are all these . . . the paramedics said if I'd waited even four minutes she might have died or been brain-damaged for life. They think she's . . . they don't think she's . . ." She started to cry again.

I tried to hold her, and she resisted. "I have to say it, okay? So they gave her Narcon, and then they had to keep breathing for her, and she started detoxing almost right away, and it was the most horrible thing ever. I can't even talk about that. We went to the emergency room, and they kept her for hours, but they said she's stable and threw us out as if she were a stray cat. We don't have insurance. They'll send us the bill. I don't give a shit. I'm so angry at her."

"You know she couldn't help it."

She took off her sad, frivolous glasses and rubbed her eyes, making them even redder. "I don't care. It's bullshit. She can help it. She has to. Mom would have said that neurochemistry is not determinism. I would say that neurochemistry is not *fucking* determinism." Completely agitated, as if she had no idea what to do, or faith that we would either, she headed back to the main room and onto the deck. We followed her, almost running to keep up. Various company members and students continued talking, pretending not to be eavesdropping. "My asshole roommates said we had to leave, they can't have any more drama. They're keeping my deposit because there was a mess and damage, and they said they'll box up my things, and I can come pick them up. I couldn't go to Jenny—she and Brandon are having major trouble. Anyway, I can't let the babies see Arielle like this. And Dad can't know. He's barely holding it together as it is."

She headed down the stairs to the parking lot. "You were right to come here," said Robert.

I said, "We have to tell your father. I can't believe you didn't call him."

"No. No. No." She shook her head, wildly. "Later, okay? Maybe? Can you help me with her?"

In the dusty parking lot, Arielle leaned against the front seat of Katya's little dark maroon Karmann Ghia. She had the window rolled down—she reeked too. Worse than Katya. She was watching the naked people making pyramids in the meadow, the Shakespeareans rehearsing the destruction of the ship.

"I think I'm still dreaming," she said. "Damn. I really fucked up." She had dark circles under her eyes, a look of shame, and, worse, of sad acceptance, as if she'd finally given up on herself. Though I'd been saying to myself all the way to the car that I wouldn't cry, of course I did. I opened the door and threw myself on her, kneeling beside her with my arms around her. Kneeling didn't work for my leg any more, but I ignored the pain spiking into my back. Arielle could have died. She could have *died*. A sensation like silvery rays shot through me, an electrocution in my brain, down my limbs, in the center of my body. Oh, what it must have been like for Eva, trying to raise these girls.

"Don't cry, Aunt Julia," said my sister's treasured youngest child. "Oh, God, I feel so sick. Don't hold me. I might barf on you." Her voice was slow and I started to take in that what Katya hadn't been able to say was that we didn't yet know what damage she might have sustained.

Robert said, "Sweetie, please try not to barf out here if you possibly can help it, not until we get you to a bathroom. Are you up to standing? Let's get you to this parlor . . . Jules, do you know where it is?"

"I do," I said. "I'll sleep there with them. You and Alyx can keep the cabin." I'd be with the girls in case anything happened—and I wouldn't have to listen to the lovebirds. "There are a couple of bathrooms in the hall next to the parlor. Let's get you two upstairs, so you can get cleaned up and have a rest."

"A rest." Arielle's voice was full of wonder. We had lunch ahead of us, and afternoon rehearsal, we were going to have to organize at least air mattresses, or, if possible, cots, and bedding, we had to get them upstairs and showered before Lenore saw them. Was I going to call Ray and rat on them? He wasn't really speaking to me—when I'd woken up after the attack, I'd been beside myself and told them all I'd known we shouldn't be in the woods, it was my fault we were there. The girls didn't blame me, and I didn't think Robert did, but Ray knew it was true. We couldn't even talk to each other now. Still, I had to call, though I didn't want to see him and his full-bore reactions to this any more than the girls did.

The day, which had seemed complicated, was now impossible. If Arielle had died. I couldn't afford to think about that. We had to function. Our students and company members were all on the deck by now. My back and leg hurt insanely. From the trees, I could hear the crows cawing. Robert said, "You'll have to move aside, Jules, so I can help Arielle."

We took them up to the bathroom, waited out a round of Arielle being sick, now down to dry heaves. We were going to have to keep her hydrated. I would have to ask Katya what the hospital had done about that. We managed to help the girls get cleaned up without Lenore becoming involved. If she said anything, we could tell her one of the new company members had the flu. That should keep her away until we had the girls back on their feet.

While Arielle slept in the parlor, Katya and I waited in one of the rehearsal rooms. I said, "I can't not call your dad and Jenny."

She was working gel into her hair, pulling it into little pink and blue spikes. She didn't seem to need a mirror but gazed out the window, her movements dreamy, automatic. Eventually, she said, "I can see that."

Sometimes, looking at Eva's children, I felt as if my bones were dis-

solving. They were extraordinarily perfect in some way I couldn't articulate—they were so exactly who they were—and yet such a danger
to themselves. They must have no idea how perfect they were, or they
couldn't possibly behave in the self-destructive ways they did.

"There's a lot of stuff in here," said Katya, looking at the altar. It
remained inert. The objects were the same as they had been the last
time Alyx and I were here but, as when I'd checked the altar earlier,
seemed entirely benign. I couldn't understand what had happened in
that first encounter. It didn't seem to matter. My focus had to be the
girls.

I waited for a mid-afternoon moment during rehearsal when the
kitchen was empty and slipped out to call my brother-in-law and, in
an undertone, give him an abbreviated version. He said, "The little
idiots. My God. My God. She took what? Is she . . .?"

"She seems okay." I wasn't sure yet, but why make it worse than it
was?

"What does that mean—okay?"

"She's pretty sick right now. I don't know if it's the stuff she took or
the stuff the EMTs gave her."

Now his rage kicked in. "Why didn't the kids call me? Why are they
with you?"

I'd been trying to think of a cover story for the hour before I called.
"I'm closer to the city than you are," I said. "You know, on the way.
It's hard for them to drive with Arielle in this shape." Silence. So I
tried, "They want you to be proud of them, to think of them as suc-
cesses. They were hoping you wouldn't have to know. Be soft with
them, Ray."

"They're my *children*," he said. "Do they think I'm hard on them?"
His voice, usually so certain, fierce or jolly or bombastic, sounded so
thin and sad that it undid me. I started to cry.

"They don't want to let you down. They adore you," I said. I'd
never exactly understood it, until that moment. He adored them too.
Shamefully, I'd always thought of them as "Eva's children."

"I'll be there in an hour. Have you called Jenny?"

"Not yet."

"That's something. I'll tell her myself," he said.

And what was I going to tell Lenore? More new company members? Thank God for the Institute's administrative disorganization. They might not even notice a couple of additional people. I went back into rehearsal, planning, so worried that I forgot myself entirely. It was only later that afternoon that I noticed the stage fright and self-consciousness had disappeared.

When Ray arrived, followed an hour later by Jenny, who had a longer drive south from Sonoma County, I led them up to the room pretty quietly. I missed the last hour of rehearsals in the process, but things were going fairly well with the old demechanization and power games.

For dinner, Arielle had broth and applesauce, while the rest of us ate sandwiches. Robert had finagled all this from the kitchen. Although we were allowed to bring snacks we'd bought into rehearsal spaces, it was against the rules for companies to make their own meals from kitchen supplies or to take food into the rooms. But when Robert's not being a pill, he can get anything from anyone. He charms people by the way he listens and invites them to share the great joke of the intractable little and great problems of life. He'd have won over anyone working in the kitchen, confiding in them about having sick company members as he heated up the water for broth. He'd have drawn them out, asking about their histories and their ideas about dance and theater. And at the end of the conversation, as a small favor, he'd have asked for a few slices of bread, some cheese, peanut butter, sweet pickle relish, mustard, and onion to make our family's favorite sandwiches. Anyone helping him would be made to feel dashing and wicked, generous and remarkable.

Upstairs, we sat around the little room, the now-harmless altar off to the side, the smell of must and incense overlying mustard and peanut butter. Arielle lay on her cot, drinking broth—we'd scored folding Swedish cots from the students' dorm supply room and shoved aside the old furniture to make room—and Ray sat on the floor beside her, eating his sandwich with one hand, the other stroking her hair. He'd already delivered his first lecture before dinner: Arielle had to know her limits, she couldn't just take painkillers like someone with a different history, she needed to let him know when she needed help, she'd had enough training and rehab that she ought to know the warning signs. He couldn't help himself, and we couldn't stop him until he was done, but now he was quiet.

Robert and I sat on my cot, not an ideal situation for my back and leg, but I let it go for the moment, and Katya and Jenny sat on Katya's cot, legs crossed, knees against each other, Katya's hand loosely resting on Jenny's knee.

Katya said, "Jen, can you please explain to us how a person can be, like, an apprentice witch? Apprentice herbalist, I get. You have to learn what everything is so you don't poison anyone. But aren't you either a witch or not a witch? Like, born with powers or else not?" She pulled a little piece of Jenny's long curly hair. Eva's middle child looked a decade older than she was, her skin weathered from all the time she spent in the sun. Or maybe it was the changes in her brought about by chemo and radiation. Or even her habitual expression of kind patience, a lavish, down-to-earth helpfulness. She looked like a woman, not a girl, unlike her sisters.

"There's a lot of very practical stuff to learn," she said, calmly. "Though someone could make it into more of a head trip if they want to. Some people are really into studying the archeology or history. Others follow the 'Elemental Magick' kind of stuff. But when it comes down to it, it's really just a nature-based religion."

Katya said, in her older sister voice, "Ju-Bu's, I know. That's a thing. Jindus. Even Ju-fis. But Ju-itches? Belonging to one of the Renewal *shuls* wouldn't do it for you?" Then, curious, "Do you work spells?"

"Are you in some sort of coven?" Ray asked.

"I belong to a couple of Wiccan/Pagan Meet-Ups. And there are some really young girls who walk around in belly-dancing costumes. Some of the people I saw on our way in look sort of like them. But there are quite down-to-earth older women. Some lesbians who really know who they are."

"So is that a dis against straight or bi women? Don't we know who we are?" Katya's tone was prickly, ready for a fight.

"And some very nurturing mothers," said Jenny, ignoring her. "I love being around all these women. I feel very at home with all of them. I don't mind the ideas about Egyptian or Druidical stuff, though I don't get into that myself. But I love our Solstice ceremonies."

Arielle made a startling sound, a hacking cough—then, very pale, lurched out to the hall.

"Should I go after her?" Jenny said, starting to rise from the cot.

Katya pressed down on Jenny's leg, restraining her. "She said this afternoon that she just wants to get through it. And let's not talk about her while she's in the bathroom. She'd hate that."

From outside came the sounds of laughter, the nightly party. And from the rehearsal hall below us rose a wailing song with a slow-motion drumbeat. I said, "The Kundalini dancers have turned out to have a great work ethic."

Ray asked, his voice rough, "Are those the girls in the belly-dancing outfits?"

"Bingo," said Robert, finishing a second sandwich. The rest of us had stopped eating.

Arielle returned saying, "It's nothing, I'm sorry. Please don't fuss."

We all fell silent, trying not to watch her. She said, in the voice of a small girl, "Dad?"

"Princess?"

We tried not to wince at this. But Arielle took his hand in hers, holding it to her cheek. He leaned toward her with his whole body. She said, "Can you tell us the story of how you and Mom met?"

"You don't want that old story," he said.

"Start," said Arielle. She closed her eyes, holding onto his hand.

"It was your mom's first semester of college. She was taking twenty units, and hardly ever left the lab. I was a senior, and had dated a few different girls, but I'd mostly been busy with extracurricular activities. War protests, labor organizing. Also studying. I'd already decided I was going to law school, so I had to keep up my grades. But one night your mom and I were at the same party. Not a student party—one of the chemistry professors was retiring. She had on a rose-colored sweater and khakis, with this little strand of pearls around her neck. No one wore pearls at Berkeley in the 80s. She had all these short dark curls and a little pointed face—like yours." He touched Arielle's cheekbone. Wistful looks flickered across her sisters' faces, and he said, "You two look more like me."

"You saw her across the room," said Jenny.

"I saw her across the room. And I thought if I wasted any time being subtle, someone would grab her before I could get there. So I poured a glass of the really good wine—I bet she would drink wine—and took it right over to her."

I said, "You said to her, 'I think I recognize you from my future.'"

"In my own defense, I have to say that I was twenty-one years old."

"It seems to have worked," I said drily. Eva had called me the next morning, and said, "Oh my God, I spent the night with this boy, and I think he's sort of a jerk and really full of himself, but I can't stop thinking about him. What do I do?" I'd said—I was eleven and thrilled by every detail of university life, at having my big sister confide in me— "You should have an adventure. It's not like you have to marry him. Have some fun."

Arielle said, "And two months later, Katya was on the way."

Katya said, "You had a family wedding, and Mom wore a flame-red dress because she said she refused to dress in off-white, as if she'd fallen in the mud in her bridal gown and had been unable to wash it out."

Arielle said, "I miss her so much," and her father answered, "We all do," in a tone that only just missed saying, "But none of the rest of us are ODing, are we?"

There was some crying, and Robert, who could never stand tears, began to gather up the dishes to take them down to the kitchen for washing.

The kitchen plumbing in the Lodge had what appeared to be one of its periodic blockages during the night. All these different people were cooking, so stuff went down the drains, which backed up. I secretly considered it a gift from the angels. Everyone who had any administrative or maintenance role at the Institute was sucked into dealing with the problem. We still had to pretend nothing was going on, even though the students had to realize that we were having a secret crisis upstairs. Lenore understood someone was sick, but she'd apparently accepted the idea that all these new people hanging around were company members; she didn't want to know any of the details of how anyone was doing. If the place had been more organized, there would have been rosters, more of a system of checking people off against initial lists. But we could have brought in Napoleon's *Grande Armée* and gotten away with it.

And though Lenore missed the drama of the arrival of our nieces, some of the company members and students had watched it happening. Anyone who hadn't seen it firsthand had no doubt heard gossip. We had to say to the company that the girls were here because of family trouble. By then, they all knew too much about our family troubles and asked the minimum of questions.

Everyone at the Institute ate salad, sandwiches, and canned food on paper plates for the next two days while workers installed new pipes. Ray and Jenny were able to come and go from their rooms in town. He wanted to take Katya and Arielle back with him, but Arielle said she was too weak and sick to move and couldn't possibly get in a car. She slept restlessly at night, napped during the day, and spent much of her time on the porch, drinking chamomile tea and watching the Shakespeareans or the naked troupe in rehearsal.

I wanted to talk to her, to find out what happened, to get a sense of how she was, but she wasn't ready yet. Maybe she talked to Katya and Jenny, maybe to her father. I don't know.

At night, though I was now used to the upstairs room, I'd lie awake like a mother afraid her baby will turn onto her stomach and suffocate in her sleep. Arielle's breath rising and falling. Her sweet, foxlike face. I said, silently, *Eva, I swear I won't let anything happen to her.* Was there any way my sister could hear me? I could remember her, so clearly, longing to have time for real work, distracted by the family. I remembered her happiness in saying she'd found empathy, that we could dissolve the boundaries between ourselves and the world, discover the neurological basis for ethics, for nonviolence. I could almost hear her voice, see her face. But, in other ways, it felt like she was long gone. All my memories of her were shrinking to a few recurring images. And I didn't want to keep returning to those woods, to the moment when I'd been timid, when I hadn't acted on my instinct and saved us.

I turned my mind to an earlier, happier walk. Eva and I, in another forest, three years before, alongside a creek. I'd been looking at the shapes of the redwoods, thinking of them as a stage set, the negative spaces and light in between, how they'd serve as a backdrop. This, of course, made me think of *Midsummer Night's Dream, As You Like It, A Walk in the Woods,* and *Into the Woods.* Lovers and warring fairies, cold war negotiators, characters out of folktales. Eva, beside me, was studying the water. When I asked her what this place looked like to her, she said, "I see a riparian community. We're in a riparian corridor here: the ferns and blackberries and poison oak have adapted to living underneath the redwoods, and insects drop from the plants and feed both the land and aquatic animals. Since we started walking, I've seen a Pacific-slope Flycatcher and Red-shouldered Hawk, a Warbling Vireo, and two kinds of frogs—California Red-legged and Foothill Yellow-legged."

We were walking in such different woods. She said, "I have an eye out for newts and salamanders. They're my favorite animals, but I haven't seen any yet this morning."

Some of my memories of her made me weep, but this one had always made me smile. It didn't seem possible that it could ever be untarnished by knowledge of that later walk, the aftermath.

I had no idea how I would keep my promise to look after her children, but I had never felt so fierce. At least we had enough space in this room. I no longer had to worry about whether getting up in the night would mean kicking Alyx or Robert in the head, accidentally or maybe not.

When I finally slept, I had strange dreams that I couldn't get hold of in the morning. Tiny shards of the images lodged in my mind, along with a sense that I wasn't supposed to be seeing, or knowing about, any of these fragments.

A pool of water I needed to drink from, but there was some decision to make.

Shadows around me, and Eva saying they (who? The shadows?) were being boiled in oil, disemboweled, their eyes gouged out, their hearts dug out of their bodies.

Standing before a powerful, frightening woman who wanted something—she had done something to her sister. Maybe I was the woman? No, that wasn't it.

Robert and I took the girls to visit the parents. River Valley was so depressing: the cheery decaying décor, the indifferent staff, except for the director of marketing who pretended to have a great interest in the residents when visitors came, to the evident surprise of those residents. We'd moved Dad to the skilled nursing wing, a gray, hospital-like place, and our visit with him was short. He was a tiny, sad gnome now, his ears enormous, his eyes peering at us, as if he were already looking back from another world. "I miss Eva," he said, weeping. "And I know how hard it is for you all." The girls and I cried with abandon, though we'd promised each other we would try to keep it together.

He was reluctant to discuss his own situation. His voice had gotten so thin and anxious, we had to strain to hear it as he said, "I think I'm losing my executive function. My brain seems to be breaking up." He gave a kind of laugh. "I was in old, old age. But I think I'm in a new country now. I'd be charting it if I could still read my writing." He took each of our hands in his own ancient, blue-veined right hand, spotted dark brown, covered with bandages where the skin had most recently torn. He was going to give us a message for Mom—they'd be wheeling her in for a visit later—but he fell asleep before he could tell us what it was.

Mom's wing was far more decorated, as if she were living in a gift shop that had seen better times. She was convinced she was having frequent mini-strokes. The doctors weren't finding neurological evidence, but her right side had weakened. She had substantial trouble walking. She wore diapers at night but wanted to be taken to the bathroom instead and was always ringing for the aides. The place also charged a per-point fortune for "personal services," which our parents couldn't afford and we couldn't afford to supplement. All very well for us to live like vagabonds, but didn't we owe them a better end of life than this?

She pretended not to know who Robert and I were, our punishment for neglect. At least I thought she was pretending. She seemed to have a clearer idea of the grandchildren. Holding Jenny's hand, she said, "I know I'm a heavy burden. I wish someone had pushed me off a pier years ago. I wish one of you would come in the dark hours and hold a pillow over my face until it's all over. I wish I had died a hundred times before I outlived one of my children."

When had she realized that Eva was really gone? Or was it a brief flash into reality that would end soon enough—should we acknowledge it or act as if it wasn't happening? Before any of the rest of us could change the subject, the entirely admirable Jenny said, "We're all sad, Grandma, but this must be so terrible for you, I can't even imagine."

My mother patted her hand, tears in her eyes. "I may be a little off from time to time, but I don't live in a cave," she said. "Your father is only a few hundred feet away. But they hardly let me see him."

Jenny leaned against Mom, resting her head on her shoulder. Saint Jenny could sometimes be manic in her usefulness. But hers was the most appealing craziness in the whole family.

The next day, Jenny went back to her farm in Forestville, and Ray back to his job. He didn't like it that the girls were staying on, but Katya said, "I know Dad can't help it. But he's *at* Arielle—he wants to lecture her all the time or wake her up to check that she's not high, just sleeping normally. She needs room, Aunt Julia. And we can't start over in a new place right now. Can we stay a little longer?"

"Of course." I hoped this was true. So far, so good. "What will you do though?" She said, apologetically, "I have to go into town and find some meetings"—from that and her smiling, definite refusals of all wine or beer at dinner or evening events, I took it that she'd gone into AA or Al-Anon or something. Nobody in our family had ever had anything to do with programmed approaches to getting help—we all preferred to fight dramatic battles by ourselves, which, it occurred to me now, had always meant losing them. But on our own terms.

She signed up with the temp agencies in town and, in four days, had found a place to go to Shabbat services, and a half-time job in the outside sales department of a family-run art and office supply store, where she could answer phones, schedule sales calls, prepare inventory lists for labels and cartons of recycled printer paper. She laid in a stock of nuts and packaged soy things for nights when all she could eat at the Institute was the salad.

Arielle was drinking quite a bit of wine with her dinners at the Institute, but she wasn't going to OD on wine. Maybe it was okay? If it helped keep her off the drugs? Within a week, having nothing else to do, feeling better, and tired of staying on the sidelines, one morning she joined us for class. The girls hadn't had a chance to go back for their clothes yet, and she wore a thrift-shop outfit that Katya had picked up in Santa Cruz, a white blouse and frilled pink crinoline skirt over feet-less tights that made her look like a 21st century china shepherdess. Her color wasn't great. Maybe she had a hangover?

After the warm-ups, we held gibberish cocktail parties, expressing social niceties in no known language, while trying to get close to those we'd decided to love and avoid those we disliked. In a foursome with Alyx, I decided everything she said was a riot, while she treated me as her oldest, dearest friend. Robert and I, in another group, each chose the other as the person we most loathed, maneuvering to avoid each other. It's easiest when you choose the same emotion, most theatrical when a person despises the one who adores them. Then you get sort of an incomprehensible Chekhovish play. Some of the students fell into the exercise as if they'd been doing it all their lives; others had to struggle with their own resistance, usually those who most depended on language, rather than tone or gesture. Arielle chased her beloveds and shied away from her enemies, but her heart wasn't in it. I couldn't see any joy in her.

Maybe the group was being harder on her, to test her. Several students chose to despise and avoid her during the cocktail party. The company members tended more toward excess enthusiasm, which seemed to make her uncomfortable. Of course they were suspicious of a family member who hadn't auditioned for the company and wasn't a paying student. And of course they both had sympathy for her and distrusted her, waiting to see what she might do next.

After our gibberish cocktail parties, we played Status Games, imagining ourselves at a big Google party, where we were celebrating our release of two major new initiatives: Google Earth, a satellite mapping program, and Mobile Web Search, which would allow people to view the results of web searches on their mobile phones. Robert taped numbers representing our social rank to our foreheads: we had to guess our own number from people's responses to us. Mostly people wouldn't meet my eyes and tried to get away from me if I engaged them in conversation. When someone asked me, in a kindly dismissive tone, if I could fetch them a drink, I figured that I had to be at the bottom of the status pile, maybe a one or at most a two. Oddly, it was helpful to have people try to avoid me. The company had been pretending nothing was wrong with my mind or body, though I could feel how uncomfortable they now were. Arielle, who wore the number fifteen, was enveloped by a crowd of eager followers but still didn't seem to be enjoying herself. Maybe she was reading their real expressions, the ways they were assessing and judging her. Probably her eerie, otherworldly beauty wasn't helping her here. She looked across at me and gave an almost invisible shrug of frustration, a silent request that I stop watching her.

By the time we were done with the Google party, everything hurt. Tired of stumping around on the canes, which limited the speed of my moves, I lay down on the floor and discovered a serpentine motion for getting from one place to another. I was pleased with this invention and could feel in the unnerving juxtaposition of seduction and brokenness the first real hint of what I might become as a performer. Feeling Robert's eyes on me, I looked up to see his small smile and decisive nod; he'd clocked this move and filed its possibilities. I looked away and then, without meaning to, back at him again. The naked wash of sadness on his face revealed how much the first professional, calculated expression of approval had been a performance. I dropped my eyes, hoping that he didn't know I'd seen, hoping that none of the company or students had caught his look, and, most especially, that Arielle hadn't seen it. I couldn't bring myself to glance over at her, to find out.

"Right then," Robert said, cheerfully. "Shall we work on Colombian Hypnosis and Sun King?"

After dinner, we stood on the deck while some of the actors tuned up instruments. From the creek came the sound of crickets and frogs. The musicians tuned a key, tried a note, asked each other whether it sounded sharp. One of the Shakespeareans began playing a mournful Renaissance air, experimentally. People had begun to gather under the soft yellow porch lights, talking, drinking, and waiting for the music to start. Arielle sat beside the musicians, sharing a bottle of wine with a few of the actors. She'd been doing it for a while, it appeared. Though she was almost grown now, she was still recognizable as the little changeling fox-child. With her alert face and her long silver-ash hair pulled back, she seemed caught between worlds. Like me, she'd gone a long way toward some other place and was still making her way back, dreamy and slow. She hadn't quite died, wasn't fully reborn.

Katya, who of course wasn't drinking at all, hadn't eaten enough at dinner, only a few vegetables, some packaged thing. There she stood, like a creature from another planet, with her sweet rounded face and cat's-eye glasses, her dyed spikes of pink and blue hair, in a thrift shop dress covered with cartoon dogs, and a yellow sweater with fat pom-pom ties. I asked her, quietly, "Not even vegetable lasagna? I thought you loved cheese."

She said—also quiet, but pent up, her words pouring out, "Aunt Julia, they take the baby calves away to make them into veal, and the mothers wail with grief. They bellow. They fight. Sometimes they stop eating. When a mother is led past the place where her calf was taken from her, even a year later, she starts fighting and wailing all over again. And they do it to the mothers over and over, so they're always pregnant or in mourning, and in about five years they're so broken down that they have to be taken away and turned into low-grade hamburger, but meanwhile we get our milk and cheese and ice cream. They're really affectionate beings, cows. They're like dogs in the way they trust us even when they shouldn't. And we totally betray them. Who are the real beasts here? I'm not going to be part of separating mothers and children."

She could never just say anything—it always had to be a speech, and though she wasn't loud, her words carried: one or two people nearby gave us bad looks. She seemed oblivious. I stepped away from them, toward the railing, pulling Katya by the elbow to a spot I hoped was out of earshot. I both wanted to cradle my oldest niece in my arms and to slap her. How was I going to help her live in the world, to keep her from throwing herself in front of every bulldozer and winding up in jail over and over again? I needed a bracelet: WWED—what would Eva do? Though Eva had had no idea what to do with her firebrand children. I said, "Okay, okay, eat your soy nuts. Let's not talk about it. I'm barely making it, as it is, Kat. I can't think about this."

"No, why would you, if you could help it? Anyway, you have to do what you're going to do. As for me, I'm going to be part of changing things, but I don't know how yet."

Arielle, tipsy, seemed to be saying her goodbyes and heading up to the room. The mosquitos were biting, though the night felt cool and dry. I slapped at my arm, killing one, which left behind a small splash of what was probably my own blood. One of the men who'd given Katya a bad look, a Shakespearean, I think, edged closer, as if he planned to join our conversation. Tall, bearded, with a solemn look. I couldn't think who he would play. King Alonso, probably, or Gonzalo.

I steered Katya down the steps and asked her, quietly, if changing things would involve lecturing the rest of us at dinner about the mother and baby cows, and she said she *hadn't* lectured us at dinner, not even about the greenhouse gases or—and her voice rose here— the egg industry. "They throw all the baby male chicks alive into meat grinders or into plastic bags to suffocate. Free range, humane, whatever. They're, like, peeping the whole time." She wasn't hearing or seeing me or the man following us, too busy peering into a nightmare otherworld, the cave of horrors. I wondered if there could be some gene for self-torture. It had come right down into Robert from Dad, but jumped Eva to show up full force in her oldest daughter.

As we reached the path, I thought I could lead her around past the creek and circle the Lodge. That would give her time to cool down. We could go in through the kitchen and upstairs without any more encounters. But the guy came down the path behind us. For some reason, she'd gotten under his skin. She was still a kid in her idealistic phase, sounding off. But he was pursuing us as if she'd tried to mug him and he were about to make a citizen's arrest. Surely he wasn't going to cause a scene?

Katya didn't seem to notice him. And he wasn't quite closing in. It felt as if he were tacitly steering us up toward the woods, menacing us silently by his very presence. That awakened a nagging, elusive memory, so I was only half listening as Katya said, "If we all ate plants, if we freed up the water and grain that goes into raising the fifty-seven billion animals we kill in the world every year, we could feed, like, four billion more people. And isn't, like, your *whole play* about shit like hunger and war? What about our war on the rest of the animals? What about our war on the planet? How can you not make the connection?"

"You're doing it," I said, "you're lecturing," and she said, "But not at dinner. Not even when that naked guy said that broccoli screams when you stab it with your fork." She made a zipping motion across her lips. "I promise to stop," she said. "Or, I promise to try. And I definitely promise not to do it at the table."

The Shakespearean, not having silenced us by his presence, now cut us off. He confronted us, his dark eyes censorious, his lips pursed, Claudius about to banish Hamlet. "I used to be a vegetarian. But my body began to crave meat—you have to listen to your body. One night I finally had a steak, and, within minutes, I could feel it coursing through my bloodstream. Within two days, I was my old self again." He had a gorgeous voice. Rich, orotund, resonant. People up on the porch had started to pay attention.

"Maybe you needed protein," Katya said, ignoring my tugging at her sleeve. "Maybe you weren't eating enough fat—that happens to people if they're trying to live on, like salad and refined pasta. Anyway, nobody gets better in two days from eating one food. And you wouldn't feel it 'coursing through your veins.' Try eating some blueberries or broccoli and see what happens. Then treat yourself to some sugar, or alcohol, or meth. You'll sure as shit feel *those* coursing through your veins."

He said, "Who are you to tell me how to live?"

"Of course you must eat whatever you eat," I said. "It's your choice." I pulled Katya away, down to the creek. "You can lecture me all you want," I said, when we were out of earshot. "Or maybe some reasonable amount. And you can absolutely lecture Uncle Robert all you want: I'd love that. But could you not lecture the Institute people?"

She said, "Do you know, I cannot stand in a buffet line piling vegetables on my plate, or, God forbid, tofu, without some guy telling me all about some vegetarian friend of his who happened to get sick once. Like, did they ever know any meat eaters who got sick? Sometimes they pick up meat and make a big thing out of eating it and saying, 'Oh, I love my bacon. Don't you wish you had some of this bacon?' They need a twelve-step program. *Seriously*, Aunt Julia."

"I'm sorry to say it, but we're on sort of shaky ground already, sweetie . . ." I trailed off, but she took my meaning. That had, perhaps, done it.

"Arielle and I don't belong here. I know. I'll do extra shifts of dishwashing. And I can garden. I bet I can master the hot tub filtration system."

"You don't have to do extra work. We have a visitor arrangement with Lenore."

"Visitors in sleeping bags on cots?"

"It could be a lot worse. We have sort of a discount for that. But it would be great if you could, you know . . . keep a lid on the animal talk." A frightful thought occurred to me. "You're not going to go blow anything up, are you? Like labs?"

"Oh, Aunt Julia," she said, laughing. "That's so Hollywood. There's like, ten billion animals living in factory farm hells. Who but a crazy person would blow up a lab to release twenty rats who have absolutely no clue about how to live outside? They'd meet some street rats and be dead in about fifteen minutes. I'll hook up with some org that needs help sending out mailings. Probably I'll go out and leaflet strangers at concerts."

Lucky strangers, I thought, picturing them out for a happy, relaxed evening and sucked in to staring at her pamphlets, full of horrible pictures of filthy, maddened caged animals coupled with jolly recipes and recommendations for packaged veggie burgers. Also a photo of happy turkeys eating pumpkin pie with cranberries out in the field of some animal rescue place, the pretty humans around them glowing with a transcendent joy rarely seen outside Renaissance paintings of saints stuck full of arrows. But everyone in our family was born to be a fanatic, one way or another. Whatever that gene was, we all had it.

Fortunately, the singing started up in earnest on the deck and we joined in, Katya too—everything from "Passionate Kisses" to "I'm on Fire," including the occasional hymn. "When I went down to the river to pray," we sang joyously, having set aside all grief and self-consciousness for the moment, entering in as if we all believed in prayer, abandoning ourselves to the sound reverberating through our bodies and the valley.

After the morning warm-ups the next day, Robert clapped his hands, "Dolphin training! The dolphin leaves the room, and we'll decide what you do. When you come back, try things out. We'll all let you know when you're on the right track. We'll be silent when you're on the wrong track and make a dinging sound when you're getting warmer."

He led everyone in a chorus of "Ding, ding, ding," and I thought, you have to hand it to him. He has zero self-consciousness.

"Right!" he said. "Let's start with someone who has experience. LaVerne?"

At first, the tasks were easy. Walk to the wall. Pick up a particular coat and put it on. Then the game grew more complex. Tanikah let herself be dinged into picking up and drinking from someone else's water bottle. Vân Anh had to circle the rehearsal hall three times. Boyce figured out that he was to inch backwards under a table singing a Russian folksong (any song would have done, we just wanted him to sing while he did it). When the dolphins did what we wanted, we uttered a chorus of dings; when they were on the wrong track, we fell silent. Almost nothing matches the eerie feeling of a room full of people watching in intense silence while you do the wrong thing and then guide yourself back toward doing the thing that works.

When it was Arielle's turn, the group rewarded her with dings as she approached a chair, fell silent as she walked around it, then dinged fairly enthusiastically as she stood on it. They were getting used to her. We waited. "I'm on the chair," she said. "That's not enough?" She began to smile. "You are a very tough crowd, dolphin trainers." She sounded like her old self, the youngest child used to taking—or at least to being given—instructions as to what to do next. She grinned in a way I hadn't seen since she arrived. Mischievous, lit up. The fox girl rampant. And although no one else in the room, except perhaps Robert, could know how enchanting that grin had looked when she was six and lost both front teeth, they were all smiling in return. She tried hopping, talking, singing, and then, finally, balanced on one foot. She said, "Once upon a time," and we dinged loudly until she raised her hands. "You want me to tell you a *story*. Cripes. I can't tell stories." Silence. She poked at her hair, which was slipping out of its pony tail.

"All right," she said, standing up very straight, "Once upon a time, a group of children found themselves lost in the woods. Every day, they strewed bread crumbs behind them as they inched away from the places they knew in search of the local circus, a feuding family that spoke to each other only in the circus ring. But one day, the children forgot their crumbs and stumbled deeper and deeper into the forest. As night fell, they got colder, dreaming of food and home. Because they sang to themselves for comfort, bears and wolves gathered to see what was happening. The children fell silent and drew together in a little circle, but it was too late. The bears and wolves tore them in shreds and ate them, and no one ever knew what happened to them. But the bears and wolves lived happily ever after. The end."

She curtsied, holding up the edges of the crinoline. "And the moral of the story is—never go into the woods without your bread crumbs."

Everyone dinged like crazy, and she had a big round of applause, which made her laugh out loud. She had color in her cheeks and hopped down from the chair like any nineteen-year-old at play, pleased with herself.

Oh, my God, how good it was to be alive. The pleasure of having students again. Forgetting the history and complications of the company and rediscovering what we did and why. Yet when I found myself laughing and applauding Arielle, I also felt a jolt of guilt. Did I think Eva would mind my laughing? People say that the dead would want us to be happy again, but I wonder if they wouldn't prefer it if the misery didn't drop and lift, if we mourned them full-time for quite a while. Nonetheless, I noticed that my pain had dropped from its usual 6-8 on a scale of 10 (doctors always wanted to know the numbers) down to around a 3-4.

Maybe, I thought, feeling actual hope, as we packed up for lunch, Arielle would be the one person in the family who'd learn from her mistakes, who at least knew that a person should take her bread crumbs into the woods, which not one other member of the family ever seemed to have figured out. We'd take fertility figurines, extra scarves, a basket full of board games and good wine, and a didgeridoo. But no one would remember the bread crumbs.

We'd been at the Institute about a month when I finally let myself skip a dance-specific lesson and the accompanying pain. Katya was at work, Arielle in rehearsal. I lay down on my cot and slid into sleep. Robert almost immediately set me on an ice floe. I said, "This is cultural appropriation," and he answered, solemnly, "All human rituals belong to all humankind." I wanted to call in the wolves but was floating out of earshot. I'd be all right if I could get to an island. A sense of menace grew around me—not from the cold, bright waves, but from the woods that encased the sea. I hadn't gotten out after all and was still in the room where something meant me harm. I sprang awake and—not fully able to focus—saw what seemed to be a gun pointing at me from the door. I cried out and reached for my canes, the cot tipping as it always did when I leaned to the side. I struggled to right it and got hold of my canes, but the gun in the doorway was gone. If it had ever been there.

The rehearsal noises stopped for a moment after my cry. Footsteps sounded on the stairs. I couldn't stop shaking. Alyx came into the room, saying, "J, are you okay? What's going on?"

She hadn't called me that in years. I held up my arms to her like a child wanting to be picked up and soothed. She sank down beside me on the cot and held me.

"A dream. I think." My heart banged away inside me. I didn't believe it was a dream. Maybe my mind was cracking from constant worrying at the edges of the hole of Eva's absence. Or maybe the Institute truly was under some malign influence. I didn't know anymore how to tell what I should be afraid of.

Through her clothes, her body pressed sweetly against mine, hard muscles under soft skin, and she stroked my hair, soothingly. My mouth went dry with desire. The pleasure of feeling her again was almost unbearable—all this time, an ocean of pleasure already existed. All I had to do to reach it was to touch her skin.

She rested her palm on my cheek, swallowing, looking into my eyes, not with her ironic, conscious self but from another being I knew well—the calculating limbic lizard, hungry and determined. Oh, how I wanted her. It had been so long since anyone really touched me. We couldn't do anything about this desire. But I felt I was going to die *right then* if I didn't have her. I leaned forward, kissing her soft, familiar lips.

We pulled back, looking at each other. "Are we doing this?" she said.

"Probably not, if we're going to talk about it first." I still had my arm around her waist, feeling her warmth through her clothes, and she kept a hand on my thigh. An eyelash had fallen on her cheek. I brushed it away, and she shivered.

She said, "I think it depends whether this is about me or about Robert."

"Forget it," I said, and after a minute, "Well, then, what are you do-ing? You kissed me back. You've been, I don't know, flirting or some-thing since we arrived."

Her voice was dry. "Evidently, I want to be a part of this family. Or maybe not."

I held her hip. She kept her hand on me, watching me as sharply as one of the crows. "It could be about Eva. Do you think I can make you less sad?"

I said, "I *felt* that we were in danger in those woods, and I didn't stop and make her leave. I should have dragged her out of there. What happened was my fault." I wanted to tell Alyx about the dreams, but felt an injunction against this so strong that I couldn't say anything more.

She said, "I know," and slid her arms around my waist as well. I pushed my face into her neck, the tears starting. She lay on her back, the cot tilting toward me, and I rolled on top of her, burrowing into her, pressing her against the wall. No one until now had been willing to leave me on the hook where I hung. Except for Ray, who couldn't help hating me, they all wanted to lift me down, pat me into shape, pretend it was okay. Like Eva, Alyx had exacting judgments, an ability to sort things out. And like Eva, she was always about to disappear into some other world where I couldn't follow. But perhaps, if I said the right thing, she'd stay.

From the doorway, Robert said, "What the fuck?" We pulled apart as he slammed into the room, locking us all in together. "Could you at least have closed the damn door? First you're yelling, and now this. What if it had been someone besides me who came in here? Do you want to completely destabilize the company?" He stood over us, hands on his hips, his face dead white with anger as we sat up and arranged our clothes. I blew my nose and wiped my eyes. "So, what, are you two back together now?"

"*No,*" we both said. It hurt my feelings that she was so quick to agree, though I'd also responded with that instant denial that comes up when you're caught, even in something as innocent as sleep. Not that we were innocent. What had we been about to do? What if Arielle had come upstairs for some reason? But if we had to be found out, did it have to be before and not after? Bewildered as I was with grief, desire, and guilt, I still felt ashamed of my resentment.

Robert said, "You *sneak*, Julia."

I said, "I am so, so sorry, Robert."

Alyx stood and reached out for him. He took a step backward and said, "*If* you are going to get back together, please have the decency to a) break off with me first, and b) keep it a secret from everyone else."

I said, "I can't believe you just lettered our options." He wanted to break off with Alyx, right? The thought didn't make me feel any better.

He left the room, closing the door very precisely and quietly this time.

Alyx stood still, tears on her cheeks. She cleared her throat. "Well, that was totally expectable."

I thought, Not expectable, *predictable,* but aloud I said, "I'm sorry."

"Me too, J. We weren't thinking, right? Robert doesn't mean all that. He's so goddamn proud. He doesn't want anyone if he thinks they don't want him. I have to go find him." She followed him out.

I wasn't about to be left alone in the room, but I didn't want to see anyone. I made my way out of the Lodge and down to the creek, leaning on my canes, watching the movement of the water over the mossy rocks, the ferns on the banks, and the steelhead rainbow trout sliding along under the surface of the water. Here's your riparian community, I said to Eva, silently. A pair of crows perched on a branch overhead, but when I greeted them, they flapped their wings and took off, flying deeper into the woods.

Robert didn't speak to me for the rest of the day, but he finally ate a good dinner. I was sort of in love with Alyx again and pining. Maybe if I could find someone else to have sex with—would anyone want to have sex with me now?—it would clear my head and cure me. I was going to be a less awful person in the future. It seemed to me I had made this vow before.

I definitely didn't want to go to sleep, and when I got up to the room, well after ten, the girls were still awake. Katya sat cross-legged on her sleeping bag, while Arielle stretched out on her stomach. Katya had toasted walnuts and gotten a huge bag of dark Bing cherries in town. The girls were playing a kind of game, eating the cherries and throwing the pits into a metal bowl on the floor between them.

"Come and have cherries, Aunt Julia," Katya said. I settled myself onto my cot, and she gave me a handful. In the dim yellow light, the altar was completely ordinary. The gun, if there had been one, had come from the doorway.

Katya was saying, "You should come to a meeting with me, Arielle. My favorite is a mixed group—it's officially AA, but has some very cool addict regulars who can't make the NA times."

Arielle winced. "I hate that word," she said. "*Addict*. It feels so generic. Like everyone who ever makes a mistake suddenly falls into this category. But I'm good now." She nibbled her way around the edge of a cherry like a squirrel—she didn't pop them into her mouth and bite down recklessly like her sister.

"Listen, though, I mean it would be smart to figure out what happened. Make sure it doesn't again."

"My mother died. So I think we can count on that not happening again," said Arielle. She threw the pit into the bowl—it struck the side and rang like a small bell.

I could almost see Katya suppressing the urge to point out that her mother had died too, and she hadn't ODed. Or even started drinking again. She looked at me for support.

"It would be a smart thing to do, and it couldn't hurt," I said.

Arielle sat up, crossing her arms over her chest. "How's your chicken, Katya? Do the meetings help with that?"

"What chicken?" I asked, but the girls were focused on each other.

"There's a little Shoreside in all of us," said Katya. "A family tradition. Or maybe the chicken was a visitor from the other world. But she's gone wherever ghosts go to rest. R.I.P., chicken. Maybe she made her point and could move on to chicken heaven. And, yeah, I think the meetings help. *Shul* helps. The way I eat helps. I feel a lot more grounded now. And at least thirty percent happier. I want that for you. It couldn't hurt to at least try some nonchemical solutions."

Arielle said, "See, I scared myself. I'm miserable. I admit it." We both leaned toward her, but she held herself stiffly, self-contained. "Oxy made me happy, and it wasn't real, but it worked. Even if I was sad, life felt like it had possibilities. There was something to get up for. I want to feel that way again. I want it every day, and I want it every hour. But I don't see myself going to *shul* and singing in Hebrew. And I definitely don't need to sit in stupid twelve-step meetings. I've done that, and it makes me worse. It makes the cravings worse. It makes me want to take drugs, to show them. I hate how all those people are acting out their own helplessness, all saying we're powerless over our addictions, that we're going to turn our unmanageable lives over to our 'higher powers.'"

She shoved her sleeves up her arms, and the redness of the cross-hatching on her arm shocked me to my roots, my chest seizing up. Before I could stop myself, I said, "Is that . . . are you . . . ?"

"They're *old scars*, Aunt Julia." She pulled her sleeves down again. "I'm doing fine. But I'm afraid of becoming one of those people who go to all the meetings, have the steps memorized. We're not supposed to be trying to teach each other anything but their stories always have a little nugget of poisoned goodness, a message for the rest of us."

"I go to several meetings a week," Katya said. "And, according to some people around here, I can't share anything without turning it into a lecture. So am I one of those people you hate? Please do let me know—I'm certainly waiting to hear."

"I don't mind your lectures, Kat. They always make me smile. You're so like Dad."

"That's great. You can't imagine how cheering that is." Katya threw two pits into the bowl in quick succession, pinging them against the sides.

"Don't be offended. I appreciate that you want to help me. But I have to get through this on my own. That's all there is to it."

I was trying to think of the right thing to say, to suggest that she could find company in the meetings. But Katya knew much more about all this than I did, and she wasn't saying anything.

Arielle asked, in a different, more hesitant tone, "Aunt Julia, after the, you know. You almost died. Do you remember anything . . . do you think there's somewhere afterwards?"

"I don't know." Even if the weird internal stricture on talking about my dreams lifted, I didn't think my nieces would want to hear them, and I wasn't sure what the dreams might mean. Ditto whatever I was seeing when I was "awake." Maybe I was never truly awake anymore. I said, "I think your mother might be somewhere very beautiful and incomprehensible. I think she might be free." I wanted to say that I thought maybe, before I'd woken, I was envying her, but even that didn't seem to be possible to say aloud. "In any case, don't you think a rest would be nice?" I could have bitten my tongue off, as soon as I said it. What if Arielle were lying about not being suicidal? But her face didn't change.

Katya said, "You sound kind of sad too. You know? Arielle and I were talking earlier. I hope you don't mind but, Uncle Robert? Like, we love him and all, but we don't think . . ." She looked at Arielle. "Right?"

Arielle said, "He runs the class and the company as if it were his. And you let him."

I wished I could talk to them all about how much I missed Eva, about the complications with Robert and Alyx, about how much I missed dancing, but I had enough self-control to keep quiet. I felt the Institute alive all around us, the menacing trees in the woods beyond.

Finally Arielle said, "Let's go to sleep. There's no point in talking about any of it anymore."

"We have to do our teeth and faces first," said their aunt, afraid to go to sleep. I watched this aunt of theirs, as if from a great distance. She was unable to help her nieces, afraid of the room, afraid of her own dreams and impulses. She spoke with the moral authority of a woman who was not attempting to cheat on her brother with his girlfriend. His girlfriend who happened to be her own ex-girlfriend. In other words, this aunt of theirs was posing as someone whose moral compass was not entirely haywire, who was not part of a perverse, essentially incestuous love triangle. I didn't wish to know this person and so found myself thinking of her in the third person. See, she wasn't me. She was some character out of Euripides, a plaything of the gods—good move, that! Not her fault at all!—the chorus turning one way, then the other, strophe, antistrophe, warning her, eloquent but unheard.

Where were Alyx and Robert right now? Angrily making love, probably. I didn't want to think about it.

The girls and I did our ablutions, got into bed, closed our eyes, and listened to each other breathe.

I'd killed Robert. Accidentally, but no one would believe me. I stood over his naked body at the edge of the creek—I couldn't leave it. The water flowed over his head, stirring his hair, trout swimming across his open, blind eyes. He would rot here. How could I have been so careless? My God, how had I done this? Where was Eva when I so badly needed her help? I took my brother's cold feet and started to drag him, feeling him catch against the rocks as I pulled. I had no idea where to hide a dead body.

HUNGER

On Saturday evening, right after "Experiments in Action: Dance-Theater Improv" ended and before "Dance-Theater Production" was about to begin, the company held a ceremony in the meadow, starting right before sunset. Each person performed a gesture, then had that gesture received and echoed by everyone in the group. We went around the circle while each of us heard from everyone what we treasured in each other.

Arielle and Katya joined us for the ceremony. The company and students had begun to take Arielle for granted. Mostly people had grown fond of Katya, too, intense and intransigent as she could be. She'd become a kind of mascot. Alyx and I were politely avoiding each other as much as possible, trying not to be obvious about it.

Night had fallen by the time we finished. Several people—including me—cried. A few students were leaving, but most were staying on to work on the production.

We had a dance in the Lodge afterward. We'd strung up colored lights, the only illumination. One of the students DJed. Our girls danced under the lights, energetic, supple. I wasn't surprised that Arielle had so many dance moves, but I hadn't expected Katya to as well. At that moment, they fit right in with the younger students. Some of the older ones joined in, off and on, taking more breaks. Others stood around the edges, drinking and watching.

Robert came up beside me. "Lovely, aren't they?" He gazed off to the side, where Alyx did a strange, hypnotic, somehow spiky little dance with Boyce and Vân Anh. They were inventing increasingly ludicrous moves, one after the other, and laughing. Robert, still not looking at me, said, "I don't think I've ever loved a man or woman the way I love Alyx. She's so unexpected, she'd keep you guessing forever. I never pictured myself getting married, but if I could marry anyone, it would be her."

It was a moment before I could breathe again. Another moment before I found my voice. "But I thought you wanted to break up with her."

"Maybe it's like when you're so hungry, you don't know if you're getting ill or you need to eat. Or maybe I've changed my mind."

"Thanks for letting me know." I was going to say, "I wish you much happiness." Or I could turn around and tear his throat out with my teeth. If I had leopard teeth. With every cell in my body, I wanted to call Eva and ask her what to do. I held very still, trying to keep the tears from starting. By then, I'd started to learn that thoughts like *I will never talk with Eva again* were a sure road to disaster, so I kept my mind very still, squeezing all my muscles together until my whole body hurt. Robert moved away then, around the edge, to get another drink. He never danced at events.

In the rehearsal hall the next morning, getting seriously down to business, we tried out different beginnings, including a post-medieval masque of war and plague. The stage would be bare, except for eviscerated skins hanging from the ceiling and a richly draped throne downstage left. The throne was medieval in shape, but the fabrics thrown across it were brightly colored, contemporary, international.

Half the group, wearing grotesque and comic demon masks, performed an exuberant stomp, like possessed puppets on the loose. The others tried dying of the plague.

Arielle joined the stomping demons. Since the dolphin training, people had accepted her more, though a sense of constraint, of kindness or faint resentment, still lingered. But as the group danced, her whirling, menacing puppet movements weren't out of place, even if not up to the professional level of the company members. Like the students, she was uneven but her inventive, distinct movements were interesting to watch and full of promise.

She and her sisters had often taken dance classes, but while Katya and Jenny later gravitated toward martial arts and yoga, Arielle had kept dancing. Ballet, jazz, tap, samba, African dance, modern. Maybe because she'd never focused on a single form, though, or because I'd missed most of her recitals, I'd thought of it as a childhood hobby. My focus had been on her troubles, as if she were only an addict. She wasn't completely formed as a dancer, but she gave herself over to it so fully that it was hard to look away from her.

Robert leaned against a wall, then lowered himself onto a chair. His one good dinner had been an anomaly. Now his weight loss showed not only in his hollowed-out face but also in his slowed movements, a need to sit more often in the rehearsal room. I'd seen the company's anxious looks, overheard murmured rumors that he might be seriously ill. No one asked me. Could I make an announcement to a few of them that he was fine and hope they'd spread it to the others? Would I be lying?

Standing behind the celebrants and plague victims, Vân Anh, Jon, and Tanikah juxtaposed statistics and quotes in indifferent voices, Jon overemphasizing them in his boyish, amazed way, Tanikah trying a deadpan approach to undercut the excess drama inherent in the material. Vân Anh said, "The dropping of the water tables. Climate chaos. Population growth. The disappearance of arable land. Underfeeding. Overfeeding. Factory farming, fast food."

Tanikah overlapped the last few words. "Nine hundred million people in chronic hunger, six million kids dying a year, fifty million American families who don't know what they will eat that week." Vân Anh raised her voice to interrupt with statistics about chronic hunger: in East and South Asia, 505 million people; in North Africa and the Near East, 41 million; in Latin America, 53 million; and in Sub-Saharan Africa, 198 million, the greatest percentage in relation to population.

Well, all that would have to come right out. Nobody would sit still for any of this—we needed some individual stories, the piece couldn't be all statistics and spectacle. Would the students see on their own how unworkable this was? Robert had brought his books on hunger. And I hadn't felt able to say no. But what, exactly, did the whole medieval plague thing have to do with contemporary facts and numbers?

"We could eat each other," said Jolene, dropping to her knees and demonstrating by bringing her open mouth right up against Boyce's calves, first one then another, and sighing loudly. Students and members of the company piled on with new gestures and sounds—lying on the ground tearing at another's belly, chewing an arm, chomping and clawing. Slow and stylized moves, with one person uttering small moans of longing, another hissing with frustration, a third clicking her tongue in well-fed satisfaction.

I made use of my strong arms and dragging leg to escape slowly across the stage, encountering one pair or grouping at a time. As they attempted to eat me, subdue me, or make love to me, I would be briefly seduced or overcome, and then, stubbornly, return to my journey toward the empty throne. The audience would realize that my inability to move quickly was real, not an imitation. Their discomfort in watching my progress—and sometimes lack of progress—from up-stage right to downstage left could maybe make a kind of narrative arc. God knows we needed one.

"Great stuff, everybody," Robert said. Alyx and I caught each other's eyes, a shared look of disbelief. We were wasting everyone's time. We might actually be in danger of doing *The Torture Chronicles Part II* if we didn't figure out a better approach.

In our first years performing together, Robert and I had spent most of our time on street theater. From the beginning, he couldn't let anyone

262 Hungry Ghost Theater

else direct him, and until we were ready to start our own company, we worked in collectives that decided everything by consensus; this took forever. Robert had fallen in love with Augusto Boal's *Theater of the Oppressed*, and so had I: breaking down the bourgeois distinctions between actor and audience, theater and life. He was fresh out of Juilliard, I was still living at home, and maybe acting together started as a kind of joke or game when he was home for a visit, but I dropped out of school, took my GED, and followed him to Brooklyn. Three years later, we returned to San Francisco. I was still thinking of college off and on, but by that time it seemed to be settled that we lived together. Never in the same room, unless it was a big group flop in some warehouse. We often didn't have hot water or electricity; we hated this, but we felt like real artists.

We joined the Electric Disciples and began performing Invisible Theater, theater as rehearsal for life, often in the midst of life itself. The corner of Market and Geary, the 38 Muni, the BofA teller line, BART trains, Fisherman's Wharf. People who'd never thought of performing became our unwitting antagonists and bit players—this was another time, before everyone was always fine-tuning their public personas and alert to any shade of irony.

Eva came to only one of our events, not long after the Loma Prieta earthquake. She was a grad student in neuroscience then, not yet obsessed with finding the roots of empathy. She'd say to me, "You should do whatever makes you happy, Julia." Doubtfully.

That evening's performance (we thought of these events as "eruptions") took place in a large hotel restaurant, in the middle of a convention of software salesmen from around the world. An artificial waterfall spilled from a balcony into a greenlit fountain, and the customers sat in soft leather chairs at glass-topped tables. Eva and I took over a table for two, examining the super-realistic fabric orchids growing out of plastic cubes: the arrangements even had moss and fake water. We ate cups of thick clam chowder sprinkled with oyster crackers and tasting of elderly bacon. Other members of our collective had scattered themselves throughout the room with their own cups of soup.

The convention had packed the place—tables, halls, elevators, and lobbies. Strangers wound up sitting together, with stiff nods of welcome and averted eyes.

We'd prepared a classic situation right out of *Theater of the Oppressed.* Robert, wearing a conventioneer's badge borrowed from an open-minded designer of video games, began the eruption by saying to his waiter, loudly, "I can't eat any more convention food. Can't you give me something real?"

"Everything we have is on the menu," said the waiter. A man in his fifties, a professional. Those around us looked annoyed, though a few seemed to have sympathy for Robert's moxie. The dinners truly looked awful, though I would have been happy to eat anything. We were always hungry. By choice, we constantly reminded ourselves. We could, theoretically, have gotten real jobs.

Robert pressed the waiter, who recommended the Continental Special: filet of sole amandine, rice pilaf, and green beans at $24.95. Robert said, "I'll have it."

All around us ran convention conversations: people who saw each other once a year, catching up vigorously, falsely. Violin-drenched Muzak created an elevated, comforting mood.

When Robert's food came, he ate it quickly, then stood, holding the bill. He called out to the waiter, "Don't worry. I plan to pay for this in full. But I don't have any money."

"You'll pay or you'll go to jail," said our antagonist, who was also our victim. He was having a hard night. Fully on the side of the Worker, we often didn't exactly take into account the actual people around us trying to do their jobs. And we'd waited tables often enough ourselves to consider even the worst customers to be a temporary nuisance. But I couldn't help looking at Eva's appalled face.

Robert was now the center of attention. "I will pay you with laborpower," he said. A quote from Augusto Boal, translated directly from Spanish, which understandably confused the waiter. After some back and forth, Robert said, "I'll work as long as I need to in order to pay for that filet of sole."

Some of the customers began to call out jokes. They started telling stories of their worst meals ever: fried snake meat with chicken and cat in Guongdong, boiled potatoes at a retirement dinner. Before they could get too caught up in their own ideas, Robert said, "I'm afraid I'm unskilled labor. You'll have to assign me a fairly simple task. I can wash dishes, for example. What does your dishwasher make an hour?"

"He makes what dishwashers make," said the waiter. "I'm going to call the police."

"Let him wash dishes," shouted a man. He waved his plate in the air. "He can wash mine!" His buddies, toasting with their glasses, said, "And ours!"

The manager, a short, balding man with a walrus mustache, appeared in the back doorway and marched toward Robert. "Excuse me, sir, but I'm going to have to ask you to come into the kitchen for this discussion."

Robert insisted, "How many hours of dishwashing will pay for the filet of sole?"

I stood up, "The dishwashers here make minimum wage: $3.35 an hour."

Robert said, "But that would be ten hours, counting tax. And tip— don't worry about that. I plan to pay my tip. But I can't work ten hours for a dinner that took me ten minutes to eat. What about gardening? How many hours would I have to garden to pay for that dinner?"

Eva had her head down, studying her plate. A collective member several tables away—by now we had one of our biggest audiences of our entire career—stood and said, "I know one of the gardeners. They're all day laborers. Except for the head of the gardening service, they make less than $5 an hour."

The manager, sweating but professional, reached out for Robert's elbow, but he pulled away. "So I would have to work a full day out in the sun or the rain to pay for this dinner?"

A red-faced man at a nearby table said, "No one here gardens in the *rain*. Get a grip, buddy."

Another member of our collective stood and said (another translated speech), "My friends, our quarrel is not with these waiters. They work like us and can't be held accountable for the prices. Who knows whether they could afford to eat here on what they make? Our quarrel is with the system itself. Perhaps we should take up a collection for this man's meal. Give whatever you can—a dollar, even a quarter. If you work for Apple, put in a twenty. And whatever's left over will go for a very generous tip to our brother, the waiter."

Some applause, some laughter, some disconcerted looks. A man bellowed, "Why should I pay for his dinner when I'm already paying for mine?"

"Are you paying, or are you on a *per diem*?" asked a jolly-looking fellow at the table across from him. "You should definitely be on a *per diem* for these things."

"I'll pay for his dinner if he also plays the violin," said an older dyed blonde in a power maroon suit, her grand shoulder pads starting to look dated.

The manager went away, presumably to call security. I was hoping we'd be gone before they arrived. If Eva hadn't been there, it might have all felt less humiliating. Or maybe her presence threw Robert off, so he didn't have his usual air of command.

Meanwhile, the hat went around. We collected more than fifty dollars, which Robert left for the waiter, who seemed inclined to refuse, disappointed at not getting us arrested.

We parted from our fellow actors—they'd paid for their bowls of soup and were now headed to the Mission to get burritos. Robert, Eva, and I went walking through the streets of the Financial District, a ghost town at night. Eva would hardly speak to us. Finally, she said, "You betrayed everyone in that room, not only the poor waiter. You think you're better than they are."

Robert said, "I think they need to be awakened."

"Who knows what it's like for them? What if they have kids? Meanwhile, their mother lives with them and they have to take her to the doctor three times a week, risking being fired from their sixty-hour-a-week job programming some wretched security system. Why shouldn't they come to a convention and eat a goddamned piece of fish without you guilt-tripping them?"

I said, "Oh, come on, Eva. They'll all go home talking about it. One of the highlights of their week."

"It's like a children's game gone horribly wrong. You two want everyone to be as miserable as you are. The whole family has bad brain chemistry. Why not see a doctor and get on Prozac like anyone else? Then you could stop blaming the world for everything."

Robert put his arm around her shoulders. "I expect you're right, Eva. You usually are. But we can't help ourselves, can we, Jules?"

Our ongoing wrestle: were we part of a larger conversation or was that self-inflating wish-fulfillment, what did it mean to be part of a conversation, was our job merely to illuminate the nature of power and its effects on people's lives? Was there anything we could do onstage to change that news at all? What if we created openings in people's consciousness or senses of empathy so that they were able or willing to take in the information already out there?

I said, "We want to change the world, Eva. One meal at a time, if necessary."

Enormous buildings surrounded us: luxury hotels, and quick lunch places that closed in the evening. We walked out toward the Embarcadero, looking across at the ruins of the old freeway, destroyed in the earthquake. After we crossed over the trolley line, we stopped for a guy juggling flaming hoops in the plaza. He had a line of patter going—chip in for a last meal before I set myself on fire, I can take my eyes off the hoops but don't you do it, I used to work in one of these banks but it was a whole lot more dangerous. That made us all laugh, together, and Robert reached in his pocket, looking for money. He shrugged and said, "Jules?" And that made us all laugh harder.

"Fine," said Eva. "Pay me back when you hit the big time." She dropped a dollar in the guy's hat and he spun his flaming wheels up into the air, nodding and grinning at us.

We headed out to the pier, looking up at the bridge, the lights of the cars, commuters on their way home, dodging each other, maneuvering to get ahead by a couple of car lengths, or maybe simply working to keep from getting hit.

"I think we're probably going to go on being invisible," Robert said, apologetically enough for him.

Eva shrugged. "You could take the rest of the evening off from saving the world." She looked as if she were about to add, "It probably wouldn't notice," but she refrained.

Evening lights slid across the ripples of the bay. Couples stood with their arms around each other, huddled in their coats against the wind, kids running up and down the pier. A guy leaned on the railing, smoking. He had white-gray hair and a big mustache, probably in his early seventies. He looked as if he had always been handsome, maybe more so now. His wry sadness showed in the angle of his shoulders, his cast-down expression. I wondered what he was thinking about. You never really know, even if someone tries to tell you. For all we knew, we were surrounded by demons and angels.

I was hoping Eva would take us somewhere for dinner. Somewhere tasty but cheap, where I wouldn't feel too guilty about her paying out of her fellowship money.

The guy leaning against the railing threw his cigarette into the water and winked. "Pretty girls," he said to Robert. "You are one lucky fellow." He looked jaunty and forlorn at the same time, and I decided—because I never thought of death then—that someone had recently left him, and he probably had a broken heart.

Three weeks before our scheduled performance of *Hunger*, with the piece still in shambles, we still had no sense of how we would create work about a subject as large and hard to grasp as hunger. Robert and I took the girls for a quick visit with Mom and Dad and then Ray drove them to Jenny and Brandon's farm. Robert and I went up to Forestville alone in our VW bus, arguing through our ideas about whether the incorporation of cannibalism trivialized the seriousness of our subject, whether statistics made the audience go numb, whether it was possible to include the story of a single hungry family and their day without becoming bathetic or crossing a line.

We arrived before dinnertime at the farm, which had been in Brandon's family for three generations. Brandon, who could build or fix anything, had rebuilt the barn and chicken coops and added a workshop out back for Jenny to brew her herbal medicines, complete with an iron, and entirely decorative, cauldron. Paintings of mountain scenes, sunlit forests, and Wiccan ceremonies hung on the workshop walls, a bucolic representation of an ideal life. The farm house felt like a peaceful, welcoming oasis. As usual, the air was full of the scents of Jenny's herbs and cooking. Ginger, cumin, coriander, and a scent of orange: her carrot-cashew curry. Also cinnamon and cardamom from the cake she'd made for dessert.

Brandon was in and out, excusing himself by saying he needed to get the most out of a rented wood chipper he had to return on Monday. Which was reasonable, except that it felt like he was avoiding us. Why were he and Jenny having trouble? Because of her mother's death? For some other reason? When he was in the room, he seemed strenuously affable, even a little too charming—possibly the practiced charm of a philanderer, though I'd also seen evidence that he had a real temper.

At dinner, Arielle drank more than she ate, picking at her food. Robert, as usual, also ate almost nothing, but no one said anything. We were all changing, physically. Between my inability to move the way I had before and the starchy Institute meals, where green salad and tomato sauce were often the only vegetables, I was continuing to gain weight. And so what? I'd decided not to be a neurotic weight-obsessed actor. I'd had only a few months left with Eva, and it made me furious that I'd wasted a moment of that time worrying about what would happen when my looks were gone. I ate three helpings of Jenny's excellent curry and her homemade mango chutney.

After dinner, we hung out in the kitchen, doing dishes and toasting Eva. The kitchen was piled high and the huge black stove still covered with enormous pots of leftover curry, rice, chutney, greens, salads, cake . . . enough that if Genghis Khan had dropped by with a few dozen hordes and we'd all been snowed in, no one would have gone hungry.

Jenny said, "Leave the dishes. We'll do them." We all nodded. But while she was putting Caro and Paul to bed, we dug in and cleaned up. I tried to pick up the curry pot to transfer the contents to a storage container, but I couldn't manage with my canes. "Robert?" He came and took the pot away.

Katya said, "Jenny hates anyone to touch her kitchen," and I said,

"I know," and kept washing. She stood beside me, solid in her tank top and low-cut jeans, tattooed snakes coiled around her arms. She seemed younger in the midst of the family, more tentative, returned to an earlier self, living in a world where any impulsive act might lead to some unexpected, life-changing victory. I touched her spikes of pink and blue hair. Tears immediately filled her eyes and spilled over. She said, "Being here, with the whole family, makes it worse. I miss Mom so much. What I keep thinking of is all the ways I let her down."

Arielle sat on one of the kitchen chairs, her legs crossed, her hair half-hiding her face. "*You* let her down? At least she wasn't here for my latest."

Brandon, who had had enough of pretending that he could bear the family, went off to his carpenter's shed. Arielle helped herself to an after-dinner glass of whiskey. I told myself that if Eva had been there, she would have considered a few drinks nothing much, a relief even, in comparison to whatever Arielle could have been doing instead, but I was worried. I didn't know what to do. I wasn't in charge of her, wasn't even sure if I should be anxious. Ray, who'd had a few drinks himself, didn't say anything in the moment, but caught Arielle outside the room on her way back from the bathroom and said, when he thought the rest of us couldn't hear, "That's enough for tonight, and you need to tell Dr. Sanders about it at the Tuesday check-up."

"I'm *okay,* Dad," she said.

Robert returned with the empty pot, set it in the sink, and poured soap into it. "What do you think? Should I pillow Mom?"

"Uncle Robert!" Katya's tender heart left her prone to constant indignation. Until she could replace indignation with ruthlessness, the odds of her transforming the world into an earthly paradise of peace were small. Okay, nonexistent. As they would be anyway. I did wonder about people who kill their aged relatives—many of them are doing just what they've been asked. But if Robert had meant to kill Mom, he wouldn't have brought it up. Anyway, the thought was ludicrous.

Arielle said, "Do you think it might be the kindest thing, in a certain way?" Now this one was going to be an artist. No, scratch that. She was already an artist.

I said, "People may say they want a pillow on the face. But they only want their fantasies of death, paradise, oblivion, to escape pain or uselessness. It's not like that." They all looked at me in surprise, and I wasn't sure, either, exactly what I'd meant or where that had come from. "I don't think it's like that. So there's no point in rushing it, for any of us."

Eva would have known exactly what to say. Though she might have riled them up, they would have listened. When I gave advice, the family argued and explained why my solutions were impossible. When I tried to tell the truth, I upset everyone. I went outside to clear my head and give them a chance to get over it. Arielle came after me, leaning on the mossy porch rail, avoiding the half-filled cat food dishes. Together we breathed in the air from the farm: manure, fresh dirt, lavender and rosemary, the musty scent of chickens. She asked, "You said before you think Mom is in a better world than this one."

"I don't know, Arielle. I hope so."

"It seems to me that if I had the chance to spend more time with her, I wouldn't make her life a misery."

"Your phrasing suggests you don't think that's true."

"I didn't think what I was doing had an effect on anyone else."

"I suppose you know how much we all love you."

"Sort of." She ran a thin finger over the mossy railing, her face hidden by her hair, like a less seductive Veronica Lake. "Mom really didn't want children. She pretended she did, but she would have liked to live all alone in a lab forever. It wasn't her fault."

I wanted to seize her, stuff her into my body, and keep her there until she was ready for a new birth. "She loved you to pieces. We all do. It would do us in if something happened to you."

"Now that's the sort of thing people say. But you know, you go on."

"Your mother loved her work, but she loved her children more. She might have liked to pretend to herself that she wanted to be alone, but when it came down to it, that was never the choice she made. Even at the lab, she ran meetings and solved people's problems. She was like Jenny that way. Everyone always counted on her."

"And I'm more like you?" She pulled her hair straight back and dropped it over her shoulder before turning to look at me, demanding something. "All we care about is making real life into make-believe?"

An idea came to me. Probably a bad idea—most of mine are. "Arielle, what do you think about people making family stories into theater?"

"What kind of family stories?"

"All kinds, really. Or, at least, the dramatic ones. Out-of-control hungers." I stood there like Cronus, ready to devour Hera, Hestia, Hades, and Poseidon. If I'd been a parent, I'd have been the kind who ate her young.

Arielle shrugged. "Why not?"

"Even addiction?"

She looked down at the railing. One of Jenny's many cats, with long black-and-white fur, half-wild, like most of them, tried to edge around the back of the deck toward a food dish but fled when he saw us turn around. Why had I said that aloud?

Katya came out on the porch. "What are you two up to?"

"Plotting criminal acts," I said. "Looking for forgiveness in advance."

"That's cool, I guess," Katya said. "We're into forgiveness. Step eight, right? Though usually I think you make direct amends wherever possible *after* you do something instead of beforehand." Arielle was now rubbing a circle into the moss. I put an arm around each niece. It was impossible to add anything about addiction to the play. I was bitterly sorry to have brought it up.

ICE

We had a big mess rather than a coherent piece and were feeling increasingly desperate. Late one morning in rehearsal, we sat in a circle to talk about hunger—back in our apparently endless loop of going over our boatload of statistics, information, images, and stories. Moving backward, not forward, away from the heart of the problem. Alyx and I, for once, sat next to each other, which was a mistake. An attempt at maturity, like the alcoholic who wants to test herself with one drink. When I glanced at her, she caught my expression. We both

went red and turned toward Robert, who'd missed neither our awareness of each other nor our immediate movement in his direction.

The girls didn't seem to have noticed. Katya was sitting in with us
for the morning, which she'd begun doing occasionally, now that her
current temp job had ended. My nieces shared an oversized pillow on
the floor. Katya, as usual, sat very close to Arielle, slightly in front of
her, as if shielding her. Arielle had her legs crossed, her chin on her
hand, long silvery hair falling all around her. The ice maiden. I tried
to imagine the hungers that drove her—for sensation? For oblivion?
What did that feel like in the body, what would that look like on stage?
I pushed the idea away and said nothing. It was her life. I was only a
bystander.

Robert stood in the center of our circle. How thin he was. A wraith
of his former self. He clapped his hands. "We need to make this idea
of hunger very specific."

Boyce wanted to do a grid of light, a slideshow of wealth and pov-
erty made semi-abstract, while we performed our cannibalistic moves.
Vân Anh had the idea of focusing on a specific country, situation,
story, and letting it stand in for the larger whole. LaVerne suggested
using photographs of individual kids in hard-hit areas, like some of
the relief organizations did.

I said, "These are great ideas. I wonder if we could collage them
with a completely unexpected element. Maybe we could lighten up
the hunger material with something older, stranger, more delicious.
Like fairy tales."

Robert waved his hand dismissively. "Let's stick to the real world in
the texts. We're already surreal enough with the movements."

It didn't help to have him standing while I sat, but I couldn't get to
my feet without a lot of business with the canes. I sat up very straight.
"If we're going to work with material from the real world, we could
use memories from the company's childhoods, memories that show
hunger of one kind or another. Something to juxtapose with the news
stories. If we need news or statistics at all."

"Childhood memories. *Very* lighthearted." His voice had gotten
acid, warning me. Against what? Was he planning to lean down and

slap me? Dock my pay? In front of the entire company and our nieces?

I smiled at him. "Not those memories. And we might even think about taking a break from the news. Because would you say that too little information is anywhere on the list of major global issues?"

"We are the *News-of-the-World* theater company. Do the Shakespeareans take a break from Shakespeare?"

That had been a misstep on his part. I said, "Sure. They do Ibsen, or Chekhov, or Shaw. Sometimes they even do contemporary work."

Some students and members of the company dropped their eyes. A few of the students seemed to be enjoying the spectacle. Jon, for one, seemed to relish the idea of a good fight. When Robert had disagreed with my ideas in the past, I'd always given way, at least in public. Later I'd tease and wheedle him into considering them, get him to decide they were his own. Why had I done that? Why did I always back down?

Alyx stuck her hands in the pockets of her rehearsal jacket, an old hoodie with a faded gold dragon stenciled on the back. She said, "Some of the company have nicer memories of their childhoods than you do, Robert. Or me, for that matter. Funny anecdotes, maybe. Maybe we should try out Julia's idea. Let's tell some stories and see what happens." She gave him her boyish, mischievous grin.

He stared at her, then at me. I wondered, later, if he thought Alyx and I were in fact sleeping together again. "I have a funny anecdote," he said, an odd look on his face: compulsion and recklessness, as if he were taking a life-threatening dare. He began to weave through the circle, talking to the whole room, one by one, gazing into each person's eyes before moving on. "Once upon a time," he began, "there lived a girl child, who, at the age of twelve, became aware that her mother was in some kind of trouble. There was no one to talk to about this. Her father was drinking a great deal and largely unavailable. In the daytimes, he went off to work. Her fifteen-year-old brother was an arrogant young bastard, her five-year-old sister a dreamy and rather spoiled child. The mother, hungry for news of the other world, longing for a better place than this one, began to receive messages. The radio told her she'd been kept apart from earthly pleasures to keep her pure for a role she would play in the unfolding of history. On the television, people winked at her, reminding her she was waiting for instructions. Spirits visited her in the daytime, as well as at night. She began to predict the future. She said a neighbor would die in order to become a messenger to the angels, and the woman did have a heart attack, though she recovered."

Sometimes you can't figure out how to justify someone's behavior, no matter how much you love them. I felt myself trembling, then paralyzed, as if I were encased in ice. My whole experience at the Institute came back: the room with the shining beaked thing, the woods and their sense of being inhabited, desires that had their own life. Apart from Alyx, none of the company knew any of our family history, and Robert and I had promised each other, long ago, that they never would. I didn't even know this entire story myself—I'd been too young to know what was going on, and no one talked about it later.

Katya and Arielle sat with their arms around each other, perplexed and anxious. Eva had always said they didn't need to know the gory details of our past. But they knew enough to figure out who this twelve-year-old had to be.

Who knew what had hold of my brother? I said, "Let's not dominate this discussion, shall we? What if everyone writes down a story on a piece of paper, no names if we don't want them, and then we write key images anonymously on white boards."

Robert glanced at me, then scanned the room with an unhappy smile. Not just unhappy. Possessed by a cold and focused battle fury. He didn't seem to be able to see anyone. Not our company, not our students, none of the people we were supposed to be looking out for. Certainly not the girls. He said, "Any story is more vivid, told aloud. Don't we want to tell our stories?"

"I don't think so," said Alyx, at the same moment that Jon called out, "Let's tell stories."

Tanikah said, "We've had enough bullshit statistics. No one gives a damn about them. The audience knows everything we do. It's not about what we know, it's about *how* we know it."

"There," said Robert, "You see? Shall I continue?"

"No," Alyx and I said, and, "Yes," said a few other people. Vân Anh added, "When we tell the stories, it makes us stronger." This idea seemed to find favor with the students.

Katya said, "Tell the fucking story." Arielle nodded and entwined her hands in a painful-looking grip.

Robert bowed to them, and to the room. "The children, of course, didn't know all the details about their mother, though the older kids naturally had begun to have an idea. The mother was instructed to show her naked self to the people in the streets so they would understand that, though we are born in sin and live in darkness, we can transcend the darkness if we awaken to our true selves."

Robert's words emerged in time with his pacing. He gazed off above everyone's heads. "If we were to stage this, I think we might not want to have the father drinking as well. It's a bit overkill, don't you think? It would be better, narratively speaking, to have him run off, so that our middle child can be feeding and dressing the family. Or maybe that's too much in a different way."

He went on, not entirely smoothly, "The mother began to keep knives handy, and so did the girl. One day, her mother picked up one of her knives, maybe to make a point, but the girl wrestled it away from her. She could not have said, even to herself, exactly what part of what happened was accidental. The knife bounced off her mother's breastbone, merely scratching her, but her screaming eventually roused the neighbors, who called the police. The mother said she'd done it to herself, to cut away the uncleanness. She wound up hospitalized. The girl was never taken into custody. To get them out of the way, they were sent off to an idyllic farm on the other side of the country for the summer."

Arielle had tucked her head into Katya's shoulder. Katya glared at Robert. He'd gone over the line, and the whole room felt it, but it was too late.

He stopped in front of me, staring down, his face gray, hollowed-out. "This scene would have to be substantially underplayed. It would be crucial not to emote. With material this melodramatic, we'd keep much of the action in subtext. Or we could fool around with tone.

The actors might sing their lines, make it overtly comic. It really is funny, in an over-the-top way. What do you think, Jules? How would this best be staged?"

Robert was either meaner than any human alive or he had completely lost his mind, cracking at last in front of everyone. Maybe he had a brain tumor. I imagined how I would grieve for him after he was gone, assuming the tumor was the kind that would kill him. If our crappy insurance would cover enough of the costs, I could keep the company going afterward. Probably the medical bills would wipe us out, and the whole company, or at least those loyal enough to stay on, would wind up performing in the streets, with an open guitar case at our feet. Who played the guitar? Boyce. The rest of us could sing.

Unable to help myself, I looked at Alyx for help, but she had folded her arms across her stomach.

Robert moved away, circling again, his shoulders hunched, focused inward. "Though the father was against it for quite a while, the middle child finally negotiated family visits for herself and her siblings as the mother went in and out of institutions, from drugs to shock treatment to operations. There's even some potentially comic business where the child sometimes hid the father's bottles of gin and vermouth, sometimes poured them down the sink. All through her teens, she fed and protected her younger sister while the mother's caregivers transferred her up and down the line from state hospital to halfway house and back."

He stopped and looked around the room, as if noticing we were there. "I wonder where the other children were. The boy was busy pretending this was not his family—he was out all the time, finding other communities and activities. The youngest child became more and more dreamy. She made up stories. Though she was a lovely little creature and had always had a lot of attention, she began to pretend to be other people. Hidden by the characters she played, the girl herself became invisible, disappearing from her own life altogether."

The "lovely little creature" remark had done it. Now the room was looking at me, or trying not to look at me, their faces pitying, shocked, reproving, some trying to hide delighted fascination. I pressed my hands together in my lap, trying to think. Having the girls there froze me completely. If I could go to them, but I couldn't, not without making everything even worse.

It was Alyx who turned on Robert. "Go ahead, have a ball. You unmitigated shit. I don't care that you've told them all about my life. A person who has no secrets is freer, in the end. Just another citizen of the post-privacy world. You can damn well post it on the Web for all I care. And I'm not ashamed of what I did to protect my little sister. I'd stab my mother again in a heartbeat. But it's completely trivial and personal. It has nothing to do with hunger."

Now the company was confused. Had they misunderstood who the story was about? I couldn't figure out what Alyx was doing in appropriating the story. Trying to protect me? The girls? I thought, watching her fierce face, I love you so much, I can't stand it. Katya and Arielle looked at me, bewildered, then at Alyx as she picked up her backpack and walked out the door.

Robert, as if he'd forgotten his cue, stood motionless, his hands hanging down at his sides, an expression of puzzlement on his face, as if he couldn't quite remember what had happened. "Excuse me," he said, abruptly, and ran out of the rehearsal room, in the direction Alyx had gone.

The paralysis, the sense of an inhabited room, vanished, and I could move again. I urgently wanted to follow Alyx, but couldn't move as fast as she did. And I had to calm everyone down: I couldn't leave my nieces, the company, or the students. I could feel the group splintering into separate beings. This was so far beyond anything even Robert had ever done. He pushed people hard and made them try out painful material, but this was different. We had no piece to hold us together: everyone needed something to do, a task.

I stood, laboriously, and said, "At this stage in rehearsal, feelings tend to run a little high. It's normal, though it's never comfortable. Why don't we take a break this afternoon? But sometime today, do write down a childhood memory or family story about some kind of hunger, and bring it back for tomorrow morning. And write down any other ideas you have for the piece. See what you discover." People stirred, shook themselves, and began making notes or gathering up their things.

The girls had already headed out into the hall. I caught up with them where they stood on the deck, looking out over the meadow. "I'm really, really sorry about that."

"That was our Mom," said Arielle. "That was our Grandma."

"Your mother was always really brave. Grandma got a lot better over the years. Some people do, and she was lucky with her medications. There's nothing to be ashamed of in this story."

Katya said, "Oh really? Then why did nobody ever tell it to us? Did they think it would be cool to wait till we were grown up and then spill it all out in public?"

I was searching for an answer. Which of us was she mad at? Robert, of course. Maybe her mother, but her mother wasn't here. I apologized, but I could see it was useless.

Katya said, "Never mind. That was a super-rhetorical question. Let's get the fuck out of here. Arielle, I'm going into town for Chinese food and a twelve-step meeting. Do you want to come?"

"You really don't quit, do you?" said Arielle. "Okay. I give up. I'll check out what happens in your meeting. Let's go hang with a bunch of addicts. Whatever."

Where would Alyx have gone? That clear sense of having found the answer, of knowing I was in love with her again, now felt muddy and unreal. This place was driving us all mad. Would Robert have said any of that if we were somewhere else? I knew I should go to the kitchen, get lunch, sit at my assigned table with the other performers, and pretend everything was okay, but I took off, navigating my way through the meadow and over the bridge, and was halfway up the path I'd chosen before I stopped to think. I needed to get out of the valley, to be up in the air. If I could get high enough, I might find the top of the ridge.

I followed the path and then embarked on the project of crossing the creek, balancing on mossy, tipping stones, occasionally slipping and going up to my knees in the cold water. On the other side, I took the widest path, which soon grew steep. I had to hold my canes under my arms and grip roots or branches to climb.

It must be possible to reach the ridge. But the path trailed away, and I discovered I'd lost sight of the creek and was surrounded by brambles, poison oak, ferns, and redwoods. I retraced my steps, painfully, until I found another path. As I climbed, more trails appeared. Was I on the right track? Maybe I would be all right as long as I stuck with the creek.

All around me the trees massed darkly, the sun above barely filtering through. My arms now ached nearly as much as my leg and hips. Even in the shade, I sweated, water drizzling down my face and back, collecting under my breasts. Stubbornly, I kept going, climbing once again, crawling when I had to. I had to get to the light, the place where the trees ended. At the ridge maybe I'd be able to see the entire valley laid out below me.

Frilled orange fungus grew up out of fallen logs. Toadstools sprouted at the base of trees. I pushed upward, startling squirrels or birds or snakes: the unseen creatures brushed away from my step. One of my canes tumbled into the creek below and began to float downstream. I had a few terrible moments of thinking it was lost, having no idea how to get back without it. I stood looking after it, hopelessly, but the cane lodged against a rock. I edged back down to the bank, pulled it out, and returned to my ascent.

When I was almost at the top of the crest, it seemed I was imagining music; then, as I moved upward, the sound coalesced into a definite song, maybe Andean, the notes of a flute, a guitar, and a woman's voice winding through them in a minor key melody both mournful and enticing. I couldn't make out where it was coming from.

The music stopped, replaced by voices and laughter, and started again. I wrestled my way up through the undergrowth. More trees, thicker poison oak, and then a clearing ahead. A series of domes shone in the sun, surrounded by beds of vegetables and flowers. On the porch, a woman out of a pre-Raphaelite painting sang, and a man with a graying beard bent over his guitar on a bench among the flowers.

In the gardens' raised beds, men and women dug and weeded, a flock of children helping. Everyone wore homemade oatmeal-colored garments, shaped like medical scrubs. Orderly rows of lettuce grew alongside tomatoes twining around their wire structures, dark red radicchio in among greens, a welter of zucchini and summer squash, and other plants, not yet bearing, that I didn't recognize. Several weddings' worth of market flowers grew up around the vegetables. I was reminded of Jenny's farm—these people were growing enough to sell at a farmer's market.

Everyone looked up in surprise as I emerged into the clearing. The bearded man set his guitar against the side of his chair. "Welcome, stranger. I'm Julian. And this is Alison. You look like you could use a rest." Sixtyish, weathered, his face had a transparent honesty, an amused patience. His heavy eyebrows gave him a thoughtful, magisterial expression. Prospero, his staff broken and books drowned. Alison, beside him, seemed remarkably unshielded, open, childlike—like a member of the naked company but without the shame or hyper self-awareness. She wouldn't survive fifteen minutes in New York City, but she was perfect here in the woods. I was already in love with both of them, and if they had some kind of harem or free love arrangement, I was ready to sign up.

They took me inside the main dome, gave me oatmeal raisin cookies and some kind of tea they'd harvested from their garden. They didn't eat or drink anything they hadn't grown. At the back of the dome, a small library contained armchairs, a hand-hooked rug, and a shelf of books on composting, French intensive gardening, vegetable cookbooks, histories of communal life, and a few worn storybooks for the children.

I asked them question after question, which they answered courteously, patiently, not too obviously displaying their pride in their life. Two families, with five children among them, lived in the compound, along with two women on their own. Julian told me they pumped their water from a well, drew their power from the high-tech solar coatings of their domes, and sold vegetables in the farmers' markets to earn money for their few bills. All decisions were made by consensus.

At about this point, the children, restless and overfamiliar with the story, went outside to play marbles on the packed dirt in front of the central dome. Julian, though, took no notice and went on. The compound read no newspapers, had no electronic contact with the world, watched no movies. They found enough to do in weaving and making clothes, tending the chickens and the garden, cooking and baking and dehydrating food. In the evenings, they played and sang while sewing. "We ask nothing from the world, and we leave as little imprint as possible."

These communards were so beautiful. What I wanted, what it seemed at that moment I had always wanted, was this spiritual life in a community. I felt it was the only true, human way to live, surrounded by the bulwark of family, knowing who you could count on, knowing that you could be counted on, having a meaningful organizing principle and a place in the structure. If I could learn to weave, they might take me in. Or I could weed very patiently. I'd get a wheelchair. Not a wheelchair—that would be like saying I could never get any better. But, temporarily, a little cart with wheels, like a go-cart, with locks on the wheels for brakes. On market days I'd sell things, make jokes with the customers, spend hours at a table stand, offering sample tastes of the berries. I could have a whole other life.

Alison said, "As the seas rise and the crops fail, humanity will continue in little communities like this one, invisibly."

"Unless everything is poisoned," I said, and smiled in apology. I was as bad as Robert. "It's so bizarre to find you right now, at the moment when my dance-theater troupe is doing a piece about hunger."

"That does sound like quite a remarkable moment of synchronicity," said Alison. "But do you know, everyone who finds us says, 'It's so perfect to find you right now. I was about to quit my job, and I didn't know where to go.' Or, 'It's so right that I'm here. I'm in the middle of a divorce, and I've been thinking about how we all live in this terrible consumer culture.' Everyone feels that we show them exactly what they most needed to know."

Julian said, "We're a blank screen to the rest of the world. A wake-up call. It's one of the functions we serve, though it wasn't part of our original intention."

How noble they were. But somewhere, in and around these paragons, some secret or flaw lay in wait. Someone was sleeping with someone's wife—or if the marriages were communal, someone must mind it bitterly, against his or her own high principles. One of the children was the most beloved, and the others ready for a small vengeance that might go wrong, with tragic results. A child might be plotting to run away to the city and its electronic networks and taco joints—yearning for the outside world, unaware of what would happen to a runaway. Perhaps one of the adults had a painful inner lump they wouldn't take to a doctor. Or the sick person, or his or her spouse, wouldn't compromise by submitting to modern medicine, and so they'd die, unnecessarily but full of a sense of their own grand and yet humble mission. The children, orphaned, would run wild.

These people were extraordinary but also a little wearying. Did I know anyone, from the naked people to these communards, who wasn't instantly ready with a sound bite, or a full speech, to explain their lives and positions? Did I even know anyone who wasn't an artist, an activist, a crazy person? Ray was a lawyer, but he had that obsession about border wars. Had Eva been a regular person? Can you count an affective neuroscientist as a regular person? Even Jenny was an herbalist and apprentice witch. So, apparently, I knew no regular people at all.

I had fallen out of love with them as quickly as I had fallen into it. I was not going to try to join their commune. Instead, like a vampire looking for her next kill, I was imagining how theater could be made from this situation. I thanked them for their hospitality and made my way down the hill in the dark, scraped by bushes, falling several times, probably into poison oak.

Finally I found the main path, which took me down to the cabin. Robert was sitting on the edge of the porch, his elbows on his knees, his chin on his hands. His face was streaked, but he wasn't crying anymore. "I told her I was sorry," he said, as if this somehow explained a key fact.

Alyx was gone, and so was her stuff. So simple! I'd pictured the three of us having time to process what had happened, but it turned out a person could walk out with no goodbyes, no exit papers. She hadn't even taken everything. One or both of them had thrown piles of her clothes and papers and some of his things over the edge of the deck with enough force that most of it landed in the creek, not far from the old tire and broken chair. Some of the paper had stuck in the trees or dropped to the bank. The deck itself was covered with bedding, old letters, and even company paperwork.

I said, "Well, I can see how well your apology worked." I waited for him to also tell me that he was sorry, but he gave me the look of a mule that's been whipped until it refuses to move.

Our camera equipment lay in the dirt below the deck, the camera's flash shattered against a rock. Still, as I examined the wreckage, I saw that it wasn't as complete as I'd expected. Belongings had all been thrown short, more performance than actual destruction. Oh, actors! Here's a question I don't know how to answer: can we help it or not?

"It was a little crowded in the cabin. Now there's more room." Robert wiped his face with the back of his hand, a rough gesture, as if he had insects on his cheeks. "Do you know what all that was about?"

I picked out a pillow from the mess on the deck and sat with him on the steps, stacking my canes beside me. "I keep asking myself."

"See, neither you nor I know. But Alyx did. She told me I'm a one-woman man, and that everything I do is somehow about you, even when it's against you. That she makes us a present of each other. She said that we've clearly inherited Mom's genetic structures and they're beginning to break through. What's your vote on that, Jules?"

Had she said that *he* had inherited Mom's structures, or that *we* had? I couldn't ask him, and I wasn't going to get to ask Alyx. In the end, he was the one she'd cared enough about to fight with. Maybe she would send me a message. But I didn't think so. "What does this do to the company, to the students? And our nieces? Did you think that was a great way to let them know a little additional family history?"

"I wasn't thinking about them."

"See, that's the thing which makes all this so impossible." I couldn't stop myself. "We're one big happy family of fucking hungry ghosts, gobbling at the trough, battling each other for food we can't even eat. Worse, we're *performing* our own emptiness. We can't help turning it into theater."

We sat in silence. I said, "I don't think we can get a lot lower than this, Robert."

"Can't we climb back up?" he asked. A real question. He needed my help.

I closed my eyes, clearing my mind, and saw a queen on a throne in the half-dark, longing for news from the sister she had eviscerated and disemboweled, a sister who'd disappeared completely after her resurrection. The image felt like an alarm going off inside. Here was what I had to do. "What if we made the piece about Ereshkigal in the underworld?"

"We did the Inanna-Ereshkigal story years ago," Robert said, but he was chastened, watching me with an unusually vulnerable expression.

"We did *Inanna's* story. We should give Ereshkigal's version. We could keep the best of what we've come up with so far and use her story to structure the piece. What is she ravenous for? Why is she so cruel to the sister she loves? What happens when she's left alone in the underworld? And what's it like in the land of the dead?" I couldn't sit any longer. I stood up, slowly, using my arms and stomach muscles. "I bet Ereshkigal herself didn't know why she did what she did."

Robert thought about this, and so did I. Why keep going back to the Sumerians? Weren't we the worst Jews (or semi-Jews, or whatever) imaginable, totally unable to even come near the material that lay right at hand? There might someday be a moment when we tackled our own family story, the story of Mom's parents, the moment when history put its hard stamp on us. But even if there ever would be such a time, I couldn't yet imagine it. Ereshkigal and Inanna were about as close as we could get.

Robert said, "We've already committed ourselves. In publicity materials and the Studio Theater calendar. To doing a piece called *Hunger.*"

"You could do anything and call it *Hunger.* Robert, I've just understood how much you've given up on theater. We wanted to transform people's imaginations. Now we're trying to *horrify* them into waking up. But it's like the Aesop fable, with the wind and the sun trying to get the man to take off his coat. Couldn't we, for once, have the nice sun role, warming the audience up in a friendly way?"

"You want to be a priestess in the Temple of Art. But we don't have time to be nice friendly suns. We have all the technology to survive, but not the will. We refuse to know what we know. Maybe it's already too late. We have to turn a ship a hundred times the size of the Titanic, and meanwhile three quarters of the people on board are madly partying. Or steering right into the iceberg."

"You can save the lecture, Robert. If we keep pushing this piece in this direction, in the time we have, we're going to wind up with nothing but another mess. At some point, we might be ready to make the piece about hunger that we were imagining, but we're not there yet. In the meantime, maybe humanity will put into practice some wonderful new solutions. Carbon sinks. Wind power. Or maybe little enclaves of civilization, or at least of life, will survive in the woods, weaving their own clothes, making their own tea, and patronizing random travelers from the outside world."

"What the hell are you talking about?" Robert had an intractable look: he sat in the rubble like a king on the battlefield, refusing to admit to his loss.

"Nothing. Forget it." My whole body ached from the climb. It was nearly three, and I'd eaten nothing since breakfast but the tea and oatmeal cookies. I was starving, my stomach much too empty for the painkillers I needed.

Robert had bullied, I had allowed it. We'd been muddled in our ideas, in our actions, by grief and fear over the family. A giant, multisided structure of loss and betrayal had risen up between us—it hadn't just happened to us, we had *made* it. Maybe, if we had been somewhere besides the Institute, our betrayals would have taken a different form. But we'd still be living with the choices we'd made and where they'd landed us.

I said, "We need to shake things up, and part of that could be doing an utterly different piece—Ereshkigal and Inanna—and having me direct it. You're not in shape to run things. And I'm not going to live like this. I don't care what happens to me. Things have to change or I'm getting out."

He laughed, an unpleasant, bitter sound. "Those were Alyx's exact words—'I'm not going to live like this.' Alas, you could never have that repetition on stage." He stood and began picking up the bedclothes and gathering crumpled papers, trying to smooth them out. After a moment, he stopped where he was. "Unless you didn't even try to make it seem realistic but had the whole company repeat it, one person after another, like a refrain. It would be perfect in the Ereshkigal piece. It could be the opening line."

"It could be," I said. We would see. The king was retreating from the field, and that would have to be enough for now. I was beyond sore and exhausted from my climb but possessed by a need to keep moving. Leaving my canes on the deck, I edged down the steps, one at a time, and slithered down the cold, muddy slope to the creek. Kneeling painfully, I rescued what I could, gathering armfuls of camera equipment, clothing, old programs from our shows. Robert moved back and forth above me, from the path to the cabin, collecting and straightening our possessions. Meanwhile, some of the company paperwork in the creek had already begun to come apart. We had, as always, brought too much with us. I leaned out over the water, scooping up the remains by the handful. As I worked, I whispered, trying to convince myself, "Indomitable, indomitable."

Sherrie, Phoebe, and Marcus left the company in solidarity with Alyx. I wanted to add something new to the rehearsal room, to change the tone before we lost everyone. Windup toys. Amulets. A smiling Buddha. A cross. But that might be like dropping baking soda into vinegar, creating a foaming explosion. Finally, I hung an old bedspread across the back of the room—pink, lavender, green, enormous cabbage roses. I asked Katya to bring back chocolate from one of her trips into town. "It has to be vegan and slavery-free," she said, and I thought I should have asked someone else, but I gave her a pair of twenties and said, "Fine. Bring me the change, if there is any."

On the surface, things continued as before, though to bring the company back to a reasonable level of functionality took about four days of chocolate, improv games, and shared stories of family memories. At intervals, various people pulled me aside to complain about Robert and to tell me more about their own lives and what his performance had reawakened for them. I listened, agreed, soothed them, and tried to find the line between explanation and justification.

Some students were rattled—we'd activated their bad parent stuff. LaVerne said, in a no-nonsense tone that reminded me how beyond us she was professionally, "I'm not going to quit and leave them in the lurch. But you and Robert need to clean up your bullshit."

Others, though, seemed to thrive. Jon said, "I always wanted to be part of a backstage drama. I thought there'd be more tap-dancing though." On the whole, I was grateful for the way he was taking it.

Jolene had said something about "your family" and looked embarrassed, but no one seemed surprised.

Katya was barely speaking to either of us. Arielle came to rehearsals during the day, and went meetings with Katya at night. She still complained about the meetings, albeit with less force, and I thought they were doing her some good. Still, she had her own drama going on. She'd stopped drinking and was flooded with unexpected emotions. "I can't believe that Mom *stabbed* Grandma," she said. "I keep saying it to myself, over and over. But I can't picture it. Do people do that stuff? It's so goddamn tabloid. Our own family? *Mom.*"

"Not really stabbed her," I said, weakly. Had she heard Mom's parents' story, the ditch at Treblinka? Some time or other, I was going to have to find out exactly what the girls did and didn't know about the family.

Rehearsals were better as we began working out Ereshkigal and Inanna, which at least had a story. As Ereshkigal, LaVerne danced on and around her throne, while I descended from level to level, stripped of everything along the way, and Robert and the company ranted about hunger in the upper world. We tried switching roles, which meant that I could sit on the throne while LaVerne descended. What did it mean to have one or the other of us flayed? Did the flaying become in one case about race and power and in the other about disability and power? Or did that depend on the audience and their reactions? Could we, whichever we decided, work with the additional and maybe unavoidable implications?

The students and Arielle were blue flames in the underworld. They translated some of the movements from their earlier demonic stomp into the new iteration of the piece. Arielle struck me as the one to watch. Not just because she was my niece. She burned harder than the others, more absolutely became the fire. Most of our performers had fully accepted her, a tribute to her gifts. Only Mel and Roxanne occasionally exchanged sidelong glances around her or made small remarks that included the words "merit" and "nepotism."

The stories and statistics still didn't quite work. We had the warring sisters, the environment of hell. We had the enraging sadness of hunger. It went together thematically, but it didn't seem to be part of a single piece. We were still looking for the final layers and connections. And I had a nagging sense of a task unfulfilled. Why? I kept seeing Arielle as the ice maiden at the mercy of her hungers. If we added a role for her as Inanna's daughter, wouldn't that sharpen what was happening between the sisters, wouldn't it give a sense of focus to the piece? How bad would it be to drop a hint and see what happened?

When the girls returned from their Thursday night meeting around 9:30, I asked if we could talk. We sat together in the parlor on the cots. I had made popcorn with nutritional yeast as a bribe for Katya. It tasted a lot better than it sounded, sort of cheesy and comforting. I said I wanted to know how they were doing and—since leaving it at that would be a lie—maybe to talk again about what they thought of putting family stories in the play. Not the one Robert had told, I added. But I wondered if it had given them a distaste for the whole project.

"I don't exactly see how family stories would go with Ereshkigal and Inanna," said Arielle. "Not that we don't flay each other from time to time."

"That's the spirit," said Katya. "Apparently, if you're going to be an actor now, you get to behave any old way you want, on or off stage."

"Don't start, Kat. It doesn't help."

"I didn't mean literally," I said. "Not the actual stories. But I've been thinking about adding an ice maiden, about bringing in addiction and different kinds of hungers." Arielle had been doing so well in the rehearsals. "Can I say this to you? Are you really all right?"

"Katya's meetings are pretty touching, really. All of us sad addicts: our big goal is to become ex-addicts. Counting the days since we last used." She looked thinner and older than she had in the spring, her eyes sad, her cheekbones prominent. She seemed to realize she'd made us sad as well, and she added, "But I like the rehearsals, and I really appreciate how you've taken care of us. I'm sorry to have been such a pain."

"You're not a pain," I said. "You're very gracious, really. We don't do much with graciousness in this family. We're always trying to tell the truth. Or, you know, the nastiest possible aspect of the truth."

"It's the part we need to look at," said Katya, uncompromising.

"Oh, honey."

Arielle said, "Anyway, I'm hanging a little with the Shakespeareans—they're teaching me to talk in blank verse. You breathe at the end of the lines—and you also have to decide, in between, whether you're going to pause or go right through the caesura. Shakespeare goes back and forth between poetry and prose, and he always has a dramatic reason. You can't deliver it in the ways that people expect. You have to keep hold of the story and the music and turn it into something they haven't heard before."

She brushed popcorn bits off her jeans and stood, her hands clasped in front of her. Her voice changed, became younger, richer, both petulant and desperate, with the faintest of pauses to mark ends of lines:

"Now I but chide; but I should use thee worse,
for thou, I fear, hast given me cause to curse.
If thou hast slain Lysander in his sleep,
being o'er shoes in blood, plunge in the deep,
and kill me too.
The sun was not so true unto the day
as he to me. Would he have stolen away

from sleeping Hermia? I'll believe as soon
this whole earth may be bored, and that the moon
may through the center creep, and so displease
her brother's noontide with th' Antipodes.
It cannot be but thou hast murd'red him.
So should a murderer look, so dead, so grim."

She had made *use* of her sadness, turned into the spoilt, pretty, well-loved daughter of a harsh, aristocratic father, awakening to an unforeseen nightmare. It was midsummer, and she was in a strange forest, without her lover, tormented by professions of devotion from a former friend who seemed to have betrayed her. Arielle had become transparent, had disappeared into another reality, in which Hermia was so lost that she could only refer to herself as if she appeared in someone else's story.

As Katya and I stared at her, Arielle said, in her own voice, "You know, Ereshkigal and Inanna, I remember them, from when I was little. It's the first play I saw. At least the first one I remember. The lights, the cold. You on the staircase."

"You couldn't understand why anyone would flay her sister." I tried to speak normally, as if I hadn't just been present for the moment when it became clear my niece was going to make it. I exerted my entire reservoir of professional control to blink away tears.

"I still don't understand." She wrapped her hair around her hands, put it behind her shoulders, exposing her face. "Are you thinking, what if Ereshkigal had a daughter or something in the play? She could carve chips of ice from the walls of the underworld and use them to live in a dream world. Making addiction one of the hungers? If we do that, I want to play it."

"Yes," I said. "Absolutely."

Katya said, "Not a good idea. Much too early in her new recovery."

"No, Kat, it's okay," Arielle said. "I think it will help. And maybe help someone else, too."

"It's cannibalistic."

"I understand how you feel," I said. "Believe me."

Katya drew a design on the floor with the toe of her sneaker. Finally she said, "If you want to do it, Arielle, then I'll be there to watch you."

We went to bed not long afterward. I was too excited and anxious to sleep in the first part of the night, then fell heavily into a dark well. Robert and I were in our sleeping bags, except that we seemed to be in a huge train station with a white domed ceiling and skylight—a contemporary Victorian conservatory full of people rushing past without looking. Robert lay on his back, red flannel pulled up to his chest, his neck and face exposed, smiling in animal triumph. I crept out of my own bag, took a pile of old programs for our performances—I knew I should remember why everything was wet—and pressed them over Robert's face. The paper became metal, cutting my hands, which seemed only right. I ought to be in pain too, if I were going to kill Robert. He thrashed wildly, giving out muffled yells, making a spectacle. No one stopped or paid any attention. Maybe people thought it was an improv.

Suddenly clearheaded, I thought, I'm dreaming, but I'm not *dreaming*. The train station, flooded with white cool light, the pale pastel mosaics in the ceiling rotunda. I had been here before; I was here at this moment, more significantly than wherever I was supposed to be. When Robert finally stopped moving, I ran away to find a train, my arms and hands aching. It was quite simple to run. I had remembered how, and everything would be fine.

Down a bright corridor of locked shops, people wheeled their suitcases, checked their watches, put on or took off the raincoats they'd need at the other end. I couldn't see where they were going. Advertisements everywhere, but no signs for the trains. Down one corridor, then another. All the doors blank and locked. I asked everyone I saw, "Do you know where I can buy a key?" But no one answered me.

The dream didn't need much interpretation. I went into town very early in the morning for the next few days and, using my phone card and every connection I had, began to make my arrangements for post-performance escape. The rehearsals, as we began to introduce

Arielle's idea, became so dramatically better that I didn't want to spoil Robert's mood by telling him that I was getting ready to move on. Having the daughter in the play changed the whole texture of the interactions. Though I'd been Inanna before, I'd somehow never tried to understand Ereshkigal, her rage, her sense that, as always, she was about to lose everything to the sister who was easier to love when she was far away. Also, I'd been thinking of the flaying as an unimaginable crime. But these Sumerian gods could, at least physically, recover from being flayed. Whether they could forgive each other was another story.

One week before our final performance, I told Robert I wanted to talk to him about the plans I was making. We sat on chairs on the Lodge's darkened deck; the lanterns had all been extinguished. A pale yellowish light from inside showed me his wary face. The sounds of very danceable rock came to us from the dorm—evidently the students were having an informal party.

I said, "I'm interested in moving away from stage performing. It's a lot for me now. And if I'm in every performance, the piece, and the company, becomes about my condition. There are already companies that do that well."

His face in the half-dark looked guilty, relieved, sad. He was so thin, an imprint on the space around him, half-faded away. "What are you going to do, Jules? You're not made to be a bit player. You're made to be an empress."

Refusing to match his tone, I said, quietly but with force, "I'm going to do this production until we take it to the next stage, and then I might want my own company. To direct my own ideas."

His kind and guilty look disappeared. "And what will I do while you follow all these plans? Retire to a farm? Open an orphanage?"

"You might like doing whatever you want, Robert. I wasn't in New York long enough for you to figure out what you could do without me. You need to find the fun in it again."

His voice shook with anger, "We're living at the end of the world, and you want me to have fun."

"Oh, Robert. You can't help anyone in this frame of mind. Why don't you try some real devised theater and be a performer among performers? You might get so into not having to be in charge of everything that you never want to direct again." His face stiffened, and he made an involuntary movement toward me, as if he had to refrain from hitting me.

I said, "Here's an assignment for you. Come up with a hundred different people, not ideas or statistics or concepts, but *people*. Alternate versions of Robert that come from some aspect of your mind, body, or life. People you would never be for some very good reason, or people you might have been in another life. A serial killer Robert, a Robert who never goes out during the daytime, a super-kind Robert, an addict Robert, a Robert who's dedicated himself to trying to erase hunger in the developing world, a Robert who became a tango dancer, a Robert who works as a night janitor for the CIA. Develop some movement, or a piece of a story, for each of them. Who else might be living inside you?"

"A hundred people is ridiculous. I don't have a hundred people in me."

"I'm not sure you know what you have in you." From the party in the dorm came the sounds of laughter, excited shouting, and Infernal's "From Paris to Berlin." All that catchy, futuristic longing made me want to get up and dance. I said, "How about thirty-five then? Anyone can find that many possible selves."

After a moment he said, "I could do thirty-five."

I smiled. "Get the whole company to do it. That's the start of your next piece."

"That's not me coming up with my own ideas then, is it?" He waited. I waited. He shrugged, not really a concession. "We'll see. And, as for you, a few months of trying to direct anything on your own, and you'll be begging to come back and be part of this."

"Fortunately, you'll be right there if I need you. All thirty-five of you." Then I said, a friendly warning, "And I think I'm going to tell a few family stories of my own. Maybe I'll write some plays."

"It's okay with me," he said, and I answered him, "No, you don't get it. I'm not asking permission."

Our end-of-summer performance—our first for the piece (in the fall we would move it to San Francisco for the last weeks before I headed off on my own)—took place out in the meadow on the final night of our closing festival. The opening night had been Shakespeare and the second night the naked people and the dancers, both doing shorter pieces. Before we started, I was ill, in secret. I remembered Piers fleeing his final performance and said to myself, as if it were a joke, "Fortunately, I can't just get up and walk away." I took the maximum amount of painkillers. I'd pay for this later, but I didn't want to be distracted during the performance.

We'd all seen scraps of everything in rehearsal for weeks, and sometimes sat in on each other's dress rehearsals and given feedback, but the performances themselves had a different level of electricity. The naked people—first shaming each other, then at last standing up to their own (and our) watching eyes—made me weep. The Kundalini dancers were unexpectedly good. *The Tempest* didn't quite come off, but the actors did well with the poetry, and the students were touching and funny as shipwrecked sailors and malevolent dukes.

We did *Hunger* in the round, as we had our first Inanna and Ereshkigal performance all those years earlier, chairs ringing the dark and hillocky grass this time, and real torches, once again, burning on all four sides. The air was already colder at night. We began at twilight, with the first line, "I'm not going to live like this," which every one of us said at some point in the performance. Once we started, I was Ereshkigal, not myself, and the panic transmuted into energy. I was *at home* and felt it through my body, cells, muscles, bones, firing nerves.

On the grass, we'd drawn a great spiral with white chalk that fluoresced in the darkness, circling the underworld where the company danced. Our students made fierce underworld inhabitants. LaVerne, as Inanna, walked the spiral into the Underworld. Robert, the Gatekeeper, confronted her, collecting, piece by piece, her crown, scepter, arm bands, and robes. Instead of crawling across the floor, I sat on a throne at the center in between two pillars carved out of ice. Tall and straight and solid, I felt like a queen, as long as I wasn't trying to walk.

We'd returned to a classic News-of-the-World technique from our very first days: some danced, a few read the hunger quotes we'd chosen. Unlike in our early days, we'd stripped away the connective tissue and allowed the quotes to stand on their own:

" . . . the 'unfathomable catastrophe' that occurred when, as a child, he saw the bulldozers arrive on the shore where he and his father fished."

"I saw warehouses in Juba overflowing with millet, dried fish, cooking utensils, agricultural tools and medical supplies, all useless because nothing could be delivered to the people who needed it."

"The death toll from hunger equals a Hiroshima bomb going off every three days."

My throne, a movable platform I could spin to watch LaVerne's passage, allowed me to look out at the audience. We'd nearly filled our eighty chairs: many people had been coming to shows all week, including a family with eight children, most of whom crawled under the chairs until the young ones fell asleep. Then there were the performers from the other companies, the Institute staff, and even a few strangers. Our family had come, of course, including Mom. I could see from her face that she wasn't following the story but was enjoying the fire of the torches, the costumes, the dancing. Ray hated it. After one glance, I made sure not to look at him again. And Katya still seemed unhappy to see Arielle performing addiction. But Jenny looked glad—she'd always hated secrecy, cover-ups, the unspoken.

Inanna's kidnapped daughter shaved off chips of ice from the pillars, swallowed them, and danced around the circle's edge, an ecstatic, dreaming girl. At last she came to the front of the throne, her eyes closed, her arms waving in the air. Robert said to the audience, "Can a girl who has dreamed our dreams go up into the light?" Though perpetually exhausted from the weight loss, when it came down to it, he was still a pro.

As Arielle danced, LaVerne neared the center of the spiral, and

Robert challenged her for the seventh time, stripping her down to her slip. When she reached the center and stood before the throne, the dancers slowed and moved to surround us. "Nothing you do will stop me," LaVerne said. "I am here for my daughter."

I raised my head in defiance, looking past her to the audience. In the front row sat a tall woman in a gold brocade coat, there for the first time. I would have noticed her if she'd come before. She reminded me strongly of someone, but I couldn't think who. She wore her dark red hair in a construction of twining braids and turned her head from side to side in abrupt movements like a splendid bird of prey. Maybe in her sixties? My guess was that she had grown up with money and had always had jobs where other people did as she told them to do. And yet I couldn't exactly imagine her in any job. In a boardroom? Performing surgery?

The company, slowly, began to dance in defense of Arielle. I said, "Leave your daughter and go. We have what she needs here." Now I was the villain in earnest, cold, triumphant. The audience shifted in their seats, tensely.

LaVerne stepped toward me, her hands raised, and I said, "Flay her." I turned my back as the dancers surrounded her, and she dropped to the ground. We'd created prosthetic wounds down her torso and sides, painting them over with latex to look like skin. Now the dancers peeled away the latex, slowly. It came off in ragged, bloody strips, leaving behind what looked like torn flesh, blood and veins showing through. The audience gasped.

Arielle stood over LaVerne and began a wild dance of mourning.

I dragged myself off my throne and slid down beside LaVerne, where I performed a solo snake-like dance lying on the grass, enacting grief and regret. Then I held out my hands to her—was I resurrecting her? Was she resurrecting herself? She rose as the company crowded around her, helping her up, uniting her with Arielle.

Lying at LaVerne's feet, I pleaded, "Please forgive me. I went mad, down here at the bottom of the world. Will you bring me up to the morning light? I can't live like this."

But Inanna, her daughter, and all the underworld inhabitants stood over me, unyielding. I curled into a ball while they withdrew one by one, leaving me alone on stage.

The audience clapped for a long time. About a third of them stood, and we had some shouts of approval. Arielle, taking LaVerne's hand and mine, as I leaned on my canes, made her bow with the rest of us. Fully alive after her dream-ridden dancing, she was a creature of the theater, a shade at home among shades. We bowed to all four sides of the audience.

In our final bow, the woman with the braids caught my eye. She wasn't clapping; she sat with her head bent. Flown with post-show self-congratulation and relief, I decided maybe she was crying. Who did she remind me of? She could have been a theater person herself, but she was more real than we were. Next to her, we were as tricky and flimsy as our costumes or the cheap light globes on the Institute porch, some of which were flickering out already. So regal. Or, really, beyond regal, queen of heaven and earth.

What kind of apology or explanation could you possibly make for flaying your sister? There would have to be a secret between them, the kind of secret only a sibling knows. A code word that leads, in the end, to forgiveness, no matter what's happened, no matter how long it takes to get over it. Ereshkigal, of course, would wait for a response, sitting by herself in the underworld. Or maybe with other gods or demons, if hells could be permeable.

As I thought about it, images began to come to me: Ereshkigal in hell, two sisters from the world above stumbling into her realm. I had the sense of *remembering* rather than inventing. Did Ereshkigal have a message for Inanna? Or was that another dream?

We kept bowing as the clapping continued, and when I next looked for the woman, she was gone. We folded and stacked the chairs, put out the torches and went off together, leaving behind a meadow full of ghosts.

Though we'd worked all summer for one ephemeral moment, I was content. Sometimes, after a successful performance—not as judged by the responses but by your own knowledge that you've found the hidden shape of the piece—you understand all this work wasn't for you after all. And it wasn't for the audience, who have become, in their silences and murmurs, their sighs and focused attention, participants and fellow creators. No matter how you imagined your task beforehand, what you've really been doing is carrying a letter from a god to a god: you did what you had to when you handed over an unopened message, in an unfamiliar language, without ever having known what's inside.

NOTES ON SOURCES

Anne Bluethenthal and Erika Chong Shuch kindly allowed me to sit in on rehearsals for Anne Bluethenthal & Dancers/ABD Productions and The Erika Chong Shuch Performance Project. I have learned so much and had so much pleasure from their work. Katie Cantrell, founder and director of the Factory Farming Awareness Coalition, has been crucial in shaping my thinking about industrial food systems. Their work has been an inspiration to me for years.

Among the works I read on theater, hunger, addiction, and mental illness, I have particularly relied on the following sources for some of the facts or ideas in this novel: Seymour M. Hersh, "Torture at Abu Ghraib," *The New Yorker*, May 10, 2004. Sharman Apt Russell, *Hunger: An Unnatural History*. Ronnie Cummins, "Hazards of Genetically Engineered Foods and Crops: Why We Need a Global Moratorium," in Karl Weber, ed., *Food, Inc.: How Industrial Food is Making us Sicker, Fatter, and Poorer – And What You Can Do About It.* Jonathan Safran Foer, *Eating Animals.* T. Colin Campbell and Thomas Campbell II, *The China Study.* Raj Patel, *Stuffed and Starved: The Hidden Battle for the World Food System.*

In the final performance, the quote about the death toll from hunger comes from Frances Moore Lappe's *Hope's Edge: The Next Diet for a Small Planet.* The quote about the bulldozers comes from James Gustave Speth's *Red Sky at Morning: American and the Crisis of the Global Environment.* The quote about the useless supplies in Juba comes from *Newsweek,* as quoted in The Hunger Project's *Ending Hunger: An Idea Whose Time Has Come.*

Augusto Boal wrote, "The artist and the madman seek the same end: to order chaos, to search for meanings. That was what God was doing on the very first day of the Creation" in *Games for Actors and Non-Actors*, second edition, many years after Sonja thinks of these words. I'm making a guess that this wasn't the first time he'd expressed this idea, and so the troupe could have heard about it. Many of the theater games and exercises come from this book or from *Theater of the Oppressed*, still others are variations of those I learned at the Berkeley Repertory School of Theater. Keith Johnstone's *Impro: Improvisation and the Theater* and *Impro for Storytellers* were also very helpful.

The story Eva reads in *The Santa Cruz Sentinel*, "Problem Children To Get Aid," was published on June 2, 1974. And some of the information on addiction and desire in "Rescue" is on the work of Kent Berridge, PhD., and his team at the University of Michigan: http://www.lsa.umich.edu/psych/research&labs/berridge/research/affecttiveneuroscience.html.

ACKNOWLEDGMENTS

This novel and its sequels have been in process for a long time, and I'm tremendously grateful for my beloved family, friends, colleagues, students, and readers for their support, help, and companionship. The list here doesn't begin to name everyone who has been central to my life and writing, but I want to offer my particular gratitude here to those who have helped me with this book.

Some of the pieces of this novel have appeared, sometimes in very different forms, in the following journals, and I am grateful to the editors for their encouragement and help: *Mission and Tenth Inter-Arts Journal, Ploughshares, Scoundrel Time, StoryQuarterly,* and *Valparaiso Fiction Review.*

Deep, deep thanks to Andrea Barrett, Angela Pneuman, Ann Cummins, Lisa Michaels, Cornelia Nixon, Ann Packer, Vendela Vida, and Steve Willis, for reading so many drafts with such brilliance and kindness, and for the pleasures of your own work. I'm grateful to, and will always miss, Nancy Johnson. Great thanks as well, for inspiration and support in reading and writing to my wonderful friends Randall Babtkis and Carolyn Cooke, Sylvia Brownrigg, Harriet Chessman, Thaisa Frank, Margot Livesey, Cass Pursell, Liz Rosner, Joan Silber, and Malena Watrous.

I was very lucky to have the chance to study with Jonis Agee, Charles Baxter, Nicholas Delbanco, Lorrie Moore, Eileen Pollack, and my MFA cohort at the University of Michigan, Ann Arbor. They saw some of the earliest beginnings of pieces of this book and taught me so much about fiction.

My colleagues and students at the Warren Wilson MFA Program for Writers and Stanford Continuing Studies, and the writers I work with one on one, as well as my former colleagues and students at New College of California and California Institute of Integral Studies, have been remarkable in their generosity and wisdom, extraordinarily devoted and knowledgeable, surprising, inspiring, and a delight to work with.

Peg Alford Pursell is my dream editor: intuitive, witty, tirelessly dedicated, full of unexpected insights and solutions. She inhabited the characters and world of this book so deeply, and with such respect, that the process of working with her has been a complete joy. My gratitude to her, and to WTAW Press, is boundless. Many thanks as well to adam b. bohannon for his gorgeous cover and book design.

I'm grateful to, and for, my whole family, and Ron's family, who have also become my own over the years. This book is for you, both my living family and those who've left us behind. You are all, every one of you, *ein Licht in den Augen*, as Grandma Bronka used to say. A particular thank you to my amazing sisters Lisa and Laura for reading drafts and commenting so lovingly and helpfully. And my deepest gratitude to Ron, my love, my light, my best friend and first reader, my other half. This book would not exist without you.

ABOUT THE AUTHOR

Sarah Stone's previous novel *The True Sources of the Nile* has been taught in courses on literature, ethics, and the rhetoric of human rights. It was a BookSense 76 selection, has been translated into German and Dutch, and was included in Geoff Wisner's *A Basket of Leaves: 99 Books That Capture the Spirit of Africa*. She's the coauthor, with her spouse and writing partner Ron Nyren, of the textbook *Deepening Fiction: A Practical Guide for Intermediate and Advanced Writers*. She has worked as a psychiatric aide in a locked facility, a graveyard-shift waitress in the restaurant where everyone went after they'd been thrown out of all the bars in town, and an office worker in an apparently haunted bodywork school in the Santa Cruz mountains. She has also written for Korean public television, reported on human rights in Burundi, and looked after orphan chimpanzees at the Jane Goodall Institute. She received her MFA from the University of Michigan. She lives in the San Francisco East Bay and teaches creative writing for the Warren Wilson MFA Program for Writers and Stanford Continuing Studies. For more information, visit her online at www.sarahstoneauthor.com.